For the best husband . . .

Cast of characters

Phil and Georgina Cooper and their son Liam

Kit Chadwick and Natalie Kennedy and their four children, Temple, Stella, Marley and Arlo

Ross and Vanessa Powell and their three children, Daisy, Jasmine and Callum

Andrew and Flick Butterworth and their two daughters, Phoebe and Zoë

Dom and Sarah Bennett and their children Mia and Dylan

Rupert and Annie Hawtrey and their three sons, William, Louis and Theodore

PENGUIN BOOKS

Other People's Husbands

Praise for *Other People's Husbands*

'A frank and believable account of friendship
and a marriage under stress. I was moved'
Adele Parks, *Sun*

'Rich and riveting . . . A perfect observation of the
complexities and pitfalls of long-lasting friendships and
their impact on family life' Heidi Swain

'Pitch-perfect. Very relatable, very real' *Woman*

'Beautifully insightful on long-term relationships
and friendships and the fractures a betrayal can cause.
A gorgeous read' Jane Fallon

'A fascinating insight into contemporary coupledom
and family politics. A page-turner full of emotion
and fabulous lifestyle detail' *Daily Mail*

'Perfectly observed, a reflection of real life we
can all learn from' Katie Fforde

'When it comes to writing about family life, Elizabeth
Noble is pitch-perfect . . . Relatable characters in a real
situation – a clever read indeed!' *Woman's Weekly*

'What a stunning story! I absolutely loved this
twisty, intriguing tale of strong, loving relationships
that begin to buckle under the strain of real life
when emotions run out of control. Evocative and
intensely moving' Celia Anderson

'Almost painfully real and thoroughly well-written' *Fabulous*

'Sensitive exploration of friendship, mid-life love, marriage and betrayal' *The Lady*

'Dramatic' *Hello!*

'A compelling, honest and uplifting tale which will have you hooked from first page to last' *Lancashire Evening Post*

ABOUT THE AUTHOR

Elizabeth Noble's previous *Sunday Times* bestselling novels include: *The Reading Group*, which reached number one, *The Friendship Test* (formerly published as *The Tenko Club*), *Alphabet Weekends*, *Things I Want My Daughters to Know*, *The Girl Next Door*, *The Way We Were*, *Between a Mother and her Child*, *Love, Iris* and *The Family Holiday*.

Between a Mother and her Child and *Love, Iris* were both Richard & Judy Book Club picks.

Elizabeth Noble lives in Surrey with her husband and has two adult daughters.

Other People's Husbands

ELIZABETH NOBLE

PENGUIN BOOKS

PENGUIN BOOKS

UK | USA | Canada | Ireland | Australia
India | New Zealand | South Africa

Penguin Books is part of the Penguin Random House group of companies
whose addresses can be found at global.penguinrandomhouse.com

Penguin
Random House
UK

First published by Penguin Michael Joseph 2022
Published in Penguin Books 2023

001

Typeset by Jouve (UK), Milton Keynes
Printed and bound in Great Britain by Clays Ltd, Elcograf S.p.A.

Jolene
Words and Music by Dolly Parton
Copyright © 1973 Velvet Apple Music
Copyright Renewed
All Rights Administered by Sony Music Publishing (US) LLC,
424 Church Street, Suite 1200, Nashville, TN 37219
International Copyright Secured All Rights Reserved
Reprinted by Permission of Hal Leonard Europe Limited

The authorized representative in the EEA is Penguin Random House Ireland,
Morrison Chambers, 32 Nassau Street, Dublin D02 YH68

A CIP catalogue record for this book is available from the British Library

ISBN: 978-1-405-93458-9

www.greenpenguin.co.uk

May bank-holiday weekend 2002

Perfect, golden days. How many of them do you truly live in a year? Or a lifetime?

This had been one.

Georgina pulled her sweater around her and leant her head on the ticking cushion, reflecting that, in this moment, she felt so happy she could sob. After everything that had happened to her in the last few years, everything she and Phil had been through, to be here, now, with these people, feeling this way, seemed absolutely miraculous. She had never thought she'd be so contented – that life would feel so . . . right. She looked around the firepit at the others, taking it all in, determined to remember every detail – a snapshot of joy for her memory.

She was drunk, of course. Well, tipsy, at least. She hardly drank these days, so three decent glasses did the trick. Georgie felt delightfully woozy. And woozily delighted. She was a lightweight compared to the others, as the growing army of empty bottles beside the bin in the big kitchen testified.

Someone had pulled a CD player to the open window

behind them, and there was music now. 'Dancing in the Moonlight'. And they were.

The whole day had had a filmic quality – like they were all stars in a wholesome movie about happy families and good friends. Georgie had thrown herself into it wholeheartedly, but also kept finding herself on the periphery, watching, soaking it in. She'd brought the clever digital camera Phil had bought her and taken hundreds of pictures, the lens lending her that precious distance. The weather had been spectacular – the May bank holiday showing off, in the twenties all day, and staying warm into the evening. There'd been rounders on the beach, the kids like a Boden catalogue in their stripy towelling hoodies, sandy sandwiches and fizzy drinks, kept cool, Enid Blyton style, in rock pools, crabbing and sandcastles in the afternoon, adults snoozing in turn, unread Saturday papers blowing in the breeze. And then a straggling, sun-kissed parade to the old-fashioned ice-cream van halfway up the hill towards home, twenty 99s with a Flake for simplicity. Splashy, giggly, bubbly baths for the kids, and enormous gins for the parents, while someone fired up a rusty old barbecue and the men got serious about the business of grilling sausages and burgers. And then, sated, pink-nosed and sleepy, the kids had sprawled in various degrees of consciousness in front of a Disney film, and eventually were marshalled into beds or settled top to toe on sofas and piled cushions.

And now the grown-ups were sitting around the firepit, lolling on rickety teak loungers and plastic deckchairs, sharing scratchy blankets that smelt of mildew and mothballs. In the absence of light pollution beyond the embers of the fire, someone who knew about stars was pointing out the constellations, and a few people pretended, good-naturedly, to listen.

It felt, to her, like she'd been initiated today. She was in this club. They were all founder members. If she was honest with herself, even though this was May and she'd known these people since the previous September, she'd had imposter syndrome almost up until this weekend. She wasn't, couldn't be, entirely sure she and Phil belonged with this gilded group. They were very ordinary people. She'd always thought so. It wasn't pejorative. At least, she didn't mean it to be. Not dull, she'd hoped, but ordinary nonetheless. She'd had what were almost crushes on these women she'd met at the nursery and school gates, and slowly, carefully, got to know over the last few months.

Sarah, with her glossy Anna Wintour bob and her perfect shell-pink manicure, was so in control, but then she had taught at the school for years, and she knew everybody and everything. She was the leader, the planner. She made things happen, even this weekend, although this house wasn't hers. She seemed so perpetually sussed. Never late. Always prepared for cake sales and World Book Day. Her husband Dom was equally together and organized. Even the man's hairline was exquisitely neat, and his blue linen shirt didn't seem to have wrinkled all day. Across from her, talking animatedly, Phil, also in linen, looked like an unmade bed. It was the way she liked him, but still . . .

Natalie and Kit were so arty and bohemian: so unmarried, unstructured and unruly. They'd started the dancing, and it was definitely bordering on the dirty kind. You felt almost like you shouldn't watch them. Natalie had the sort of untamed curly hair, the glossy kind that oozed sexy and made women like Georgie try perms. When she grew impatient with it and piled it on her head, secured with a pencil or, once, a twig from the playground, it just stayed there, and looked like she'd come straight from a modelling shoot.

Their laid-back hosts Annie and Rupert – the Hawtreys – were so posh they were almost aliens. Easily the grandest people she'd ever known. Apparently this house, this effortlessly glorious coastal home they were all in now, was where Annie had spent summers for most of her life, messing about on boats with her long brown legs and boys from Eton and Harrow. This weekend – this extraordinary, pinch-yourself weekend – was just a regular Saturday and Sunday for her.

Flick was just wild and funny. Her husband Andrew was the only one who'd seemed distracted during the day they'd just shared – his Nokia mobile phone kept ringing and she'd seen him several times circling by the groyne, holding it aloft, an expression of exasperation on his face. Flick just teased him, and he didn't seem to mind: he'd grin, throw the phone on a pile of towels, and give the kids three or four minutes of high adrenalin attention, bellowing, and swinging whoever was nearest over his shoulder, before he went back to the phone. They'd been married less than a year, she remembered.

You could see the newlywed sparkle between them – the tenderness. His proud eyes followed her everywhere she walked. Or swayed. She'd definitely drunk the most, of the women at least, but it didn't make her sloppy or embarrassing, like a fourth glass might have made Georgie. She just became her funnier.

Vanessa and Ross seemed terribly clever. Properly intellectual. The type who read more than one newspaper, even on weekdays, and listened to Radio 4 instead of Radio 2. They'd met at Cambridge, she knew. She imagined all their other friends were professors and junior government ministers and book editors. Georgie was pretty sure she wasn't smart enough to get into a serious conversation with them. She wasn't quite as sure who made her feel that way – was it them, or did she do it to herself?

But here she was. Here they were, the three of them, her, Phil and Liam, curled up now under a crochet blanket on an ancient green velvet chaise-longue at the foot of the bed in the room they'd been given. Liam, her beautiful and precious little boy, with his ginger curls and his dusting of pale freckles, was, it seemed, her golden ticket into this particular club.

They wouldn't have been her friends at school or university, these women – she was sure of it. She'd have envied them, imitated them, admired them, maybe even despised them.

It was different for the guys. Men didn't evaluate, didn't keep score. Not in the same way, she thought. They might all have been on the same football team, or propping up the same bar, and it would have been easier for them to be friends. An architect, a designer, a doctor, an entrepreneur, a house-husband and an insurance broker walk into a bar ... They'd fallen, it seemed, into a quick and easy, matey friendship. If they had less in common than their wives – maybe if they *only* had in common those wives, their children and their postcodes – it didn't seem so obvious.

It was always more complicated for women. It always had been. But then Liam had been lined up between Natalie's Stella and Annie's Louis, and been invited to play with Vanessa's Daisy, and shared a lift to Sarah's Dylan's birthday party with Flick's Zoë. And over a few months, via dozens of playdates, a hundred cups of tea, and a Christmas fair committee, all this had happened, and now they were 'a gang'. She'd even used the word, on the phone to her mother, turning down an invitation to stay for the bank holiday. 'We'd have loved to, but we're away with the gang.'

And there were years to come. Years and years. These children would grow up together. And these people were going to be her friends. Hers and Phil's. She wanted to savour every moment, but at the same time, she couldn't wait. And it could only get better, right?

Spring: This Year

I

'Cheers!' Six champagne flutes clinked. Annie always added, 'Chin chin,' because she was posh, and, with Natalie, it was a dramatic '*Na zdorovie*', in a deep Russian accent, not because she was Russian but because she was, well, dramatic. These were the things you knew about people when you'd been drinking with them for almost twenty years. Celebrating, commiserating, commemorating. You'd notice if they didn't do it, but you didn't particularly notice when they did.

'To Phoebe.' This was a beaming Sarah, the orchestrator. 'To Phoebe and her James.'

'To Phoebe and her gorgeous James. And to the perfect wedding going off without a hitch this summer,' Vanessa added.

Flick, her eyes closed, raised her empty hand towards the heavens, fingers crossed. 'Amen to that.' Then laughed her raucous, loud laugh.

'How is Andrew?' Georgie asked.

'If that poor gorgeous man hasn't had an aneurysm by August I for one will be very sodding surprised.' Flick laughed and rolled her eyes.

'Sssh. Don't even joke.' Georgie always shushed superstitiously, especially about health, which was not a laughing matter. *That*, she knew, was her thing. She

9

wondered if they would miss it if she didn't do it. Probably not.

Flick laughed again, that contagious, easy, throaty chuckle. She put her hand on Georgie's arm. 'Oh, he's fine, honey. Don't worry about him. Truthfully, he's in his element. Loving it. He's got staff.' She made air quote marks. 'The marquee people, the flower people, the booze people, he's running his own little wedding business already and he hasn't had this much fun since he retired, which I always said he'd done too early, by the way. He's got a flippin' clipboard. At this point, as you well know, it's less a wedding, more a project. And they've only been engaged five minutes. Pity me . . .'

The other women nodded entirely without pity. This information did not surprise them. They'd all known Andrew a long time. The kids had in fact been engaged for almost a month now, although this was the first time the five of them had been able to get together, using the happy news to hook on a day at the spa. Flick put her spare hand on Sarah's arm this time, and patted her appreciatively. 'That's why I'm so eternally grateful to you, Sarah, for setting up today. When I woke up this morning and realized I'd be luxuriating in a delightful spa with my best girlfriends instead of spending another Saturday with the dreaded lever arch file, listening to a twenty-minute discussion of whether or not the hornbeams in the tent should all, in fact, be ten or fifteen feet tall, I was bloody ecstatic.'

'There are going to be real hornbeams in the marquee? Seriously?' Vanessa was wide-eyed.

Flick rolled her eyes. 'There are indeed. Four of them. More in the church.'

'Blimey.' Georgie couldn't help wondering what they had cost. What it would all cost. One person's wedding day, another person's two-storey extension . . .

'Poor Andrew. It's a very short engagement by modern standards.' The wedding date was set for August. 'Brides usually need a year. Some venues are booked out for two.'

'Ah, the beauty of having it at home, and a lucky break at the church. Which may or may not have been an unlucky break for someone else, since it was a cancellation, but let's not dwell. And poor Andrew my arse. Absolutely no need for sympathy. He's in his element.'

'Still, though, there's not long for all the other stuff. I'm seriously impressed he's managing to put it all together so fast.'

'People will think it's a shotgun wedding.' Annie giggled.

'Annie! So old-fashioned!'

'Is it, though?'

Flick smiled. 'Nope. They're far too sensible for that kind of mistake. Far too work-oriented, too, I should think. Just two crazy-in-love kids in a hurry, so far as I know. And I was there when she chose the dress – and it's *not* an Empire line. It's definitely the sexy side of demure, barely room for her breakfast, let alone a baby bump.'

'All right, Hercule Poirot. I for one think long engagements are unnecessary. When you know, you know.'

'I couldn't agree more.' Flick nodded heartily. 'I mean, I was engaged to Craig for years.' Craig had been her first husband, her daughter Zoë's dad. 'Marriage lasted considerably less time than the engagement. Andrew, I met and married within a year. You'd think I'd have been more cautious, maybe. But, like you say, when you know, you know. With Craig, hand on heart, I'm not sure I'd had that moment of absolute certainty. With Andrew, absolutely. And we're still married, twenty-odd years later.'

'My mum and dad made me wait, but only because I was so young.' They all knew Annie had been married at twenty-three. They all knew most of those things about each other. 'I'd have married him after our first date, though.' They knew that too. Knew that Annie tended to live her life in a Georgette Heyer haze. Rupert was a good man, though – on that they would all agree. And for all his male bluster, just as soppy about his wife as she was about him.

'We saved up for the deposit on a house first.' Georgie smiled, tongue in cheek. 'Sensible.'

'Nothing wrong with sensible,' Vanessa chimed in. 'It would be better if kids thought that way these days. Saving up for stuff – not really a thing for some of them, I'm afraid. Too many gadgets and clothes and exotic holidays to go on.'

'God, we sound old and judgy.'

'We *are* old and judgy.'

'Speak for yourself . . .' Flick hoicked her considerable bosom up in the swimsuit that was cut for someone maybe two or three cup sizes smaller. 'I'm just judgy.'

They all laughed.

Then it was back to the wedding, for Annie at least. 'Are there going to be fireworks?'

Flick nodded. 'I bloody love fireworks. Only the noisy ones, mind you. I like a bang.'

The others raised their eyebrows at Flick's very obvious innuendo, but didn't take the bait. It was too exhausting.

Flick continued, 'I believe a ten-minute display, along the back fence, at going-home time, is under discussion.'

'Which is? Going-home time, I mean. Are we talking all-nighter?'

'Carriages, dahling . . .' she made her voice much more posh than it was '. . . are at midnight, I think. Half past? Something like that. We'll have been at it all day. Not sure I could keep going all night. As I left, someone was being commissioned to write out all the timings and stuff on a pallet in modern calligraphy, whatever that is. They're having a monogram, you know!' Flick drank again, deeply, and snorted.

Annie clapped her hands in delight. 'Well, I can't wait. It all sounds amazing. I love weddings. All weddings. But what was it that Simon Callow says in the film? You know. About the weddings of people you really love being the best. And we *really* love Phoebe.' Poor Annie should have had a daughter to go with her three strapping sons. She, perhaps more than any of them, was the quintessential mother of the bride and, ironically, she would never get to be one.

Phoebe, Andrew's daughter, and Flick's step, although no one had ever used or even considered the distinction,

13

was adorable. She'd been sweet-natured all her life. Always a peacemaker. The sort of kid who always sat with the child who was on their own.

'She's the first, too,' Annie added, before she remembered Natalie's elder daughter. 'Apart from Temple, of course.'

If they were honest, they didn't all love Temple in the same way. But, then, they didn't really know her. Natalie's daughter Temple was the oldest of all their children by some years. She was already married, to Max, and had been for a couple of years now. She and Natalie's youngest child, Arlo, just eight years old now, were 'the outliers'. The other thirteen kids ranged from seventeen to twenty-five, and they had always been treated by everyone as an amorphous body of child. This group of mothers and fathers had been the village that raised them. You wiped a nose, and even a bottom, if it needed doing, regardless of parentage. You fed whoever was in your kitchen at teatime, and you drove however many kids you could fit into your car wherever you were going. That was how it had been, the glorious, chaotic magic of it. Temple had already been a prickly teenager when the group had met and become a gang. Her nose piercing and her pink hair and her unbiddable psyche had seemed so alien to the rest of them, still dressing very small children in stripes and Start-Rite shoes, never imagining a time when they might not be in control and able to fix everything that went wrong.

For Temple's part, she had viewed them all, over the years, with cool detachment, which occasionally veered into disdain and even embarrassment. She had a cool dad, and he lived in London, where she preferred to be. She'd always been on the periphery, although she'd grown up to be a warmer and easier person than her teenage demeanour had promised, and she and Natalie, they knew, adored each other. Arlo, nine years younger than his next nearest in age, had been the bonus baby they'd all cooed over and loved a cuddle with while silently grateful they weren't being kept up at night and still carrying a pantechnicon of gear wherever they went. Natalie had bookended the group with the oldest and the youngest child. By rights she ought to look the oldest, or at least the most knackered. She was lucky they didn't hate her because she looked neither.

'And we weren't at Temple and Max's wedding.'

'Even I only just made the cut for Temple's wedding,' Natalie joked. Georgie remembered the photographs of an achingly cool Shoreditch warehouse celebration – all neon signs, houseplants and smoke bombs.

'Do you think they'll all get married? Eventually? That we've got years and years of lovely weddings ahead of us?' Annie looked hopeful.

'I doubt it.' Natalie sounded cynical. 'Statistically speaking. Isn't marriage dead?'

'I thought it was making a comeback.'

'Nope.' Vanessa shook her head. No one ever questioned Vanessa's authority on issues like this. There was just a general assumption that she'd be right. 'Marriages are going down, have been for years. But, then, so are the number of divorces. Falling fast.'

'Well, we're relentlessly happily married, aren't we? Bucking the trend, this little group. Just me, huh, in this gang?' Flick was laughing. 'The one scandalous divorcee . . .'

'Ah.' Natalie raised one eyebrow. 'You all forget Kit and I aren't married.'

'That's *right*.'

'We *do* forget that . . .'

'I wasn't married before either, so I've never done the engagement thing, the wedding thing, the divorce thing, none of it.'

It was odd, when you thought about it. Natalie was the most obvious centre-of-attention person of all of them, although she had some competition from Flick. But then she was, too, the least conventional. The most bohemian.

'You *seem* married,' Annie persisted.

Natalie laughed.

'Has Kit ever asked you?' Sarah sounded surprised as she spoke. A new question. A missing piece of information. That felt rare to them all – they could mostly tell each other's stories.

Natalie laughed again. 'Once or twice.'

'And you turned him down?'

Natalie waved a hand. 'Oh, they weren't exactly conventional proposals. There was never a bended knee or a ring or anything like that. Nothing to turn down. Not Kit's style, maybe, but I suppose I never really thought he was serious.' She shrugged, and she was smiling, although a careful observer might have thought it was a

16

weaker, less genuine expression than before, with less sparkle in the eye.

'Too bourgeois for you both, maybe,' Georgie supplied.

Natalie winked. 'Totally.'

'So . . . five of us relentlessly happily married, bucking trends all over the shop, one relentlessly bohemian unmarried –'

'And the one wicked stepmother, to boot.'

'Less of the wicked, thank you.' Everyone knew Flick adored Phoebe, the daughter she'd taken on when she married Andrew. Phoebe had been six years old, all doe eyes and crazy curls, and ridiculously easy to love. Andrew had often joked that Flick only married him for his daughter, although Flick had had one of her own – Zoë – just three years younger. She always concurred.

Everyone was suddenly reminded, amid the joking, that Phoebe's mum, Samantha, wouldn't be there for any of the planning or the day itself, and the mood quietened almost imperceptibly. She'd died when Phoebe was born, from a haemorrhage so swift and so catastrophic that she'd barely seen her daughter. They hadn't known her, of course. It sounded so unlikely, so Victorian, to die in childbirth. No doubt Vanessa could have produced some statistics on how often it still happened, but it horrified them, nonetheless. And it was deeply sad for Phoebe – they all felt that on her behalf. Held at bay, most of the time, by Flick, and the family she'd created of the four of them, but something that reared its head on certain days and some occasions, so that they lived

17

happily as a cohesive, bonded four, but with the faint shadow of a fifth person always behind them.

Flick's face softened: she knew what they were all thinking, because she'd been thinking it for weeks, ever since they'd made their announcement at Sunday lunch, James standing up formally and putting his hand on Phoebe's shoulder, although he'd obtained Andrew's permission a week before over a pint in the pub, dear old-fashioned boy that he was.

'I've been thinking about it too. About how to make her feel her mum's presence on the day. Andrew too. I think that's why he's working so damn hard for her. I know I make fun of him, but he's not just doing it for himself, or because he loves a project, or even for Phoebe, bless her. He's doing it for Samantha. I know she's there with him in every decision. Phoebe's grandparents will be there, of course, and Sam's brother and his lot. And she'll be wearing Samantha's veil.'

'Aw. That's so lovely.'

'It's beautiful, thank goodness. Stunning Chantilly lace. It'll go great with the dress she chose. It's plain, the veil is fancy. They're gorgeous together. And of course Phoebe is shaped like bloody Gisele Bündchen, so that helps . . . And after we went for the first fitting last week, I took the dressmaker Sam's wedding ring and she's going to sew it into the bodice – it's got all those corset stays, you know, boning stuff. The ring is going to be sewn over Phoebe's left boob, over her heart, with a tiny piece of blue ribbon.' Flick patted her own bosom. 'She doesn't know yet. I'm not even sure she knew her dad had kept it for her all these years.'

'God's sake.' Annie's eyes had filled with tears. 'Tell the poor girl the day before, will you? Give her a chance to have a cry before she gets her make-up done.'

She put her arm around Flick and kissed the top of her head. 'That's lovely.' Flick leant against her friend for a moment, then shook her off, rubbed her eyes, and sniffed.

'Enough of that, you soppy bugger. Always you with the waterworks. Who wants to try the thalassotherapy? I've been writing articles all week. The knots in my neck have knots. And I'm banning the subject of the wedding from this point on. We *do* have other things to talk about. We have our own lives, you know!'

'And we have Dorfest to plan.'

'My very favourite weekend of the year!'

'All our favourite.' If there were dissenters in the group, they wouldn't have said so.

They'd done it every year since 2002, the first time they'd all gone to the Hawtreys' place by the sea. Annie's tentative suggestion that they repeat the exercise across the May bank holiday of 2003 had been leapt upon eagerly, and by 2005 it was, it seemed, an inviolate feature in all their diaries – it had become Dorfest at around the same time, the name coined by no one remembered who, but it had stuck. Apart from 2009 when Ross's appendix had burst the week before, so the Powells had missed, and 2011 when business had kept Andrew away, although Flick was there, they'd spent the same weekend together every year since. For a few years, Annie had half dreaded someone dropping out, but no one ever had.

It had most often, although not exclusively, been the Hawtreys' holiday home that they returned to, and they had loved being part of a big marauding gang. They'd slept, or not slept, in two big tents erected on the lawn, delightedly feral. In recent years, their offspring had inevitably faded away, building their own lives, and now it was just the twelve of them, and the world was their oyster.

Planning for the next year began over a few bottles of red around the table at the one before. No one remembered who'd suggested they go *away*-away, but everyone had keenly agreed. Empty nests didn't need feathering, and it was a novelty to make plans that didn't require elaborate childcare arrangements. Natalie, who still had Arlo at home, also had Kit's sister Maggie, who had never married or had children and worshipped her brother's, but especially Arlo, whom she often babysat. He was usually more excited for the weekend than they were. So they were free. The Eurostar to Bruges, beer and mussels, the train to Edinburgh, last year cheap easyJet seats to Barcelona and a sweltering tour of the Gaudí cathedral, which reduced Annie to speechless tears. Like so many things in the life of their friendship, a rhythm had imposed itself – one year they stayed in England, braving whatever the bank-holiday weather in Dorset offered up, the next, a city break. In part, this arrangement reflected the fondness they all had for the

Hawtreys' home, and the memories it held, but also it relieved the financial pressure some may have felt – Dorset with a boot full of food and supermarket wine was a good deal cheaper than flights, hotels and restaurants in a European capital.

This year was to be a Dorset year.

'The long-range forecast is crack the flags.'

'It's a while off yet. The long-range forecast is almost always hopeless. You can't predict weather months out.'

'Nah. Not this time.' Natalie spoke in Betty Boop's voice. 'It's gonna be gawjus . . .'

'Sunscreen and raincoats then.'

'I'm bringing the picnic stuff.'

'I'll do cakes and brownies.'

'Didn't I say I'd do salads?'

'Hey, don't start making lists when we're in this hot tub. I need to write stuff down . . .'

They all laughed, and someone sent a spray of water at Sarah, who always wrote stuff down.

2

It was dusk when they hugged goodbye and got into their own cars to drive home. Natalie let them all go first. Windows were down, and her friends drove away, their waves and kisses, and see-you-soons fading on the breeze. They'd had a good time – they always had a good time. Her skin had that faintly medicinal herbal-spa smell to it, and her nails were neat and shiny from the manicure as she stared at them on the steering wheel in the dying light.

She minded that she felt melancholy. It had been a long time since Natalie had thought about not being married to Kit. And a long time since she'd lied to her friends. Actually, maybe she'd never lied about something important, just told the little white ones everyone told.

But today she had lied. The truth was that Kit had never asked her to marry him. Properly or not. And she wasn't sure why she had felt she needed to lie.

There'd never seemed anything sinister about it. Kit had had been in two long-term relationships before her, the second of which had ended about eighteen months before they'd met – and he hadn't been married to either of those women. His parents – both dead now – had been happily married for at least fifty years so there was no dark, twisted antipathy towards the institution. His sister Maggie hadn't married, but Natalie hadn't tried to add two and two to make five out of that. You could hardly have accused him of fear of commitment. Their lives were tightly, inextricably woven together, just like those of the others. Like they had all said, Kit and Natalie *seemed* married. Their home – the house here and the tiny flat they kept in London – were jointly owned, they had shared bank accounts, children together, all of whom he'd wanted and welcomed. Well, he'd perhaps taken a bit of persuading to feel enthusiastic about Arlo, who was born when Kit was fifty-five. But once the boy was here, he'd loved him as easily, and as completely, as he had Stella and Marley before him. It wasn't the same with Temple, but Temple wasn't his and she understood that. Or, at least, she tried to. No – their lives were undeniably as enmeshed and intertwined as any of the others'. It had, apparently, just never been about marriage.

She'd come to the relationship with Temple in tow. Perhaps she had let go of girlish dreams when her daughter had arrived and things had fallen apart with Temple's father, Toby. It was hard to remember now.

She'd thought he was going to ask her – just once. After Stella was born. Hers had been a relatively straightforward birth – much easier and quicker than Temple's had been nine years earlier. Then, she'd had a firm but kind Scottish midwife who had assured her, when she first got to the ward, that really young women gave birth like shelling peas and she'd be grand. She'd gone off shift, was back on again the next day before Temple was eventually delivered by ventouse, had wiped her patient's brow admiringly and apologized for her false promise as the young doctor sewed Natalie up. 'But, oh, you were a brave wee lass.'

Natalie was cynical of the proclamations midwives made about second babies, and had expected the same with Stella, who had slithered obligingly into the world three hours after her waters had broken in the freezer aisle of Waitrose. Ordinarily they'd have all been allowed to leave the hospital later the same day, but Stella had a touch of jaundice and they wanted to keep her overnight, just as a precaution. Dads were sent home, and Natalie had been able to take a glorious hot bath, and even sleep, so she remembered feeling like a serene, even beautiful Victorian new mother, in a fresh and pretty nightdress, with combed hair and clean teeth, when Kit had come back in the morning. He'd burst in with an enormous bunch of the palest pink roses, the ones he knew she loved far more than red ones, and a tiny Cartier box. She'd been surprised to feel her heart leap with girlish excitement. It was a beautiful pair of diamond stud earrings. She recalled a quick swoop of disappointment, a tightening in her chest. But then the lovely midwife had wheeled a tiny Stella in, and put her glorious baby in her arms, and it had been, of course, pushed far back into the recesses of her mind by more visceral and real things. She didn't look for a box after Marley, or after Arlo. And it went away, the vague feeling of somehow being unfinished. How could they be? They were a family, and that was so much more than a couple, wasn't it?

She could have asked him, and she'd thought about it from time to time. But why would you ask someone who was so clearly uninterested in the institution? There were points, she was sure, when he would have said yes. But then she'd never have known whether he was agreeing for the right reasons, and she told herself she didn't want that. So she put it away. The way you needed to put things away to make stuff work. The way everyone did.

They'd last talked about marriage several years ago, just after Temple had announced to her over tapas one Saturday afternoon that she and Max, her boyfriend of just less than a year, were engaged. Her daughter had giggled delightedly, uncharacteristically uncool in the moment, and waggled her left hand across the *patatas bravas*. Natalie felt tears springing to her eyes. The ring was as unconventional and as beautiful as she was – a big cabochon aquamarine on a narrow gold band, with tiny pavé diamonds sparkling unevenly around the edge. It was far too big, and kept sliding around her finger towards her palm – Temple had already developed the habit of twisting it back into place. Her eyes had been bright with tears of her own, and alight with joy, and Natalie had found herself unprepared for the clash of emotion the sight evoked in her. Her happiness was contagiously bright, but for Natalie it was tempered with uncertainty about Max as her daughter's choice, with a tiny stab of sadness at this underscoring of her child's adulthood, and something else, something she was surprised to realize was envy.

Kit's reaction to the news when she got home from lunch and told him had been characteristically low-key. Stella had squealed delightedly, much younger than eighteen in that moment. He had looked up from the newspaper he was reading, nodded once or twice, and said, 'Crikey. That's a bit quick, isn't it?'

'I love weddings!' Stella exclaimed. She'd only been to one, a couple of months earlier – a schoolfriend's big sister was marrying at home and she was the friend's plus one. She'd evidently had quite the night at the reception. 'And I bet Temple's will be amazing! Ooh, ooh, who do you think Temple's dad will invite?' Her excitement crescendoed at the notion of rubbing shoulders with A-listers from Toby's address book, and she scurried off to look people up on Instagram.

'You don't really like marriage, do you?' She was emboldened, later that evening, by red wine and mild irritation at his nonchalance.

'I never said that.' Kit looked over his glasses at her, an expression of mild amusement on his face that did nothing for her mood.

'But you don't.'

'I just don't think it changes things. I don't think it's a panacea.'

'Nor do I. Did you ever want to marry me?'

Now, sitting here, she couldn't remember. She couldn't remember what his answer had been. She remembered that he'd turned it around, like he could, made her laugh, and that the evening had ended with the two of them making love, and that they hadn't talked about it again.

But she couldn't remember what he'd said when she'd asked him.

He was right about it not being a panacea, was the thing. Here they were, a couple of years later, and Temple and Max were as unhappy now as they had seemed happy that bright, stylish day in Shoreditch. At least, she felt sure Temple was. She didn't really know Max.

Her phone rang. She pushed the button that answered it while she was driving, and put the car into reverse.

'You on your way, Nat?' He always started in the middle of a conversation. Never said hello.

'Just leaving. Should be home in half an hour. How's Arlo?'

'He's fine. Good day, I gather. Chatting nineteen to the dozen when I picked him up. He was ravenous so I gave him some food. He's done his reading. So he's on the iPad.'

'Oh, well done. You're a hero.' Why did women do that, she wondered briefly. Treat husbands like babysitters, heaping praise on them, when they'd really just been parenting their own children.

'It gets better. I've cooked for us.'

'Wow!'

'Don't make it sound so rare.' A slight hurt tone in his voice. Affected or genuine, she couldn't tell.

'No – I mean, great.'

'I figured you'd have been on rabbit rations at the spa, so I've made my famous chicken korma.'

Was it famous? She didn't remember eating it before. 'Sounds amazing. Thank you.'

'Had a good time with the girls?'

'Fabulous.'

'Great. I'm glad. I'll see you soon.'

She rang off, and drove. He had a way of doing that. Of being kind and good and even ideal. Just when he needed to remind her he could be. Like he had some sixth sense.

3

The weather forecast for the May bank-holiday weekend turned out, surprisingly, to be completely accurate. The sun had been shining all week before they set off, long enough for even the English to go to bed without assuming it would have broken by the time they awoke the next morning. On Friday, the relentlessly cheerful weather person on BBC *Breakfast* waved her arm across the green weather map like a magician's assistant, conjuring up that most elusive of tricks: a glorious bank-holiday weekend in prospect.

Annie had gone down mid-week 'to open the house up', so it had been agreed that Dom and Sarah, who pretty much passed the Hawtreys' house en route to the Hawtreys' other house, would swing by and pick Rupert up. The Powells were to drive the Coopers in their bus of a family car, and the Kennedys and Butterworths would make their own way. Andrew and Flick were delayed by a wedding-cake tasting, Flick had reported, in an emoji-laden WhatsApp, with heavy use of 'cake' and 'woman with head in hand in despair', and, traditionally, no one would offer to share a ride with Kit and Natalie, because it would be unbelievably stressful. They never left, and thus never arrived, when they said they would.

Rupert was empty-handed, although Dom had opened the boot to receive his bag.

'What? No gear?'

'Have you met my wife?' Rupert raised an eyebrow to go with his two empty arms, then shut the boot and climbed into the empty front seat. 'She packed for all eventualities and took my stuff down with her on Wednesday.'

'You are the last Victorian husband, d'you know that?'

'Grateful and unashamed every day to be married to the last Victorian wife.' Rupert smirked.

'As well you should be.' Dom laughed.

'Hey! You'd hate me choosing all your shirts, and shorts, and taking your shaving brush three days early.' Sarah's tone was indignant.

'How would you know? You never tried,' Dom teased, incredulous.

It had never occurred to any of them that comparison of husbands or indeed wives might be not only, as the inspirational quote had it, the thief of joy, but the creator of trouble. That their banter was anything other than fond, observational, harmless.

A full hour behind them on the road, Kit and Natalie bickered about service-station coffee shops. The scratchiness between them had started earlier, before Maggie arrived to scoop up Arlo. It was a well-rehearsed argument, this one. Natalie had been on the phone with Temple when they were supposed to leave. He hated how she always dropped whatever she was doing when Temple called, disappearing with the handset behind a closed door. He was jealous, Natalie said. He wasn't fucking jealous, he said. He'd just like to be on time for once in his life. In their life. He'd been in the car with the engine running when she'd finished and come out. She minded that he didn't ask how Temple was. He minded that she didn't apologize for keeping him waiting. And it segued effortlessly, easily, after years of practice, into sniping about soy lattes. Natalie laughed, but it sounded shrill, even to her.

'My God, Kit. Even our arguing is mundane. We used to make each other laugh in the middle of a fight. Remember? Stop the squabble just like that.' She clicked her fingers in front of his face, and although the gesture didn't disturb his vision, he tutted irritably and moved his head, as though she were being dangerous and irresponsible.

'If we can't laugh each other out of it, can we at least fight about things that matter? Do it properly. Can't we scream and hurl things?'

'On the A303?'

She hated the amusement in his tone. It was patronizing. As if she was a silly child. In those moments, in that tone, was the acknowledgement of the age difference between them. Funny how she had never felt it at the beginning. It was his easiest, his first defence.

'Anywhere. Turn the volume up.' Frustration pushed at her ribcage. She raised her hands to the heavens.

Kit narrowed his eyes. In that moment he looked as if he didn't even like her. Then, deliberately misunderstanding, he slowly turned the knob on the car radio.

She should have taken the joke. It was exactly the kind

31

of tension breaker she'd been talking about. Determined that this was him doing exactly what she wanted, even though it wasn't and his eyes were the proof. She should have been cajoled out of her spiky mood. She would have been. She had been, many times before. Today, she just didn't want to be.

She felt old. And helpless. Temple's unhappiness with Max weighed on her. She couldn't shrug it off. When Temple had called lately, it was always to cry or rail or worry, and it felt to Natalie as if she had spent the duration of the phone call absorbing it all. It hurt that Kit didn't seem to care, or didn't want to hear about it. Temple wasn't his daughter, and their relationship was nothing like the one Andrew, say, had with Zoë, or Flick with Phoebe. With them, you couldn't tell where blood ended and love began. It never had been like that with Kit and Temple. Temple had always had her own father, and Kit had never tried to replace him, practically or emotionally. Once that had seemed wise, considerate. But they'd known each other a long, long time and now she wondered if it had been unkind. Lazy, perhaps. If Temple had felt rejected by Kit's indifference, even as she gave a very good impression of not wanting anything else from him. And, of course, if it was Natalie's fault. Had she ring-fenced Temple, and not let him inside the steel barrier? She used to watch Andrew and Zoë, feel real envy for the easy affection between them, and blame herself for it. But maybe that wasn't right. Temple was his children's sister. Her daughter. They were both her family. His disinterest felt so unkind. She resented him for not helping her help Temple, and she couldn't seem to make him understand.

So she didn't turn the radio down and let the mood change, like she once would have done. She opened the window a crack and leant her head against the door frame and watched the landscape change. She hoped that by the time they arrived, she would feel less like crying.

'Opening up the house' was what Annie said when she meant 'have a couple of precious days to myself in my happy place' and everyone knew it. It took only a few hours to get it ready for guests. There was a lovely woman in the village called Suze, who came up and did the beds and towels, and gave everywhere a good clean. Annie filled jars with flowers, and baked treats on the range, listening to folk music on the ancient radio. This particular week, she spent hours in the garden, loving the feel of the warm spring sunshine on her skin. It couldn't be true, she knew, but it seemed like it was always glorious here. Her parents had bought the place when her older brother Giles was a toddler, before they could really afford it, but knowing money would get easier. She had all the yellowing documentation in a box in the master bedroom, so she knew what they had paid in 1963 and what it was worth now, and it had been a good investment. And, much more, the most joyful place to grow up. Giles hadn't wanted it, thank God, when their parents died, too young, and barely a year apart. Somehow, he had never loved it like she had, and their parents had sensibly left him their London house. When he'd immediately sold it to buy a ski-in-ski-out chalet in Chamonix Annie hadn't minded the loss or the shocking lack of sentimentality because her favourite memories of her parents were in this place. They'd been older when children had come along, and her father had been a judge by the time she was born, studious, absent and serious in London – altogether different here. Here, he'd had time for her, and they'd fished, and walked, and made things in the small workshop in the garden.

The house was an early Victorian rectory on the edge of a village within reach of Lyme Regis, sitting high in its plot, so the walk down to the sea was steep, but the views were wonderful. The greenstone walls and slate-tiled roof were a little shabby, and the paintwork peeled in places, but in May the whole front of the house was engulfed by the blue flowers of an ancient gnarled wisteria. It was so pretty it took her breath away every year.

Inside, it had hardly changed, although Rupert had persuaded her, in recent years, to replace the bathrooms – her own parents had done the same when she was young, but as this had happened in the 1970s, and the house had not been listed, the bathrooms she inherited from them were sky blue and avocado green. Natalie had recently assured her they were fashionable again, but she wasn't convinced. Everything was white now, with decent showers fed from a big, efficient water tank. There was a new kitchen too, built by a local joiner around the big red range of her childhood. She had her mother's Aga cookbook – an edition printed in the 1950s – and her collection of copper pots and jelly moulds.

Rupert was inclined, she knew, to rip everything else out now they had time and money, start all over again before grandchildren – he was far more into that sort of thing than she was. He started a conversation every other year on this weekend with Dom, an architect, about how you might take the back off the kitchen and push out into a big orangery, or add a dormitory level in the roof space. Dom contemplated and sometimes sketched, but it never went further, and if it did, she had her power of veto. Rupert knew how Annie felt about it. He'd won one battle, over a swimming-pool, after a particularly happy family holiday in the Dordogne, where the house they'd rented had a very pretty and very safe fenced pool out of sight of the house. He'd been right about the pool – the boys, then three, six and nine, had been in it every day for hours – but she'd put her foot down about orangeries, dormitories and everything else. She liked familiarity and comfort, the fact that there were memories in every corner, and she wanted the grandchildren she longed for to see it as their fathers had seen it when they were boys, and how she had seen it before them, even if that meant things were a bit musty and threadbare.

When she 'opened the house up' alone, she slept those nights in the wrought-iron single bed in her childhood room, with the original rose-sprigged wallpaper, instead of in what she still thought of as her parents' room, where Rupert had installed a vast bed with an eye-wateringly expensive super-king mattress. As comfortable as that undoubtedly was, she liked it in here when it was just her. They were nights of pure nostalgia. Besides, their bed was too big without the lovely warm, familiar length of him in it alongside her. Not even Rupert knew she did that.

She loved the house best of all, though, when it was full of people and, as she sat on the wooden bench in the front garden nursing a coffee and waiting for everyone to arrive, she reflected that these were among her favourite people with whom to fill it. Second only, probably, to when the boys and boisterous crowds of their friends and various girlfriends descended. This was a lucky group. Lucky to have found each other, lucky to be such good friends, all these years later. Luckier still to be well, to be together, to have happy, healthy children. That had to be unusual.

There'd been challenging times, of course. Life was a roller coaster, not a steam train, and there wasn't one family among them that hadn't had a rough patch. Most of them had lost a parent, and a handful were middle-aged orphans now; they'd been there for each other through those sadnesses. Her own boys had practically lived with Andrew and Flick when she was nursing her own mother through the end stages of the heart failure that had killed her. Kids had been ill, been hurt. When Ross and Vanessa's youngest, Callum, had developed meningitis as a toddler, they'd taken turns to have his sisters Daisy and Jasmine for sleepovers so his parents could stay by his bedside during that frightening week in the ICU, cooked casseroles and baked brownies. Georgie had gone round, done the laundry and changed all the beds so that when the news was finally good, they could come home and fall into a dead sleep in clean sheets.

And they had all done it for her, more than once, when Georgie had been going through the gruelling treatment for breast cancer a few years back. Natalie had wanted them to shave their heads in solidarity but Flick had said that was easy for her because she clearly had a nice-shaped head, and she knew she wouldn't suit bald, so she was on her own. In the end Georgie hadn't lost her hair: she'd worn one of those cold caps that prevent it. Annie remembered then that Flick had tied an ice pack on her head with a jaunty ribbon when she showed up for the chemo session and said she'd take the solidarity points there and then, thank you. God, how they'd laughed at that. Even Georgie, who felt like crap, had laughed until fat teardrops rolled down her face.

There had been vicissitudes in their friendships too. It was a lot like marriage, a friendship with longevity. Any relationship that really mattered, come to think of it. There were bad patches. Of course there were. There were hot buttons, and pinch points. Sarah could be bossy, and Natalie was sometimes exhausting – Annie knew Vanessa was occasionally irritated by what she called Annie's 'Pollyanna complex'. Georgie's worried pessimism was sometimes repellent to be around, while Flick could certainly be OTT. Annie herself had struggled when she left nursing. Retraining as a therapist had taken it out of her – it had been hard, much harder than she had thought. She'd stepped back then, to focus.

They'd given her the room to do that, without judging her for it.

The kids had fought with each other sometimes – fallen out. There'd been dangerous moments in the women's lives – through exams and university – when competitiveness, defensiveness and protectiveness had gnawed at some of the ties that bound them. 'We're all mammals after all,' Flick had once said. 'Mumma Bears.' She was right about that. They all had other friends, a life apart from the group – jobs, families, neighbours, older friends, and newer ones too. In that way it was very different from marriage – you could take time away, step back, have a breather. So far, they'd always gravitated back to this closeness. There'd been trial separations – if you were honest and looked back across the years you could see them – but no one had wanted a divorce from the gang. Or from each other, thank God. Annie had seen the collateral damage divorce caused when her brother Giles and his wife Hannah had split up a couple of years ago. The thought made her shudder. It would be a hand grenade.

They were all invested. They all understood the preciousness of the emotional ecosystem that supported them all.

And there had never been a bad day when they'd all been here. Scarcely a cross word – any bickering confined to couples, and not much of that. Generally, they all arrived, enjoyed, and went home warmed, if not by the Dorset sunshine, then by the glow of camaraderie. So Annie sipped her coffee, and waited.

*

Andrew and Flick were first to arrive, just before midday, honking the horn joyously as they turned up the steep driveway. Then, scarcely a few minutes later, Phil and Georgie appeared with Ross and Vanessa. No one unpacked or bagsed a room – Annie decided in advance who would sleep where – but there were bear hugs and fresh coffees poured, and the same old view to be fussed over as everyone stretched their limbs after the journey. Rupert, Dom and Sarah weren't far behind. Annie had Rupert on FindMyFriend, so she could track their progress through his phone. No one really expected to see Nat and Kit for another hour or two, so gradually, slowly, rooms were occupied, cars emptied, food and drink supplies unloaded into the big fridge. Someone – probably Phil, the music connoisseur of the group – synced his phone to a wireless speaker he'd bought, and there was music. As she looked around at her kitchen, full of friends, and her handsome husband whispered that he'd missed her, and that she must have finished 'opening up' early, because her freckles were out, Annie felt truly happy.

It was around two thirty when Natalie and Kit finally rolled up. Everyone was outside by then, changed, and beside the pool. Annie had laid out charcuterie on the long grey teak table – she'd cut a picture out of a foodie magazine, and recreated it: two big wooden boards with hams and salamis and cheeses and Marcona almonds and good olives from the deli – and someone had opened rosé wine. They'd all thrown swimming costumes on under shirts and sundresses, and most had been in the water already, even if just to dangle their legs, hot from the long drive.

Sarah was in the kitchen searching for the sunscreen Annie thought she had left over from last summer when she heard Kit's car on the gravel. She watched from the window, unseen, as their car doors opened and the pair climbed out. Spied on unaware, they were stony-faced and silent. Kit rubbed his forehead, one finger on each temple, as though he had a headache, then ran his hand through his hair. Evidently Annie had heard the car too, her hostess ear primed, and she came scuttling down the side of the house in her ancient striped kaftan and flip-flops. From her vantage point inside, it was only Sarah who saw Kit and Natalie instinctively rearrange their faces into broad, warm smiles as Annie opened her arms to embrace them each in turn.

'You made it!' Sarah heard Annie exclaim, through the open window. 'Welcome, welcome!' She pulled them both towards the back of the house. 'Come on, come on. Everyone's out here – there's bags of food left. We've only just started really . . .'

'Aha, last but not least!' Rupert, too, was expansive in his welcome.

'Sorry, everyone. Arlo . . .' Natalie began her excuse. After all these years, she still offered one, although no one raised an eyebrow about their late arrival.

Andrew raised a hand to stop her. 'You're here now.'

Phil had poured two glasses of rosé and passed them one each. 'Here, you two. You're not far behind. You can catch up.'

'Let them at least get their gear,' Annie protested. But Kit had clinked his glass against Phil's, just a little too hard, and drunk his in one.

Natalie didn't even sip hers, just smiled her thanks at Phil and put her glass on the edge of the table.

'You'll want to change. It's sweltering. The water is delicious. Come, come . . .'

Sarah, who'd put the full water jug down, couldn't tell whether Annie had sensed the tension or was just being the consummate host.

'Is your car still unlocked? I'll get your stuff. You're in the downstairs double.' Rupert pulled a T-shirt over his head, and scrabbled under his chair for battered deck shoes.

Natalie let herself be led inside and Sarah followed.

The 'downstairs double' was Annie's dad's old study with a double bed in it. His law books and political biographies were still on shelves against the back wall, and the room smelt of libraries. A big window looked out from the front of the house towards the sea. Natalie went over to it and stared out at the view.

It was when Natalie was quiet that her friends knew something was really wrong. When she was vocal and melodramatic, things were usually fine.

'You okay, Nat?' Annie joined her at the window.

'It's so beautiful here, Annie. Why do I always forget?' She sounded wistful, but then shook herself. 'I'm fine. It was a bit of a stressful morning is all.' She sighed.

'How's Temple doing?'

Natalie's eyes filled with sudden tears.

'Oh, my darling.' Annie stroked her friend's arm. 'What's going on?'

Natalie took a deep breath, hesitated, then waved a hand in front of her face just as Rupert appeared in the doorway with two leather bags. He took in the scene. When Annie shrugged at him, he put down the bags and turned tail.

Natalie seemed to change her mind after the interruption. 'Do you know what? I do want to talk to you guys about this. But not now. I just . . . I just want to have a peaceful, lovely, happy weekend with all of you. Does that . . . is that okay?'

Sarah nodded vigorously. 'Of course. Of course.'

'Yes, darling. Whenever you want to talk, but not at all until you do. You just put on your cossie, or whatever, come out when you're ready, okay?' Annie had lifted the bags Rupert had left onto the bed and joined Sarah at the door.

Natalie looked at their kind, concerned faces, and smiled gratefully. 'I'll be there. Give me five minutes.' She held up her hand, palm splayed. 'Five.'

The two friends backed out of the room, shutting the door gently behind them, and headed back towards the pool.

Once they were out of earshot, Annie shook her head. 'Poor thing. That didn't sound very positive, did it?'

Sarah pursed her lips. 'We've got all this ahead of us, I suppose.'

'You think you'll stop worrying about them, don't you, when they're launched . . . grown-up?'

'Never happens, I don't suppose.'

'It's like a set of juggling balls, isn't it? And we're the jugglers. And our babies – however old our babies are – they're the balls and we've got to keep them all in the air. Or, at least, we need them to be in the air for us to be okay too.'

'Don't forget the husband ball.'

'Steady!'

Sarah laughed. 'The husband ball, the home ball, the job ball . . .'

'The bloody menopause ball!'

They were at the pool now.

'Too many balls, not enough rosé!' Sarah and Annie laughed.

'What the hell are you two cackling about?' Dom raised his sunglasses.

'Oy! We don't cackle. We laugh in attractive peals. Balls, if you must know. And we were saying we need more wine . . .'

It actually took Natalie another half an hour to appear. By the time she did, the nibbling at charcuterie had mainly finished, and a companionable silence had descended on the group, lazy in the heat. Flick was lying on the edge of the pool, her arm behind her head, one leg dipped. Sarah was swimming leisurely lengths, her stroke barely breaking the surface of the water. The others were in various stages of doze in the selection of teak loungers and ancient plastic chairs, although Ross was half reading a copy of *The Times*, and Andrew, lying on his front on the grass, was on his phone.

They mightn't have noticed her arrival, if it weren't for the slam of the back door, and they might have ignored it, if it hadn't been for the way Natalie was dressed. At the spa, they had all worn swimsuits under their terry robes, the utilitarian ones that came with motherhood, and just sort of stayed, most often from the Boden catalogue, with good support and sensibly cut legs, in primary colours and thick fabrics. The ones that didn't make you self-conscious when you had to bend over knee deep in the leisure lagoon to pick up a child swallowing mouthfuls of chlorinated water. A tankini, maybe.

Today, though, under her diaphanous white shirt straight out of Saint-Tropez, unbuttoned, Natalie was wearing a bikini. None of them had ever worn a bikini within the intimacy of this group. Strangers around a hotel pool, or family members – perhaps. Even Georgie might have worn one then. Not here. It was an unspoken, probably unconsidered thing. This was a radical change. A red triangle bikini with ties at the neck and back, and at the high hips. A very deliberately sexy bikini. It felt like a rude gesture made to them all.

Everyone affected not to notice. But everyone did. Except, perhaps, Kit, who didn't even look up at his partner. It felt, to the women, each separate with thoughts they wouldn't articulate, disloyal somehow. Unsisterly. She had the best body, for Christ's sake. They all knew it. Women always did, right? She didn't need to wear the bikini to win hands down. This victory almost – just almost – had spite in it.

Natalie was the youngest of them. The slimmest. The most blessed, physically – olive-skinned, and smooth, with long legs, and a small, high chest that had refused to succumb to gravity, even after four babies. There were no broken veins or dimples or stretch marks or rolls. She looked . . . well, extraordinary. It made even Flick want to sit up and pull her shirt on.

Later, home again, Sarah told her daughter Mia about the red bikini. They were chatting over coffee. Mia had come home to steal stuff. She had her own flat now, and was systematically removing pieces from her childhood bedroom, and sometimes from the living room, a cushion at a time. Sarah was aware, and unconcerned. She wanted new cushions anyway and was just enjoying the fact that a trip home from her eldest child no longer seemed to involve a bag of laundry. Dylan had not entered that phase yet. Mia asked about the weekend, and Sarah found herself talking about the bikini. About how she thought it had made them all feel peculiar.

Mia made her feel strange too – as though it was her problem. 'I wouldn't feel that way about one of my girlfriends. I'd be glad for them. If I even noticed. We just don't feel threatened by that shit, Mum. My generation is more sisterly than that – more supportive, more collegiate. We raise each other up. All that "special place in Hell for women who don't help other women" stuff. You know, Ruth Bader Ginsburg.'

'I don't know if Ruth Bader Ginsburg ever wore a killer red bikini in front of her close girlfriends and their husbands – and, actually, it was Madeleine Albright who said that, and I'm pretty sure *she* wouldn't have.'

Mia rolled her eyes and stuck out her tongue. It was a very Mia gesture. Maddening and disarming in equal measure. 'You're overthinking. Really. Have a word with yourself. Maybe she just didn't want the tan lines, Mum. It's not like she got naked, you bloody puritan. Besides, what are you worried about? I'm sure Dad and the other guys barely noticed. And, anyway, you look pretty good in your black one-piece, for fifty-four, I mean.'

The back-handed compliment – almost an afterthought, she imagined – had made her laugh, and they moved on to a different subject. Sarah thought she was pretty sure she'd have said the same thing, when she was Mia's age. When they were all, by the way, bloody gorgeous, unravaged by life and time and it was a far more even playing field. Things changed. Women changed. It had meant something, the red bikini.

Natalie's hair was up in a loose bun atop her head, tendrils escaping down her neck onto her shoulders. Her eyes were hidden behind huge black sunglasses, and there was a certain set in her jaw. She knew, Vanessa mused, as she gazed at her from behind her dark glasses, over the top of a Victoria Hislop novel, exactly how amazing she looked.

Rupert stood, and offered her his chair. 'Here. Here you go.' Annie loved him fiercely in that moment. Because of the chivalrous manners, and mostly because he seemed to take absolutely no notice of the bikini.

He'd have offered his chair to whoever appeared and didn't have one. Without a lingering glance.

'I think I'll swim, actually, Rupes, thanks.'

She slipped the shirt off her shoulders. Then she walked slowly to the far end of the pool, stood on the edge, raised her arms slowly, and dived in, swimming the whole length underwater, and finally, eventually, surfacing at the shallow end where Sarah was sitting, hugging her knees on the circular steps. She rested on her back, her elbows supporting her, on the top step, the water lapping at her flat, smooth belly, and, tilting her head back to the sun, closed her eyes.

Everyone, except maybe Rupert, had watched the whole set piece. They just didn't necessarily understand what it meant.

4

Later, Natalie feigned sleep behind closed eyes and found her mind drifting backwards. The others were chatting quietly, except Kit, who'd said he needed to make a call and gone inside. It was him she was thinking about. Him as he'd been. Them as they'd been. She did it like people walked, in their minds, through old houses they'd lived in when they were trying to sleep. For comfort. The story of us.

They'd met in the private members' bar at the Ivy. Natalie had been twenty-six, Kit fifteen years her senior. She'd been with the cast of *Hamlet* – at least, the director, Laertes and Polonius. A few weeks earlier she'd been given the part of Ophelia. They were still in readthroughs, spending their days on camp chairs in a big draughty rehearsal room off Garrick Street. They'd finished at five, and had already had a couple of drinks in a pub around the corner. The group had got smaller as people had peeled off and the director suggested his club.

Kit was with colleagues celebrating a deal they'd just signed in an office block the other side of Tottenham Court Road. Neither he nor Natalie was a member of the club – both just guests. Neither had expected, or even particularly wanted, to find themselves there that evening. Afterwards that had made it seem like a miracle to them both – their meeting. It was so random that they were both there. For years afterwards they loved to tell the story – both speaking at once, interrupting and adding details. Of how they'd been sitting with their groups on sofas with the piano between them. It was noisy, and jolly – Friday night. He was drinking champagne, which he actually hated and would never have ordered for himself, and she was drinking gin martinis, which she loved then and loved still, and they were both eating olives, although they were ravenous and wishing there was more food. Laertes and Polonius were flirting shamelessly with her, but she'd taken a vow years earlier not to get romantically involved with cast mates – a vow she tried terribly hard to keep, although it wasn't difficult with Laertes and Polonius. On her first job, a much older Norma Desmond type had warned her, charmingly, not 'to shit where she ate' but the advice hadn't come home to roost until too late, when a love affair had lost her a part and gained her a baby – Temple.

Natalie was hardly a child star, but she'd had one great meaty part in an acclaimed BBC mini-series when she was sixteen – and people still knew her for it ten years later. There'd been interviews, and a piece in the *Telegraph* about up-and-coming actors in designer outfits. She'd fallen completely in love with Toby Carpenter, the actor who played her brother, before filming had finished. He was beautiful and sexy, raised in an acting dynasty, and seemed so sublimely confident and assured. She'd fallen stupidly, easily pregnant with Temple at seventeen, and been blissfully happy about it. She turned

49

eighteen the month before Temple was born, and that, too, had attracted media attention, more tabloid than broadsheet, and cost her the next big role. It hadn't lasted with Toby. Neither of them was really mature enough to settle down to parenthood, but only one of them had any choice in the matter. She'd been horribly hurt, and frightened, but time had passed, and by the time she met Kit, she thought she and Toby were good at being friends, and he shared custody of their daughter, whom he had always adored. He was actually pretty famous in his own right, and critically successful, these days, and he was unfailingly generous.

Natalie couldn't regret what had happened – Temple was the whole world to her – but it had been hard trying to balance work, especially the kind of work she really wanted to do, and a small child. You couldn't drop everything and fly to Croatia to film for three weeks with a child, and you couldn't necessarily say yes to a theatre gig that had you out every night for months. Temple was almost eight by the time Natalie met Kit, and well used to moving between her mother's and father's homes. Toby had encouraged her to take the part, and Temple was spending more time with her dad while Natalie worked. She missed her giggling, wide-eyed daughter, but she had to admit that she was loving being utterly absorbed by acting again. Kit liked to say he hadn't known who she was when he met her, and it would have seemed insufferable for her to doubt that it was true, although she might have wondered . . .

Now, when they told the story, they said how she'd

gone to the bar to get more olives because it was busy, and the piano was loud, and the waiter hadn't seen her waving, and how Kit, who'd been watching her from the other side of the piano and couldn't concentrate on what his colleagues were saying because he thought she was just so pretty, took the opportunity and just started talking to her.

That, they liked to say, was that. After all, they were hungry. Chatting at the bar became hasty excuses made to their companions and a table at Mon Plaisir, so impossibly French and old-school that you were bound to fall in garlic-scented love by the time you ordered one crème brûlée and two spoons.

It wasn't quite that filmic, of course.

But almost. Ophelia was her last big part in theatre. She'd fallen pregnant with Stella by the end of the year. Not accidentally, as had been the case with Temple, but because there was no reason not to. They were madly in love, and she trusted it more, she knew, because they were both older, especially Kit, who was forty-one. She'd moved into his riverside flat in Fulham. Marley had followed reasonably quickly in 2000, her beautiful millennium boy, and that second baby pushed them out of the city and into the life they still had now. She'd been surprised when he suggested it – he'd seemed as urban as she considered herself, but she'd worried about it. They bought a tiny flat off Shaftesbury Avenue as a bolthole, and at the beginning she thought she'd be there twice a week, gulping polluted air gratefully.

The new home was a big barn conversion on three

acres – authentic on the outside, and cleverly converted within, full of curios, mid-century furniture and the modern art Kit liked to buy: huge canvases of bright colours. She hadn't gone full-on cliché – there were no chickens, and she hadn't planted raised vegetable beds or a cuttings garden – but the space, it turned out, was glorious even without those trappings. And the peace . . . She marvelled that she'd reached her thirties before she'd really heard birdsong, or noted where the sun rose and set, and discovered that those things did more for your serenity than any Zone 1 meditation workshop ever could.

She'd adjusted more quickly and more happily than she'd ever thought she would. Temple had spent more time with them then. Toby was working in the States a lot – playing a villain in a superhero television show that kept him in LA for months at a time. She'd worked a bit, in those early years, small television parts. At first she told herself she was taking a break, while Stella and then Marley were young, but she had never really gone back to it. She was too happy, too comfortable. This was a good life. Then she was too scared, maybe.

When she'd fallen pregnant with Arlo, Stella had been fourteen and Marley twelve. Arlo had been her wonderful bonus baby, for sure, but he'd also been, she knew and perhaps the others suspected, her tiny human shield against going back to acting, to putting herself out there to be appraised and judged. Kit had never minded that she didn't work – never actively encouraged her to go at it hard, find a more ambitious agent, do the rounds. She suspected he preferred that she was at home with their little family. There was something the tiniest bit old-fashioned in his view of family life, despite his ostensibly bohemian persona. He'd never admit it, but there was. And, then, he hadn't really wanted to share her.

Those school-gate friends had been key to her contentment. A lovely surprise. At Stella's nursery in London parents had been in a perpetual hurry – dropping, racing away, running late. Their determination to do and have it all could make them condescending to someone whose work was unconventional, as though it were easier. It was the same at Temple's trendy private school, where she'd never really found friends, more cliquey frenemies. Here, things were just calmer – plenty of working parents, of course, and maybe they were swans, less keen to advertise their multitasking, serene above, frantic below the surface, but there were mothers not rushing off too, interesting, funny, smart women, who had time for a coffee or a walk and a chat.

She'd met Flick first – she was freelance 'and never before midday', she'd said, when they first lingered after drop-off. Flick had recognized her, and said so, but wasn't overly interested, which Natalie was surprised to find she liked. A chat by the cars led to coffee, then lunch, and Flick became her entrée. She was probably the Queen Bee at that point, Flick, although she'd have hated the title. Someone always was. People gravitated to Flick because she was loud and funny and energetic, but she was also kind. She had the knack of carrying a crowd along with her because she was such fun. It was through Flick she'd met Annie and then Vanessa, who was on maternity leave from her banking job with her third baby, Callum, when they first met. Usually, Flick explained, it would be Vanessa's husband Ross at drop-off and pick-up. She called him the 'honorary mum'.

She'd introduced herself to Georgina, when she'd found her sitting forlornly on a bench while Liam, her son, cried pitifully for her at the window. Georgie had been close to tears herself. Natalie had offered to report on when the little boy's tears stopped – which turned out to be precisely one minute after his mother had disappeared from view. Georgie had seemed starstruck at first – she had the DVD series Natalie had made when she was sixteen – but she'd got over it soon enough. Everyone knew Sarah. Ms Bennett. She taught year six, but she'd also met Annie at NCT classes, when Annie had been pregnant with William, her eldest, and Sarah with Mia.

There were lots of others, of course, and the six were perfectly friendly with many of them. Who knew why a group distilled and honed itself as it did? Within a relatively short time, though, everyone else was peripheral. Not overtly, or unkindly excluded. There were plenty of drinks parties and sports days and class outings. But this was the core. She fitted here, to her complete astonishment. She'd had Temple so young, and actresses were competitive with each other, and she hadn't had the freedom to run in a pack with them. These women – Sarah, Annie, Flick, Vanessa and Georgie – were her best friends. She'd do almost anything for any one of them, and she believed they would for her. They were family.

5

It was after 2 a.m. when the last of them went to bed. Phil and Georgie had gone first, which was pretty standard, Natalie and Kit not long after, and not entirely as one. Sarah and Vanessa left Dom and Ross with the others at around half past midnight. Inertia kept the rest up, draped over sofas, and the thick rugs on the floor, talking nonsense, until two, when Annie stood up abruptly and turfed them all out. 'You know I can't go to bed until all of you do. Hostess with the mostest. So bugger off, do.'

In their room, Flick pulled the striped curtains, turned on the bedside lamp, then went back to the door and switched off the overhead light. Andrew was rummaging in his case for his washbag, pulling it out triumphantly, and sticking his toothbrush into his mouth. 'What was all that, then?'

'What was what?'

He took the toothbrush out. 'What was that crackling tension this afternoon, by the pool?'

Flick raised an eyebrow. It had to have been serious for Andrew to notice. He was usually oblivious to that sort of thing.

'Kit. Nat. The whole Pamela Anderson bikini thing?' he added.

She peeled off her dress and slipped her long cotton

nightshirt over her head. It was striped too. Alarmingly like the curtains. 'Oh, so you noticed the bikini then, huh?'

'We all bloody noticed the bikini.'

'All right, down, boy . . .'

'I don't mean like that.'

'Sure you don't!' She looked at him archly, but not seriously.

'I most certainly do not. My eyes do not wander, my love. Never have, never will.'

'Eyes are one thing . . .'

Andrew raised his hands in a gesture of surrender. 'Not just eyes . . .'

She took his hands, and pulled them around her back to rest on her waist. He winked at her and dropped them to her bum, squeezing gently.

'Had they been arguing?'

'You're so nosy.'

'You've got to admit, the whole vibe was weird . . . Kit, Nat. Nat, the bikini . . .'

'Let it go, Andy.' She slapped his arm, but gently, and he didn't move away. 'I had a nice day.'

'Right. I forgot. The code. Loyal to a fault, you lot. Forget I asked.'

'You didn't have a nice day?'

He'd given up on information now, distracted by her closeness, and made mellow by good food and plenty of wine. He kissed her neck. Then her earlobe.

'Nice of Annie to put us in the Shagging Suite . . .' The room they were in had been called that for years. It was the furthest from anyone else's. Two of the bedrooms were on the ground floor, in repurposed reception rooms, another three were off the main landing, and this one, an en-suite, was tucked into the eaves upstairs. It was probably Kit who'd coined the term originally, although they all called it that now. 'We haven't been in here for years.'

'Do you think everyone does it when they're in here?' Flick had her hands on the back of Andrew's neck now. The balance was tipping – playful to serious – and, sleepy though she might be, she was happy to let it.

He whispered right into her ear, 'Not as well as us . . . Loving the nightshirt, by the way. Very Laurel and Hardy vibes.'

She giggled. 'Right. Which one am I, then?'

He squinted and tilted his head appraisingly, even as he started to lift the nightshirt up and over her head. 'The sexy one . . .'

Sarah was fast asleep by the time Dom came to bed, although the bedside light was still on, and the novel she was reading was open on her chest. She'd fallen asleep with her glasses still on, and one more pillow than she usually slept on. She'd get a crick in her neck if she stayed that way all night. Dom eased it out from behind her head, then put the spectacles on the shelf next to the bed. She didn't stir during either procedure. He envied her the oblivion. He wasn't remotely tired, however late it was. He felt, in fact, distinctly wired.

He started to undress, then realized he couldn't face finishing the process and climbing under the sheets. It was still and close in the room. Pulling his jeans up again, he grabbed his cigarettes from the front pocket on his bag and crept back out. Annie kept a small lamp on in the kitchen all night in case people came searching for water. He took a box of cook's matches from the windowsill, and eased the back door open.

Lighting up, he took a deep drag and exhaled slowly. Sarah hated the smoking. So did Mia, in that militant, righteous way your own kids adopted when they disapproved of you. Dylan, he suspected, smoked like a chimney when he wasn't at home, and said nothing about it. Dom loved it still, although these sensible, middle-aged days he hardly did it. He bought maybe a pack a month. If that. Hot days made him want to smoke most of all. He was twenty-one again, drinking beer and smoking on a beach in Greece, that evening's dinner and where to buy it the most complex decision he had to make all day. Funny how a slim tube of burning tobacco could summon up the taste of that freedom so acutely more than thirty-five years later.

Dom lay on the grass, bare feet crossed, one arm behind his head, and smoked slowly, gazing up. Behind him lights went out one by one until the back of the house was dark, and the night sky twinkled with stars. He tried, and failed, to find any of the constellations. Not his thing, but it was pretty. And successful at making you feel small and insignificant within the universe. A welcome oblivion, just for a minute or two.

This dissatisfaction. This non-specific disquiet, a brain fidget. It wasn't going away. It wasn't how he expected to feel. Life for Dom, at fifty-seven, was, on paper, exactly what twenty-seven-year-old Dom would have hoped for, in almost every single way. Healthy, strong, he still had hair, and even an approximation of a six-pack. He hadn't, like most men his age seemed to have done, succumbed to the allure of a road bike, with its ridiculous Lycra get-up. He still liked the gym, and a game of squash: old-school. He was, by anyone's yardstick, successful in his field – almost the architect he'd dreamt of being as an idealistic and unrealistic young man.

At twenty-seven he'd just finished his degree – an arduous seven years: a four-year BA first, two years as a postgraduate, twelve months of work experience in a firm near his parents' home. A slog, for sure, but the time had done nothing to dim his enthusiasm for his chosen career. He was bursting with ambition, full of plans. And he'd done it – his own small practice by the age of forty, a portfolio of buildings and projects he was proud of. He was no Richard Rogers, but he didn't just do extensions and blocks of flats, and he was his own man. He liked his work. Far, far more good days than bad in the last however many years. He'd paid off his mortgage, built up a good pension. He could stop at sixty, easily enough, if he wanted, and what a joy to reflect that it might not be what he wanted. How many people could say that about their working life?

He had friends and interests and skills beside work. His diary, and their life, was full, and he was still curious about the world. He kept a list in a Moleskine notebook of places he wanted to see, and it was a long list he was beginning to tick off. And the kids. The loves of his life. The kids were doing well. They were good kids. Dylan was a bit shiftless, but being shiftless at twenty-two was no bad thing in this day and age – he would have a good degree behind him, and he'd figure out what he wanted to do eventually. It felt good that he could back him, instead of quietly panic about him. Mia was completely sorted, like her mum.

Her mum. Sarah. She was an exemplary wife. He was a bloody lucky man, and he knew it, and other people often told him he was, in case he needed reminding. When he'd made a speech at their silver-wedding party a couple of years ago, he'd said, and almost totally meant it, that he couldn't have asked for a better one. That she was a brilliant mother to his children, a wonderful teacher, an inspirational educator who'd made a positive impact on hundreds of kids, the best cook, the best companion, the best friend . . . and it was all true. She'd worn a shimmering silver dress – he'd called it sequined but she'd corrected him: they were paillettes, she said, whatever the hell they were. He remembered her standing at the front with Mia and Dylan flanking her as he spoke, their arms through hers, her eyes brimming with tears, and her beaming smile . . . He remembered. She hadn't fundamentally changed. She was all of those things.

So what the hell was wrong with him? What was missing from that picture?

And why the hell couldn't he get the sight of Natalie in that red bikini out of his mind?

6

Phil bashed the pillow and turned it over to find the cool side. Beside him, Georgie was still sitting upright against the rattan headboard. 'What you doing?' He was trying to sleep before the wine of the night before became the vague queasy headache of the next morning, but the blue light of his wife's phone was bothering him. There was no ambient light at all here, and it was too bright in such deep blackness.

'Texting Liam. Make sure he got home okay.'

Phil sighed, and rolled over. 'He'll be fine.'

'Just checking in with him.'

He was tempted to say he might have brought a girl home and not appreciated a text from his mother in the wee small hours, but decided against opening that particular can of worms. She wouldn't sleep at all if he planted that seed.

She finished click-clack typing, and put the phone down.

Sliding into the bed, she patted his arm. 'Sorry. Done. You know I worry.'

Oh, yes. He knew.

Phil couldn't pinpoint the exact moment he had first realized his wife was capable of embarrassing him. He'd been so proud of her once. She was better-looking than he was – quite a lot better-looking. He'd always known and never minded, although at the very beginning, before they were engaged and then married, he'd worried that it couldn't last and viewed all handsome men as a potential threat. It made him feel good to be seen with her.

She was still more attractive, although objectively, unfairly, the ageing process had narrowed the gap between them.

It was fairly specific – this embarrassing behaviour. It was her parenting. He was embarrassed by the way Georgie parented. Or, at least, by the way Georgie talked about her parenting and their son. He'd been listening to her do it for twenty-two years now. She was the Alastair Campbell of parenting. Grains of truth about their beautiful boy embellished with gallons of spin, exaggeration, distraction and the occasional downright lie. It had helped a bit when he'd realized that almost everyone else did it too – the mothers, that was. Not the dads. Competitive parenting, it seemed to him, was a sport for some women. But Georgie was Olympic level to everyone else's mere town or county standard.

Phil had always operated on what seemed to him the sane and simple basis that no one but he and Georgie felt about Liam the way they did. He was their miracle, their greatest achievement, their pride and joy. Everyone else had their own. Most men he knew were utterly immune to the charms of other people's children, and certainly profoundly disinterested in hearing about them in any detail.

Particularly when hearing about them was 80 per cent

boast and 20 per cent mitigation. If you were keeping a tally – and he knew well enough by now that women were – Liam was a Mensa-worthy genius, with a prodigious musical talent, a gift for public speaking, demonstrated enviable sporting prowess in the pool and on the pitch, and did it all with a humanity and sensitivity well beyond his years. He was accompanied by an ever-faithful gang of loyal friends, adoring girlfriends, and an affinity for animals and the environment. Meeting Liam after that would be, well, underwhelming. Liam was great. He was kind. And bright. Phil was completely proud of him and, what was more, he actually really, really liked him. But Liam was not the Dalai Lama.

'He's not the Messiah,' he used to say, in his best Eric Idle voice. 'He's a very naughty boy.' Georgie didn't like it when he did that.

She'd been doing it tonight. He'd tried to head her off, but she'd doggedly continued with some story about Liam curing cancer, single-handedly shrinking the ozone hole, or brokering peace in the Middle East. Or was it getting to the final stage in an interview process with a marketing firm? Yes, maybe it was that. Eyes were glazing over. How odd that she didn't notice. Odder still that her friends were still her friends. How they managed to overlook this particular fault in his otherwise lovely, worried wife was a constant source of amazement to him and had been for years. It was not an attractive quality. Liam did not enjoy it either. He blushed an angry red when she did it in front of him, and stared at the floor. He'd noticed that her friends smiled, acknowledged and then broadly ignored whatever she might have been saying. Which was exactly what he did. Or tried to do. He wondered if Georgie even noticed.

It was the IVF. His mother, a wise woman, had told him that twenty years ago. 'He's a hard-won baby, that one. He's very, very precious. You're just going to have to make allowances.' Occasionally Phil wondered whether Georgie imagined they might have sprinkled some magic dust into the test tube in which the scientist had swilled Phil's less than robust sperm with her artificially swollen and brutally harvested egg, but he tried not to be unkind. It wasn't him, after all, who had had to subject his body to the relentless wretched cycle of injections and hormones, even if he had ridden the same waves of excitement, hope and crushing disappointment for the four long years it had taken Georgie to conceive Liam. He'd tried to hold his wife up even when he felt himself buckle under the weight of it all. She had been a total warrior. Unbelievably resilient and brave. He'd been in awe of her. She'd never, throughout, let go of the dream of their child. A dream that had remained tangible and solid for her when it had shimmered and started to evaporate for him, like a mirage. He could never, he knew, thank her enough for what she had been prepared to put herself through to conceive Liam. The relief that had coursed through him when she said she couldn't face it again had made him feel guilty. He would have done it, if she had asked him to – he would have gone through it all for her. But he was so glad he didn't have to. Liam was enough. Liam had to be enough.

And he did know, really, why they were all still her friends. Brilliant friends to her. She was the kindest woman – she would help anyone. She was rock solid and loyal. And brave. That was why he put up with it and why they did too. People were not perfect – ever. He knew his own flaws. God knew how she put up with him. She had curled up now and fallen easily and quickly to sleep, her hands, palms facing, under her cheek on the pillow, like a child. Looking at her face, he felt a rush of love and guilt – the two always completely mixed after everything they'd been through. He kissed her cheek softly, and stroked where he'd kissed, and she murmured, 'Sleep tight,' and moved a little closer.

The next morning, Vanessa was already up, dressed, and in the kitchen when Annie appeared. She was carefully drying the wine glasses they'd hastily washed up the night before, and putting them one by one into the dresser they had come from.

'God. You angel. Look at you. You shouldn't be doing that.'

'Why on earth not?'

Annie rubbed her eyes sleepily, and squeezed her friend's arm. 'Rupert brought me tea in bed this morning, around seven, I think, and I drank it and turned over again, for God's sake. It's after nine now. Everyone will start appearing in a minute. Better get breakfast going.'

'Might be a few slow to start, Ross included – I left him groaning softly.'

Annie smiled at her as she filled the kettle. 'And how are you?'

Vanessa winked. 'I'm grand. One wine, two water.'

'You sensible creature.'

'Boring.'

Annie had only seen Vanessa truly and properly drunk once in all the years she'd known her. She'd been out with the girls after Callum was born, when her tolerance was extremely low after nine plus months of sobriety. It had been a total accident. Too much booze, not enough food. She'd been gloriously unguarded, and completely hilarious. She was normally so together. They'd all loved it, but it hadn't happened again.

'They need to get up. It's going to be the most gorgeous day. It's almost hot already. We're so lucky.'

'It's not lucky at all. It's *always* like that down here, you know!' Annie joked. She had her head in the fridge now, and soon emerged with a big pack of back bacon. 'Shall we entice them out of their pits with the smell of bacon frying?'

'Good idea.' Vanessa put the last glass in the dresser, then took two pans down from the hooks above the range.

It took another hour for the stragglers to be lured to the kitchen, a bit longer for them to finish breakfast. People ate in shifts, some not even sitting, but grabbing a sandwich over Annie's shoulder as she cut them on a wooden board. Rupert took his that way, and beamed at her as he bit into it, ketchup dripping on his chin. She wiped it off with her finger. Someone made coffee in the big cafetière, and the teapot was filled and refilled. Annie put the last plates in the dishwasher and set it off. 'There. All done. Someone up for going into the village for fresh bread for lunch?'

'Me. No problem,' Dom answered, very fast.

'I'll go with you, if you like.' Natalie smiled at him.

No one raised an eyebrow, least of all Annie, who'd asked the question. Why would they? Most of them didn't even hear the exchange. They weren't even all in the room. Some were dressing, some already pottering in the back garden. At least one person was swimming – you could hear the faint sound of splashing, even in the kitchen. The people in the room weren't listening, not particularly. They were reading the news on their phones, or wondering whether it was a good idea to take one paracetamol now for a vague headache to negate the need for two later once it had really bitten. The first night was always a big night.

'Give me a second. I'll grab my keys.'

'I'll get my bag. Meet you out there.'

Back in her room, Natalie stared briefly at herself in the mirror. She grabbed a hair tie from the dressing-table, and put her hair up, then decided against and took it out again, combing it back from her face with her fingers. She grabbed her basket.

There was no one left in the kitchen as she crossed to the hallway, and out to the front. Dom was already in the car, with the engine running. She opened the passenger door and jumped in, smiling at him.

Escape.

They didn't speak until he'd driven the three miles or so into the village. Natalie wound down the window. The radio was playing music, but she didn't recognize the song. There was a small car park, completely full. Dom lapped it once, but there were no spaces.

'I can jump out, if you like. The bakery is just round there, isn't it? You could wait.' She willed him not to agree.

He wasn't about to. 'No. No need. Wouldn't mind stretching my legs. Might get the papers . . . Hang on. This lot's going, I think.' A family meandered towards their car, eating ice-cream cones. Dom pulled in and put his indicator on, and they waited for the mother to strap the youngest child into a car seat, then climb into the front. Dom glanced at Natalie and gave a broad grin.

There was a short queue at the bakery, and Dom nipped into the newsagent next door while Natalie waited. She bought three baguettes and a soda loaf, stowing them in the basket she'd brought with her. She held it open for him to put in the armful of broadsheets he'd bought, and when he had, he took the bag from her, and put it on his shoulder. The errands were done within ten minutes. Both of them tried to think of a reason to stay out longer.

Dom's glasses were on top of his head, despite the bright sun. His eyes were crinkled, their hazel irises speckled with amber and green in the light. They were facing each other on the pavement, looking right into each other's eyes. 'Fancy an ice cream? I'll stand you a Ninety-nine with a Flake before we head back.'

She laughed, gesturing at the bread. 'We've earned it.'

They strolled down the street to the sweet shop. The freezer containing the ice creams was at the front, and a miserable-looking teenager served them two cones.

By unspoken agreement they wandered a few yards beyond the sweet shop, where the high street tapered and gave way into a small park, with a fenced playground. They sat on a bench. It was quiet – most people must have been at the beach. One couple cooed and fussed over a baby wedged into a swing, and two older, unaccompanied kids stood on either end of a seesaw, trying to balance.

'We've eaten a few of these over the years. Sat here often enough too.'

'For sure. They loved this playground, the kids, didn't they?' You had to walk past the playground from the beach en route to the car park, and home. They'd seldom managed to pass it, when the kids were younger. However tired they seemed to be after the sea and the sand, and however damp they were, the slides and swings, and quite often the ice cream, had beckoned.

'Come rain or shine, they certainly did.'

The conversation they had while they ate their cones was not electrifying. They barely spoke, and didn't look at each other much. Just occasionally, each sideways. No meeting of eyes now. They sat apart on the bench. They didn't touch, the whole time, from the moment she climbed into the car until they pulled in at the house again, and went back into the cool of Annie's kitchen.

There was nothing remarkable about the couple who weren't a couple who bought bread and newspapers and ate an ice cream on a bench on a bright, warm bank-holiday-weekend morning.

You'd have to be inside their minds to begin to understand how they each savoured those minutes. Inside their bodies to feel their heart rates. To notice how Natalie had waited one or two beats, earlier at the house, before she'd said she'd come with him. How both of them had held their breath, hoping that no one else would decide to tag along. To realize why they were quiet, on the drive. Because there was so much to say it was safer to say nothing at all.

The truth that no one knew and they'd never acknowledged was that there'd been something between them for a long time. A very long time. Something they had never acted on, but something significant that ran like a sparkling thread through the fabric of their lives.

And if they were both honest, it had started the day they'd first met. All those years ago, when life seemed good, happy, settled. When there shouldn't have been room for such feelings, and yet, suddenly, everything shifted and there was. No one could have been more surprised than the pair of them.

It would have been daft to call it 'love at first sight'. Any use of that expression was daft, as far as Natalie was concerned. People confusing love and lust – sure. People determined to differentiate their own stories from everyone else's – always. People with a penchant for romance and fantasy – well, who was she to mock?

But Natalie believed in the something at first sight. The electrical crackle. The almost imperceptible time shift. The slight click of your world on its axis. The thing was, you had to be open to it to feel it, to see it. If your head and your heart and your loins were completely consumed, you wouldn't even notice it. Your busy, happy brain would register that that man, the one you'd met earlier, the one who was married to your new mate, was nice-looking, or had a great smile, or even seemed to be a surprising husband for your friend, not at all what you were expecting, or was sweet and patient with his young children. Whatever it was, you'd notice and it wouldn't mean anything. You'd file the thought with all the others to chat over with your husband later, over the glass of wine you poured even as you were kicking off your heels. If you weren't completely consumed by the life you were leading and the man you were leading it with, if there were the tiniest cracks or gaps or spaces unfilled by what you already had, and who you already had, then that chance encounter could freeze-frame you in a second while everyone carried on, oblivious, around you. Your own personal JFK moment, your Princess Diana: you would never forget where you were and what you were doing the first time you saw them. But Natalie wasn't naïve – it wasn't love.

It had happened with Dom.

And neither of them had ever done anything about it. In all those years.

Almost eight years after that happened, the day you first met him, you were sitting next to him at a dinner party. You were often placed next to him – people knew you enjoyed each other, but they didn't think about it any more deeply than that. Someone else was telling a story about that day, and everyone was remembering, and laughing. He smiled just at you, just for you, and leant over and very quietly and quickly described your dress from that day. 'It had pink flowers.' And you remembered, but it was shattering to know that he did too, and you had to excuse yourself and go to the loo so you could grip the edge of the basin, and smile at your reflection, wondering if you had ever before felt so . . . noticed. Whether four small words, spoken low and quiet, had ever got you so riled up before.

And you did nothing about it.

Once, when you were in a big group, all merry on wine and clique fumes, noisily hugging and kissing each other goodbye in the sudden darkness outside a bright restaurant, when it was your turn he missed your cheek, and briefly, oh-so-lightly, kissed the edge of your mouth. It could almost have been an accident, but you both knew it wasn't. He'd angled your bodies just the smallest amount, so no one could see, his hands on your upper arms.

Another time, you were squashed into the back of a cab, and you took his hand in yours, under his coat. He curled his fingers around one of yours, like a baby might, exerting almost no pressure at all. Your neck tingled at the very slightest touch, and your stomach felt like it lurched into your pelvis disquietingly, and it seemed like it might have been the sexiest stroke of your life.

These encounters, if you could even call them that, had happened hardly ever. Every couple of years, even. Months and months passed between them. Their lives brought them together often – at parents' evenings, at dinner parties, on the sidelines of various sports pitches, in pubs, at concerts. Often. Mostly, absolutely nothing out of the ordinary happened between them, and yet the possibility of it always hung in the air. Natalie usually thought of him when she dressed before those meetings, when she shaved her legs in the shower, when she applied eyeliner. She did that thing of scanning rooms with seemingly no agenda, looking for him. She knew where he was at any given moment in any room they were both in. But usually nothing happened between them. Nothing either of them would ever need to confess.

Her mother was fond of a saying – she seemed to have one for every occasion: 'It doesn't matter where you get your appetite, so long as you go home for your dinner.' That was one. She told herself that was all it was. That was all she was doing. That probably other people did it too. Someone may feel those things for Kit. Or anyone else. It was normal enough, wasn't it? Maybe it was the Chippendales, maybe it was Ryan Gosling, maybe it was the guy at the petrol station. It was all okay, wasn't it, as long as you didn't do anything about it? As long as you were just working up an appetite.

It wasn't true, though. It wasn't okay. She sometimes

thought about him when she made love to her husband. That was not right. She thought about him when Kit was asleep, and she was wide awake in bed. She played out fantasies in her head – dreamt up scenarios where the two of them ended up alone.

She'd rushed to grab her bag when he said he was going to drive into the village, and she'd willed the others to stay away, and she could have sat on the bench in the park with him all day.

And she wanted him to touch her.

The only person she could ever speak to about Dom was Dom. And she daren't do that. She told herself no good could come of it, and she knew it was the truth.

Back at the Hawtreys', Dom put the car into park, and pulled up the handbrake. She knew she needed to open the door, climb out, but she didn't move.

He said her name once, and when she looked directly at him his face was stricken. 'Are you okay? Nat? You seem sad.'

She looked at him. His hand was still on the handbrake, and hers were in her lap. Suddenly he went to put his hand on them. It hovered there, and they both looked down at it, as though it was important, as though, if he put it down on hers, it would have crossed a line. It felt like there was a humming forcefield between them.

She heard the gravel crunching before she saw Vanessa come up behind the car. She'd been running, there were AirPods in her ears, the wire attached to an armband. She was sweaty, and breathless.

Dom pulled his hand away abruptly.

'I'm fine. Really.' She opened the door, and stepped out just as Vanessa came level with the car.

'Hiya, you two.'

Natalie opened the back door to retrieve the basket, and wondered whether her cheeks were pink, although Vanessa seemed oblivious as she stretched, one hand above her head in a big lean.

Natalie felt shaky. This was uncharted territory. She'd wanted to stay with him, tell him everything, anything. Smooth the errant curl above his ear with one finger. Count the colours in his eyes. She went into the house without looking at him again, deposited the bread with Annie, and escaped to her room, grateful that Kit wasn't there. She sat on the edge of the bed for a few minutes, and took several deep breaths.

Kit seemed to be in a more conciliatory mood when she found him in the garden. She suspected he didn't really know how exasperated she had been the day before. Funny how she could feel that the tone of their squabbling had changed lately while he was oblivious to it. She hadn't carried on the argument when they'd gone to bed last night. And he would never have raised it. He'd kissed her perfunctorily on the cheek, and fallen asleep with his back to her. But it seemed all was forgotten today. He had pulled an old deckchair into the shade, and his Panama hat was across his face, but he sat up when he heard her voice greeting the others, and smiled, gave her a small salute-like wave. She waved back, but stayed by the house. Dom had changed into his trunks and a T-shirt, and she tried not to catch his eye. Later, in the afternoon, when Annie insisted on a walk, she cried off. She was relieved when Kit agreed to go, and disappointed when Dom did too. She chided herself. Ridiculous girlish behaviour. Get a grip of yourself, Nat.

She called Maggie to check on Arlo, who clearly wasn't missing her at all. Texted Temple, then Stella and Marley, and felt tetchy with herself for checking her phone every few minutes, cross that they didn't reply, and cross for minding. They were adults, with their own lives. She was needy and sad. It was too hot in the garden, and she went inside to lie on her bed, where she was suddenly cool, and had to pull the old quilt around her. Her mum, Sylvia, used to say, 'Oh, my sweet girl, you don't know where to put yourself,' when Natalie was agitated. She really didn't.

7

Supper was to be a barbecue, another part of the Dor-fest tradition, even in a year when golf umbrellas were required for the hapless chefs. Cue the habitual jokes about how the men would burn the meat, then take all the credit for the meal after the women had made the salad, the dessert, the marinades, the sauces . . . the comfortable and familiar gentle humour. They'd united against their children when they were teenagers, full of militant views, completely black and white in intractable opinions, and so adorably, infuriatingly certain that they were right about everything. They all remembered long, good-natured arguments around the pool, where playing devil's advocate was like shooting fish in a barrel. The kids were gone now, though, and had succeeded in changing nothing about the old-fashioned dynamic before they left.

So, the guys were outside in the sunset, drinking cold beers, and peering conspiratorially at the coals Rupert had set, and the girls were in the cool of the kitchen, companionably chatting as they prepared the food, except Flick, who was mixing margaritas. She took her role as cocktail-maker very seriously, and had commandeered one end of the table for her task, where she was painstakingly dipping rims into egg white and then into salt. She'd even brought glasses from home, knowing Annie was ill-prepared for the exotic. Sarah was cutting fruit for Eton Mess, while Vanessa and Georgie put together a huge salad. Annie was mixing a dressing, and collecting condiments on a rattan tray. Natalie prettied cheese and grapes on one of the big wooden boards from last night. The Mamas and the Papas were playing through the speaker, and there was singing along, and even some dancing that the kids would have found excruciating. Rupert came into the kitchen at one point to find some tongs, and swept Annie into a brief spin on his way through.

Flick passed each of them an elaborate wide-rimmed cocktail glass, and they said, 'Cheers!', just as Mama Cass took it down a notch, and the mood mellowed with the music.

Natalie sighed, and addressed them all now, ready to canvass their opinions.

'I think Temple's marriage might be in real trouble.' She'd alluded to things being difficult – certainly Sarah and Annie had known things were near the surface when she'd arrived yesterday afternoon – but this was the first time she'd said something concrete to all of them. As she had known they would, they all locked on in engagement straight away, empathy on their faces, small noises of understanding.

Annie, of course, was the most stricken. 'Oh, Temple. Bless her.'

'Bloody hell, Nat. They've only been married five minutes.' Flick exhaled sharply. 'Poor kid,' Georgie added.

'Do you know what's going on with them?' Vanessa's analytical mind didn't make her any less sympathetic.

She blew a breath out of puffed cheeks. 'Not everything, I don't suppose. I haven't spoken to Max for ages. I've only heard Temple's side of things.'

'Which is?'

'Oh. Well. It's vague, at best. She's just sad. Most of the time. It sounds like they're living increasingly separate lives. She says he doesn't want to plan things with her – not holidays, not big stuff, not even redecorating the flat.'

'That's not a good sign.'

'I don't think so either.'

'Has he got stuff going on outside the marriage? At work?'

'You mean an affair?' Natalie's eyes widened in horror.

Sarah put up her hands. 'No! No. I didn't mean that! At all. Sorry. I meant like pressure, problems . . . you know, distractions.'

Natalie shook her head. 'She hasn't said so.'

'He might not have told her.'

'But isn't that weird? Don't you tell your partner pretty much everything?'

'I do.'

'Me too. First person I want to tell anything, good or bad news.' The others murmured in agreement. Natalie thought sharply of that morning, and of wanting to talk to Dom. She couldn't look at Sarah. Of Kit, tired, it seemed, of hearing about Temple.

Rupert came into the kitchen looking for something

79

else, followed closely by Phil in search of a bottle opener, and the moment passed.

Much later in the evening, Flick sought her out.

'She'll be okay – Temple. You probably just have to be there for her, right? Ready to listen. Ready to hold her hand, if that's what she needs.'

Natalie was grateful. 'Can't tell her what to do, can I? She's an adult.'

Flick's eyes narrowed, and she tilted her head. 'If you could, what would you tell her?'

'I never thought he was right for her,' Natalie murmured.

'That's tough. I can imagine. We've got James – and James is perfect for Phoebs. They've got the whole yin-yang thing going. I know nothing's guaranteed, but I'd lay money on it lasting. I think we'd have both hated it if we didn't see that.'

Thinking back now, the very first time Temple had brought Max home, Natalie remembered she'd had a sinking feeling. Temple had been so excited about him, breathless on the phone, boasting about how gorgeous and funny and sexy he was. Admittedly, anyone would have found it hard to live up to the billing. He was a good-looking boy, for sure, all thick dark hair forward across his forehead and cat's eyes. They made a handsome couple and they patently couldn't keep their hands off each other, to the extent that it made everyone else at the table uncomfortable. Temple seemed almost giddy with joy. 'I think he might be The One,' she'd whispered excitedly, helping Natalie clear the table.

Natalie instinctively hoped not. She wouldn't necessarily have been able to articulate what she didn't like
about him. He had edge. He did this thing where he
added something to almost everything Temple said – it
wasn't that he was contradictory, or critical, it just grated
with her. It was like Temple needed editing. Once, when
she spoke over him to embellish a story he was telling,
Natalie watched as he quietened her with one finger on
the back of her hand, and she stopped talking. And
when she moved around the room, he didn't follow her
with his eyes.

Later, although she thought they'd be staying overnight, and had made up a clean bed, Max and Temple had
caught a train back to London to see some show someone Max knew was starring in. Natalie had tried to talk
about some of what she'd seen, but the kids had scat-
tered to avoid clearing up, and Kit batted away all her
small criticisms, as though he was Max's counsel. She
persisted, frustrated that he didn't agree with her. As the
two of them were getting ready for bed later, she was still
trying to talk to Kit about her misgivings. Kit laughed at
her – not unkindly. 'Classic mother reaction. You're just
pissed off because you thought they were staying longer.'

'I'm not!' She pulled her nightdress over her head,
indignant.

Kit's expression challenged her. 'Don't you think
you're programmed to find fault – you know, there's no
one good enough for your precious girl?' He didn't wait
for an answer, just wandered into the bathroom and
picked up his toothbrush.

She followed him. 'No. Not at all. I'm not a cliché, Kit. But don't you think it was a bit odd how he made absolutely no attempt to impress us?'

'Why does he need to impress us?'

'You don't think he should give a single shit what we think of him?'

'Not really.'

Kit had gone back to brushing his teeth, and she'd stared at his back, annoyed.

'Well, I'll remember this conversation when it's Stella bringing back someone serious.'

He spat, rinsed, and dried his mouth on a towel. 'You do that.' He was aggravating.

She'd driven Stella to college the next morning. Stung by Kit's reaction to her, she'd determined she wouldn't say anything about Max, slightly afraid she'd face the same accusations from her daughter that she'd had from her husband.

She didn't need to. 'Not my favourite Temple boyfriend, not going to lie,' Stella had said, unprompted. There had been a few, over the years, and she had developed crushes on most of them.

Natalie had kept her eyes on the traffic, and her tone casual. 'Oh, really? Why's that?'

Stella shrugged, fumbling in her cavernous tote for something, only half concentrating. 'He didn't ask us a single question. Not one that I can remember. Max's favourite subject? It's not even Temple. Max's favourite subject, I think, is Max.'

Funny how even a kid could sometimes nail something

perfectly. Stella had pretty much skewered Max that morning in the car, and she'd been right.

Flick nudged her back into the present. 'Hey. Hey, just try and stop fixating on it for now, Nat. You're there for her. That's all you can be. That's the job, now.'

'Easier said than done.' She smiled weakly. 'But you're right, I know.'

Following Flick back to the others, Natalie felt a tiny shiver of shame. It was true that she was worrying about Temple. But it was a background noise in her mind this weekend, not the dominant sound, and it wasn't the real reason for her distraction or her melancholy. That was much closer to home, she realized, and much, much harder to explain.

On bank-holiday Monday, the tradition was to have one last lunch together, at a local pub. People packed beforehand and set off for home from there, all hugging and saying their fond goodbyes in the car park. Rupert and Annie had come back to sort out the house a bit before they headed back. Two of their boys were planning to come down next weekend, filling the rooms with mates.

'One last cuppa before we go, love?' Rupert had called her downstairs. There were a couple of brownies left too, and he'd brought those out to the table in the garden. Annie, hot and bothered from stuffing all the sheets and towels into the big laundry bags she used, appeared in the doorway and smiled gratefully. 'Come and sit down with me.'

Annie joined him on the teak bench, leaning into his shoulder. He slipped his arm around her, and she rested her cheek on his broad chest. Rupert kissed the top of her head. 'It makes such a lot of work for you, darling.'

'And it's worth every minute. You know I don't begrudge a second of it. It's my happy place, and it's happiest full. Besides, I'm not exactly taking the washing down to the stream to rub it on the rocks, now, am I? I'm just taking it down the road to drop it off.'

He chuckled.

'And you work hard too.' She tapped his chest. 'There's the barbecue and the pool and stuff . . .'

'Good point. I'm exhausted, now you mention it,' he teased. 'You should have made the damn tea.'

'It was fun, though, wasn't it?'

Rupert nodded. 'It was indeed. Most people were on great form.'

'Most?' She probed. Annie had always been grateful to be married to a man who noticed things. It was much more fun that way.

'Well, probably nothing much, but I thought Dom was out of sorts, to be honest.'

'What? Did he not get excited about sketching out an orangery and kitchen extension?' she asked in mock horror. 'He normally *loves* that.'

Rupert pinched her shoulder gently. 'Oy. No.'

'What do you mean, then?' Annie hadn't noticed anything.

'Ah . . . Hard to put my finger on it.' He thought for a moment. 'Restless. He seemed restless to me.'

'Okay.' She pondered that. 'You don't think it was because he didn't want to be here, do you?'

'No. Not at all – probably a work thing. That's a very Annie concern, if I may say so.'

She smiled, acknowledging that he was right. She was, she knew, the consummate pleaser. 'Sarah seemed good. Fine. The only rumble on the girls' end was poor Nat. I think things are going wrong with Temple's marriage. She was sad . . . a bit.'

'I'm sorry to hear that.' She wondered if he'd mention the red bikini. He didn't.

'I know . . . Horrid . . .' They sat, for a moment, in companionable silence. 'I'm looking at that water and thinking it's tempting. One last brief wallow, maybe, before we do battle with the A303?'

At home several hours later, Dom peered into the fridge. 'Dinner?'

Sarah scoffed. 'How can you even think about food? I've eaten far too much this weekend. Must have put on half a stone.'

Dom sighed, and took out a pack of Cheddar. She'd done nothing of the sort. He was used to hearing her mithering about the odd pound here and there, though in truth she was still pretty much the same size she had been since Dylan was born. And that was probably no more than a size up from the girl he'd married. He found all the pre-holiday and post-Christmas dieting joyless. It was like there was always a price to be paid.

She intercepted him on his way to the breadbin. 'I put

the loaf in the freezer before we left. You'll have to defrost a couple of slices if you're making a sandwich.'

'I thought Kit and Nat seemed a bit off song.' He realized he was working hard to keep his tone nonchalant. He also knew she was only half listening as she moved around the kitchen. Despite the day, she was in Sunday-night mode. He'd tried to talk to her earlier, in the car, but she'd been asleep beside him most of the way home. Not that he'd minded. He'd been deep in thought – deep in imagining, at least – pretty much the whole way.

Sarah's response was sharper. 'What do you mean?'

'Just a bit stroppy with each other.' He was fishing.

'Nah.' Sarah paused to consider, then dismissed his concern with an airy wave. 'Didn't get that, particularly. You know Kit. He's usually got that vague thing going on. I think Natalie's just preoccupied by Temple. Trouble in paradise with her and the husband, I think. Pickle?' She held up a jar of Branston.

'Thanks.'

'I'm going to unpack. And give the kids a call.'

He didn't mind that either. He knew she wouldn't relax until those things had been done.

He took the thawing bread and the other things he needed for his sandwich to the table, propped his phone up against the fruit bowl and opened *The Times* app.

8

A few days later, Natalie was clearing up after giving Arlo his tea, and wondering what she might cook for herself and Kit later, when the phone rang. The landline. She assumed it would be Sylvia, calling for a chat, or Kit, heralding his return.

But it was Dom's voice she heard. 'Nat?'

'Hi, Dom. How are you?'

'I'm good, thanks. You?'

'Fine. Fine.' She couldn't think of anything beyond the normal pleasantries to say to him. She remembered his hand hovering over hers in the car. 'I presume you're after Kit?' She looked at the clock on the kitchen wall. It was early.

The line went quiet long enough for her to wonder if it had gone dead. 'Dom?'

'I'm here. Is Kit in, then?'

'No. You've missed him, I'm afraid. He's not back yet.' Another interminable pause.

Then, 'I was calling to talk to you, actually.'

'Oh.' The thought occurred to her that in all these years that had never happened. Not just Dom, none of them. Phil, Rupert, Andrew, Ross: maybe once in a blue moon one of them would call to ask a birthday-related question or, in desperation, a child or food favour or something. But not to chat. They did that with each other sometimes, but not with each other's wives. And vice versa. How strange and archaic that suddenly seemed.

Dom spoke in short, staccato sentences. He sounded nervous. 'You seemed a bit upset, I think. At the beach. Last weekend. I wanted to . . . I was just . . . I wanted to check that you're okay.'

It was her turn to pause. The question took her by surprise.

'I wanted to listen to you, you know. But there wasn't any more time . . .'

She couldn't speak.

'Sorry. I shouldn't have called.'

She tightened her grip on the handset. 'No. I love that you called . . .'

Silence. At the other end, she heard him breathing.

'I would have liked to talk to you.'

Neither of them dared say more than that. They both sensed the danger in the harmless words.

She heard Kit's car on the gravel driveway outside. 'Kit's home. He just pulled in.'

'Okay. Okay. I'll see you soon, Nat.' Then, a new forced bonhomie in his tone, 'Think we're all meeting up at Flick's, aren't we? Next weekend? Yeah, so I'll see you then.'

'Bye, Dom.'

Later, when Arlo was sound asleep in bed, and Kit was half watching *Newsnight*, she took a long, deep bath.

Normally she'd have read a magazine, or listened to a podcast while she wallowed, but tonight she lay in silence in the scented water, her eyes closed, imagining, over and over, the conversation she and Dom hadn't had but could. She was a little thrilled, a little frightened, a little dizzy with it.

When she finally climbed out and into her nightdress, Kit was already in their bed, reading one of his heavy-weight biographies. He looked up and smiled, but only briefly, without speaking. She climbed in and rolled onto her side to watch him. His hair was messy, and she reached out to smooth one side, above his ear. Kit twitched, but carried on reading. She watched him for a few more seconds, wondering if he would notice, but all he did, as he turned a page, was absently reach out and pat her arm. She stifled her sigh, and turned back to lie flat against the pillow. Everything felt hot, and the sheet was instantly tangled around her legs, so she kicked at it impatiently. She sat up, and fiercely bashed the pillow before lying down with it balled under her ear.

'You okay?' Kit finally responded to her disruptive fidgeting, his tone neither annoyed nor particularly concerned. But he didn't stop reading.

She murmured that she was, and turned her back to him, her eyes wide open, and sleep very far away.

9

Natalie hadn't been quick enough to come up with an excuse when Flick had called to invite them over the following Saturday night. It was the last thing she wanted to do. Except that it wasn't. Her stomach was twisted with excitement at the thought of seeing Dom.

'Come on! You've got to come! Everyone else is. I need you. It's like a rehearsal for VIPs. That's you lot.'

Apparently the caterers Andrew and Phoebe had chosen for the wedding were providing a tasting menu for approval and the florists were doing dress-rehearsal centrepieces. Also, Andrew wanted everybody's opinion on the wine he was planning to serve.

'The others have said yes so you've just got to come. Don't even think about giving me the babysitter excuse. If you can't find one, you can always bring Arlo and he can curl up in the TV room. Say yes! Oh, and don't dress for the actual wedding. We don't need approval over your outfit, although at some point I will, apparently, be given a colour spectrum of shades for my frock. For the photographs, you know. For fuck's sake! Just come casual. Fascinators optional.'

There was nothing casual about the set-up. A long wooden trestle table stood on the lawn just beyond the patio doors. Each place setting, in front of a Camargue chair, had a folded card with a name in calligraphy, along with a bewildering array of wine glasses and a huge periwinkle blue linen napkin. Elaborate floral displays in pinks, blues, whites and apricots were dotted down the middle of the table, and candles of different heights and matching colours in etched hurricane lamps filled the gaps. Approaching down the side of the house, Natalie saw a team of caterers hard at work in the kitchen. Someone in chef's whites was leaning over tiny plates on the breakfast bar, wielding a large pair of tweezers and a plate of nasturtiums and pansies. Flick was wearing one of her flowing summer kaftans and greeted them with an expansive gesture. Looking far more excited than she pretended to be whenever the wedding was discussed, she kissed each of them on both cheeks.

'You two! You made it. Last – *plus ça change* – but hardly least. Just in time. We eat in about five minutes.'

'This looks like it's straight from a magazine, Flick!' Natalie gushed. 'It's amazing!'

'Right! Welcome to my mini wedding. I feel like Franck from *Father of the Bride*. I've half a mind to renew my vows with Andrew while it's all so pretty.' She gestured to a young man in a grey linen apron holding a tray. 'Have something bubbly!' Kit took two glasses and passed one to Natalie with a smile, then wandered in the direction of the men, congregated at one end. Dom had his back to her. Kit patted him on the shoulder, and then Dom turned, just a fraction. His head inclined in a small bow, just for her. Flick put her arm through Natalie's and pulled her gently in the other direction, towards the women.

'It's fantastic!' she said. 'They normally just do all this for the couple, maybe their parents, if they're the ones paying, but I thought this would be more fun. It's the most well-oiled machine. I haven't been allowed near the kitchen since three o'clock this afternoon. It all smells divine, looks even prettier, and I had all afternoon to make myself over as Alison Steadman in *Abigail's Party*. What a time to be alive. Just as long as it doesn't bloody rain. Come and say hello to Phoebe! James has been hijacked by Phil and the others. God, it makes you realize how old-school we are. Boys over there, girls over here . . .'

Phoebe was surrounded by mother figures, all evidently telling wedding stories. If she found it overwhelming, she hid it well. She was beaming.

'We never did any of this in our day, you know. Vol au vents, chicken with grey vegetables and a slice of fruit-cake. That was pretty much standard.'

'Come on, Uriah Heep! And a bag of winkles for the night bus home?' Flick nudged Georgie playfully.

'Night bus? Are you joking? It was all over by five o'clock, and we were in a car heading for Cornwall.'

'What – no Maldives?'

Georgie giggled. 'I wish. A week in St Ives. Rained nearly every day.'

'Course it did.' They all laughed.

'I love it.' Annie looked even more delighted than Flick. 'Being engaged used to just be the bit where you booked the village hall and the vicar read your banns. Now it's a whole thing! And what a pretty, pretty night.'

Natalie kissed Phoebe. 'Hello, darling. You're looking

very beautiful.' She did. Natalie had dressed carefully, and taken time with her make-up and hair, but Phoebe had youth on her side, and no amount of time or expensive product could compensate for that. The look of having it all in front of you.

You silly woman, she told herself. What on earth are you playing at?

Annie concurred. 'I told her that. She's got the glow, right?'

Phoebe blushed, which made her even prettier, of course. 'And I told her it was the facials. I booked a series of them running up to the big day.'

'Bollocks,' Flick interjected. 'It's love, not bull semen or whatever they put in those facials you get charged silly money for.'

Phoebe made a face. 'I hope that's not what's in it. You've put me right off.'

Sarah kissed Natalie on both cheeks, and squeezed her shoulder kindly. She smelt, as she always did, of Jo Malone's English Pear and Freesia. 'You doing all right?'

Don't you be kind to me, Natalie thought. I don't deserve it, not from you. It was the first time she'd felt ashamed. She struggled to assimilate the feeling, sipping nervously at her glass, and smiling at the conversation she wasn't really listening to. Did she really think she'd been noble, all these years, leaving Dom alone?

Someone knocked on a glass with a knife, sending them in search of their places at the table. Natalie found she was holding her breath as she wandered down one side, trying to seem casual.

'You're this side, Nat. Next to me.' Phil smiled from one end. Natalie's heart sank, but she beamed back as though she'd won the lottery, and walked around. Phil was nice enough.

'And me.' Dom smiled, pulling out her chair for her. Kit was on the same side as her, but right down the other end. She was opposite Andrew, who was now explaining to Vanessa on his left how he'd come to choose the white they would be having with their starter. Phoebe and James sat beaming in the middle, bride-and-groom style. Flick stood behind Andrew, her hand on his shoulder and her glass raised. 'Welcome all,' she said. Then, with a little shrug, she took her seat beside her husband.

Natalie unfolded her napkin and put it on her lap, smoothing it across her knees, suddenly nervous. Dom did the same, deliberately letting his fingers brush hers under the cloth. She looked at Sarah, but she was talking animatedly to James, across from her. She snatched her hand back, and turned her shoulder towards Phil. She was afraid colour was rising across her chest and throat. She couldn't look at Dom, and she daren't make eye contact with Flick in case she'd noticed any of the exchange. She might have done. Of all of them, Flick was probably the most observant.

'How did Liam get on with that interview you two were talking about in Dorset? I haven't had a chance to get properly caught up with Georgie yet, and I think she's been busy with work, right?'

Now their thighs were touching. From knee to hip.

94

The food looked exquisite, like art on a plate, but it all tasted like cotton wool in Natalie's mouth. She felt like an idiotic teenager. She'd moved away, at first, but he'd migrated nearer and nearer. She hadn't wanted anyone to notice, so she'd returned her leg to its initial position, and let it happen. Dom was talking to Annie and Phoebe. She didn't know whether she was impressed or appalled by his ability to seem so normal. And she couldn't believe that she could be sitting still and talking at a table where her husband sat, where Dom's wife sat, where all their friends were, all celebrating love and romance. And she didn't care. She wanted never to stand up from the table.

It was dark when they finished. Walking back up the garden to where the cars were parked, he let his fingertips brush hers again, just for a moment, until Ross stepped between them. And when he kissed her goodnight, like all those years ago, his lips touched the edge of her mouth before he pulled away.

Summer

'Hello, my darlings.' Natalie's mother stood beaming on the doorstep of her cottage, her arms open wide. 'All my girls together! How wonderful! What a treat!'

Sylvia had moved to this house in a small market town soon after Natalie's father had died, more than fifteen years ago. They'd sold the bigger family home, most of the books and a lot of the furniture, and she'd started again here. So Natalie hadn't grown up in this chocolate-box house, with its neat thatch, and pretty garden, but it still felt like home, because her mother was in it.

With admirable spirit, Sylvia had changed almost everything about her life when her husband had died. They had loved each other, Natalie knew, but robbed of an old age with him, Sylvia had refused, in her own words, to act as though she had died too. She'd moved to a new home in a new town to build a new life. It was a style of house and a place she said he wouldn't have chosen, but that was why she had, so she wouldn't have to regret, every day, that he wasn't there with her. Natalie had never been sure she herself could have been so brave.

Sylvia had taken up things she'd always wanted to do and had never found the time for, like painting and pottery. Hobbies had become passions, so the house was filled with her eclectic, colourful efforts. She'd joined a walking group and a bridge circle, and, although there'd been no shortage of keen widowers over the years, she had refused any offers of anything more serious than dinner or a trip to the theatre. 'Your father wasn't perfect, God knows, darling,' she always said, 'but he was perfect for me all those years. Death has made him even more so in my mind, and I shall never replace him.'

Natalie often thought that she worried about her mother, alone, in her early eighties, less than she'd have been inclined to worry about both parents if her father were still alive: she seemed to have more energy, and a busier life, than the pair of them had had all those years ago. Everything faced outwards, not inwards.

They usually saw each other every few weeks, to shop, or for lunch, or a play, but it sometimes felt as though it was harder to find space in Sylvia's diary than in her own. There were the sacred weeks she took Arlo, as she had done the others in their turn, Christmases and Easters, the odd long weekend. But Natalie hadn't seen her for ages, and she couldn't remember the last time it had just been her, the girls and Mum. Last Christmas, Temple had been with Max's family, and Stella had been in Austria, skiing with friends, so it had just been her mother and the boys. She'd been looking forward to today.

Natalie had persuaded Temple and Stella to join her in a belated Mothers' Day celebration: she would have taken Sylvia out, just the two of them, but she'd wanted to include the girls – Sylvia adored them. They'd tried to make it happen in April, but Sylvia had been on what she called – without irony – a girls' weekend in Seville. 'She definitely has a better social life than me.' Stella had giggled. So June it now was. Natalie's two daughters had caught the train down together, and she had met them at the station to drive them the two or three miles to her mum's house.

Parked in the station's pick-up point, Natalie watched Stella and Temple as they walked out arm in arm, their faces obscured by large dark sunglasses, like celebrities. It always made her heart glad, seeing her two girls together. Separated by nine years, with different fathers, raised in quite different ways, it delighted her that they were – mostly – friends as well as half-sisters. She remembered the first time the two had met – the tiny infant and the excited child. Toby had been away, filming for six months in Romania, so Temple was with her full time throughout her pregnancy. Sylvia had moved in with her and Kit around week thirty-eight, so she could look after Temple when Natalie went into labour, then help when she brought the baby home.

She'd done all the 'right things' when Temple came in to visit them at the hospital, although she was nine, not a toddler. Stella had been in her plastic crib, and Natalie had opened her arms wide for Temple, who had barely acknowledged her, squealing with delight as she sped to the other side of the bed to peer instead at the new baby. That fondness had endured, even when Temple had switched to spending the majority of time with her father as a teenager, despite the differences between them. Stella had been a happy shadow when Temple was around, and Temple had been patient and kind with her. Today, they made as unlikely a pair as ever. Temple, six inches shorter than her younger sibling, had left her hair wild and curly, and was wearing wide linen trousers and a skimpy T-shirt, an enormous black bag slung across her body, while Stella was her usual neat and smooth self in a pink sundress and rope wedges.

Stella had graduated from Edinburgh University the summer before, and been at home for a few months while she job-hunted, but once she'd found something, she'd moved into a three-bed flat in Brixton with a school friend, Joanna, and Sal, a mate from uni. With Temple in London, and Stella and Marley at university, Natalie had been beyond grateful for Arlo, the last fledgling.

There'd been shades of the cuckoo in the nest when Stella came back after finals – it was odd for them all, the independent, self-determining young woman, the parents and sibling used to her absence. They'd had some fun while she was at home, but they'd had some hideous rows too, doors slamming for the first time in years. They'd all been ready for the job and the flat, when they came. Even Arlo. Of course, Natalie had missed Stella horribly, and had had to get used to her being gone all over again.

She was trying, now, to adjust the balance of their relationship – to be more her friend than her mother. It was the hardest part of parenting, she thought, stretching the umbilical cord without severing it. Across a couple of decades, you needed to demote yourself from being their absolute everything to the thing they happily, healthily left behind, and you had to do it seamlessly, without, somehow, diminishing yourself for yourself. It wasn't easy. She wasn't sure she'd quite managed it with Temple, so there was no reason to suppose she'd be any more successful with Stella, but it seemed right to try.

With Marley it was much easier. She loved him passionately, as she did all her children, but he was so easy. A long, lanky eating machine when home, an almost entirely silent absentee. She couldn't remember the last time he'd brought her, or Kit, an issue or a problem, and although she read all the stuff about mental health in young males, and tried to be alert to any signal, Marley seemed, to her relief, to be a straightforward, easygoing, happy guy who required neither her vigilance nor much of her input.

Stella didn't often thank her for her input, but hadn't quite lost the lifelong habit of requesting it either. It could feel cruel, and Stella could be bombastic.

Sylvia had laughed heartily when she heard her granddaughter described that way the first time. 'Buck up, Nat. She sounds just like you. I used to pray I'd live long enough to see you dealing with someone just like you, and here she is!'

Sylvia had chosen the venue for their lunch – a gastropub with a large conservatory at the back. Today, all the doors were open. They sat down at their table near the outdoors, and Natalie ordered a bottle of Prosecco.

'To you, my darling girls. To all of you!' Sylvia made the toast, when the glasses were filled, and they clinked.

She leant in, her eyes sparkling. 'I want to hear every tiny detail of your lives – anything you want to tell me, of course. I don't meddle.'

They laughed because, of course, she did. She knew exactly which questions would make you squirm the most, and she loved to ask them.

'What about a young man for you, my beautiful Stella? I cannot believe suitors are not swarming around you like bees to honey, darling!' Sylvia exclaimed.

'Such a grandmother thing to say, Gran.' Stella laughed, rolling her eyes. 'Suitors? Which century are we in?'

Sylvia rolled her eyes. 'Is there any century in which manners and romance are not to be desired?'

Both her granddaughters knew better than to argue with her. She had a very low tolerance for anything remotely 'woke'. The very word, once she had understood its twenty-first-century meaning, made her sputter with indignation. Marley had been heard saying that he loved his grandmother – now his only living grandparent – but that she was the actual definition of political incorrectness. 'We're not supposed to ignore it. We're all supposed to correct her,' he'd said, a tiny bit exasperated, one Christmas. 'Otherwise we are part of the problem and not part of the solution.' No one thought that was a good idea. Not even Marley.

'Course not.' Stella indulged her. 'We love manners and romance, right, Temps? Unfortunately, Gran, no suitors on the horizon. Just don't seem to be batting them away just now.'

'Nonsense. You can't have noticed, that's all. You're

gorgeous, just like your sister.' She patted Temple's knee. 'But seriously, darling, you've got to kiss a lot of toads before you find your handsome prince.'

'Gran! I'm only twenty-two.'

'I was married to your grandfather by the time I was twenty-two, my sweetheart.'

'Oh, my God.' Temple and Stella grimaced at each other. Sylvia caught the look, and raised a finger in their direction. 'Hey. I see you.'

'I'm going to the loo.' Stella stood up.

Temple jumped to her feet. She had no intention of drawing the fire in her sister's absence. 'Me too.'

Watching the girls retreat, Sylvia leant in conspiratorially, and narrowed her eyes. 'How is she doing, really?' Natalie knew she meant Temple now, and not Stella.

She shrugged. 'Not great, I think, Mum.'

'She looks tired.' Natalie had thought so too, when the dark glasses had come off in the restaurant.

'You're right. She did say she hadn't been sleeping that well.'

'So what's she going to do about it?'

'I don't know about that either.'

Sylvia sighed, and spread her hands, palms up, in front of her. 'There are two ways this can be fixed. By staying together and working at what is wrong. Or by calling it quits. I don't really know Max. I think your hunch is that the latter would hurt our girl the least in the long run. Better sooner before it hurts her any more, before there are children who will be hurt if it doesn't work out, before she starts to believe it's normal to be married to someone who doesn't at least want to try to make her happy. I had friends who lived their whole lives that way and, believe me, it's no damn good. It makes for wrinkles, and bitterness. Everyone should expect more.'

'I know you're right. But I can't tell her.'

'Nonsense. Of course you must tell her. Even if she is furious with you.'

Natalie smiled. She made it sound easy.

The door swung open and Stella and Temple started to weave their way through the tables towards them. Sylvia fixed a smile on her face, but leant in closer and whispered,

'Can't you take her away somewhere? Just the two of you. Get the whole story out of her?'

The girls were back. 'What are you two whispering about?'

'None of your business, sticky-beaks.' She picked up the folded menu. 'Now, who is having what to eat? I don't want to hear any rubbish about diets. And, afterwards, their chocolate mousse cup is legendary . . .'

Later, when they'd dropped Sylvia at home – which had taken a time, as there were flowers in the garden to be admired, and a new gouache drawing of pink peonies to exclaim over, they laughed at her, fondly, en route back to the station.

'She's a one-off.'

'Safety in numbers. Easier to deal with her as a threesome. She's like the Stasi with a blue-rinse one-to-one.'

Natalie laughed. 'Oy! That's my mother. She'd be really offended about the blue-rinse bit.'

Stella sniggered. 'But totally fine with the Stasi?'

'She likes to know what's going on. She's invested.' She stopped short of the air quotes, but the girls knew what she meant.

'Okay. We'll call it that. She's a riot. I can't imagine her not being around.' Temple remembered her grandfather well, but Stella's recollections were more from photographs and stories told – she'd been so young when he died.

Natalie hated the thought of her mother's absence, and refused to entertain it. 'I'm so glad you came, girls. I've loved today. Thank you.'

'Hey – thank you! Free lunch. Catch up with my sister. It's been good.' Temple smiled.

'I was telling Temps on the train, Mum – Sal's being seconded for six months, with work. It's amazing. She'll be in Bristol. They'll put her up in one of those executive lets there, all paid and everything. Very cool. Will definitely be going for weekends. Bristol is fantastic, she says. She'll keep up the rent and stuff in Brixton in case she wants to come back at weekends, but I don't know – she'd make a lot if she sublet it, and she could always share with me or Joanna if she was back in London. Not like either of us is seeing anyone – as Gran has painfully reminded me!' She made a mock-rueful face.

'To who, though?' Temple asked. 'You wouldn't advertise for strangers, would you?'

Stella shook her head. 'No. Don't think so. She doesn't

need the money, really. But it might be nice for her and for us, huh? And, well, we had drinks a few days ago – me and some of the Dorfest girls, Zoë and Daisy. Phoebe and Mia showed up too. They'd been for a wedding-dress fitting around the corner.' Stella was momentarily distracted. 'Oh, she wouldn't show us a picture, but I've seen a swatch of the fabric, and oh – my – God. It's gorgeous. She's going to look amazing . . . and, anyway, Mia was saying she wasn't really loving her flat at the moment.'

'No? Where is she, again?'

'Hampstead? Somewhere up there. I've never actually been. She only moved this year. She's almost six months into a contract. Breakout clause time. One of her flat-mates has a boyfriend, who sounds like a bit of a creep, and he's always there, apparently. She was talking about moving out when the six months was up, but she didn't really know what she wanted to do after that, so . . .' she took a deep breath, finally coming to her point '. . . it might work for her.'

'What did she think of the idea?'

'I haven't said anything to her yet – I need to speak to Sal first. Good idea, though, huh?'

Natalie couldn't have explained why it made her anxious to think of her and Dom's daughters living together. But it did. Of course. Because it's too close to home. All of it. You stupid woman. That's precisely why you cannot do anything about it.

Natalie decided she'd be more proactive with Temple. It was everything she was trying not to do with Stella, but maybe that was a mistake with her elder daughter. Sylvia was right. She asked to see her again a week or so after their lunch. And she was glad she had.

It was too warm and too lovely to take the Tube, so Natalie strolled to the Overground station. She was in no hurry, and that feeling was always a novelty for a young mum. Not that she was that young. But Arlo still was. For years and years, even the loveliest days were bisected by duty. You didn't leave until after the school run. Tried to be home for tea, bath and bed. But now term had ended and the long summer holiday had begun. Arlo was with her mum. That tradition had started when he was really young: as soon as the term ended, Sylvia took him somewhere for a week or so, just the two of them. They talked about it for months beforehand, planning and scheming. This year they'd taken the train to Edinburgh. They were coming home on the sleeper. Arlo was desperately excited about it all, but especially about the sleeper train.

She'd made this plan to spend some time with Temple once she knew Kit wasn't going to be around. In the past, he might have avoided this particular week – the two of them might have slunk away to one of those snazzy places in the New Forest or the Cotswolds for a day or two. When she'd learnt he'd booked a trip with two old college friends, he'd pretended he hadn't realized it was the same week, and she'd pretended she minded he wouldn't be around.

('You never said.'

'Why didn't you just know? It's the same damn week every year.')

She didn't even notice she didn't mind until he'd said it. She might even have started to reproach him. Even then, she told herself it was just because having a few days in a row all to herself was such a novelty, a real treat. Complete self-determination was rare for wives and mothers. She tried not to think about the faint, creeping sensation that she was glad he was going.

She'd wondered about booking a hotel for her and Temple, or a day spa or a show, like Sylvia had suggested. She wanted to do something special, something indulgent, for her daughter. But Temple had said she only really had time for lunch just now. Work was busy. She felt a slight sting of rejection, but she hadn't said anything.

In the end, though, the two of them had had a quick lunch outside, in the park, then seen an exhibition at the Royal Academy. There wasn't time to unpack anything substantial, but at least it reconnected them. Temple seemed a bit happier. She looked bright-eyed, even, and less tired than the last time. She was dressed for work and Natalie realized she hadn't seen her with hair and make-up done, in a pretty dress, for a long time. She was beautiful both ways.

She and Max were seeing a counsellor, she said, right at the beginning, before the waiter had even taken their order. He'd been resistant to the concept at first, but they'd done several sessions and she really thought they were starting to make some progress with their 'issues'. One of Max's, she said, staring at the tablecloth and colouring vaguely pink, was that he didn't feel comfortable with her talking about it to Natalie. Natalie swallowed her indignant snort. She bet he bloody didn't. He'd much rather keep Temple locked in an echo chamber of his own pronouncements.

'So can we not talk about him, Mum,' Temple had implored, 'about any of it, just for today?'

Natalie felt that sting again, but she smiled, patted Temple's hand, and replied, 'Of course, darling. Whatever you like. I just wanted to see you, my beautiful girl, and spend some time just the two of us.'

And that was what they had done. And it had been a happy couple of hours – light and giggly and funny. If Temple had needed to talk for hours on end about Max, Natalie would have listened, of course. But this was better. It needn't always be about him, and sometimes a break from whatever was going on in your head was best. Just before they'd parted, with Temple about to descend the steps to the Underground, Natalie had brought up the idea of a weekend away. 'Wherever you want!'

Temple had agreed immediately, and pulled out her battered diary to look for a date. In the era of electronic calendars, she still had an actual diary – it was one of the sweet, old-fashioned things about her. She suggested one only a few weeks off, when she thought she was free, and marked it with a small pencil. Sylvia was right, Natalie thought. She might get her to open up more there, whatever Max thought about sharing.

After Temple had gone back to work, Natalie had wandered happily through some of her old stamping grounds, dipping into the fabric shops and costume outlets on Berwick Street, and spent a wonderful hour browsing in Liberty. It felt like ages since she'd had nothing in particular planned, and was free to linger. She'd thought about staying the night in their flat. There was no reason not to – no one to rush home for. She had what she needed there – a toothbrush, clean knickers for the morning. But on balance she'd realized she'd rather go home to the countryside and wake up, the windows wide open, to the sound of birds, not traffic. The thought made her smile. Twenty-six-year-old Natalie would have been incredulous.

She stopped halfway across the Thames, on Waterloo Bridge. She always did, if she was walking. It was still her favourite view of all the vistas she loved in London, facing east to St Paul's Cathedral and the big curve in the river, and west to Parliament and the London Eye. The day was still very warm, but there was a breeze. Below her, a river bus sailed serenely beneath the bridge, full of tourists and commuters.

There were several trains each hour at this time of day, so she wasn't rushing, and she had no plan as she strolled off the bridge and up the wide staircase to the station concourse. If there was a wait, she'd just buy a big coffee, a copy of *Vogue* . . .

And then, just like that, there was Dom.

She told herself – no, that wasn't true. She'd stopped lying to herself. She told *other people* (or she would have told other people) that it had started by accident, that no one had meant for it to happen. She might even have tried to score points for resisting so long – the force of her feelings. Their feelings. It wasn't true. It wasn't really an accident. It was just exquisitely slow, played out over years and years.

Perhaps it was the unfamiliar surroundings, or the unexpected nature of the encounter. Seeing him walking towards her, a smile of recognition breaking slowly across his face, her stomach dropped and her heart raced. She was utterly surprised – she hadn't seen him since the night at Flick and Andrew's and the soft good-night kiss. They hadn't spoken on the telephone again and there'd been no message – of course there hadn't. But here he was, right now.

'Nat! Hello there. What are you doing here?' He looked flatteringly delighted to see her. He bent down and kissed her cheek quickly and she was surprised again that the smell of him was familiar. She felt stupidly aware of everything. Hyper-aware. The slight prickle of his five o'clock shadow on her cheek, the briefest sensation of his breath across her skin, and the light touch of his hand on her shoulder as he kissed her. Like a young girl. Like an idiot.

'I've been up in town for the day.'

Stupid, obvious answer.

He cocked his head on one side, and his smile was teasing now, his sarcasm lightly delivered. 'Really?'

She was flustered, for God's sake. Which she almost never was. She wondered if her make-up was okay. It was hot, and with the walking, she wondered if she looked a mess. She quickly ran a finger across her upper lip in case it was beaded with sweat. Ran her fingers through her hair, pushing it back from her forehead, and hoping it was more tousled than tangled.

He wasn't looking at her while she did these small, self-conscious things. His gaze was fixed above her head at the board.

'Christ.' His voice was exasperated. 'They're all up the Swannee.'

'I see that. I thought I'd probably catch the five-thirty.'

'No such train this evening.' He smiled wryly. 'I was going for that one too. Knocked off early. Serves me right. Looks like the next has been cancelled too. Shit.' He glanced at his watch, then back up at the board, and then gazed at her. It felt like he'd deliberately rearranged his features – the irritation was gone, and he was smiling again. 'So, you're up in town?' Again with the slightly teasing tone. 'Business or pleasure?'

'All pleasure, I'm afraid. A completely self-indulgent day. Kit's away. Arlo is with his gran. They've gone to explore Edinburgh. It's my "me" week so I'm making the most of it. I met Temple in the West End, and we had lunch. A look round the Royal Academy. A bit of window-shopping on Bond Street and I popped into Fortnum's.' She lifted a small turquoise bag containing the tiny marzipan fruits she could never resist to vouch for her.

'Good for you. How is Temple?'

She smiled. 'She's good. Doing okay.'

'I'm glad.' He was still grinning at her.

'You? Working?'

'Indeed.' He raised his briefcase as she had raised her spoils, and gestured at his navy blue suit. He wasn't wearing a tie – the top couple of buttons of his white shirt were undone and she tried not to stare at the blond hairs springing at the top of his chest. She pictured the rest of the hair and the pattern it formed, remembering him in swimming trunks in Dorset a few weeks ago, and wondered if she was blushing. God – she was such a cliché. Far too bloody old to be coquettish. It was unseemly. Embarrassing.

She started to speak, but the station announcer began an utterance at the same time, and he raised a finger to his lips, cocking his head to hear. Around them the station concourse was getting steadily more crowded with milling commuters. The announcer finished. She hadn't caught any of it.

'This has happened far too bloody often lately. The infrastructure's had it. Signalling in Surbiton.' He rolled his eyes.

'How long does it normally take to sort itself out?'

'That depends. Hours sometimes.' He looked at her, and it was quite a look – steady, intense even – suddenly quite serious after the grinning. Then he took his phone out of his pocket, and punched a key. She knew who he was calling. 'Sarah? It's me.'

She looked away when he said Sarah's name, but the pressing crowd was keeping them in close proximity, and she could still hear him.

'Yes, fine. Okay. But the trains are buggered. Some sort of signalling Armageddon somewhere. The usual. Probably melted tracks. You know, the chocolate ones can't take the heat.' He paused, listening. When he spoke again, she turned back, and he was gazing directly at her. She watched his mouth while he talked.

'Listen, it's beyond crowded here and more than a little unpleasant. Think it'll most likely take a couple of hours to sort itself out. I think, if it's okay with you, I'll cut my losses and get a pint or something. Maybe grab a burger. Sit it out in the sunshine, and just be home when I'm home. Is that okay?'

He paused again. From his expression, she knew he wasn't just asking his wife. He was asking *her*.

Finally.

She felt the sensation you got when you were on a roller coaster and it made that sudden deep swoop. And she nodded at him.

She couldn't hear Sarah, but then he dipped his head. 'Just me.'

As he listened to whatever the answer from home was, he raised an eyebrow at her. It was disconcerting. She shrugged in response, and smiled, accepting.

'I'll see you later. Me too. Thanks. Bye.'

So. It was the first lie. It would have been a perfectly normal coincidence to have bumped into her. No big deal. He should have said, shouldn't he? It would have been fine to say that *they*'d grab a drink, wouldn't it? But he hadn't done that, and he'd wrapped her up with him in the first tiny knot of deceit.

She didn't need to call anyone, and she was glad she needn't lie, except later when she already knew she would lie by omission.

She should have felt troubled. She just felt excited.

'Let's get out of here.' And he took her hand.

The warm sunshine and the station chaos meant that there were already crowds in the bars by the Thames. By unspoken agreement they kept walking, further from the station and the people, and they kept holding hands, long after it had seemed a necessary and sensible way to guide one another off the crowded concourse. Her hand felt small within his grasp. He switched the hold now – lacing his fingers between hers. She felt his wedding ring against her skin.

They bought pizza slices and small bottles of champagne from an old-style silver van parked on the side of the road, and sat on the patch of grass by the river, in the shadow of the London Eye. Lots of people were doing the same, and there was a laid-back, funky atmosphere she had always associated with her youth, and with London on a warm mid-week evening. It was the kind of evening she'd missed when she'd first got together with Kit and moved out of the city. A few times, cooking fish fingers for Temple, tired from school, bouncing a baby Stella between feeds, she remembered looking at the clock, seeing 6.30 p.m., and missing this, exactly this, but she'd given up doing that years ago. Now, though, it was exhilarating to be there again. Natalie felt dangerous, and she liked it. She'd brought a shawl with her, although the day had turned out much warmer than she had expected, and she spread it out now for them to sit on. Dom took off his jacket, and rolled up the sleeves on his shirt. He folded the jacket carefully, inside outwards to protect the wool, and laid it neatly beside them. It was very like him – that careful detail – and she smiled.

'What?' His tone was playful.

'Nothing.' She kicked off her mules, letting her toes sink into the grass.

He sat across from her, leaning back on his elbows. She was very aware that her feet, with their bright pink toenails, were close to his shoulder. It seemed suddenly very surprising, and very intimate. She'd been his friend for twenty years. They'd been at parties, and funerals, up mountains and on beaches. They'd seen each other in black tie and pyjamas, swimsuits and ski suits. But this was completely different. They'd been alone maybe three or four times, and never for long. The others hadn't been far away. This was different. And he felt it too. She could sense that. And he had made it happen. He had started it. This. Whatever this was. He stared at her foot.

Then, when he sat forward to open the champagne bottles, he laid his hand across the arch of it, just briefly. Deliberately. Like his fingers curling possessively around hers in the back of a cab for ever ago, it had the same startling and disproportionate effect.

This time they didn't talk lightly about the past – about the times they'd been in London with the others, about summer-in-the-city recollections. Not about anything they'd ever done as a group, with Sarah and with Kit. They talked as though they hadn't known each other for almost twenty years. As though they didn't know the minutiae of each other's lives – spouses, children, domestic details. But about none of that. For now, some loyalty, unspoken, still held.

Without the interjections of others, or the sense that the length and depth of their conversation was inappropriate, without the policing of company, they just talked.

And two hours passed.

'We've got to go.' She desperately didn't want to. The thought that it might be another twenty years before she could be alone with him like this seemed absurd. And unlikely.

He groaned, equally unwilling, it seemed.

'It's been so nice.'

He groaned louder. 'Nice is a terrible word.'

'Stop fishing for compliments.'

'Give me another word, and I will.'

'Amazing. Okay. Amazing.'

He looked down at the grass. 'I'll take that.'

For a moment they were silent, and then they looked at each other.

'Is this okay?' Dom asked, although he knew the answer.

She shook her head slowly. 'I don't think it is.'

'Do you want to go?'

She shook her head again. More slowly. 'No.'

'I don't either.' He laughed. 'I want to stay here. I want to just sit here with you, sipping champagne, on this glorious evening. I want to look at you. Keep looking at you.'

'Dom.'

'You're so beautiful, Nat.'

'I don't think –'

'You are. You always have been. You get, in fact, and somewhat unfairly, more beautiful with time. To me.' He held her gaze.

'Thank you.'

'I've wanted to tell you that so many times. It feels bloody fantastic to tell you now.'

She didn't know how to respond.

'It's always been there, hasn't it? Something.' He wouldn't let her not look at him.

She didn't want to make him stop. The answer was obvious. 'Yes.'

That was the truth, after all. There always had been. There was relief in admitting it.

It was another line crossed, too.

It was Dom who was bolder, and his voice was genuinely curious. 'What is it, do you think? I mean, have you thought about it?'

'I've thought about it.' She laughed ruefully. 'Of course I have.'

'So have you figured out what it is, from your

perspective? Do we just fancy each other? Is it that superficial, d'you think?'

One last try. 'We shouldn't be having this conversation, Dom.'

'But we are.' He took her hand. 'I declare an amnesty. Please just . . . please answer.'

She took a deep breath. 'I think . . . it's always been more than that, for me.'

He looked relieved. 'For me, too.'

He offered his other hand, to pull her to her feet, but kept holding it after she was standing, her arm close to his side. It seemed obvious that they were going to kiss but, still, it took a long moment of standing that way. Maybe they were giving each other a pause to step back, step away. Maybe each was hoping the other would come to their senses. Maybe they were just savouring the delicious weight of anticipation.

She hadn't kissed any man other than Kit since she'd met him all those long years ago. Perhaps, asked, people might have cocked their heads, appraising, and guessed that she, of all of them, might have done, but she had not. She only knew how to kiss him – she'd long forgotten there was any other way. She didn't know how to kiss anyone else. Not, like this, on the mouth. His mouth felt more different than she had thought it would.

And she had almost completely forgotten how a kiss could start so gently and softly and slowly – could be so tentative and careful – then grow in intensity without you moving apart once. That wasn't how married people kissed. This felt as if the kiss was everything, all there was going to be. How lips were the fixed point around which the rest of you moved – hands through hair to the backs of necks, chests together, hips rising.

She felt like she'd forgotten everything. Like she'd been dormant.

That's all that had happened, the first time. They were like kids. Kit would have called it a snog. She'd never liked the term, but it worked well for what this was. They broke apart eventually. Stood smiling at each other.

Dom nodded decisively. 'Okay, then.' She wasn't sure what he meant.

Then, reluctantly, they began retracing their steps towards the train and their lives.

The lights in the station seemed unnecessarily bright after the twilight of outside. They looked dishevelled, interrupted somehow, and they'd smoothed down their hair, rubbed their mouths. She felt the graze of his stubble on her face and hoped she wasn't red. Anyone observing them on the platform, waiting for the announced train to disembark, would have guessed exactly what had happened between them, not by how close they stood, but how consciously apart, yet there was, miraculously, no one they knew tonight. They took seats opposite, not side by side, on the train, as the carriage filled. The cram of disgruntled commuters with their bags, unnecessary mackintoshes and newspapers meant that no one could see how his large, black-leather-clad foot was just touching her smaller one in its blush pink mule. Even if they had, it would have seemed like an accident. Neither let show on their face how it felt to have their feet touching that way.

They were careful again when they got off the train at the station. Anyone could be here. They were parked in different directions in the car park. Hers was further away, the closer spaces having gone to the early arrivals. Their fellow travellers milled in both directions. Someone brushed by Natalie too closely, and for a second she thought they were trying to get her attention, someone she knew.

'I'll walk you to your car.'

'No. No need. Thank you.' She didn't trust either of them in the dark corners.

He didn't argue with her. Perhaps he didn't either. When he said goodbye, Dom's voice was a fraction too loud, like an actor projecting to an audience. 'Well, Nat, great to see you. Have a good night.' And the kiss on her cheek was chaste, and dry, and far from the corner of her mouth.

She didn't know what she'd expected, but she felt achingly flat, and disappointed.

At home, having gone straight upstairs to bed, Natalie couldn't sleep. The windows were all wide open, but the air was still and the room didn't cool much. At eleven, exasperated, she threw back the sheets and took a shower, but that didn't help. She lay on the covers, restless, her mind whirling. At five she gave up, and wandered downstairs in her linen dressing-gown to make tea. She took a mug out onto the terrace, and sat in a wicker armchair, her knees hugged to her chest. The air was finally cool, and the sun was rising. It was beautiful – a painterly wash of pinks and oranges and blues in a cloudless sky, and she felt calmer than she should. She had the strong feeling that the night before had been momentous. That her evening with Dom had broken a sort of dam inside her. There was guilt, and anxiety, a sliver of sorrow, but they weren't the dominant emotions, not now, not yet. Whatever happened next, and she had no idea what it would be, things would never, couldn't ever, be the same between them.

Her phone buzzed from inside on the kitchen counter, and she went inside to get it. It was a text, from Dom. He'd sent a photograph, and she clicked to open the attachment. It was a shot of the same sunrise she was watching. There was no message, but she thought she knew what he was saying. She held the phone close to her chest, and went back to the garden.

12

Almost a week had passed. Five days. Often a week flew by, measured in loads of laundry, and steps counted on your Apple watch, and episodes of your favourite show. Hell, whole months could go by like that. This one, though, had dragged.

What was he thinking? Natalie told herself that once that beautiful sunrise he'd shared with her wordlessly had passed, and Sarah had come down to make coffee, he'd been suffused with regret at his, at their, foolishness. He should be. She could have messaged him herself, but she didn't. Several times she started a text message, then deleted it. Was she pretending to herself that letting him make the contact somehow absolved her of guilt? Or was she just not brave enough?

And then he did. He left a voicemail, asking her to meet him for a late lunch. He said the place, and the time, as if he'd already booked a table, and his confidence should have seemed arrogant, maybe. So sure she'd go.

But he was right. She'd thrown her phone onto the sofa, as if it was suddenly burning hot, stared at it for long minutes, fighting with herself, before she picked it up again, and typed, yes, she'd meet him. She'd be there.

That night, Natalie slept badly again. She'd dreamt vividly, and she wished she couldn't remember what had been in the dream, but she could, like it was a film she'd watched. The kids had all been young, at their most marauding-gang stage – a giggling gaggle of inter-changeable, irrepressible, excitable innocence. A friend of Vanessa's had been the stage manager at the local theatre – she'd always arranged a block of tickets, really good seats, for the first weekend of the pantomime. She and the other girls had taken them all, every year. It was one of their cherished rituals. Leave half an hour at least for them to fill pick-and-mix bags in the foyer, then div-ide and conquer them in the seats, and wait to see who brings their blankie and curls up on your lap instead of their chair, and who falls asleep, and who is a bit too young or too timid and cries when the special effects go bang. Leap up in the interval to be at the front of the queue for ice creams – those cardboard pots with the spoon in the lid. Don't let the kids choose – you'll be there all day. Get half chocolate and half strawberry and hope for the best. Take up to half the group to the loo at an inopportune and uncharacteristically quiet moment in the story because they honestly, truly didn't need to go in the interval. Emerge blinking into the cold dark night, with the kids on a sugar high. Collapse with large glasses of Merlot.

Except instead of a dame and two ugly sisters, it had been her on the stage when the heavy red velvet curtains opened. Her and Dom passionately kissing. The dream ended when she broke off the kiss and turned to curtsy to the audience, only to see the horrified children, mouths gaping. And there in the middle, Sarah. Except not the Sarah of ten plus years ago. Present-day Sarah, looking right at her.

Natalie sat up against the headboard. She felt clammy, and her nightdress clung to her uncomfortably. Beside her, Kit was still asleep.

She stood up, moving slowly and quietly so as not to disturb him. She took her phone from the nightstand, and crept downstairs into the laundry room, where she could shut the door. She texted Dom. She'd changed his number in her phone. He was listed under U, as Upholsterer. She'd done it the day after the South Bank, when he'd sent the picture. She wondered whether he had done the same. What disguise he'd have chosen for her.

Can you talk?

He came back immediately.

Shall I call you?

She dialled his number. He answered in his normal voice. 'I've been playing squash. I'm heading to my car. You still okay for later?'

Her voice was a whisper. 'I don't think so.'

'What's happened?'

'Nothing's happened, not as such. I just think . . . Dom, we can't do this. At least, I don't think I can.'

'Don't say that.'

'Don't you think what we're doing is wrong?'

He paused. 'It doesn't feel wrong.'

'That's not the same thing.'

'Meet me. We can talk about this. We can decide what to do.'

'Don't you hate yourself, just a little?' She looked out

of the window, across the lawn, to the field beyond. Rabbits ran back and forth in the early silence. She'd been enchanted by the sight of them frolicking when she and Kit had first moved here, before she discovered they ate everything she planted. 'I think I hate myself.'

'You have to come, Nat,' he implored. 'Just say you'll come. Please.'

Perhaps he knew what she did too. That if she wasn't going to meet him, she'd have texted. That she needed him to pull on her once more. To tug her out of what was right, and habitual, into what was wrong and wonderful.

He read her answer in her silence. 'I'll see you at two. Okay?'

She didn't agree. She hung up.

13

Natalie had heard a group of the older girls, years ago now, discussing the three-date rule. She couldn't remember whether it had been all of them, but Mia, Phoebe and Daisy definitely had been involved. Maybe Zoë was with them. She'd been relieved that Stella, that little bit younger, had been somewhere else with Jasmine. She had no idea where the boys were, but at that time, the two groups seemed to repel each other. The girls had been lying languidly on the grass at Annie's one day, all long limbs and short shorts, imagining the grown-ups were distracted. She had no recollection of why she was in the garden – she certainly wasn't snooping. She almost wished she hadn't heard, because it had placed on her the uncomfortable responsibility of whether or not to relay it to their parents. She wasn't one of the disciplinarians, that was for sure.

She'd decided against. Perhaps it was just talk. Showing off. Sex education as gleaned from episodes of *Friends*. It had been a bit shocking, she recalled, that any of them might have thought they were at *that* stage. Wasn't that parenting? You were always two steps behind. To her, they were too young to be having sex, however ready they thought they were. Ross had once said that a part of him always wanted to take boyfriends

Daisy and Jasmine brought home around the back and kick the shit out of them, however nice they were. Flick told a hilarious story about mild-mannered Andrew squaring up to one of the girls' prom dates and telling him, *sotto voce* gangster style, that he wouldn't mind going back to prison. She said it might have been more menacing if the lad hadn't had four inches on Andrew. Stella, she believed, had waited until she was sixteen or seventeen, some time after the third date. That boy had been sweet, and they'd been together through sixth form. Mostly it worked out, and perhaps ignorance was, to a degree, bliss. They all seemed to have come through it okay.

And now here she was, years later, a grown woman, considering the three-date rule.

She wanted Dom. He made it very clear he wanted her, and that made her want him more. There'd been a lot of hot and heavy, all outdoors, all in public. It was very like being a teenager with nowhere to go. In the cold light of day, it was – what would Sylvia say? – unseemly. She couldn't help it.

It couldn't have happened in winter. Would it still be happening in winter? What, even, was it?

If they were to find themselves alone, it would happen. It would definitely happen. The thought was both delicious and terrifying. You could never undo it.

If Natalie's emotions ricocheted, Dom's were consistent. He was so, so sure. She spent half the time feeling lightheaded with desire, driven by appetites long dormant, the other half almost nauseous with guilt and fear. A silly woman, trying to live a double life. She didn't have the constitution for secrecy. It plagued her at night. There was already so much to confess. So many lies – they piled up like cars in traffic jams. When she was with him, it all faded away. But it soon flooded back, its whoosh loud in her ears.

If Dom felt any of that, he didn't confess it to her. He was pushing her. Pulling her with him. Oh, the things he said. She'd never known, even when she'd acknowledged the forcefield of attraction around him, how beautifully he could speak, how he could make her feel with words. She'd never heard him talk to Sarah that way. She didn't want to wonder whether he ever had. She didn't want to talk about Sarah at all. Their paths hadn't crossed in a while, and she was glad.

With each hour they spent together, it was getting harder not to take it further. She didn't know how much longer she could wait. It was inevitable. Whatever she said to herself, or tried to tell either of them that it couldn't happen, it was like they both knew it would.

14

She should never have taken him to the damn flat. What the hell had she expected would happen? No excuses. No blaming Dom, or the moonlight, or the wine, or even Kit. It was her. Just her. She'd told herself it was the middle of the afternoon. That they were middle-aged. Middle-aged married people didn't commit adultery on weekday afternoons in broad daylight. That it was safe. It was laughable. That was what she'd told herself. Pathetic.

It had all been so very easy.

Lunch outside, a stroll down to Trafalgar Square, a spontaneous flit around the National Portrait Gallery. At least, she'd thought it was spontaneous. Dom might well have planned it that way. Kit used to like galleries. She couldn't remember the last time they'd been in one. A client party at the top of the Tate Modern a couple of years ago, but he scored no points for that. He'd wanted to get home, not to linger and look at art.

All Dom wanted to do was linger. He suddenly had all the time in the world. He didn't want to look at art. He wanted to look at her looking at art. He couldn't take his eyes off her, and she loved how that felt. She'd never felt more desirable in her life.

London was hot and busy. It was suddenly peak

tourist season, and everywhere was crowded. There seemed to be queues for everything – a cold drink, an ice cream, a seat outside a coffee shop. The flat was so close.

Almost as soon as she'd suggested they went there for a cup of tea, with the promise of an oasis of peace and quiet, she saw what she'd done. She knew exactly, even if she tried to deny it to herself. Dom accepted the offer casually, but he felt it too, she knew. They'd been chatting all afternoon, but now they said barely a word to each other. They'd been strolling, but now he took her hand, and they walked purposefully.

The flat was on the first floor, off a small green courtyard you might not know was there. It was a modern development – just six little flats on three floors, with the patch of outside space, and tiny balconies, just wide enough for a couple of folding chairs.

She'd been already today, earlier, before she'd met Dom, to drop off her bag. She'd told Kit she was planning on staying the night. She'd put fresh sheets on the bed. She'd bought a small bunch of yellow roses when she'd picked up milk and sparkling water, and arranged them in a jug on the round café table.

They were timid again once they were inside. The change in setting made them nervous. Natalie opened windows, and poured glasses of cold water.

'This is great! I'd sort of forgotten you had it.'

'Thank you. It is great. We're so lucky to have it. Truthfully, we don't use it enough, really. When we bought it, you know, when we moved out, I thought I'd be here all the time but, you know, life.' She shrugged. 'I haven't slept here in months. The kids probably use it more than we do. It's a shame, really. A waste. It's such a lovely flat.'

The walls and units were painted white. There were a couple of black-and-white framed landscape photographs. No books. Barcelona leather chairs, and a simple rug. Through the open black Crittall door a big bed was made up with white sheets, and a gauzy linen voile curtain billowed slightly in the breeze. The yellow roses on the table were the only colour in the space. It was almost monastic. 'It's very different from your house.'

She smiled. 'Yes. I like things a bit minimalist. Especially in a tiny space. The house is much more Kit's. Maximalist.' That felt disloyal. 'I mean, what he's done there really works . . .' Her voice trailed off, and she shook her head.

'It's beautiful.'

She laughed. 'It's too small to swing a cat in, really. There's just this room, the bedroom and a minuscule wet room through there.'

'The perfect pied-à-terre.'

'I suppose . . .' Natalie felt jittery. 'I'll get us that cup of tea.' As if that might save her. The kitchen part of the room was a small U shape at one end. She filled the kettle, and took mugs from a cupboard.

It was almost, but not quite, unbearable.

And then Dom was right there, behind her. He reached around, gently prised the mugs from her hands, put them on the counter and took her hands in his. He kissed the side of her neck, and his breath on her skin was hot, then cool where his lips had been. He gradually spun her around. Took her face in his hands and kissed her deeply, leaning into her so her back arched over the worktop.

Then he stopped, pulled away, and looked into her eyes.

Something snapped in her, and she was kissing him back, all at once oblivious to anything except him.

And it was Natalie who took him by the hand and led him to the bed.

In the end, it wasn't as either of them had expected, or might have chosen it to be. Films and a certain type of novel peddled dreadful lies about sex. The first time two people who aren't familiar with each other's bodies or desires have sex, it is more likely to be awkward, unsatisfying, Natalie thought, than violins crescendoing, waves crashing. Limbs get in the way, preferences are as yet unknown, small doubts and worries pierce the mood.

And that was how it was for the two of them. A bit awkward, and too fast. Too much pressure. It was fast, fumbling, amateurish sex, with too many clothes in the way, and over far too quickly – before any kind of seduction scene either of them might have had planned could even get started. No conversation. Like virgins whose virginity had become burdensome, they just needed to get it over with. He'd laughed, his face buried in her neck, by her collarbone, and she'd laughed too, and stroked his nape, and it had made it all right.

Then she shifted slightly to lie against him, his arm

around her shoulders, fingers stroking the top of her arm, her hand on his chest. He groaned. 'I'm sorry. That was rubbish.'

'No! Not rubbish.'

'Not exactly great.'

'It's okay. I didn't bring my score paddles.'

'Thank God for that. I think a six would destroy me.'

She giggled mischievously. 'You think it was a six, do you?'

He flipped her over onto her back, and lay across her. 'Hey. Don't push your luck, Nat. You're dealing with the fragile male ego here.'

He didn't feel fragile. He felt solid, and strong.

Later in the afternoon, after a glass of wine, it was better. Much, much better. He'd gone slowly, slowly and appreciatively, exclaiming over her, telling her softly that she was beautiful and soft and sexy so often that she truly felt all of those things. Exploring, discovering . . . all of the wondrous things about learning a person. Sex with Dom that second time, and the third and the fourth and the fifth, felt like making art, whereas sex with Kit was painting by numbers. The latter got the job done, and could even make a beautiful picture, but it wasn't exciting or creative. It required no input from your mind, and minimal energy.

When you listened to every sound the other person made, gauging their pleasure, watching their face, moving slowly and so carefully, you could make it right for them. However good she had felt with Kit, she hadn't felt *this*,

this extraordinary powerful excitement, in years and years, and it was, here and now, completely consuming.

Afterwards he lay with his head on her breasts, one leg thrown across hers, while his heart rate and breathing slowed. 'Thank you.' She felt like a goddess. He kissed her briefly, a tiny dry kiss on the skin just above her nipple, closed his eyes, and slept. She felt it, the moment when oblivion descended. It took Natalie a lot longer to drift away. She felt too alive.

She fell asleep eventually, but several hours later, something unfamiliar woke her in the darkness. The room was lit only by moonlight through a gap in the curtains she'd hurriedly closed earlier, and from outside, she could hear the noise of glasses being moved, and cars. For a moment, she completely forgot where she was, who she was with. It took a few seconds to orient herself in the bed, in the room, in the flat. Dom was awake too, beside her, on her side of the bed. He was sitting upright against the headboard. Slenderer than Kit, less hairy, blonder. Now, suddenly, the comparison occurred to her. Earlier, she hadn't thought of Kit. Dom had blocked out everything.

'Are you okay?'

'I can't stop looking at you.'

She smoothed her hair back, self-conscious.

'Don't. Don't do that. You're wonderful, Nat.'

She laid her head back on the pillow, holding his gaze.

'I can't believe I'm here with you. It's like a dream. I sound stupid, probably. I am stupid, probably. But it's dreamlike, in the sense that I have dreamt of it.'

15

When she got home, Natalie went straight upstairs, relieved that neither Kit nor Arlo seemed to have heard the car, or her key in the lock. She turned on the bath taps so no one would hear her throw up. She'd known she was going to ever since she'd stood up on the train, and it had been a race to get here, to be alone, before the nausea overtook her. She felt dizzy with guilt, and very sick.

They'd stayed in bed until noon, her and Dom, talking and kissing and laughing and dozing. At some point, he'd put clothes on and gone out to buy breakfast, and they'd had croissants and coffee in bed, pastry flaking onto the crumpled sheets. They'd showered together in the tiny wet room, learning each other's bodies, then gone back to bed, damp and slippery.

It was like being drunk. At times she felt she couldn't take any more and then that she could never get enough.

He'd had to go around three. He held her and kissed her and suddenly couldn't speak.

Natalie wanted to cry as she stripped the bed, and put the sheets in the washer-dryer in the kitchen. Crumbs of breakfast fell on the tiled floor and she knelt to pick them up.

Being on the train home without him was like sobering up. As if she'd been under a spell in the flat, and it had been instantaneously broken as the train powered her towards her life. By the time she alighted at the station, she was ill with reality.

For a few minutes, she sat with her head resting against the toilet seat, waiting for the queasiness to pass. She unbuttoned her dress, and unhooked her bra. Her underwear felt too restricting.

When the bath had filled, she took off the rest of her clothes and climbed in, although she'd made it too hot, and the queasiness returned. She drew her knees up and held them to her chest, her eyes tightly closed, but the room kept moving.

'Nat? Is that you?'

Kit was outside. She heard him turn the knob, glad she'd locked the door. 'Are you okay?' His voice was full of concern.

She groaned. 'Think I've eaten something dodgy. Been sick. Just riding it out in here. Sorry.'

'Oh, bloody hell. Poor you. Let me in?'

'Not a spectator sport, love. Besides, I'm in the bath. It'll pass, I'm sure. It's just food poisoning. I'll be fine in the morning.'

'Okay, okay. I'm sorry. Look, don't worry about anything. I'll sort Arlo out. I'll sleep across the landing, let you have some space. I'll hear you, if you need me.'

'You're a star.'

'I'm just sorry you're not well. Did you have a nice time before that, at least?'

She moaned by way of response.

'Okay. You'll tell me later. Call me if you need me, okay?'

He went away, thank God. She sat stock still for maybe ten minutes, maybe more. The hot water left her skin red. There was a tidemark, where she'd held herself stiff. Gradually, everything calmed, and the sickness passed, although a throbbing headache in her temple took its place. Climbing out, she swallowed paracetamol from the bathroom cabinet, and pulled her dressing-gown over her damp skin.

Kit had left a cup of tea on her bedside table, along with a bottle of mineral water. He'd closed the door of their bedroom, and pulled the curtains over the window, so it was almost dark. She climbed onto the bed, curled into a ball, and let sleep overtake her.

It was hours later when she stirred. Kit had come in quietly, and had the back of his hand on her forehead, assessing her for a fever. She kept her eyes closed, and he smoothed her hair back from her face, then left her alone again, and she willed herself back into oblivion.

The next morning, she woke, as if she'd been asleep for days, to the smell of bacon grilling. She waited a second to see if it made her queasy: it made her hungry. She climbed out of bed, and opened the curtains to a blue sky. She retied the dressing-gown around her waist, and looked at her tousled self in the full-length mirror. She didn't look any different from the day before. No scarlet letter, no tell-tale marks of the journey his hands and his mouth had taken around her body. She felt an unexpected jolt of lust at the visceral memory of the day before, and turned abruptly away from the mirror. She didn't want to look at herself any more.

Downstairs, Kit and Arlo were sitting together at the kitchen table. Kit had spread the newspaper across half of it, and Arlo was breakfasting with two Power Rangers. She kissed the top of his tangled head. 'Hello, darling boy.'

He squirmed out of her embrace. 'Are you better, Mummy?'

'Much, thank you. All better.'

'I'm glad. Dad's burnt the bacon.'

'Oy!' Kit complained. 'What happened to the boy code, Arlo?'

Arlo smiled. 'You did, though, Dad.'

'I did.' He nodded his confession. 'Cup of tea? There's unburnt bacon too, if you want some.'

'Tea first. Then I'll see.' She smiled gratefully.

There was nothing strange in his behaviour towards her. Why would there be? In every other way, this was a normal weekend morning. Just like all the other mornings. This was their life.

The day would get busier, noisier. Arlo had cricket this afternoon, she remembered. They'd both take him, most likely, and she'd watch a few overs from the boundary, chatting to the other parents between balls, although Kit would stay for the whole match. Arlo kept wicket, and she worried about cricket balls hitting him. His coach said he was pretty good, Kit said proudly. She'd shop, later, for food, and, if there was time, she'd maybe browse the boutiques on the high street, try something on. Maybe if they weren't busy, she'd get her nails done at one of the bars that had sprung up at regular intervals. Pale pink, and squoval, like always. She'd buy an armful of whatever flowers looked loveliest from the market stall on the corner. Talk on the phone with one of the older kids, if they answered.

Cook something for Arlo, and brief the babysitter on bedtimes and snacks when he arrived. Arlo loved Charlie, who was cool and sixteen, lived up the road, and would throw an unconcerned wave over his shoulder when Kit and Natalie left, already lost in whatever computer game he and Arlo had loaded. Kit and Natalie were having supper with Flick and Andrew – Flick wanted to try a new Vietnamese place that had opened in town. Natalie would drive the four of them, and have one glass of wine. Flick, Andrew and Kit would drink a bit more than that, and they'd laugh, and eat, and later, when she'd dropped off the Butterworths, and they got home, she'd pay Charlie, ask about his GCSEs and his mother, and see him out. By the time she'd turned out all the lights, checked the locks and gone up to bed, the wine would have anaesthetized Kit, and he'd almost certainly be asleep, flat on his back, snoring. And while she might normally roll him, or complain, she wouldn't tonight, because she wanted him to stay asleep.

And the day would have passed. And she'd have got away with it. And she was risking it all. And she missed Dom, which was ridiculous, because how could that be? And she was sorry and she wasn't sorry. And she didn't know what was going to happen next.

'So . . . *brocante*.' Flick said it with a thick, ham French accent the kids would call racist. 'It's just a fancy word for a flea market, right?'

Vanessa nodded. 'Yep. Sounds much better in French, though, doesn't it?'

'Doesn't everything?'

Vanessa was a self-professed Francophile, who dreamt of retiring to the Loire, although the others thought Ross might have something to say about it if she ever tried to move there. She'd been learning French on Duolingo for years. It was always what she had playing in her AirPods when she ran. If you looked closely, you could see her mouthing words while she jogged.

'Do you know, for example, that the French for slut is *Marie-couche-toi-là*?'

Flick laughed. 'What?'

'It means "Lie down here, Marie." That's much nicer, right?'

'Good to know. I'll remember that the next time I need to call someone a slut. Always good to hurl insults prettily . . .'

'*Ah, zut alors, rosbif*,' Annie chimed in, mischievous.

Vanessa was stern. 'Things they definitely *don't* say in France.' Annie stuck out her tongue.

'But we're talking basic junk? The stuff we got rid of when my gran died – all those knick-knacks from the corner-display unit?' Flick looked unimpressed.

'Rupert calls them spinster *tchotchke*s.'

'It's not just that. There's bigger stuff too. And, anyway, I say one man's trash is another man's treasure.' Vanessa's tone brooked no argument.

'And you lot have been to these before, have you? How have I missed out?'

'We've only been once. Last summer. I'd heard about it from a friend who got these amazing benches there. You were away, I think.'

'It wasn't anything like as sunny,' Georgie added. 'I bought that tin bath I put hydrangeas in on my patio.'

'Yep. Took one of those to the tip from my gran's too.'

'More fool you. You probably threw away a fortune.'

'Fashion is a funny thing. I give you the avocado bathroom suite.'

Sarah smiled. 'I bet you'll find something you absolutely love.'

Flick grimaced. 'Not sure about that.'

'You're a cynic, Flick Butterworth.'

'I'm just saying.'

It was the hottest day of the year, and clearly half the country was out on a Sunday trip. They'd come in tandem, in two cars, in case they needed the boot space, and although it was still early, they'd had to drive right to the bottom of the field to park. Now they were all trudging towards the adjacent field where the stalls were set up. Annie was wearing a straw hat, and Natalie quite envied her. The sun was already strong on the back of her neck. Earlier risers were heading back already, their arms full of treasures.

Vanessa appraised all their purchases as they passed. 'I knew we should have come before breakfast.'

'Not a chance. It's Sunday.'

'Hope the good stuff isn't all gone.'

They'd reached the entrance. Everyone dutifully laid down a ten-pound note. As she did so, though, Flick mouthed, 'Ten pounds,' silently and incredulously, rolling her eyes.

Once inside, she put her arm through Natalie's. 'What are you after?'

'I don't know until I see it. Piece of stained glass. Old French bakery sign. Enamelware. That's what's so exciting.'

'I need new terracotta pots for the garden,' Annie announced.

'And I'm hoping for a Pimm's.' Flick was slathering sun cream on her arms as she walked.

'Almost everything on this man's table seems to have come from a skip.'

'Ssh. He'll hear you.'

'He won't – he's busy fleecing that couple with the rusty sign.'

'You're incorrigible. I'll just walk away!' Sarah threatened.

Natalie held back and watched her friends from a distance, weaving among the tables and the crowds. This was their schtick. Flick was outrageous, the others pretended they minded, but they'd mind a lot more if she wasn't. She didn't want to look at Sarah, but at the same time she wanted to study every little thing about her. She'd known her for so long, but now everything about her physicality fascinated her. Her hair, pulled into a high ponytail. It looked coarser than Natalie's, and she wondered how it felt to touch. Whether it was long and thick enough to form a curtain around them when she was moving on top of him. Was she ever on top of him? She'd never noticed how long her eyelashes were. She wasn't wearing any make-up, and the sunshine showed up the blondeness and the length.

Sarah leant forward to look at something, and inside her scoop-neck T-shirt, Natalie saw her beige bra with its sensible straps and smooth high cups. She felt creepy, and sick. She was comparing herself to Sarah. Wondering how Dom did. An image of him kissing her, holding her, flashed into her mind. She tried to push it away but it persisted. She felt queasy. What was she doing? What the hell was she doing? She felt afraid, now, all of the time.

'You're quiet, Nat.' Georgie had slipped back to where she was. Natalie hadn't noticed until she appeared right in front of her. 'Are you feeling okay?'

She smiled, meaning it to be bright and unconcerned. She sounded insincere to herself. 'It's hot, right? Annie had the right idea with that hat.'

Georgie smiled back. 'Want to find some shade?'

'And miss out on all this?' She gestured to the table of horse brasses they were strolling past. Ahead of them, Flick and Vanessa were examining a dilapidated printer's drawer. Annie and Sarah had crossed to a stall stocking old zinc milk churns.

Georgie giggled. 'Don't you start. Come on. I spy the ice cream. They're bickering. Either they'll never notice we're not behind them or they'll catch up with us.' She linked arms with Natalie and pulled her forwards towards the refreshment tent.

They bought two choc ices. Seating was under umbrellas on hay bales, and they found a spare cluster in the welcome shade. Georgie was easy enough to sit quietly with – of all the group, she always demanded the least. The others found them soon enough. Annie had bought something from the milk-churn stall for the garden, and Flick had a cabbage-shaped soup tureen in her arms. She raised it aloft, like a trophy, then gave a small bow. 'I take it all back. I am the *brocante* queen. Everything old is new again. This was a total bargain. Twenty quid. One tiny little chip. These cost more than a hundred quid at Divertimenti and places. I shall buy the refreshments as a penance for being such an Eeyore. What are you all having?'

Natalie turned her head away. She was about to cry. She pulled her sunglasses down from where they were resting in her hair, and bit hard on her bottom lip. Anything to make it less obvious.

She loved this. She loved these women. All of them. She loved days like this. The monstrous stupidity of risking it all had just hit her like a freight train. She'd been thinking about Kit and the kids – about her domestic life. Sitting here now, listening to them tease and giggle and just enjoy each other, a whole new possibility of loss and pain had just hit her hard. It almost made her dizzy.

17

Natalie didn't know how long Kit had been standing in the doorway. She hadn't heard the car or the front door. She and Arlo were in the garden. He'd been bouncing on the trampoline, demanding she score his jumps and tricks. She wasn't watching, not really, awarding everything an eight or above and hoping he wouldn't notice. He'd given up eventually, and now he was lying on his belly in the grass, chatting to himself or to whatever insects he'd found. She was curled into a wicker chair, her arms hugged to her chest, her eyes fixed on the horizon. Kit made her jump when he appeared behind her.

'Penny for them?' Dropping his case and his linen jacket onto a chair, he came over and planted a quick, soft kiss on the top of her head.

She smiled. 'Not sure they're worth that much.'

'Ah . . .'

'I didn't hear you come in.' She looked at her watch. 'You're earlier than I thought.'

'Traffic was light.'

She nodded. 'Good day?'

'Meeting went well. It's always a good day if I'm home before bedtime, right? How's the boy?'

'He said he was exhausted. But he's just been flipping on the trampoline for the best part of an hour so he has a somewhat different concept of tiredness from mine.'

'Ah, youth. Wasted on the young, don't they say?'

'They're not wrong.' She fell silent again.

Kit put his head on one side and looked at her hard. 'You okay, Nat?'

She tried to smile reassuringly. 'Why'd you ask?'

Kit shrugged. 'You've just seemed a bit distracted lately. Not unhappy, exactly, but not very . . . not very you.'

I was thinking about Dom's hands on me. I'm always thinking about Dom's hands on me. This is me now. I'm a person who takes a train to an eleven-foot-square bedroom with a clean white bed and sleeps, although we don't really sleep, we just rest, sated . . . has wild, athletic, tender, amazing sex with a man who isn't you. Who loves and hates being that person in almost equal measure. So that distraction you see, that's me contemplating literally being torn in half.

'I'm sorry,' was all she could muster.

Kit raised a hand. 'No need. It's fine. I was just wondering whether I could help. Whether you wanted to talk about it.'

His hand was on her shoulder. She turned her head and kissed it. 'Thanks.'

'But no thanks?'

She smiled. 'I'm good.'

He nodded slowly. 'She's good.'

Arlo came hurtling down the garden. 'Dad!' He leapt into Kit's arms and let his father hold him for a moment before he squirmed free. 'Can we make pizzas for dinner? Please? I'll help. Can we?'

'What does Mum say?' Kit turned to her. She nodded, and Arlo cheered, and the two of them headed towards the kitchen hand in hand.

But she wasn't good. The day before, at exactly this time, she'd been in the bed in the flat, wrapped in Dom, watching sunlight on particles of dust in the air, feeling the sheen of sweat on her skin, waiting for her breathing to slow and still. And she couldn't stop thinking about what he'd said.

'It's like this – this, right here, right now, with you – this is my real life. Everything else is made up. Here, now, with you. This is who I am. This is where I am meant to be.'

When he'd said it, she'd been lost in him, and she had felt powerful, and extraordinary, and moved by him. Now, remembering the words, she just felt panic.

18

A matter of weeks since the day at the flat, and she could start a tour of illicit spaces within walking distance of Waterloo, like a Victorian prostitute. He'd pulled away from the station entrance, and she knew she'd missed the train she'd told Kit she would be on. They'd walked down a hidden Georgian street of tiny terraced houses. She had never known it was there. It was like being on a film set. There was a pub on one corner, and he'd stopped there and pushed her to the side to kiss her one long, last time before they took the train back to their lives. It was like being drunk.

Pressing her hard against a brick wall still warm from the sun, Dom kissed her until her knees were weak and she forgot everything she ought to remember. How did that work? You could be resolute, as certain as you had ever been about anything, and the resolution could crumble into dust and blow away on a breeze just like that.

They'd met at her place five more times. She kept an almost obsessive count. Things between them hadn't cooled down at all, whatever each of them went through when they were apart. It seemed absurdly easy to forget when they were together. They couldn't get enough of each other, pulling at each other's clothes impatiently the second they were through the door. They barely ate or drank, and seldom left the bed except to shower. They did that together, too.

It hadn't been hard to get away without anyone being suspicious. Not yet, at least. Kit never delved, when he thought Temple might be involved. If anything, he seemed vaguely pleased she was taking time for herself, and perfectly happy to spend some with their son. She didn't specifically know what Dom told Sarah, but she knew they'd lived independent lives before, so she imagined there wasn't close questioning going on for him, either. He'd always stayed in London for odd nights – work dinners, early starts or seeing old mates.

It was surprisingly easy so far.

She couldn't – wouldn't – think too far ahead. They never did that out loud either, the two of them.

When they were together, they were obsessively self-contained. And having sex. 'It's never been like that for me before, not with anyone.' He stopped short of saying Sarah's name, but it hung in both of their minds like a spectre. 'I'm, like, totally consumed by you, Natalie Kennedy. You're my red mist.'

It hadn't been like that for her, either. With Toby, she'd been so young, full of romantic ideals and barely free of adolescent fantasy before she was pregnant with Temple. With Kit, she'd known, so quickly, that they were going to be together. Love, of course. And lust. She wouldn't pretend otherwise. She'd tried to remember details, but they were fuzzy at the edges. Stella had come along, then Marley, and they were a family. And her feelings for Kit were all wrapped up in that. In how good a father he was, and how comfortable their life was, how safe and how contented she'd been all those years.

This was different from either of those relationships. This was her in middle age, and this was stark and separate and selfish.

'God. My God, Nat.' He groaned as he pulled away from her. She reached to smooth her hair and her dress.

'Listen, I want to take you somewhere next weekend. Can you manage it, do you think? I can get away for the night.' They'd never met at the weekend.

He didn't tell her why he could get away for the night, and he didn't need to. She knew because Sarah had told her. On the phone a couple of days ago. She was excited – school was over, and she was free for the summer holidays. Mia was moving, and Sarah had offered to help her, then stay. They had tickets to *The Book of Mormon*, and they were going to queue up and eat at Dishoom. She'd invited her, for God's sake, to join her with Stella, for bloody Bombay Potatoes. Then on Monday morning, when Mia went to work, Sarah was going to Liberty to buy fabric for some sewing project she was planning, and then meet an old friend for lunch.

And she knew because Stella had told her. Mia was moving in with her and Joanna, into Sal's vacated room. She was really excited about it. They were friends, but Stella and the others in the group who were her age had been just slightly in awe of the older kids – Mia and Phoebe, and Annie's boy Will – the three years that seemed such a vast chasm of an age gap when you were thirteen and they were sixteen, or when they left for university and you were stuck doing your GCSEs.

It was all so oppressively near. They were such fools.

'I can't.' She shook her head. 'I'm sorry. I just can't.'

'You can.' He kissed her again.

She put her two hands on his chest, and gave him a small push. 'I really can't, Dom. I'm taking Temple away for the weekend.'

He paused, frustrated. 'Where are you going?'

'To the Cotswolds.'

'For how long?'

'Just the two days. The weekend. We're staying Saturday night.'

He looked crestfallen.

'I'm sorry.' She took his hand.

'No. I'm sorry.' Dom pushed his hand through his hair. 'I don't mean to sound needy and demanding. I got ahead of myself and I shouldn't have pushed. I'm sorry. Of course, I know you need to spend time with Temple right now.'

She put her hand on his head. He leant his cheek into her palm.

'I just so wanted to be with you. I think about it all the time . . . All these snatched bits of time. I want more. I want to spend the whole night with you, and wake up in the morning with you next to me. I really, really want that, Nat.'

Natalie looked at him. It was intoxicating, his desire to be alone with her. It was flattering and exciting. If she closed her eyes and shut everything else out, the two of them, naked in a big white bed, the thought made her breathless.

But it was frightening, too.

Not just the lies, the excuses. Not just the come-down she'd be fully expecting. He was like a drug. When she got home, when the effect of him wore off, she always felt ill. It was the sense that he was moving faster than she was – she knew it was true. Too far and too fast.

He turned to her and kissed her. Like every time before, it blotted the rest out. Literally made her weak at the knees.

'What about Sunday night?'

'What?'

'Could you stay away another night? Without that seeming weird?'

'Dom . . .'

He ignored her warning tone. 'Please. We're away for two weeks after that.' Natalie felt a small, unexpected needle pierce her heart when he said 'we'. A streak of jealousy. 'Then it's Phoebe's wedding and the summer is practically over.'

'I don't know.'

'Don't say no without thinking about it. I could book us somewhere. Near where you'll have been. I could meet you, after Temple leaves. We could have dinner, a night. Just us. Like a real couple. You'd be home Monday.'

She hesitated. 'We're not a real couple, Dom.'

'Please. Just promise me you'll think about it,' he begged.

She smiled. She already was.

19

Natalie and Temple managed to keep straight faces while the smiley, chinos-wearing 'team member' gave them the tour of their accommodation, outdoing each other with delighted coos and exclamations. Only when he left them to it did they dissolve into helpless giggles. Temple threw herself onto the mattress, a kid again. It was lovely, her mother thought, to hear her peals of laughter. It had been a while. It might be worth a cramped night, and a bath and toilet you had to go outside to get to. Natalie had always wanted to stay in something like this – her favourite childhood author had been Rumer Godden, and her favourite character Kizzy, the brave girl who lived in a bright wagon with her gran. She'd had a bit of a thing for the romance and whimsy of shepherd's huts like this one, long before cool, posh hotels and David Cameron had hijacked the concept, but she'd never managed to persuade Kit into one. Now she was wondering how the two of them – petite women with little overnight bags – would manage even one night. The hotel's wide-angled lens had definitely been in play when they shot for the website.

'They looked bigger online,' Natalie explained apologetically.

'I can't help thinking these are for lovers, Mum.' Natalie had a fleeting image of herself tangled with

Dom. 'He probably thinks we're a lesbian couple. Did you see him sort of wink when he was telling us how to work the hot tub?'

Natalie laughed. 'You're probably right. I'm sorry. Shall I see if they can move us? They might have rooms in the main house.'

'No. No. Don't be *that* person. Besides, they definitely won't. This is a dead trendy place, you old hipster. And it's a glorious July weekend. They'll be full. Anyway, I beyond love it. It's cute and girly and fun. And shepherd's huts are desperately Instagrammable. Apart from David Cameron's, obvs. Instaperfect.' She made a frame with her hands, like a film director, and clicked her teeth. 'We'll make it work.'

The hut was set on its own, down a steep bark path, on a hill overlooking the valley, spread out like the proverbial quilt below. Huts were dotted all over, safely distanced, a barn-like building off to the left housing the bar and the restaurant. It was, Natalie acknowledged, a space far better suited to a pair of lithe lovers than a mother and daughter, but it was sweet, all faded vintage quilts and enamel coffee cups. The hot tub was less neon-lit wife-swap spaceship and more wholesome Swedish vibes. Still, she couldn't help reflecting that Kit would say it was money for old rope, and even Dom might call it twee.

The two of them had spent the day browsing and pottering in a few of the picturesque Cotswolds villages she loved, all mellow stone, climbing roses and houses you'd kill to live in. If Natalie had an agenda, as Sylvia had reminded her she should have when she'd called, she was determined not to bulldoze. Better, in her experience, to let Temple relax and unwind, and see what came to them. She'd said, in London, that she and Max were making serious attempts to improve things . . . and perhaps they had.

'Come on, then. Hot tub it is.' She dipped her hand in to test the warmth of the water. 'Lovely and warm. Can't *not* have a soak, can we? You brought a swimsuit, right?'

Temple shook her head. 'No! But I don't care. Nudie Rudie. Remember?'

Natalie remembered. They'd called her that when she was a toddler. She'd been particularly keen on divesting herself of any clothes at the earliest opportunity, almost regardless of climate or company. One of Natalie's all-time favourite photographs of her daughter showed Temple in the garden at Sylvia's, naked but for a pair of bright red wellies. Her sundress and tiny pink pants were strewn across the lawn in the background. 'Never really leaves you, that urge.' She laughed.

'The less I know about that the better,' Natalie retorted, heading inside to grab her costume. When she returned, Temple's sundress and tiny pink pants were strewn this time across the willow screen shielding the hot tub from the pathway, and Temple was already in the water, her head back against the rim, and her eyes closed.

'I brought us a glass of fizz.'

Temple sat up and took the glasses while Natalie climbed in, then handed her mother a glass, and took a sip from her own. For a bit, they just sat, enjoying the silence and the way the warm water soothed them.

Temple turned to Natalie. 'Thanks for this, Mum. It's been great. I feel very spoilt. Not to sound entitled, or anything, I feel like I've really needed it.'

'It's lovely for me too, darling.' She took a breath. 'Things no better? With Max?' Then instantly wished she hadn't framed the question in negativity.

Temple gave a small, tight laugh. 'Aha. No. No better.' A long pause. 'Considerably worse, actually.'

'Oh, love. I'm sorry. I was hopeful, after I saw you in town, that you two were on the right track.'

'Me too. Actually, probably not, if I'm honest. You know what? I think I was just kidding myself. I really, really wanted it to be true.'

'What's happened? If you want to tell me, I mean. I don't want to pry.' She was being so careful. She could hear Sylvia scoffing. 'Pry, damn it, Natalie. She's your child, and it's your job. Pry.'

Temple put her glass down on the edge of the tub. 'The truth is, Max has been seeing someone else. For ages, actually. Full-on cheating on me. And lying to me. Coming to therapy, spouting a load of bullshit, at two hundred quid an hour, mind you, and then sloping off to see his girlfriend. Lying to my face about wanting to make it work with us.'

'Christ.' Natalie was blindsided. The hot tub was suddenly too hot, so hot she felt faint. She moved over to the step. The cooler air hit her shoulders at once, but did little to make her feel less odd.

'Yup.' Temple's voice broke. 'Didn't see it coming. God. So naïve. You'd think I'd have seen signs. Been just a bit suspicious. I feel incredibly stupid. I didn't think he'd do that. But he did.' She took a deep breath. 'So I've thrown him out of the flat. And, well, it's over. Irretrievably over. He couldn't say anything ever again to me that I would believe.'

Natalie wasn't sure where to start. But Temple was still speaking. She'd brought her legs up under the water, and was hugging them, her chin resting on her knees. She looked, to her mother, five years old.

'I mean, you can't let them stay, can you? Not when someone thinks so very fucking little of you that they're shagging someone else and coming home to climb into your bed.' Her voice was small, and angry.

Natalie's stomach dropped.

Temple looked up at her mother. 'Do you know where he met her?'

'Where?'

'Tinder. The bastard was actively looking.'

'I can't believe he'd do that.'

'Well, he did. Ought to be some consolation, I suppose, that he was lying to her too, poor cow. She didn't know he was married. There isn't, really, though. Same storm, very different boats.'

'I'm sorry, Temple.'

Temple sniffed. 'So, I'm thinking there's something wrong with me. There must be.'

'Hey.'

'No. There is. Because people cannot love me. Not properly. Not permanently.'

'What are you talking about?'

'It's never happened, for me.'

'Temple! What on earth do you mean?'

'You don't know, Mum.'

'What? What don't I know?'

'That it never works out for me. It never has, when it comes to love.'

'What are you talking about?' Natalie slid back into the water, and laid her hand on Temple's head. 'What don't I know?'

'That something about the way I love people makes it easy for them to hurt me. Not just Max. Every boy before Max too. Every man.'

Natalie's mind raced, trying to remember Temple's relationships before her husband. There'd been a few boyfriends, of course. She was a pretty, bubbly girl. It had always seemed to Natalie that they swarmed around her. Only one or two had seemed to last more than a few months, maybe. She'd remembered Sylvia saying that she mustn't get invested in boyfriends – that they'd come and go, and that it would be no good for her to fall in love with one and be heartbroken when it didn't work, any more than it would be for her to hate them and wish them gone, because then Temple would have a stick to beat her with when things fell apart. So boys had always been welcomed, fed and watered. Once Temple had passed sixteen, she'd told her mum that Toby let boys sleep with her in her room, and she'd been too proud to check that information with him, so she'd let her too, even though Kit had never really liked it. He'd never let Stella or Marley do the same. Boy- or girlfriends they brought home slept in the guest room. And she'd met Max young.

'I don't know where this is coming from. I don't understand why you're blaming yourself for other people's bad behaviour.'

'Because there's a pattern, you see.'

'I don't see. Help me out, love. Who? What do you mean?'

'Do you remember Todd?'

'Todd?' She didn't. 'I'm sorry.'

'It's okay.' Temple smiled ruefully. 'I was with Dad. We weren't that close then, you and me.' God, that stung. It wasn't said with malice, but it hurt Natalie nonetheless. 'I think I was jealous. I know I made out that London was cool and where I wanted to be, and that living with Dad was great. And there was great stuff about it, I won't lie. But, really, I think a big part of me wished I was with you, Stella and Marley. I wished Kit wanted me.'

'That's not fair. You were always welcome.' Natalie tried not to sound defensive.

Temple squinted, and tilted her head. 'Come on, Mum. That's not quite how it was. I felt like I didn't fit in.'

'Oh, God.'

'Look, Mum. I'm not saying this to make you feel like crap. It was on me.'

'No. It's on me. You were just a child.'

'You were this happy little unit. The world revolved around Stella and Marley, and I got that. At least, as much as a kid that age can get it. And I was a pretty difficult teenager.'

'*My* teenager.'

'It was easier to be in London with Dad. Dad wasn't big on boundaries.'

'What do you mean?'

'He was too liberal. He didn't ask enough questions, you know. He didn't make enough rules, and he didn't enforce the rules he did make. I see that now. I didn't see it then – I was a bit wild . . .'

'How wild?'

'Nothing too dramatic. I drank way too much. There were drugs. Never anything really bad, not really.' She paused. 'A lot of boys, and I mean a lot.'

'Oh, love.' She'd known, she supposed, that some of that had been happening. The drink-and-drugs stuff. Lots of parents knew it was, but maybe they mostly buried their heads, like ostriches, and just hoped it would pass without doing lasting damage. That was all you could do, wasn't it?

'And boys who weren't very nice to me, necessarily.'

'I'm so sorry.'

Temple felt for Natalie's hand under the water, and held it tightly. 'I promise I don't think it's your fault. I didn't then, either.'

Natalie sighed. 'It is, though. You're my daughter. I just . . . I thought you were happy. You always seemed, when you came to us, like you couldn't get back to your fabulous life fast enough. Truth is, Temple, I was jealous too. I felt rejected by you then. Sounds pathetic, for a grown woman, but it's true. We were just small-town people, suburban, quiet, and you seemed to find us so dull.'

'You were a family.'

'Oh, God. Will you tell me about Todd?'

Temple shrugged, and hesitated. For a moment, Natalie was afraid she had shut her down, but then she spoke.

'I was almost fifteen. Still a virgin. Just. It felt like everyone was doing it. Even if they weren't, they were lying about it. I was mad about him. Really gone. I thought he was mad about me. He said he was. I wasn't ready. You know?' Natalie nodded. 'And he said he'd wait. He said I was worth waiting for. He made me feel special. I hate how that makes me sound. Pathetic.'

'Not pathetic. What happened?'

'One night we were at this party at someone's house, and he was really drunk or stoned and . . .'

Natalie brought her hand to her mouth.

Temple shook her head quickly. 'No. No. Not that. He tried. Just persuasion at first. Then he got a bit more physical. I had to sort of shove him to get him off me. I mean, he got pissed off with me when I wouldn't. Called me a cock-tease. And he left me upstairs in a room on my own. He went down and told everyone I was a frigid bitch, and then slept with one of my friends. The same night. That's exactly how special I was.'

'I'm sorry that happened. I wish you'd told me.'

'I didn't tell anyone, Mum.' Temple sighed. 'But I didn't say no, not really, to anyone, not again.'

Natalie felt hollow with sadness. She opened her arms, and Temple moved through the water into them, and she held her, rocking her gently in the warmth, rocking them both.

'There were too many, and they didn't care for me. Because I didn't care for myself, I suppose. With each one, I just felt a bit less special.'

'My poor love.'

'It's okay. I'm okay.' Temple smiled. 'Max stopped doing the therapy just after I found out. I've kept going. And it's helped, Mum. Everyone should have some. We've all got our own shit. It's made a lot of sense of a lot of stuff. Would recommend. I feel like I've started, finally, to get my head straight. To reclaim the self-worth I chipped away at for so long.'

'And?'

'And I see how I set the tone, kind of, if that makes sense. It's like if you expect to be treated badly, if you accept that, then it's likely that's what will happen. It's very Hallmark, but it's true – you have to love yourself, and you have to know your worth. I'm starting to under-stand that now.'

Natalie had never felt so worthless.

'And I'm not absolving Max. He's a total shit, and I'm going to be well rid of him. He honestly did raise self-absorption to an art form. I'm fuming that I wasted the time on him I did. But I set the pattern, before I even met Max. It started with me.'

'You amaze me.'

Temple smiled. 'Nah. Took me longer than most people to get here.'

'I don't believe that for a second. Trust me. Some people never get that close to understanding themselves.'

*

166

After that, they talked, laughed and cried for most of the night, curled up in dressing-gowns and the quilts on the bed. Now that she was talking, Temple had a lot to share about those missing years. It was hard to hear. A lot of it made Natalie feel wretched, but she didn't say so. It wasn't Temple's job to comfort her. When Temple eventually slept, it was curled into her mother's embrace in the small double, her hand cupping her face as it always had when she was young. Propped up on pillows, Natalie could see her by the light of the small lamp above their heads, and watched her closely. Sleep was almost impossible for her. There was too much new information to digest. Her chest hurt, and her mind raced.

Her heart ached with love for her child. Temple was so wrong. She had loved her dearly, from the second her slippery body had been put on her chest. Live-for-die-for love. But she felt like she had failed. She must have failed, for Temple to see herself in that way. Why was she even here with her now?

And she was enraged. She was angry with Toby – he'd kept too much from her, and that she found unforgivable. He should have told her. She was pissed off with Kit for not trying harder with Temple. She was more than furious with Max. How dare he? But she reserved her harshest admonishment for herself, and it swelled like a balloon behind her ribcage.

For years and years now, she'd defined herself as a partner and mother, been sure of who she was within those arenas. And now it felt as though it had all been blown up. She was a person who had let down her daughter when she'd needed her most. She was a person who could, it seemed, cheat on her partner and was still able to walk and talk and function. A liar.

How had Temple put it? Thought so very fucking little of Kit that she'd shag someone else and then climb into bed with him. Eloquent.

In the morning, they'd dozed. Sundays usually started with Arlo, unfeasibly alert by 7 a.m., but despite the extra hours, Natalie came to feeling heavy and anxious. Conversely, Temple seemed lighter. Breakfast and the Sunday papers were delivered to the hut in a wicker hamper, and Temple, exclaiming over the tiny pots of ketchup and Kilner jars of milk and orange juice, seemed young, and even happy. She cooked back bacon on the electric grill and sliced baguettes for sandwiches.

When they'd dressed and checked out, they walked – a long purposeful yomp – through the vale. Natalie wondered if Temple had more to say, but she kept the conversation bright and simple. She was grateful – her brain was full already. Dom had texted her with the name and postcode of the hotel he'd booked. *Cannot wait*, his message read.

Heading back to where they'd parked, Temple put her arm through her mother's and laid her head, briefly, against her arm. 'Thank you.'

'For what?'

'For this. For listening.'

'I should have been listening much more acutely long ago.'

'Stop it. Please don't do that. It wouldn't have mattered if you were. I wasn't speaking. That wasn't your fault.'

Natalie didn't respond.

Temple squeezed her hand. 'It *wasn't.*'

'Are you going to be okay now?'

Temple hesitated. 'No. Not for a while. But I'm starting to believe that I will be. What's that song?' She hummed a few bars, but Natalie was none the wiser. 'Come on! It's a real ear worm. You know . . .'

'Not a clue.' Natalie laughed.

'Not broken, just bent.'

'One session in the hot tub and you've got your head straight?'

It was Temple's turn to laugh. 'No! You're good, Mum, but you're not that good. I'm paying someone, no offence. My head is absolutely not straight. It's not going to be a straight line. Wavy as fuck is my guess. But, God, Mum, it helped, talking to you, being with you. It really, really helped.'

Natalie shook her head. 'You're just trying to assuage my guilt.'

'I'm not. That's yours, I'm afraid. I can't fix it for you just by telling you not to feel it. I'd been bottling up a lot of that crap for too damn long. You know? Lance the wound, the infection starts to heal. Something like that. I feel better. Baby steps.'

'First baby step? You know you can come home. Because it is your home. Wherever I am will always be your home. You know that, right?' Natalie had stopped, to make her point.

Temple smiled. 'That's too babyish a step, though, Mum. I'm too old to run home.'

'Try telling Sylvia that. I still run home,' Natalie said ruefully. It wasn't true. She hadn't run home lately. Sylvia knew nothing about the new life she was living.

'And having you on the end of the phone – priceless. But, nah, I'm going to stand on my own size fours.' She stood, legs spread wide, arms raised. She looked like Julie Andrews in the opening credits of *The Sound of Music*, about to whirl around the Alps. 'Stand up to Max. Stand up for myself. I've got work, and friends, and I still look bloody good, though I say so myself. And I promise you, Mum, I'm going to be okay.' Temple hugged her hard. 'And now, you need to go. We both do. Back to our realities. They'll be missing you at home.'

Natalie looked at her daughter's open, sweet face, and thought that she might actually hate herself. She hadn't told Temple she wasn't going home, of course. There were too many lies already. She reasoned she needn't fabricate a story for her – Temple never called the landline at home. Just her mother's mobile. Still, she felt like a fraud and a liar. I am a liar now, she thought. That's my life.

20

Natalie drove slowly between the two hotels. Passing a layby with a panoramic vista, she pulled in impulsively, and sat staring out at the view for almost an hour with her phone silenced. She had a lot to process, about Temple and about herself. She felt tearful, and fraudulent, and almost overwhelmed.

Dom had already checked in when she arrived. She was sure the young receptionist raised an arched eyebrow just a fraction when she asked for him by name. Wouldn't you normally say, 'I'm meeting my husband here. Has he arrived yet?' Asking for Dom Bennett was a giveaway. The girl scanned her hand, taking in the diamond eternity ring she wore in place of a wedding band, as she handed her a key with a bright smile, and directed her to the lift around the corner. Not that she'd care, Natalie knew, or that she hadn't seen the same thing before. The point was that *she* cared. She had *never* done this before. This place had a very different vibe from the one she had just come from. It was smart – flashy even. A country-house hotel given a Versace makeover, full of art made with gold, and slightly naff bronze sculptures of animals not native to the area. Not her sort of place at all. She wouldn't have thought it was Dom's. Perhaps the anonymity had been deliberate. Maybe everywhere else had been full at short notice.

The lift pinged and the doors opened on the second floor. She stared at the signage, which seemed unnecessarily complicated. She was tired. It had been a very strange and wearying night. All she really wanted to do was to douse herself under a powerful shower and sleep a long, dreamless sleep. She wondered whether she should knock, but then she looked down at the key in her hand and decided to let herself in. It was a big, bright room, more tasteful than the public spaces, with a large picture window looking out over the gardens and car park below. Dom was lying on the vast, high bed. It had one of those tall, statement headboards that were so fashionable, upholstered in a vividly coloured fabric. He'd taken off his shoes, but he was dressed, lying on top of the covers, his phone in his hand. For the first time since this had started, her stomach didn't lurch at the sight of him.

'You're here!' He stood up and padded over to her, sliding her bag off her shoulder onto the floor with one hand, and putting the other arm around her waist, pulling her in to kiss her. She didn't melt into the embrace, but he didn't seem to notice at first.

It was when he started pulling at her clothing that she stiffened and took a step back.

His face registered something like shock, then quickly rearranged itself.

'Yeah. You're right. For once, we have all the time in the world. Well, twenty-four hours, at least. That feels like such a luxury. I've been so excited to see you. What shall we do? Want to have food, something to drink? Are you hungry? There's a gorgeous terrace. We could walk.'

He sounded so eager, like a puppy. Natalie wasn't sure what to say. The bedroom, with the big bed, seemed the wrong place to be. Claustrophobic and suggestive. 'Let's walk.'

If he knew by now that something was wrong, he was determined to ignore it. He slipped his shoes on, pulled a sweater over his head.

There were a few people already having drinks on the patio at the back of the hotel. Signs pointed towards the gardens. It was a ridiculously pretty place – a perfect pastoral English setting. Wonderfully romantic. Dom held her hand, fingers scissored with hers. No one looked at them – why would they stare at a middle-aged married couple? They didn't know a thing about them.

Natalie didn't trust herself – all the way here in the car she'd been rehearsing what she might say to him. What she should have said weeks ago. What had suddenly become crucial since last night, with Temple. But here, with him, she could feel her resolve weaken. She had to get it out before it was too late.

She waited just a couple of minutes more until they were out of sight of the other guests, hidden by a high yew hedge. Across the lawn, a wrought-iron bench enclosed the trunk of an ancient oak tree, and she headed them in that direction.

They sat down. She felt Dom's arm come up to embrace her shoulders, so she angled herself towards him. He took her hand instead. 'What's wrong, Nat? You're wistful. Did something happen with Temple?'

It was Temple. It was Kit. It was Sarah. It was all of it.

It was enough. She took a deep breath, and exhaled slowly. She had to do this now.

'I need to say something, Dom.' She turned to face him. 'It's not about Temple. It's about you and me. And you need to listen to me. Please.'

'Okay.' He spoke slowly. She saw fear on his face, and effort. He knew, and he wanted to stop the words coming.

'You know this has to stop, don't you?'

This time he didn't answer.

'It's wrong.'

'It doesn't feel wrong.'

'It doesn't feel wrong when it's just the two of us. Just in those few hours, I do know what you mean. But the rest of the time? We are hurting people.'

'No one knows.'

'Christ, Dom. No one knows *yet*. How long do you think it's going to be before they do?'

'I don't think about it.'

That was a lie, she knew. 'But I *am* thinking about it. And I can't think about anything else. Not any more.'

'I can't stop. I'm in too deep with you, Nat.'

'We have to stop. We should never have let it start — that's the truth of it. We're not kids, and we're not free. There are too many people involved in this, and we can't keep pretending it's just the two of us. Actions have consequences, and these actions *will have* consequences. You're being unbelievably naïve if you keep burying your head in the sand.'

'Look, you're upset. I don't know what's happened.

What you and Temple have talked about to put you in this mood. I want to know. I want you to tell me. Everything. So you have to stay here with me and tell me. Talk to me. You can't go. Don't do this now. That can't be all I get.'

'I'm sorry. I don't want to hurt you.'

'If you do this, you will be hurting me. More than I have ever been hurt before. Please.'

'Don't do that. Don't make it you versus me. Don't leave it all to me. You know I'm right. You do know it.'

He shook his head. He wasn't listening.

'We are not these people. We are not cruel and we are not destructive and we are not dishonest. This is not who we are.'

'Why are you saying these things? That's not what we have. That's all wrong.'

'No, Dom. This is all wrong.'

She stood up and began walking towards the entrance to the hotel. Dom had no choice but to follow her.

He shut the bedroom door and leant against it, as though he thought he could keep her with him. Natalie stood calmly in the middle of the room, but her heart was racing. She was horribly afraid she was going to cry, but she couldn't. If she cried, he would comfort her, and if he touched her, she would never leave. 'I can't stay here with you. And not be with you.'

Then he looked around, the penny dropping. 'You didn't bring a suitcase in. You were never going to stay.' His tone wasn't accusatory, more surprised.

She looked down at the carpet. 'No, I didn't. I wasn't. I'll go, Dom. It's my fault.'

He shook his head. 'No. It's ours. I don't want you driving in the dark. You stay. Please.'

He picked up his bag, and took his jacket from where it was hanging on the back of a chair. She thought he might leave without saying another word, but at the door, he stopped and turned back. His eyes were full of tears. 'I hate this.'

She didn't know how to respond to that. She hated it too. But it would be unfair to say so. He waited for a moment, his hand on the door, his back to her. Then he opened it and was gone.

Natalie exhaled with something like relief. For long seconds she breathed slowly in and out as her heart slowed. Part of her, a huge part, wanted to run after him, call him back. She laid her forehead against the window and waited. A few moments later, he appeared on the gravel below, and headed for his car. She watched him unlock the boot and stow his bag. Then he turned and scanned the building, unsure of which window opened into the room he had just left. She leapt backwards, behind the curtain, so he wouldn't see her, and didn't look out again until she heard a car start. Dom reversed out of the space too fast, then hesitated, turned left. And then she couldn't see his car any more.

She took three steps backwards and sank onto the bed. She was too exhausted to cry. Too exhausted and too sad. It was done. It had had to be done. Tomorrow she would think about what damage might already have occurred. Tonight, she just needed to rest her brain.

When she woke up, it was dark outside, and her neck hurt. She kicked off her shoes and padded to the bathroom to run the shower. She needed to wash away the day. Back in the bedroom, she fumbled for her phone. She'd been asleep for hours – it was just after eleven now, too late to call home. She had three new voicemails. She was tempted not to listen to them, but her habit persisted and she pressed the play button. The messages played one after the other, each voice completely familiar to her.

Hi Mum. Home safe. I loved every minute of the time we spent together in our little shepherd's hut. I've come away so relieved that we talked the way we did. I'm sorry I took so long. Promise me you won't dwell on the past and all the crap I've told you. It must have seemed like a lot. No more secrets, I promise. I'm all good. At least, I know I will be. I've got some housekeeping to do, but I'm up to it. I love you, Mum. Thank you.

Nat, hi, it's me. I hope you're having a good time. We're fine here. Where are Arlo's cricket whites, by the way? I can't find them in his room and they're not in the wash – I checked. Ping me a message if you know. Otherwise I'll keep looking. See? We can't manage without you. We miss you. I miss you. See you tomorrow.

Natalie, where are you? I've got so many things I want to say to you. I can't believe it's over. It can't be over. I know you need some space. I'll leave you alone. And I hope you'll realize that this isn't over for you any more than it is for me. I'm going away with my family, but I'll be thinking of you every moment, and wishing I was with you. I'm sorry if that makes me a shit, but it's true. I love you, Nat.

Dom hadn't said that to her before. Maybe he'd come close to it. There were moments, lying in his arms, when she'd felt he was thinking and feeling it, but he hadn't said it. His voice had cracked with emotion in the message.

The three strands of her life, there on the phone. Ropes, wound around her head, her heart, her whole self. It made it hard to breathe.

21

It was a great villa. You never knew, did you, until you arrived. Brochure pictures only told the best half of the story. This one was just about perfect, and Sarah felt a hunter gatherer's pride at having sniffed it out. Pretty, with bougainvillaea growing up the walls, and vivid geraniums in pots around a wide terrace surrounding an appropriately turquoise swimming-pool. It was spotless, and comfortably furnished. No wafer-thin mattresses or broken garden furniture. The location was great too: the house was in a quiet enclave, but still an easy walk from the beach and the square, which was dotted with appealingly authentic-looking restaurants. There was even an extremely decent supermarket a short drive away. Sarah felt a pleasant surge of relief and pride. She always booked their villas.

They'd been taking this type of holiday for a good few years now – probably since Mia had left home. They were masters of what she thought of as the speculative family holiday. Taking a villa for one or two weeks in the summer. One with three to five bedrooms. That way, the kids could come. Bring a friend or two, if they decided to. No pressure, kids, there if you want it. If you were near Faro or Mallorca or Pisa, the budget airlines had loads of flights – you could get one last minute, and mates could join you cheaply.

It wasn't the only sort of holiday they'd been on since the kids were teenagers – there'd been the odd 'big family trip' to California one year, to Thailand another. She and Dom had been on holiday just the two of them, of course they had. There were the weekends with the Dorfest gang. Dom had been cycling with mates from the Lycra fraternity . . .

But there had been some version of the speculative family holiday, too, most years. It was Sarah who couldn't quite let go of 'the family holiday'. A cottage in Hay-on-Wye for Easter, once a chalet in Méribel. She felt guilty not inviting the kids, although they didn't seem to feel the same qualms about not using any of the 'well-appointed en-suite guest rooms' if it didn't fit in with their plans, or if they got a better offer. Dom snorted when they even said 'plans'. Planning, as grown-ups thought of it, seemed to be anathema to young people. Everything was last-minute. Committing in March to a fortnight in July was seemingly impossible to them. It made Dom grumpy. He was given to chuntering that they had more stamps in their passports than he did. Sarah, though, always clung to the hope that they'd come. She liked her family – her life – best of all when it was complete.

This summer, though, there was no Mia. At twenty-five, she'd made it clear earlier in the year that she'd be doing her own thing in the summer. Dylan had (over) compensated by bringing three friends from Warwick.

In fact, he hadn't brought them: they'd flown in on a budget flight three days after Dom, Sarah and Dylan, so Dom had had to drive back to the airport at stupid o'clock to pick them up. They were nice enough boys, but they ate everything that wasn't glued down, requiring trips to the nice supermarket every other day, and they left towels, goggles, glasses and those ghastly plastic slide shoes all over the place, never in pairs. They went out to the square every night after dinner, and came home trying – and spectacularly failing – to be quiet in the small hours, meaning they slept until midday, and were monosyllabic until dusk. Not one of them ever offered to empty a bin or light the barbecue. They'd have done it quickly enough if asked, but that wasn't the same thing at all.

Dom parked at the supermarket, sighing deeply. He'd hardly spoken on the drive over. They'd left the lads playing cards by the pool. The fridge was empty again.

'I'm sorry. I should have gone on the car insurance. Then I could have done the shopping on my own.' She was a safe driver, but she had always hated driving abroad.

'What would the point of that have been? You're a perfectly good driver at home. On the Continent you turn into a quivering wreck. I've no idea why.'

'You don't have to come in, then. I'll be quick. I just need a few bits.' She felt she should sound apologetic, even as the voice inside her head immediately rejected the tone.

'Okay.' He pulled out his phone.

She'd expected him to turn down the offer and come in with her. But she'd expected a lot this week that hadn't come to pass.

Dom was often tense in the days before a holiday. That was the familiar rhythm of their life together. She knew the responsibility of having his own business meant he had to leave things in good shape, and she never minded the long days he usually worked running up to their departure. She did her best to lighten his load. He'd certainly never bought sunscreen or printed off boarding passes. Christ – she'd even have packed for him, if he'd asked her to.

But usually, a day or two in, he relaxed. Almost visibly. He'd stop shaving. That was his tell, really. She liked him with a bit of stubble, especially now that it was salt-and-pepper. She liked who he was when he stopped shaving. He'd lie in the shade listening to podcasts or reading. Fall asleep after lunch. By day three or four, they'd have found a wonderfully comfortable level of intimacy and closeness, and she'd cherish it. She was always sad to come home, where life seemed to drive, day by day, inch by careful inch, a very tiny wedge between them until the next time they stepped off the conveyor-belt. But they weren't unusual, were they? Wasn't life like that for most people, if they were honest about it, at least with themselves and to each other?

This week, though, he just hadn't relaxed. She'd wondered if he didn't like the boys, but they were fine. It couldn't be that. She'd asked him, a couple of times, if things at work were worrying him. Even if he didn't feel well. He'd brushed her off each time – not unkindly but as if she was making it up, looking for a problem, and with a note of exasperation, so she'd stopped asking. She couldn't put her finger on it, but he just wasn't . . . here with her. He wasn't sleeping well, she knew. She never slept better than on this type of holiday. She swam for an hour every day, drank two or three glasses of wine with dinner, and slept like a baby for nine or ten hours easily. But a couple of mornings he'd been gone when she woke up, and she'd seen a pool towel and a cushion on the sofa downstairs, as if he'd tried to get back to sleep there. He'd gone for long walks on the beach, most days, and not invited her. She knew he took cigarettes, imagined him smoking out of view, and she minded.

She took a trolley and went up and down the aisles as quickly as she could, grabbing just what she needed for today and, hopefully, tomorrow. When she got back to the car, he didn't get out to open the boot and help her, even though there were big packs of water and Coke in the trolley. She tried not to mind. But Dom was the kind of husband who did that. Who'd always done that.

He seemed to have percolated irritation while she was inside the shop.

'I don't want to do this again. Not any more.'

'What do you mean?' Was he talking about the supermarket?

He paused, and looked at her intensely. For just a second, she felt afraid. She didn't know of what.

'This. The whole villa thing. Bring other people's kids away with us. Bring our kids, for God's sake. They're adults. We've done years of it, Sarah. I don't want to pay for all the damn food and booze. Or spend my holiday in a bloody concrete car park.'

'Calm down!'

He sounded exasperated. The nought-to-sixty nature of his mood was alarming and out of character. 'I don't want to calm down. I want you to listen to me. I know what you say, Sarah. I know why you make us do this. But *I* don't want to do it.'

Sarah felt shaky. She was already worrying about how she could appease him before they got back to the house. She didn't want him to act like this in front of Dylan's friends. It would embarrass her and it would discomfort their son, and it would ruin the atmosphere, probably for the rest of the holiday.

'Okay. Okay. I'm listening.' She put her hand on his where it rested on the gear stick of the hire car, but he snatched it away.

'I mean it, Sarah.'

'I can tell.' She smiled, hoping he would smile back, but he was looking ahead now, so he didn't see her expression.

He turned on the ignition, and roughly jammed the car into reverse.

Later that night, she was already in bed, sitting up, sticky with after-sun cream and deep in a novel, when he came in. She'd gone up early, exhausted by the effort of compensating for his quiet sullenness, and he'd waited until the boys had gone out for the night in their haze of Lynx.

He'd made her a cup of tea and brought it round to her side of the bed to put it down on the side table. He sat on the edge of the mattress, but he pinched her thigh as he did so, and she pulled her leg out of the way. God . . . everything was awkward.

'I'm sorry.'

'It's okay.'

'It's not okay. I was a shit. I know you do so much work on holidays like this. It's frankly outrageous of me to complain.'

'Dom, it's really okay. It's meant to be your holiday too. I've heard you. I promise.'

He smiled at her. 'You're lovely.' He leant forward, leaning on both hands either side of her hips, and kissed her gently on the lips.

She tried to kiss him again, pushed herself gently towards him, opened her mouth slightly. But he stood up and moved away towards the bathroom, and she went back to her book.

'Cheers-ears.' Flick clinked her glass against Natalie's. 'Here's to tomorrow going without a hitch.'

'It will. And if it doesn't, no one will notice.'

'Exactly. I'll drink to that. Thanks for coming with me, Nat. It's nice to see you. You've been lying a bit low this summer.'

Natalie shrugged. 'Summer's always a bit like that, isn't it?'

'True.' Flick held her hand, fingers splayed, in front of her face. 'What do you think? Round, square, squoval?'

'I like round on you.'

Flick raised her eyebrows and gave it her best Mae West. 'Just as well, honey. That's my look.'

Natalie laughed. 'You're incorrigible.'

'Which just happens to be the name of this lovely red colour.' She held up a bottle of nail varnish.

'You're going red?'

'Nah. One's colours are pastel, dahling. The whole day is like a bag of sugared almonds.'

She picked up another bottle. 'This one is for real called Mother of the Bride.'

'Meant to be, then.'

Flick handed the bottle to Leah, who was currently filing her nails. 'Thanks, love.'

Natalie laid her head back against the chair. It had a massage button, and she'd switched it on. She could feel the knots in her neck as the chair pummelled them. She closed her eyes.

'So what's up with you, Nat?'

She replied without opening them. It seemed easier. 'What do you mean?'

'You've been off. Just a bit. For ages. I'm missing the drama.'

Natalie laughed. 'Is that what I am? The drama?'

'You know what I mean. Megawatt Nat. Your bulb's been a bit dull.'

'Ouch.'

'It's not a complaint. It's an expression of concern.'

'I know.'

'I love ya. Just checking in.'

Natalie sighed, trying to figure out how to answer. 'Oh, I don't know. You're right. I know. I suppose I am in a bit of a trough.'

'Anything you want to talk about? Anything to confess?' Natalie looked at Flick sharply, but she was clearly joking.

'Nothing specific. I've been really tired.' It was true. She'd never been so tired.

'Have you been to the doctor?'

'No. It's not that bad.'

'Could be menopause, that's all I'm wondering. In which case HRT.'

'Am I that old?'

'Afraid so. Maybe. Peri-menopause. Who even knew?

You can have that crap going on for ten years, apparently – thank you, God. Who is, by the way, very definitely not a woman.'

'Maybe . . .'

'Just a thought. An MOT can't hurt at our age. I mean, I know you're way younger than me . . .'

'Not way younger.'

'Ten years. That's pretty much a generation.'

'For God's sake, Flick. You're extraordinary. You look younger than me.'

'Well, that's bollocks. Although, to be fair, in the arse versus face debate, I definitely went for face.'

'I hope I'm just like you when I grow up.'

'As if. Not a chance. You're going to age like Twiggy. I'm more Mrs Tiggywinkle.'

It was impossible not to giggle when you were with Flick. It wasn't menopause. Or even peri-menopause. When she'd last seen her gynaecologist, he'd informed her she was still ovulating, and could still, therefore, fall pregnant if it weren't for her coil. Christ help her if that happened.

Some part of her wanted to confess. Change the names, change the dates. Flick would be furious, she knew. She'd been on the end of an affair. People who'd had it done to them were unforgiving, not interested in reasons. And she'd be right not to be. No excuse. There was no excuse.

Dom had sent messages from his holiday. Lots, at first. He missed her, he said. He wanted – he needed – to talk. She hadn't replied to any of them, and he'd stopped.

And when he'd stopped, she was relieved, but she also missed him. She was dreading tomorrow. It would be the first time she'd seen him since the wretched day at the shiny hotel, and she hadn't a clue what to expect from him.

Kit was as he had always been. They hadn't taken long summer holidays for a few years now, preferring to stay home and head somewhere hot in October half-term, or at Christmas. It made her almost angry that he hadn't noticed anything. She felt out of control of herself, an emotional maelstrom, and he, apparently, couldn't tell. Which was obtuse and unkind of her, she knew, since she was putting so much energy into appearing completely normal at home. He'd asked her, just that once, and he'd accepted her answer, that there was nothing he could help her with, so readily. To her, the equilibrium was entirely changed. To him, apparently not. Or did he just not mind enough to keep asking? The awfulness of being fed up with him for not being suspicious of her was not lost on Natalie. Arlo was his boisterous, rambunctious self. Off at day camp with mates from school, coming home exhausted and happy.

She spoke to Temple more regularly than she had before the night in the shepherd's hut. Max had moved all his stuff out, and she was talking about getting in a flatmate. She had been to see a lawyer about a decree nisi, and she said she was still seeing her therapist. An old girlfriend had asked her to join a party on the Île de Ré and she was there now. She'd been sending photographs of an idyllic house and ripe market produce in net shopping bags. And of herself, with freckles across her nose, squinting in the sunshine. She checked in with Stella and Marley more frequently too. She knew she was compensating, but she needed to do it, and they bore it with equanimity.

Natalie had been avoiding Sylvia, and she felt bad about that. She couldn't lie to her mother, and she was horribly afraid that she'd collapse and dissolve entirely if she saw her, and told her, and that it might be impossible to rebuild herself in the same shape.

And she could no longer sleep through the night. Ever.

23

Andrew wasn't in the house when Flick got home later that evening, fingers and toes sparkling with Mother of the Bride. The house was spotlessly clean, unusually tidy, and strangely quiet. The round table in the middle of the hall was adorned by an enormous and artfully casual vase of flowers in Phoebe's colours. She rolled her eyes fondly, even as she took a deep sniff at one of the blowsy roses. Guests weren't even supposed to come *in* this way – there was a pathway of coir matting with tiki torches and arches to guide them around the side of the house to the back. Something would have gone wrong – and that seemed highly unlikely – for anyone to see these flowers. Flick dropped her bag in the hallway, although she probably shouldn't – there would be tutting later – and walked through to the kitchen, which was similarly immaculate, and the bifold doors leading to the garden.

The serious work out here – planting, training, pruning – had started, she swore, within minutes of the engagement announcement, and it really did look like something from a magazine. She'd be hard pushed to name much of what was out here, doing its harmonious, weed-free thing, but she could appreciate the beauty of the overall effect. Domestic matters had never been her thing, inside or out. She hadn't the patience for gardening, or the tolerance for housework, which struck her as the most colossal waste of time and energy. She'd always lived in a sort of organized chaos, slightly grubby around the edges, until Andrew. Her student digs and bachelor pads had always been a mess – no fairy lights and scented candles for her. Pointless.

She and Zoë had been renting a garden flat in a dodgy-ish part of Wimbledon when she met Andrew. Her divorce settlement hadn't left her with a lot – the marital home had been mortgaged to the hilt. Rent, bills and occasional nanny charges when she couldn't work around Zoë ate most what she had. Not that Andrew had had money back then. That had come later, when he sold the company he'd started. When she first knew him, most of what he was making was being ploughed back into the firm.

That was how they'd met – he'd been identified by a business magazine as One to Watch for the new millennium, and Flick, working as a freelance journalist – sporadically since Zoë had been born a couple of years earlier – had been commissioned to interview him for a piece on the tech *Wunderkinder* who were going to make it big in the twenty-first century. She hadn't been particularly enthusiastic about the piece – he was her third One to Watch that week, and the other two had been bloody hard work – the first so arrogant and conceited she'd had trouble even sitting through the interview without chucking her coffee over him, and the second so introverted and geeky she'd had far better chats with the ticket inspector at Wimbledon station. And then there was Zoë. Flick had tried to cancel Andrew at first – citing a cold that was making Zoë cranky and unwilling to be left. He'd been very understanding for a man, she thought, quickly establishing that he had a daughter of his own around the same age and understood perfectly. In fact, he'd offered to meet her in Wimbledon so she could get it done in an hour. Told her to bring Zoë if she wanted to. She didn't. Zoë wasn't really cranky, so she'd left her with the sitter, but she'd taken him up on the offer to stay local. Why the hell not? It was just an hour.

She'd stayed for two, and only left because she had to pick Zoë up from the childminder. Not only did he manage to make his business chat fascinating without seeming like a wanker, but he'd made her feel fascinating too. That was more of a feat, given what the last couple of years of her life had looked like. Her kickass had deserted her when Zoë's father, Craig, had left her for an intern when she was seven months pregnant. He'd taken her mojo with him, and left her with a vast belly, swollen ankles, a chip on her shoulder, and a borderline sociopathic aversion to men. All of them. It was going to be her and Zoë for the next eighteen years or so, and then just her, and maybe some cats. Thank God for Andrew. She had done, every day since.

Flick pushed back the bifolds, and stepped out onto the terrace. Andrew was walking out of the tepee, and he waved, then beckoned enthusiastically. He opened his arms to her as she approached. 'Good time, darling?'

'Fabulous. Got my lady nails.' She waggled her pink manicure at him. 'I'm officially relaxed.'

'I'm glad.'

'It was bliss, love. Thank you so much for suggesting it. Just the job.'

He kissed the top of her head, his arms around her. 'You smell of scented candles.'

'You certainly don't.'

He laughed. 'Nope.' He put one arm up, Popeye style. 'I smell of triumph.'

'Triumph. That's the new creed, right?' She nuzzled playfully into his neck. 'How's it been, gorgeous?'

'All go.'

'All good go?'

He nodded happily. 'Almost without a hitch. Nothing we couldn't sort, anyway. They've been a great team.'

'You must be knackered.'

'Not really. I'll probably collapse tomorrow night, after Phoebe leaves. Right now I'm running on love and adrenalin. Besides, we're mostly done, until the caterers and the hair and make-up people turn up tomorrow. And the photographer and the videographer . . .'

'And Uncle Tom Cobley and all.' Flick laughed, and ruffled his hair.

'My list is one long series of big red ticks, Flick. I'm officially *ready*. You timed your return brilliantly as ever – everyone just left for the night, literally moments before you drove in. The girls are off getting their nails done now. They'll be back in a bit. Come and see what we did.'

He took her hand and pulled her into the tent.

And it was beautiful, as she had known it would be. Perfect. Meticulous in every tiny detail, from the floral arrangements on the tables, their colours picked up in the napkins and the water glasses, to the fairy lights strung around the poles of the structure, to the modern calligraphy on the signs: exactly the vision he and Phoebe had settled on when she'd got engaged in April. Andrew was beaming. He'd so loved doing this, she knew. Doing it for his beloved Phoebe, yes, of course. And she knew he'd have exactly the same pleasure doing it for Zoë too, although somehow Flick couldn't imagine her daughter wanting the same traditional things. They'd embraced their mutual step-parenting so entirely when they'd married a year after they met that, if it wasn't for Phoebe's white-blonde and delicate prettiness and how sharply it contrasted with Zoë's dark looks, no one would know they were a blended family.

But he'd been doing it for himself too, she knew. After he'd sold the company in 2005, there'd been no need for him to work, but the idea of early retirement had been anathema to him. The golf course did not beckon, and a round-the-world cruise held no appeal whatsoever. He'd held various non-exec positions, volunteered and mentored, but he was a man who was always looking for the next project. The new challenge for which he would have boundless enthusiasm and incredible energy. She loved it about him, and understood long ago that he would never stop entirely.

'Aw, love. It's completely beautiful.' It was. She felt a lump in her throat. 'You've missed your calling. I definitely see a new career. Wedding planner.' They'd all watched both versions of *Father of the Bride* across the last two weekends when the girls were home for fittings and hair appointments. Cinematic 'homework' was an Andrew introduction that had continued throughout the girls' childhood: *Home Alone* before a trip to New York, *It's a Wonderful Life* every Christmas Eve, war films on VE Day and Remembrance Sunday. He had owned hundreds of DVDs that Flick had only recently been able to persuade him to get rid of, and they'd always had the biggest television he'd been able to talk her into. The original 1950 version of *Father of the Bride* with Spencer Tracy and Elizabeth Taylor had come out ahead of the Steve Martin remake for them all, except for the hilariously OTT wedding planner, Franck, which was what Zoë and Phoebe had called their dad ever since.

'Forget it. I've got one more in me. Zoë's. If she wants one, that is . . . That's it.'

'Aw, go on. You love it.' She punched his arm playfully.

He wrapped her up in another of his bear hugs. 'It's going to be a great day, huh? I'm so bloody excited.'

'Me too. Can't wait. You hungry?'

He nodded. 'Starving. You?'

'God, yes. It was all a bit lettuce leaf and half a cherry tomato at lunchtime. I fancy a curry.'

'Already ordered. Sag aloo, brinjal bhaji, tikka for you, korma for me. And I've put a bottle of tomorrow's champagne in the fridge for us.'

'You're an amazing wife – you know that, Andrew Butterworth?' Flick kissed his cheek, and laughed. 'I'd marry you all over again.'

24

Apart from Andrew and Flick, they were all there, five pews from the front, bride's side, except Kit and Natalie, which surprised no one. The two of them would doubtless slide in last minute, like Hugh Grant and Charlotte Coleman, in a delicious cloud of Natalie's Coco Mademoiselle. As in the film – and such was its cultural significance to anyone of a certain age that it was impossible to attend a conventional English wedding without reciting lines to yourself and remembering Kristin Scott Thomas's vast pink hat – there was a certain greatness to their lateness.

The rest of them had been there in plenty of time, of course, in their finery, sitting outside the pub a hundred yards from the church a respectable forty-five minutes before the service was due to start, watching the other guests arrive from their choice vantage point. Georgie, the chronicler, had brought her camera, and snapped away. They scrubbed up pretty well, she reflected. James, the young groom, was there too, with his raucous ushers and his best man, looking grey around the gills with anxiety, or maybe last night's drinking. When Georgie approached them with the camera, his best man threw an arm around his shoulders, beaming, and James managed a fixed grin.

The kids were here too – most of them, anyway. Zoë, the bride's sister, and Mia, Dom and Sarah's girl, the bridesmaids, were with Phoebe, of course, back at Flick and Andrew's home. Just Temple and Arlo were missing, the latter having been included with his parents, but wisely having eschewed the invitation in favour of a sleepover with a mate and an afternoon of football. The other ten, having landed back in their hometown from various flats and university halls the night before, had admittedly arrived with their parents, but the second the cars had been parked, they'd moved like a shoal of fish to separate themselves, heading straight for the beer garden at the back of the pub.

'We scrub up well, for old codgers.'

'Speak for yourself. I'm neither old, nor a codger.'

'Course you're not. You're gorgeous. We're all gorgeous. In our prime.'

'And just look at the kids we produced.'

'Now they really *are* gorgeous!'

'Our babies are starting to get married. Christ, that makes me feel old.'

'I love a wedding.'

'Me too. Especially when I really, really love the bride.'

'You said . . .'

'It'll be like your twenties, when you seemed to be at a hen do or a wedding every weekend from May through August. Just the next generation.'

'And we'll be doing the dad dancing at the reception.'

'Exactly. Showing them how it's done.'

'I hope they've got flip-flops for the dancing. I can barely walk in these heels.'

'I hope they've got a space away from the music where you can hear yourself think and actually carry on a conversation.'

'Oh, for God's sake. You actually *are* an old codger!' Everyone laughed.

A swanky beribboned car pulled up, and Flick climbed out, holding her feathered hat on her head carefully with one hand and waving like the Queen with the other. She was followed by Mia and Zoë, ethereally lovely in strapless beaded dresses with pale aqua tulle skirts, clutching posies of creamy roses and white ranunculus.

'Wow. Look at you all. Stunning.'

Flick gave a little shimmy, and a deep chuckle. 'Aren't we just! Drink up, you reprobates, and get into that church. They aren't that far behind us. Or at least they won't be, if Andrew stops crying.'

'Have you seen her?'

She nodded. 'She's a vision. He's a state.'

'Blimey. She wasn't kidding about the trees – didn't realize they'd be quite so *foresty*,' Sarah whispered, as they filed obediently into the church under the elaborate floral arch adorning the entrance. 'Jesu, Joy of Man's Desiring' was being played by a string quartet set up in the transept. 'Classy. Of course.' Out of the bright sunshine, it was cool and almost damp inside. Hornbeams lined the aisle and garlands of eucalyptus and ivy dressed each pew. 'That Kate Middleton has a lot to answer for. Trees in church.'

'Sssh.'

The music stopped. Annie fumbled in her clutch for tissues. The congregation hovered in anticipation. And here, as if they had timed it that way precisely, were Natalie and Kit. They must have sashayed past the bride in the porch. Smiling apologetically, shushing themselves theatrically, sliding in, and forcing the others to squish up to admit them. Ross, on the end, was pushed uncomfortably up against a pillar. It was annoying, Georgie reflected, that Natalie – always the most glamorous of them – should be so late, and still so matte. Not so much as a bead of sweat on her upper lip, and no red cheeks. Just her normal, gorgeous, late self, resplendent in expensive baby pink and dove grey, air-kissing each of them in turn from her vantage point on the inner aisle.

By general consensus a hush settled over the whole congregation, the doors that had been briefly closed opened, and Bach's No. 1 Suite for Solo Cello began. There were four bridesmaids – besides Zoë and Mia, the bride had chosen a mate from university and another from law school. Georgie caught Sarah out of the corner of her eye, gesturing that Mia should carry her posy lower, at her hip, not her chest. Mia rolled her eyes at her perfectionist mother's silent instruction, but fondly, and did as she was told. They made their way, one after another, up the aisle, smiling shyly left and right, and filed into the top pew on the left. Flick turned back, and Georgie saw that she was crying, all her bluster and sarcasm forgotten in the loveliness of the moment. Then she turned, too, and watched Andrew bring his daughter down to James at the altar.

It was incredibly moving, it turned out, watching a young woman you had known as barely more than a toddler, ready to take this absurd, optimistic, huge step, and Georgie felt tears well in her eyes. Andrew looked perilously close to sobbing. His jaw was set, and one corner of his bottom lip was bitten firmly between his teeth. He studiously avoided eye contact. Flick put one arm around him and left it there, gently stroking his side.

And then, with a 'Dearly beloved', they took their seats and the vicar began . . .

Afterwards, they spilt out and stood among the gravestones.

Georgie put her arms around Annie. 'Come here, you soppy mare.'

'Can't help it. Wasn't it lovely?' Annie dabbed carefully at her eyes.

Georgie and Sarah nodded. 'And she looks beautiful.'

'Completely. Like a young Audrey Tautou.' Natalie always invoked actresses.

The kids had been out of the church before them, sloping around the side – for sneaky cigarettes, some of them. They rambled around to the front now, wondering when the photographs would be done and the drinking would begin. Two of Annie's boys, Louis and Theo, hugged her briefly in turn, each dwarfing her. 'Waterworks, Mum? *Really?*'

'To the Batmobiles,' Kit cried, raising his car keys.

'I'm dying of thirst, and parking at the Butterworths' is going to be a bitch.'

Watching Dom from across the busy space, a wave of lust washed over Natalie, her body betraying her. She had feared it would, the moment she turned her gaze in his direction. She'd scanned the seating plan for his name, even before she'd searched for her own, knew exactly where in the room he was. But she'd saved it, dreaded it – the moment, the feeling. Hadn't turned. She knew she would be more or less in his exact line of vision, and she knew he'd be watching her. She'd waited until the speeches, when she could legitimately angle her chair towards the top table to listen. Just a few degrees more, and he was in her peripheral view, and she wasn't listening at all. It was easy enough to laugh when others laughed, and to *aw*, sentimentally, when her neighbours did.

Sex was all she could think about. It felt like sex had been all she had thought about since it had started. She should be thinking about romance and tenderness and loyalty and joy. But she wasn't. When he was in her orbit, she was thinking about sex. About the last time they'd made love. For that short period of time, he'd been her drug, and the withdrawal hadn't worked. She hadn't known it was the last time, that last time in the flat. It was Temple who'd unknowingly pushed her towards ending it so abruptly. She hadn't had time to be ready.

God, it was different with him. Night and day. Some-times she tried to remember how it had been at the beginning with Kit, the one she was supposed to sleep with, all those years ago. Had it been as good with him, then? Was it impossible to have sex with your partner as good as sex with your lover? Was it just the illicit frisson, the danger, the novelty? She hadn't the vaguest idea of how she felt. When she had been with Dom, she didn't know which of them she loved. Maybe both. Maybe neither.

Love was a bloody big word. An enormous, expansive, generous word with a million applications. You loved your husband, your children, your parents, butter and Marmite on a crumpet, Coral Charm peonies in May, a cigarette with a sundowner on a beach, Beatles ballads, that blue dress, *The West Wing*, some of your friends, and Prosecco.

'Lust' was a small, specific word. A laser beam. Throbbing, tense, radiating intensity. An obsession.

Love could apply to so many people, all at the same time. Lust demanded specificity.

Love was fabric softener and mown grass, your child's hand in yours and a cashmere stole. An afternoon in a hammock. Lust was everything prickly and sharp and disquieting. It didn't want you to keep still. It was a bed of nails.

Love had never overwhelmed her, even in the moments of her life when she had felt it most strongly. Because love buoyed her. Lust wanted to hold her under. Lust could drown her at any time. Buckle her knees, race her heart, make her insides rushing hot liquid.

Lust was in danger of making her hurt people she

loved. Today, here in this tent dedicated to love, she felt lust was winning.

Experiencing that whoosh of desire in this room was practically shameful. It was the Wicked Witch of the West skulking around while Glinda the Good Witch held court. A ribbon of red in a sea of pastel. Was that what made it feel so bloody good?

It was odd to her that no one noticed. She felt as if the current between them should be visible, like heat wobbling the horizon on a summer's day. A sizzle, a crackle. A superhero green flash. It was the biggest thing in the space. But no one noticed.

That was what she told herself. Even then, she didn't quite believe it.

It was still warm once darkness fell. Lucky weather, as everyone said, although they would have said the same if it had rained, even as they pulled pashminas around themselves to keep warm. The cake had been cut, the toasts and speeches delivered, the first dance, slightly self-conscious and sweet, had been danced, and the party was in full swing. There were three distinct canvas structures, all connected: one for eating, one for dancing, and one in the middle set out with hay bales covered with blankets for 'flopping', as Annie would doubtless put it. All of the wooden supports were wound with fairy lights and several firepits were ablaze. To the side, an outdoor barbecue area had been set up where the catering staff were busying themselves making pizzas, although not even the most vigorous dancer could possibly still be hungry after the three-course wedding breakfast they'd had. Piles of shawls and blankets were dotted around, and lots of the older guests had positioned themselves cosily around the fires, where the music wasn't so loud.

Will stubbed out his cigarette in the terracotta pot where he'd been leaning. He'd just seen his mum, Annie, slightly tipsy now, coming back from the loo. She'd held his face between her hands and told him how handsome he was, and how much she loved him, and how much she was looking forward to dancing at *his* wedding one day. He was a foot taller than her, and well used to her affectionate gestures, but he'd resisted her attempt to lead him back onto the dance-floor where her friends were mum dancing. He was far too sober for that. Come to think of it, he was almost totally sober, which was surprising. He'd been in the middle of the young throng, totally at ease in the company of lifelong friends, not so much dancing now as jumping sweatily in time to tracks of their youth, but he'd escaped to process the singular thought that had occupied him since about 2 p.m. that afternoon.

He was looking for her. For Mia. Second bridesmaid on the left. The girl he'd known since they were in nursery.

Eventually, miraculously, she came out of the tent alone. She was still wearing her bridesmaid's dress, of course, that spectacular dress, but the high heels had been replaced by her Converse, so the dress was now a bit too long, and she had it bunched up in one hand to avoid stepping on the hem. The headdress-thingy she'd had on was gone, and her hair was messy, not smooth. It all made her look more like Mia, yet no less extraordinary. He had the same jolt he'd had when she'd walked down the aisle in the church. The same punch in the stomach, how-have-I-not-*seen*-her-before feeling. Seeing him there, she came towards him, smiled at him, her wide, dimpled, infectious smile, and reached out with her free hand. He let her arm slide down his, then took her hand and stood straight, pulling her back in the direction of the music.

'Hey, Will.'

'Dance with me, Mia.' He didn't care what they did, just wanted to be close to her. She laughed. 'I've *been* dancing. Where were you? I'm completely knackered. Seriously. I've been at this bridesmaiding lark since dawn. Tough gig. And I'm actually seriously contemplating a pizza. They smell amazing. Need to soak up some of this booze and have a sit-down.'

'Dance with me,' he repeated, more serious now.

She let him pull her towards him and twirl her, and he didn't know whether she had noticed the change in his tone.

'No dancing. Sit with me,' she implored.

'Done.' He hadn't wanted to dance, not really. There was a bench a few feet away. She flopped onto it, her back against the arm, her knees hugged to her chest. She always sat like that. He sat next to her, feet on the ground, and rested his nearest arm on her knees, ever so casually. She was completely familiar to him, and completely new.

It was messing with his head, but in the most wonderful way.

'It was fab, wasn't it?'

He nodded.

'Phoebs – she looked incredible, didn't she?'

He honestly hadn't noticed Phoebe. Bad wedding guest. '*You* looked incredible.'

'Aw. Go on.'

She rested her head briefly on his arm. He reached around with his other hand, laid it gently on her neck. He'd have touched her a thousand times over the years – an arm around her shoulders, a brush against a leg in the back of a car. All those times, he'd never noticed, never counted. But never her neck.

Emboldened by the fact she wasn't looking at him, he carried on: 'Serious. You looked amazing. Couldn't take my eyes off you.'

She raised her head and then they were gazing into each other's eyes, closer than they were used to being.

'Stop!' Her tone was playful.

'Shan't.' His wasn't.

He really wanted to kiss her. It must have shown on his face. She looked quizzical, then confused. Then she moved back. 'Ew. You're being weird. Stop.'

'I'm not being weird.' He didn't move backwards – held her gaze. Suddenly brave. Or stupid.

'You definitely are. You're, like, my brother. I knew you before you shaved. You knew me before I had braces, for Christ's sake, Will.'

'And?'

'And so it's weird. And inappropriate.'

'You sound like your mum. That's a word she'd use. Has used, of course. Many, many times. I do shave now, though. And your teeth are perfectly straight.'

'And still . . . incest. Incest, Will.' She was half laughing. He took some comfort from the fact that she could have moved further along the bench, but she hadn't.

'Did I miss the part when we found out we were related by blood? Or even marriage?'

'We're related by shared history.'

'We're *not* related, Mia. Trust me when I tell you that at no point – not one – in the last however many years that I've known you have I considered, for one single second, you as a sister. Or even a cousin.'

She cocked her head and looked at him hard.

'And never less than right now.'

She didn't break the stare.

'Our parents are friends. Best of bloody friends, sure, but friends. We've known each other for, like, a really long time.'

'Our *whole* lives.' Her tone was earnest.

'Okay, *most* of our lives.' He drew in a deep, slow breath, then exhaled. 'Have you seen yourself today? I mean, was there a mirror where you guys were, before the whole wedding thing?'

She giggled, and stared down at her hands.

'When you walked into that church today, Mia, you looked . . .' he seemed to search for the right word '. . . shattering.'

'Interesting word, Will.'

'That's exactly the word I mean. It's like something . . . exploded when I saw you coming down that aisle.'

Mia shook her head, still laughing. 'You are *so* drunk. When you remember this crap in the morning, you're gonna die. Die. Trust me, you idiot. You're gonna be texting me literally begging me not to tell the others.'

'No. I won't. I'm not remotely drunk, Mia Bennett. But you are still shattering. And in the morning I'll be sober and you'll still be shattering.'

'Are you paraphrasing Churchill?'

'See? I love that you *know* I'm paraphrasing Churchill. Beautiful *and* smart.' He felt emboldened. 'Enough, though, of this chat. This is a party. You need to dance with me. And then you need to kiss me. Not necessarily in that order.'

'What I *need* is pizza.' But she looked confused now, and, he told himself, almost disappointed that he was bringing the conversation to a close.

'And stop giving me the brush-off, will you?'

He stood up, and offered her his hand. She took it. When she stood too, they were close together. She was shorter than him, and she tilted her head back to look at him. The shawl she had had wrapped around her shoulders slid off one of them, and he leant forward the tiniest amount to move it back up, and it was then, when his face was nearest, that she kissed his cheek. It was gentle, and soft, speculative, perhaps, but – and he almost smiled to himself – not at all how you would kiss someone in your family. There was definite lingering. He'd take that, for now.

*

Inside, Vanessa slid gratefully onto an empty chair with Annie and Sarah at either side of her. She hadn't seen Natalie for ages. She'd just passed Georgie on the way back from the loos. Andrew and Flick were dancing. Flick was whatever you were between tipsy and roaring drunk. A good dancer sober, she was pretty mesmerizing uninhibited by alcohol, and Andrew could only try to keep up in her rather fabulous orbit. They'd been on a table nearer the action for the wedding breakfast and the speeches, but they'd commandeered this one shortly after dinner ended and the table's original occupants had moved on – it had a good view of the comings and goings and the dance-floor, but it was far enough away that you could still hear yourself think, and each other gossip.

Annie sniffed an empty glass, shrugged, and filled it with wine from a bottle on the table, then topped up her own. She clinked Vanessa's glass before she'd even picked it up, and a spray of white wine sloshed across the cloth. For a posh girl, Vanessa thought, she could sometimes be surprising. That was the thing, though, that undefinable posh thing. It was why the richest people from the best families wore the oldest hats and flat shoes to Ascot.

She kicked off her distinctly not flat shoes, and, tucking her dress between her thighs, rubbed her sore feet in turn, ruefully. 'This is always my favourite bit of a wedding . . .'

'That's so typical of you, Vanessa.' Sarah laughed. 'You like *this* bit best. When we're all a bit bleary and pissed. And I'm teetering on melancholy. Not the minute the groom sets eyes on the bride, or the father wiping away a tear, or the heartfelt speeches . . .'

'Oh, I love the speeches. Wasn't Andrew fucking brilliant?' Annie swore when she was tipsy. Hardly ever when she was sober, except when she was in the car: then she had a sailor's vocabulary.

'Or the food? Which was spectacularly good, as mass catering goes,' Sarah said.

'Nope. None of that. Seen one, seen 'em all.'

'So cynical.' Annie shook her head in mock sadness.

Vanessa's eyes twinkled. She didn't mind the criticism in the least. To her, cynical was more a compliment. 'I like the drunken, messy, slippery slope to carriages at midnight. It's when all the interesting stuff happens.'

'Remind me why we're friends?' Sarah laughed.

'Because.' Vanessa took a large swig from her glass. 'That's my job. That's how this group works. You know that. All groups have a dynamic. Everyone has a job. We're like . . . like cogs in a wheel, you know. Moving parts in an automaton. Sharp-eyed, sharp-tongued cynic is mine.'

'What's mine?' Annie looked mildly alarmed.

'You're the sweetie-pie. Everyone's favourite. The soppy one.'

'I'm the wetty, you're basically saying.'

'In the best possible way. Yes. Wouldn't change a hair on your head. None of us would. Sarah's the organizer. Sergeant major. Keeps us all in line.'

'God. You make me sound like a schoolteacher.'

'Sarah, you *are* a schoolteacher.'

'That's my day job, for Chrissakes.'

'That's your personality type. It's not a job. It's a vocation.'

Sarah considered for a moment, then raised her hands in surrender. 'Can't deny the charge.'

'Nat's the glamourpuss, sometimes the drama queen. Georgie's the worrier. Flick's the anarchist. There. That's the set.'

'Right. I don't know what to say about that.' Annie raised an eyebrow at Sarah, who patted her on the shoulder.

'It's not a bad thing. It's the magic. It's why it works. Do you think we'd all still be close if we only had our addresses and our kids in common? No way. Look at everyone else who's fallen by the wayside over the years. We have a magic formula. We're like a complete friendship experience . . . We're the – the avocado of friendship.'

They sniggered. 'You're talking utter bollocks, you know that?'

'Maybe, but I'm right. Think about it. If you want a cuddle and sympathy – Annie. Fun – Flick. Hard truth – me. Your arse in gear – you, Sarah. Catastrophizing – Georgie. And Nat – drama and fashion tips, I suppose.'

'That's a bit bloody reductive, if you don't mind my saying so, Vanessa. I can be fun,' said Annie, plaintively.

'And I'm sympathetic.' Sarah pouted.

'Yes, yes, we can all do bits of each other. We just don't tend to when we're all together. No need, you see. We've grown together, over the years, too. All those things, those qualities, those accommodations, have been magnified. It's like companion planting in the garden.'

'Huh?'

'Where you plant one species and it makes another one grow. Like symbiosis.'

Sarah snorted, and raised a hand. 'Okay, Vanessa, enough. Enough psychoanalysis. Enough big words.'

'Enough bullshit.' Annie laughed. 'Where the hell are our husbands? We need to be rescued. We need to dance. Or eat pizza.'

'Smoking cigars behind the tent, most of them, I expect.' Sarah wrinkled her nose in distaste. 'Like we won't know they've been doing it from the smell on their clothes. I just saw them.'

'And our glorious children? What are they up to?'

'Mostly dancing, passed out on the grass or . . .' Vanessa wasn't sure she should say anything. Three glasses of champagne ago, she almost certainly wouldn't have done. Loose lips sink ships. And she wasn't quite as blunt as she had just claimed to be.

'What?'

Too late now.

'Well . . .'

'Stop being coy, Ness. Aren't you the straight shooter? What?' Annie was wide-eyed.

'I'm sure it's nothing, but I did just see your Will and your Mia . . .' She nodded at Sarah.

'What?'

'Nothing. Just . . . talking.'

'If they're just *talking*, what's the big deal?'

'They looked . . . close.'

Annie's eyebrows were almost in her hairline. 'You are being so mischievous, Vanessa Powell!'

'Well, would it be a problem?'

Annie and Sarah looked at each other across their friend. Weighing it up. Sarah giggled. 'I don't know. Would it?'

Annie pursed her lips. 'I love Mia. She's absolutely gorgeous.'

'I love Will.' It went without saying that Will was gorgeous too. All Annie's boys were – tall blond Vikings of young men just like their dad. Annie had once told them, years ago, that a mentor of his at medical school had discouraged him from his first choice specialism of obs and gynae on the grounds that no woman with a problem would want someone that handsome between their thighs brandishing a speculum. They had concurred. It was true. You really wanted an ugly bald gynae.

'So . . .' This was Vanessa. 'Not convincing, ladies.'

'No, no. I'm not saying anything. You're being naughty. It would just take a bit of getting used to, right?'

'Yeah, I mean . . . they've grown up together.'

'Exactly.'

'It's funny that this is the first time. If it is the first time – what would we know? All these kids, all the same age, how come none of them have gone out together before?'

'Cos they're like brothers and sisters.'

'Aha. So you *would* think it was weird?'

'No. Stop it. You *are* a bloody disrupter. This is an entirely hypothetical situation anyway, so no one needs to get their knickers in a twist. They're just talking, they're friends.' But Annie was laughing. 'Besides, weddings have different rules, don't they? Shall we go and see for ourselves?' She stood up.

Sarah followed her. 'Oh, yes, let's – that'll be helpful.'

'Come on.'

The two women linked arms, and pulled Vanessa out of her chair. She just had time to grab her heels before they marched off in search of scandal.

Outside, though, there was nothing to see now, except their happy husbands, heading back towards them stinking of Cubans, and a small line of people with the munchies queuing for the pizzas.

'Dance with me.'

'No.'

'Dance with me.' Natalie looked around. The floor was packed. She couldn't see her friends, but they might have been in there, in the crush. Or outside. It seemed most people were drunk, or just tired. They'd all been going for hours now. Some were eating pizza. The waiting staff were weaving between the tables, clearing place settings and uneaten desserts. The DJ had already played 'My Way'. Phoebe and James were still there. She thought they were leaving on honeymoon tomorrow.

Dom held out his hand. 'Dance with me, Nat.'

She took it, because she didn't want him to make a scene, and because of the way he looked at her, and because she found she couldn't not take his hand, and he walked her to the dance-floor. The song was a slower one now. Groups split into swaying couples.

In the throng, he put his arm tightly around her waist,

pulling her to him, her arms around his neck. She could feel him. They'd stood this way alone and naked, his fingers splayed in the small of her back, possessively, and she couldn't think about anything now except how that had felt.

'I miss you. All the bloody time.' He said it close to her face, just to her. She felt his warm breath in her ear, and she groaned softly. His hand moved dangerously down, tipping her ever so slightly inwards, and she fought not to grind herself against him.

'Oh, God.'

She'd have gone outside with him. There and then. He could have laid her down in the grass and done whatever he wanted to her, whoever was watching. She was that close.

She was oblivious. She'd told herself it was over and she'd meant it. In that moment it felt like it could never be over. He was all there was.

And then the music changed again. Suddenly Flick was there, dragging Andrew, her hands moving his hips in time with her own. People were lifting Phoebe and James into the air. Sarah joined in, Ross holding their clasped hands in the air. Everyone was singing.

Natalie took a step away from Dom, letting her hands fall from around his neck, and felt his hands loosen, then release her. People moved between them and the moment was gone. She felt empty, and hollow and confused, like a hypnotist's victim, back in the room.

25

At twenty-five he'd had a few girlfriends, a few more flings and the odd encounter but, waiting for Mia that evening, Will didn't remember ever being quite so nervous before meeting a girl. Being nervous at all, for that matter. Or having had to work quite as hard as he had to get the date in the first place. This evening was the result of more negotiating emails and persuasive texts than he would normally invest.

Girls liked him – he'd always known it, although he'd tried not to be a dick about it. One, a pretty redhead called Ruth he'd been with for a time in his first year at uni, had told him it wasn't so much that he was good-looking, although, she had quickly added, he completely was, but because he was kind and fun and had the knack of making girls feel like they were the only one in the room when he was talking to them. She'd been great, a straight-talking Yorkshire woman with a coarse turn of phrase. 'I'm not gonna lie, Willie,' she'd said, lying beneath his arm in the cramped single bed at his student halls. 'It's a knicker-dropper combo. You should teach workshops. Please teach workshops.' He'd always treasured the compliment. He and Ruth hadn't lasted long romantically, but they were still friends, the very best of friends, thank God, and he knew that was to his credit as well as hers. They were flatmates too – they'd started after graduation in a house with four others. Now, at twenty-five, with proper jobs and decent salaries, a party house held no appeal, and it was just the two of them (and their occasional overnight guests) in a relatively civilized garden flat in Battersea with a Nespresso machine and a Sky subscription.

He figured he lived what he had learnt. His dad was a gentleman – he had always treated their mum like precious china – and it had rubbed off. They all adored their mum – his dad and his brothers, Louis and Theo. To the three boys, without sisters, she'd seemed a tomboy in some ways – always on the touchline for football and rugby matches – but there was no doubt that she was their dad's princess. In a good way. He'd never want her to be disappointed in him, and that had had the effect of checking his behaviour since adolescence when all his mates were gladly sacrificing chivalry for results. Ruth said he was old-fashioned, and that was his USP. She knew his other secret, though – that his standards were impossibly high: once he knew a girl wasn't going to meet them, he sometimes spent weeks or even months trying to let her down gently. She said she could tell within five minutes of seeing him with a girl whether the roller coaster was on an upward climb or the swooping fall . . .

That evening, Ruth had been home before he'd gone out. When he'd come into the living room in a carefully curated outfit, she'd been cross-legged on the sofa with a bowl of pasta and the *EastEnders* theme tune. She'd looked at him appraisingly over the top of her thick black glasses. 'Who's the lucky girl?' she'd asked. He'd been single for about six months, which was nudging unusual.

'Mia.'

Her eyes widened. 'As in Mia home-friend Mia?'

Will nodded, trying to be nonchalant. 'The very same.'

She looked puzzled. 'So how come the Casanova kit? You've washed, and everything, I can tell.'

'Rude.' He threw a cushion at her, and she had to hold the pasta bowl high in the air. 'What d'ya mean?'

'I've seen you on your way out to meet your home mates. Millions of time. You're usually dressed like a tramp. And there's normally a gang of them. Not sure I've seen you do it in your best shirt smelling of . . .' she sniffed the air suspiciously '. . . your best Penhaligon cologne.' She pronounced it col-og-nee on purpose, her flat Yorkshire vowels drawing out the word comically.

'All right, Inspector Clouseau. Imagine if you used your powers for good instead of evil.'

She gave a dastardly laugh. 'So Mia has a cute friend?'

'Nope.' He shook his head. 'Just me and Mia.'

Ruth considered this, lips pursed. She picked up the remote and muted Danny Dyer. 'Dish.'

'Bugger off.'

She held up her free hand in surrender. 'Okay. Okay. Touchy much?'

He checked his phone, and ran a finger around his collar. Ruth was right – he'd showered after work but he felt sweaty again already.

'Touchy and nervous.' She narrowed her eyes.

Will sank onto the sofa. 'Okay, okay. You got me. I'm both. Mostly the latter. Really, really nervous. I've got five minutes. What do you think?'

'About what?'

'So, yes, home Mia. But at Phoebs's wedding –'

'That one you went to a couple of weeks ago?'

He nodded. 'She looked, well, phenomenal. It was like I was seeing her for the first time, you know?'

'The thunderbolt?' Ruth nodded sagely.

'Kind of. Does that sound ridiculous?'

'Not to me. Then again, I do have a serious rom-com addiction.'

'So, I mean, I've known her for ever, that's true. Her parents, my parents, all that jazz – but we've seen much less of each other since we all went to uni and stuff. We've all grown up. I don't know *adult* Mia all that well. Not really.'

'And you'd like to?'

Will smirked. 'So badly.'

Ruth nodded again, thoughtfully, like a doctor hearing symptoms and preparing to give a diagnosis.

'So, what do you think?'

'Well. Since you're asking . . . Point one. Weddings do weird things to you. A rich seam Richard Curtis has been mining for decades. Play with your brain. If this is the first time you're seeing her since, she might have gone back to being Mia your mate. Might. So be warned. Point two. And this directly contradicts point one. You're right – sometimes you can't see what's right under your nose. Point three. It's just a date. Did you tell any of the others? George? Timmy? Anne? Dick? Julian?'

He realized a second too late that she'd segued from serious advice back into making fun of him. 'We're not the bloody Famous Five.'

Ruth was laughing. 'I don't know. It all sounded a bit bloody lashings of ginger beer to me, to be honest.'

'You're useless.'

She stopped laughing. 'I'm sorry. Sorry. Being serious now, mate. Why the hell not? Relax. It's just a date. You're not proposing, are you, you great lump? Go and find out.'

And now here he was, nursing a lager and wondering if she was going to stand him up. He'd been early but she was very nearly late. He was acutely aware of the time, and plotting his graceful exit if she didn't show. And then she was there, and even though the bridesmaid's dress and professional make-up had given way to a more familiar Mia – jeans, sneakers and a high ponytail – he still felt the same as he had at the wedding. Maybe he hadn't appreciated the way the jeans hugged the curves, and the sneakers revealed a slim, golden ankle, or how shiny the hair in the high ponytail was. Christ, he was in trouble here. He was gratified to see that she looked slightly flustered, and as she hung her bag over the back of a chair and slid into it, she pushed back her fringe and said, rather breathlessly, 'Sorry. Bloody Tube. Sat between stations for ages. No air conditioning. Like it wasn't already hot enough.' She flapped her white broderie-anglaise blouse to cool herself. He briefly saw a sharp collarbone, the lacy edge of her bra, and felt quite peculiar. 'I thought you might have given up on me and gone home.'

'Never.' He picked up a copy of *Captain Corelli's Mandolin* from beside him. He'd grabbed it from the bookshelf in the front hall as he'd left. It was Ruth's. 'I was ready to wait for ages.'

Mia nodded, impressed. 'Aw. I love that book. Awful, awful film. Gorgeous book. Isn't it amazing?'

He hadn't read a word, but he nodded enthusiastically, fervently hoping there'd be no more questions. 'A classic.'

The business of drinks and food took a couple of minutes, and broke the ice. When her vodka, lime and soda arrived he made a toast. 'To persuading you to come out.'

'To being persuaded. Glad I was.' She smiled, almost shy now.

Conversation was easy while they waited for their food, and then ate. He always thought of chat on a first date as a game of tennis, and theirs had plenty of rally shots. He didn't like girls who didn't ask questions – the kind who sat there as though they were the prize, that their good make-up and smooth, glossy hair should be a substitute for conversation. Like being with them ought to be enough, and they needn't try to be engaging. In the Venn diagram of women, the intersectional overlap of pretty and dull was far bigger than it should be, he thought.

Mia wasn't like that, although she *was* distractingly pretty to him. Had he never noticed before how her mouth moved when she talked – slightly, disarmingly, asymmetrical?

She was animated and funny and bright. By mutual agreement they steered clear of home talk, or reminiscence of time spent together over the years. This was new. She told stories of her office, and her flatmates, and talked about places she wanted to travel to. He was surprised and delighted to discover common ground he hadn't necessarily expected – they both loved schlocky horror films and weepy country ballads, and hated sushi and New Year's Eve.

When Mia excused herself and went to the Ladies, Will checked his phone. There was a message from Ruth. A thunderbolt emoji, and several question marks. He typed the middle finger emoji in return, deleted it, paused, then pressed the red heart. And then the arrow. And *then* the middle finger emoji. No point denying it to her – she'd be able to read his face the minute he walked through the door.

They were still chatting easily as they finished their dessert and coffees. The waitress brought them together, and Will felt irritated – he wanted the evening to go on and on. He was gripped by a sudden fear: the date was nearly over and, lovely though it had obviously been, the whole encounter could still, apart from the odd slightly long look, have qualified in the friend zone. He very much did not want to be in the friend zone. As if she could read his mind, Mia stared into her empty coffee cup, and said quietly, 'I always had a bit of a crush on you when we were at school. Did you know?'

He shook his head. 'No. Not a clue.' He genuinely hadn't.

'Honestly? I didn't think I was that subtle. I always acted a bit of an idiot around you – at get-togethers with our parents and stuff.'

'Passed me by.' He shrugged. 'I cannot imagine for a moment, as I sit here, why I would ever have been oblivious to anything you did, Mia, but I promise I never once thought of you as an idiot.'

They'd been a school year apart. He knew he'd been slightly disdainful of the younger girls at times. How had he not looked properly at her until now?

'We all sort of did, I think. Me and my mates, I mean. They were jealous that we were family friends, actually. You really didn't know?'

Will laughed. 'Wish I had noticed.'

She smiled when he added, 'I'm noticing now.'

Around them, the restaurant had almost emptied of other customers. He'd had no idea they'd been there so long. He waved a waiter over, but the guy had already printed out the bill, and it appeared immediately. Mia reached into her bag for her purse and tried to pay half, but she gave in graciously when he refused to let her. She didn't make it awkward, like women sometimes did, so that when he got to the door of the restaurant he'd have no idea whether he was a shit if he held it open for them or a shit if he didn't.

'I'll just have to take you out next time, then.' She had her head on one side. Her tone was sweetly shy flirty.

'Next time?'

She nodded decisively. 'I liked it.'

'I liked it too.' They held each other's gaze.

'Are you going to tell the others?'

She was close to Phoebe, who was probably still on honeymoon, now he came to think of it. He would normally drop details of his love-life into chat with his younger brothers over a pint, as they would with him. They hung out with Liam, Daisy and the others. They could all, potentially, know about this date in days – in hours, if it was deemed hot enough gossip. One was bound to tell a parent, accidentally or very much on purpose, and, Christ, those women, their mothers, they would *definitely* tell. And he could hear his mother's studied nonchalance on the phone. 'Seeing anyone new, darling boy?'

She shook her head vehemently. 'Hell, no.' She seemed to realize her emphatic delivery was open to misinterpretation. 'I mean, not . . .' She was flustered.

He put up a hand. 'I agree. I feel like we should just keep this between us for now. Is that okay?'

There was something in the care they were taking of each other. Something that meant it needed protecting, shielding from the scrutiny of the vast, nosy group they were a part of. They both felt the shift to 'us and them'.

Will smiled broadly at her, and she mirrored it. He imagined that, to the tired waiter, they might look like the cats that got the cream.

26

Vanessa parked early at the nature reserve, her car facing the view, and turned off the engine, Radio 4 with it. In the silence, she could feel the blood rushing in her ears. She'd zipped her sweatshirt high – she'd probably have a red rash across her chest and neck: she always did when she was anxious. Dog-walkers came and went in pairs, chatting by their open car boots, and runners passed, red-faced from their exertions. The Indian summer of last week seemed set to continue for a while longer but, so early, it was still quite cool.

She often met friends here on a Friday morning since she'd moved to four-day weeks. She couldn't shake the habit, formed over a thirty-year career in the City, of getting up before six, but people didn't want to meet then. Sometimes, she'd make a Thermos of tea, and come here at seven for a long, solitary run before she met someone for a walk at eight thirty. She'd tried persuading Ross, but he had his own morning rituals. They'd learnt not to try to merge too much. That was how it worked best for them. When Daisy and Jasmine had still been at home Ross had been breakfast chef, drill sergeant and chauffeur. He and Callum had a different ritual now, which seemed to involve Callum rolling out of bed ten minutes before he left for the train to college clutching a hastily buttered slice of bread folded in half, not exchanging a word with anyone, and Ross would most likely be in the garden with his fancy Japanese secateurs dead-heading or pruning.

Natalie might feel ambushed. She'd lured her there with an innocuous invitation – the kind she had issued before. A leisurely walk, an easy conversation, an instant coffee in a paper cup from the concession by the car park. She *would* feel ambushed. Vanessa didn't care. It *was* an ambush.

Alone in the silent car, waiting, she felt the pure rage well up in her again. It wasn't lurking far beneath the surface. By the time Natalie pulled up, her habitual ten minutes late, she was bubbling with it. Vanessa watched as she climbed out. Natalie never wore Lycra outside a studio or class. This morning she was in a bright green mohair jumper, oversized, with a woollen plaid scarf tied around her neck, and Grenson boots. So bloody stylish. She opened the back door so that Simon could scamper out, his lead trailing behind him, and was scrolling on her phone as she locked the car and turned to look for Vanessa's. When she saw it and waved, Vanessa opened her own door and climbed out.

The dog ran at her, and she dropped down to her knees to greet him. He was old now, a little whiter every time she saw him. Vanessa remembered him as a glossy puppy, barely twelve weeks old and crying for his mother in Natalie's arms. 'Hello, lovely boy.'

When she looked up, Natalie was in front of her, smiling. 'Morning, darling. How are you doing?'

'Good. Good.' Vanessa suddenly didn't know where to start. The conversations and accusations she'd rehearsed in her head seemed clunky.

'Anyone else coming?' Nat looked around for other familiar cars. It wasn't unusual for them to be a larger group. Not Sarah, of course, unless it was the holidays, but often Annie or Flick, and sometimes Georgie, might ordinarily have been there. In long ago half-terms there might have been a dozen or more of them – a noisy, happy scramble of gossiping mums and kids prepared to walk for ages, as long as there was an ice cream in the immediate future.

'Just us. Actually, Nat, I really wanted to talk to you.'

She was obviously managing to keep the anger and urgency out of her voice, because Natalie didn't immediately seem suspicious. Or she hid it well.

Vanessa released Simon from his lead, and the two of them set off in his wake.

'What's up?'

'Oh, Nat. You have to know what's up.' There. It was that easy. There really was no point in prolonging it. She'd come to say things, and no amount of small-talk or buying time would help. Don't lie. Don't lie. Please don't lie.

Natalie stopped, and her shoulders dropped. She seemed to sink a little. For a sickening moment, Vanessa thought she might be about to fall and put her arms out automatically, shocked at the sudden drama, but then Natalie straightened. She couldn't look at her. Then she turned, and there were tears in her eyes. 'I'm sorry.'

She looked pitiful, but Vanessa didn't want to pity her. She wanted to stay angry.

'Can we sit?'

There was a bench about fifty yards in front of them on the wide path, angled to make the most of the pretty view across the fields to the hills, a bench with an inscription – an invocation of love and devotion. They walked to it without speaking, and sat down. Simon lingered, puzzled at the truncation of his walk, then scampered down the hill among the bracken in search of rabbits to terrorize or fox poo he could roll in.

'So. You know.'

'I know something. I don't know what I know yet. I'm hoping you're going to tell me.'

'Did you guess?'

'I put two and two together. I've been suspicious for a while. But the other night I knew I was right.'

Natalie was almost wild-eyed. 'How?'

'Does it matter?'

'I'd like to know. Do the others? Does Sarah?'

Vanessa felt red-hot anger at the mention of Sarah's name. 'Not from me.' She paused. 'I saw the two of you dancing. It looked a bit hot and heavy for friends. And then I was watching you when you were saying goodnight. Everybody was pissed, but I wasn't. You kissed him. But it wasn't the kiss. You kissed Ross and Phil and Andrew and Rupert too. We all kissed each other, for God's sake, like we always do. Except you two. It was the hand. He put his hand on your cheek, his fingers were on your ear, in your hair. It wasn't the kiss. It was the hand.

It was possessive. It was intimate. He made the kiss a peck but he forgot the hand. And that was how I knew.'

Natalie was staring at her hands in her lap. She wove her fingers in and out nervously, turning her palms over and over.

'I just don't know what I know. I don't know what's happened between you two. Not the full extent, I mean. Clearly it's something that shouldn't have done. So tell me. What the fuck are you playing at, Nat? What are you doing?'

Natalie sighed. 'It's not a game, Ness.'

'Damn right it's not a game. I can't believe you'd do it. Either of you.'

'We didn't mean –'

'We?' She could hear the fury and the sarcasm in her own voice. Her heart was beating out of her chest. 'What exactly are you doing? Are you sleeping with him?'

Natalie couldn't meet her eye.

'Fuck. You are.' She'd hoped she'd caught her in time. Wanted to shake her, talk sense into her. Save them all. 'How long?'

'I don't want . . . I don't think I should –'

Vanessa gripped her arm tightly. 'How. Long?'

'The summer. This summer. Not long. A few weeks, a couple of months.'

Vanessa exhaled slowly, her mind racing. 'Dorset?'

Natalie shook her head vigorously. 'No. No. After that.'

Vanessa rubbed her forehead. 'That's an affair, Natalie.'

'I know.'

'I seriously thought you might just be being dumb,

you know. Flirting. Taking flirting too far. But you're telling me you've been meeting in secret. That you've been . . .' Vanessa almost couldn't bring herself to say it. Didn't know what word to use. '. . . sleeping together.'

Natalie didn't speak.

'I can't get my head around it, Nat.'

'I didn't mean . . .'

Vanessa was so angry she had to make an effort to keep still, not to shout. Two walkers passed within a few yards, staring at them. She waited for them to move away, then hissed, 'Don't give me that crap.' She heard herself – harsh, strident. She wanted to shake her. 'You certainly didn't bloody mean not to. But you *are* doing it. To Kit. To Sarah. To all of us, for Christ's sake. All of us. The kids . . . I can't believe you'd be so stupid . . . so destructive . . .' Her voice trailed away with the enormity.

There was nothing Natalie could say to defend herself. 'I know.'

'So why?' Vanessa tried to calm down. 'What's it about?'

'I thought I might be in love with him.' Natalie screwed up her eyes.

'You *thought*?'

'It was mad. I know that. I ended it.'

'It didn't look ended.'

'I hadn't seen him for a while. Until the wedding . . .'

'And what?' Vanessa's voice dripped with disdain and sarcasm. 'You just got caught up in the romance of it all?'

'You're being cruel.'

231

'Pah.' Vanessa sat silent for a while. 'And Dom? What does Dom feel? Is he in love with you?' She couldn't keep the cynical tone out of her voice.

'I don't know.'

'And he's not with Sarah? Suddenly? Just like that?'

Natalie tried to defend herself. 'Not just like that. There's been something there, for, well, for ever. We've never acted on it. Never.'

'You're acting on it now. You've chosen, the two of you, to lob a bloody great grenade into the middle of all of this.'

'Are you going to tell her?'

Vanessa didn't answer. She didn't know. She hadn't expected this. Naïve, perhaps, but she'd thought this was something else. Flirtation. Dancing a little close to the edges of harmless. She thought maybe Natalie would have cried a little, confessed to being in a rut with Kit. Maybe something a little deeper than a rut. But she found herself deeply shocked. She felt foolish. And she had no idea what to do next.

'Are you?'

'Are you going to stop?'

'Yes. I promise. That's the point. I have stopped it. I stopped it before the wedding. You have to believe what I'm telling you. Give me a chance, will you? Let me make good on that promise. Please, please, don't blow it all up.'

'If I don't, it won't be for you. Or for Dom. I want to bang your heads together. It would be for Sarah. For Kit. For all of us.'

'I know. They're who I care about too. You are.'

'I swear, Nat. I'm serious now.' Vanessa stood up and moved away from the bench. 'I can't look at you, Nat. And I don't know if I can ever forgive you. But it isn't me you need to worry about. I'm a bystander at this little show. What about Kit? Kit loves you. Everything you have together, you two. Arlo's still in primary school. He's a little boy.' She paused. 'And Sarah. Your friend Sarah. My friend Sarah. She doesn't deserve this.'

Natalie was crying softly now. Vanessa hated that she cried prettily, a single tear rolling down her cheek. 'I don't have anything to say.' She turned to walk away without another word, Simon following her.

'Please, Vanessa,' Natalie implored, but there was no reply.

27

Natalie had never stopped sleeping with Kit. Never on the same day but, still, she'd done it. She'd lied to Dom when he'd asked her, possessive and intense. It wasn't his business and she didn't ask about Sarah. He'd volunteered, just once, that their sex-life had tapered off in the last few years, but she'd stopped him, told her she didn't want to know. That it was disloyal of him to say and disloyal of her to hear things about Sarah. What a bizarre thing that was, she realized. She thought she knew anyway. Dom was so emotional about sex – always almost tearful in the aftermath, almost grateful when she enjoyed it as much as she clearly did. He seemed so obviously a man who wasn't having a lot of sex at home. But she and Kit were. She'd only stopped initiating it. In the years since Arlo, that which had once been a reasonably fifty-fifty split had become more seventy-five twenty-five, but that probably wasn't what had given her away. Nor had she learnt any new tricks from Dom to betray her. But it seemed he had guessed anyway.

Tonight, she'd initiated it. She wanted to blot Dom out. And it had been a while, with her and Kit. Kit had grilled steaks on the barbecue. It had been one of those very precious late-summer days, positively warm in the middle when you feel compelled to be outdoors all day.

They'd put the sprinkler on, and Arlo had been running through it for hours, long after the sun had gone down and it was too cold. Then Kit had lit the firepit, and they'd wrapped themselves in blankets, toasted marshmallows and drunk red wine. Arlo had fallen asleep, and Kit had carried him up to bed, and come back to where she was sitting, staring into the embers. He'd been quiet all day, and now she was too.

When they'd let the fire die down, she'd taken his hand on the stairs, and slid her hands under his shirt to stroke his back, and down and down. He'd moaned, and pushed her back on the bed, and they'd made love. It seemed to Natalie that it made Kit feel quite overcome: his shoulders shook when he held her, and he buried his head in her neck when he came, holding her so tightly he almost hurt her. She clung to him, and for the first time in ages she believed they would be all right. That Dom and the feelings he evoked in her might recede and that her old life could be enough, could be more than enough. Not settling. Being really okay.

Afterwards, though, when Kit would normally roll onto his side, away from her, but stay close, keeping one hand on her hip, he stood up, pulled on his boxers and a T-shirt, and sat in the armchair in the corner watching her. It unnerved her – no one really sat there: it was more an upholstered clothes horse. Once upon a time he'd watched her a lot – sleeping, showering, putting on her make-up. She remembered then that it had felt intense and possessive and sexy as hell. That wasn't what this was. He was thinking, not feeling. Thinking so hard she swore she could hear it. And the expression on his face wasn't kind or appreciative or sated or full of wonderment and love. It took a moment for her to settle on the right word, because it was so unexpected.

Rage. Quiet, barely controlled rage from across the room. It didn't suit him. His nostrils were white, and his lips were smaller. The anger made him uglier. His chest rose and fell too fast. And it made her brave. Anger was easier to face than sadness.

She sat upright, drawing the sheet around her, her back straight against the headboard, exhaled, and tried to speak. But what she said would be the first domino in a long, winding, terrible conversation, and she didn't want to push it over.

'I know, Nat.'

'Know what?'

'I don't want you to lie to me. Please don't lie to me.'

He filled her silence instead. 'How long?'

She wondered if Vanessa had spoken to him, but somehow she knew that wasn't it.

It wasn't the beginning of a conversation, and it wasn't enough of a clue. How long have things been going wrong between us? How long have you been unhappy? How long have you been cheating on me?

'Kit . . .'

He spoke into the silence she was meant to be filling. 'How long have you been sleeping with someone else, Nat?'

She took a deep breath, but didn't answer.

'Don't you know? Are you trying to figure it out?'

There was cruelty in his voice, and it shocked her. His eyes, though, were sad, and she thought she knew that he was forcing the spite into his voice to stop himself crying.

She felt physically sick.

'I'm sorry. I'm not.'

'Please.' He spat the word out.

'It's over. I promise it's over.'

He just stared at her.

'Kit, I am . . .' She started to move towards him, acutely aware that she was naked, but he raised a hand to stop her.

'I don't want apologies, Nat. I want to know how long.'

She picked up her dressing-gown, put it on and tied the belt around her waist. Then she sat heavily on the end of the bed. 'Will it help?'

He made a strangulated sound. 'Help? No. No, I don't suppose it will. Still, though, I'd like to know.'

She didn't want to tell him. She didn't want to give details, and she didn't want him to have them. 'How did you know?'

'I didn't, for sure. Not until just then. Not know, exactly. I've been nursing my suspicions, my fears, for weeks now. I'm probably ridiculous to you. How many lies have you told me? Straight to my face. It takes some pluck, Nat, to live a parallel life. I didn't think you'd do it. I didn't want to believe you would. But I didn't know until I saw your face, just now. You've no idea how badly I wanted you to laugh at me, call me a stupid old man, because it wasn't true.'

'Shit.'

'Yes. I'm sorry. Inconvenient', his voice faltered, 'that my hunch was right. Is it galling for you that I still know you well enough to be aware when something's wrong? Does it work better for you to tell yourself, to tell *him*, that I don't know you any more, that I don't understand you? That I don't give you what you want, what you need? Is that what you say to him?'

And then he just crumpled. It was like the anger had been his backbone, and it slipped away, and his shoulders lurched inwards, his chest concave and suddenly old-looking. It caused her physical pain, as if she'd been stabbed in the heart, to see him like that. He put his face into his hands, so she only heard, couldn't see, him sob.

'Don't you love me, Natalie?'

This was the moment. She had to tell the truth. She had to cling to the certain knowledge that telling the truth about how she felt was the only way not to make this worse.

Natalie took a deep breath. 'I wasn't sure I did, for a while. I was in very odd place, Kit.'

He recoiled, almost as if she'd hit him. 'Odd. Wow.' Like she'd winded him.

'I don't want to lie to you any more, Kit. I want to be honest.'

The sound he made was strangled. He was trying for sarcasm, but pain meant he didn't reach it.

'But I do love you. I have loved our life. Our children. I do love you. Of course. But I was confused. About whether I loved you like I'm supposed to. If it was like it's meant to be.'

He stared at her. She knew she had to keep talking. She had to try to make him understand what she meant.

'If that was all there was, you mean?'

'Maybe. And I fell for someone. I know that will hurt to hear, but I have to say it. Someone was making me feel things I thought I'd forgotten. And I got confused. I thought that if he could, then you couldn't. I'm not making excuses, Kit – I'm not. But it's like a bit of madness. You stop being you. I mean, you know what you're risking, who you might be hurting, the damage you might be doing – the horrible, irreversible damage – but it's like it's worth it, in that moment.'

'And is it?'

'It wasn't. Not even close. I've hated myself almost every minute of every day.'

'Except the minutes you've spent with him?'

She shook her head. 'Some of those too. I've told you, it's over now.'

'Just like that? You're not confused any more?'

'I know how that sounds. I don't think you can be any more disappointed in me, and more angry with me, than I am, Kit. I never . . .' her voice was breaking now '. . . I never thought I was capable of doing this.'

Kit was crying now. She'd only seen it a handful of times in their whole life together. Mostly happy tears. This was pain, etched on his face. Betrayal. Her chest ached. She'd done this.

'And I don't know if you can forgive me. Or even,

actually, if I can forgive myself. I might have holed our marriage below the waterline. I've hurt you. I've hurt me too. I've been someone I never thought I could be. I've got to come to terms with that. I've been trying to believe that everything else, everything good and wonderful and important about us, can be enough. This home, our family, our life . . . But I know that it might not be. I know you deserve more. I want more too. I've been selfish and I've been cruel and I know that. And that can't, can't be right. It can't be the right thing to do.'

'And the affair?'

She hated the word. 'That's over, Kit. Can't you see it on my face?' She wanted to say that he had to know because he knew her. But did either of them know the other?

Kit rubbed his face angrily, sniffed hard. He kept his back to her while he pulled on sweatpants and walked out of the room without another word. He still hadn't asked who it was.

Autumn

28

'Come all the way out.' Mia had put her head through the curtain of the changing room. She'd zipped her mother into a dress she hadn't wanted to try on, and she was trying to coax her out of the cubicle. They were in a shop Sarah wouldn't normally consider, but she'd had a glass of wine over lunch, and she and Mia were having fun. She hadn't seen her daughter for ages and she needed something to cheer her up. She'd been in a funk for quite some time. Probably since the holiday. It hadn't been the happy fortnight she'd planned. Dom's bad mood had persisted. The long walks he'd taken on the beach had become whisky-fuelled sessions in his office since they'd got home, jazz music playing, the door firmly closed. He didn't get drunk, and he wasn't mean. It was like he was anaesthetizing himself. Keeping himself from her. And he smoked in there too, though she'd asked him not to. The smell of stale tobacco clung to the curtains. She was waiting for him to tell her what was wrong.

Meanwhile, she'd had work to keep her busy – the start of term was always frenetic – and Dylan to pack off to university. It was a lot. It always had been, but a morose husband did not help. Today was just for her and Mia. They'd had lunch in Soho, then wandered up to Regent Street, and along Carnaby Street, where Mia had seen a dress in the window of this boutique and insisted her mother try it on, which Sarah had only agreed to do on the condition that Mia tried on something too.

'Really?'

'There's no one here.'

They had the fitting room to themselves. Sarah stepped out, and stared at herself appraisingly in the long mirror.

'You look fab!' The dress was fashionably cut, more fitted than she would normally choose, and, sitting just on the knee, shorter, too.

'Not too mutton? Could I wear it for Annie's fiftieth, do you reckon?'

Mia frowned. 'Not at all mutton. No politically incorrect theme this time?'

Annie's fortieth, famously, had been quite possibly the last vicars-and-tarts party held in England. She still got flak for it, but was reasonably unapologetic, on the grounds that it had been huge fun, that she'd classed it up by making it vicars and tarts from history. Annie had been Cardinal Wolsey, with Rupert a six-foot-three Anne Boleyn, complete with extra finger.

'No. No vicars and tarts this time. Not even historical ones. Annie's woke, these days.'

Mia laughed at the notion. 'Right. Okay. So, yes, you could definitely wear this to Annie's fiftieth. You'd be beautiful in it.'

'I don't know . . .' She didn't feel particularly beautiful.

Mia sighed. 'It's hardly a Spandex tube dress, Mum. The colour is gorgeous on you. I love the arms. Have you got a shawl or something to go with it?'

Sarah considered.

'Look, this is the one. I'll buy it for you, if you won't.'

She held up her hands in surrender. 'Okay. Okay. Sold.'

'Good. I'm gasping. In need of a wee and a cup of tea. I'll go to that place over there, and grab us a table.'

While the sales assistant wrapped the dress in tissue paper and put it into a bag for her, Sarah watched Mia cross the road, and go into the coffee shop, feeling a familiar surge of maternal pride. She was a lovely-looking girl, her Mia. And a lovely girl. She seemed on fine form, and Sarah was glad. She'd missed her company lately. She hadn't come on holiday this year, which might have helped where Dom was concerned. For all his protestations, and that extraordinary temper tantrum in the supermarket car park, he adored his only daughter. Mia had claimed to be too busy with work and with Phoebe's wedding . . . They hadn't had a day like this for too long. She wished Mia would come home with her and cheer her dad up.

'I've ordered us two English breakfast teas, and one of those cupcakes, two forks.'

'Cake. Just after I bought that dress in a fourteen.'

'Stop! You're insane. It's a wonder I don't have an eating disorder. Are you ever not thinking about what you weigh, Mum? Ever?'

Sarah thought Mia was joking, but the rebuke stung just a little.

'Hey.' Mia reached across the table and squeezed her hand. 'Sorry. I'm just saying. Be more Flick.' Sarah laughed. She knew exactly what Mia meant. Flick was every pound of a curvy sixteen, never, ever said no to cake, and didn't give a damn. Mind you, Andrew still looked at her like she *was* cake . . .

The waitress appeared almost immediately with their order, and Mia stirred milk into her tea, then sat back in her chair. 'So, Mum, I've got something I want to tell you.'

She was smiling, so Sarah knew it must be good. She put down her teacup and folded her arms on the table. 'Oh, have you? And what might that be?'

'I've – I've started seeing someone. And he's lovely.'

'I'm so glad, love.'

'Me too.' She beamed.

'I thought you had a bit of a glow about you today.'

'You did not!' Mia preened a little, pleased with the compliment.

'I actually did. When you met me at the station.'

'Well, maybe I have. He's making me very happy. Very, very happy.'

'I'm excited for you. How gorgeous. Tell me all about him.' She corrected herself: 'Well, tell me what you'd like to tell me about him.'

'The thing is, Mum, you already know him.'

'I do?' Sarah looked puzzled. 'Is he a friend? One of the uni guys? Is it Ben?'

Ben had been on her course at Manchester, and never, at any point, a love interest. They'd shared a house in the second and third year, with some others, and he was now a qualified quantity surveyor living happily in Shoreditch with a girl called Marianna. Sarah had always liked him, and always been slightly hopeful they'd get together.

'Not Ben, Mum. I told you, he's got a girlfriend.'

Sarah was still thinking. 'Who then?'

'I'll tell you but you can't tell your friends.'

'Okay.'

Mia hesitated. 'It's Will.'

'Will Hawtrey?'

'Will Hawtrey.' Mia studied her mother's face for her reaction.

Sarah remembered some nonsense Vanessa had been spouting to her and Annie, at the wedding, about the two of them talking outside the marquee. She'd forgotten it until just then. 'Seriously? I mean, how?'

'It just sort of took off after Phoebs's wedding. I mean, nothing actually happened that night, but there was a spark that just hadn't – genuinely – ever been there before. Not for either of us, I think.' She paused, as though she was reflecting again on the miracle of that night. 'Anyway, he asked me out. We went out. It was amazing, and we've been seeing each other ever since. I mean, a lot. It's gone a bit fast, I suppose. But, Mum, it feels right.'

'Oh, Mia. Bless you.'

She was laughing, a little nervous, but also clearly surprised to find herself slightly tearful. 'I feel like . . . like I just know. And I don't worry about anything. Because I know. And he knows. And I know he knows. And he knows I know. Wow. That's a lot of knowing, right? Does that sound ridiculous to you?'

'Not at all. I'm just . . .'

'What?' Mia looked alarmed.

'Trying to get my head round the fact that it's Will. Little Will.'

Mia raised a hand. 'Okay, so let's not call him Little Will ever again, please.'

'Point taken. Sorry.' Sarah took Mia's hands across the table, the cupcake forgotten. 'Darling girl. Good for you. Annie is one of my best friends in the world. She and Rupert have raised the kind of young men your dad and I would pray for you to bring home. I am so, so happy to hear you got one, without your dad having to offer Rupert, like, goats in exchange for your hand.'

They laughed, still holding hands.

'Do they know? Annie and Rupert?'

Mia shook her head. 'You are absolutely the first, apart from Ruth – Will lives with her. Not even my flatmates. It's pretty new. Don't tell them, will you? Please don't even tell Dad yet. I mean, I can't make you not tell Dad – you guys are married. But I wish you wouldn't. Just for a bit longer.'

'I understand.'

'You do?'

'It's a delicious secret. I get it. Won't Stella know soon, though?'

'We haven't stayed there. Just his place, so far. I mean, I'm more of a squatter than a full-blown tenant at Stella's. I don't want to take the mick.'

'I see that.'

Mia exhaled loudly, through puffed cheeks. 'I was a bit nervous about telling you, to be honest.'

'Why?'

'In case you thought it was a bit close to home, that if it didn't work out, it could make things awkward for you

248

and Dad, and the Hawtreys. I just . . . I wanted you to be pleased for me.'

'And I am. And you think things are going to work out, don't you?'

Mia's smile was coy. 'Did you know that Dad was the one, Mum?'

My God. Sarah thought for a long moment. Where she was now, it was almost impossible to remember experiencing the feelings that were radiating out of Mia. It was almost thirty years ago. The palpitations, the jittery butterfly sensation, the complete certainty, the overwhelming joy found in the company of another person. The magic. Had she? Had he?

A totally unexpected wave of sorrow broke over her that she couldn't quite explain, even to herself.

She looked at Mia's beautiful shining face, and made herself mirror her expression of pure, untrammelled happiness. 'Of course I did, darling. Of course.'

It wasn't true, though. She'd taken some persuading to go out with the architecture student who'd started sitting opposite her in the university library all those years ago. She'd been studious and ambitious then, and still a bit bruised from a sixth-form romance that had ended badly the year before. He'd shown up every day for a week or so, taking up residence on the other side of the wide oak table she'd chosen because it was tucked away and it had a nice view across the rooftops of the city. She hadn't taken much notice of him at first, except to feel a mild irritation at having to share the table. After a few days, when his attempts to catch her attention in the library had failed, he had followed her out into the sunshine one afternoon, rushing to shove his books into a rucksack.

'You tie knots in your hair when you're concentrating.'

'Do I?' She touched her head self-consciously.

'You do. They slide straight out. But you do. You tie knots in your hair and you speak under your breath while you're writing.'

'You don't seem to be doing much writing. Or much concentrating.'

He'd laughed, and dimples formed in his cheeks. They made him look younger and less cool. 'All your T-shirts have stripes.'

He raised an eyebrow, as if to say, Aha, so you have noticed me, after all. 'I only have two. I wear them on rotation.' He laughed again, and she liked the sound. 'So come for coffee with me.'

She shook her head. ' I have a lecture.'

'I'll wait.'

'You're weird.'

'I'm not. I can provide character witnesses. Not just my mum, either.' It was her turn to laugh. 'Is that a yes?'

'If I have one coffee with you, will you stop stalking me in the library?'

'If you have one coffee with me, you'll want to sit with me for ever.'

'Oh, my God. Does that line ever actually work?'

'I don't know. I just used it for the first time. Does it?'

She cocked her head, and smiled. 'You know, it might.'

29

Kit hadn't left. She had been terrified, at first, that he would leave her, but he had stayed. He hadn't slept in their room since that awful morning. He'd moved a few things – not so much that Arlo would notice – into Marley's room, and he'd slept there every night. It had been Arlo's habit to climb into his parents' bed early most mornings, but this year, he'd increasingly eschewed a warm cuddle for TV or the iPad. She remembered feeling sad that her last baby was growing out of such a delicious habit, but now she was glad she didn't have to answer questions about where Dad was.

Things were normal when Arlo was about. And horridly strange when he wasn't – when he was at school or in bed, they were like polite strangers. She'd tried to talk again, but he'd warned her off, his face fierce. 'You have to stay away, Nat. You have to give me space.' She hadn't tried again.

If they focused on the normal, she could remind him, remind them both, that they worked. That they could work. So she walked on eggshells, and waited.

She hadn't seen any of the girls in a while. The thought of spending time with Vanessa or Sarah terrified her, and she didn't want to make any plans with Georgie, Annie or Flick either. She'd dodged invitations on

WhatsApp, to talk or meet for lunch, keeping her responses easy and breezy so no one worried or pushed. Having one child way older than the others and one way younger made a pretty effective smokescreen, and her excuses about seeing Temple up in London or having sporty or school things with Arlo weren't challenged. And, despite their closeness and the longevity of their friendships – or maybe because of the longevity – they'd never completely lived in each other's pockets, so she told herself it wasn't obvious she was dodging them. Annie's fiftieth birthday party, however, was unavoidable. She'd had the date in her diary for a year, for God's sake, since Annie had first told them she was planning a big celebration. The invitation had come weeks ago and had sat propped on the shelf by the front door. She wondered if Kit had noticed it, if he would raise it. But he didn't, and she was afraid to. They didn't talk about it until the morning of the party.

Kit had come in to get some clothes. He'd knocked, which felt wretched to her. She'd been woken by it. Her sleeping habits were dreadful – she was lying awake until three or four, then falling into a very deep, drugged kind of sleep from which it was increasingly hard to emerge to face the day. She heard the knock from twenty thousand leagues under the sleep sea, and hauled herself up against the headboard, running her fingers through her hair, and trying to come to. She pulled the sheet up and clamped it under the arms when he came in, but he didn't really look at her, just went straight to his wardrobe. The cupboard door hid his face.

'It's Annie's fiftieth tonight, Kit. Do you remember? There's a whole tent thing.'

Kit answered without looking at her. 'What is it with your friends and marquees?'

So they were 'her' friends. She sighed, and bit back the 'our'. 'Let's go. Together. Please.'

She thought he'd look at her now, but he stayed facing his shirts. His hand, on the edge of the wardrobe door, stiffened slightly, but when he spoke, his voice was calm. 'You must be bloody joking. I'm not going. Are you quite mad?'

'Fine. I can't make you go. But I'm going. I have to go.' She paused. 'I wish you'd come with me.'

Now he rounded on her. He shut the door, too hard. 'Why the hell would you care whether I come with you or not?'

'Kit. Don't. I do care. Of course I do. I care about you. And I care about our friends, about our life . . .'

He snorted. 'You're the one who chose to implode our life, Natalie. It's a strange time to start caring. They're your friends.'

'Kit.' She couldn't bite it back now. 'They're our friends.'

He snorted. 'They're your friends and their husbands. Six guys who have been forced into decades of friendship because their wives happen to get along.'

'That's not true.'

'Isn't it? What do we all really have in common, Nat, except you lot?'

It wasn't true. He liked them. It was her he didn't like right now. She didn't want to argue with him.

'Kit?'

'What?'

'Please. I'm sorry. I'm trying.'

'Trying to what? Put on a show?'

'No.' She shook her head. 'Not that.'

Kit hit his forehead with the palm of his hand. 'What am I saying? What an idiot. You've *been* doing that, haven't you? Putting on a show. I almost forgot that you're an actress. It's a compliment, my dear. You're *that* good. The mask only just started to slip.'

She was trying to breathe through these moments of bile and spite. Most of the time there was a careful skirting of each other, an odd formality and an unnatural politeness in the way they spoke only about the minutiae of life. She was ready to answer anything he wanted to ask, however hard that might be, because she owed him the truth, but there'd been no questions, no details sought. She didn't think she'd have been able to exercise the same restraint, had their positions been reversed. She imagined she'd have been obsessive about the details. Arlo was an oblivious whirlwind, and focusing on him helped them both, she thought. Maybe Arlo was the reason he had stayed, and she'd take that. She wanted him here. But from time he time, like now, he swatted at her. It was like a slap.

The door opened slowly behind Kit. It was Arlo. Natalie had thought he was still asleep. He clearly just had been – he scratched his messy bed-head, and stretched his arms, so an expanse of round belly appeared between the top and bottoms of his pyjamas. He was holding the torn grey muslin scrap he still took to bed every night. He looked much younger than eight, as he stood there, and she knew exactly how the top of his beautiful, dishevelled head would smell if she pulled him into her lap. If he let himself be pulled.

He looked from one of them to the other. 'Are you two fighting?' His tone was reproachful.

He'd heard them. She'd thought they'd just been quietly hissing to each other. Natalie wondered whether he'd been outside for the whole conversation. What had they said that he might understand?

She looked at Kit, who opened his arms wide, and Arlo went to him.

His father picked him up, and sat him across his lap, burying his head in his warm, soft neck. 'A bit.'

'Stop it, then.'

Kit nodded gravely at his boy. 'Okay. Want some breakfast?' He ruffled Arlo's hair.

Arlo nodded decisively, as though business had been successfully concluded. 'I want pancakes.' Then he corrected himself. 'I would like pancakes. It's the weekend.'

'Pancakes it is, then. Let's you and me go and make pancakes, shall we, and let Mummy get dressed?'

Arlo nodded again, and slid off Kit's lap, taking his hand, and pulling his dad towards the door. 'I'd like chocolate chip. Please.'

'Coming right up.'

'And then, later, it's Annie's party!' Arlo loved a party. 'Mum told me there's going to be a bouncy castle for the children, but I expect Annie'd let you have a go, if you wanted to.'

Kit looked at Natalie across Arlo's head, his expression unreadable, and Natalie held her breath.

'Don't you think I'm a bit big for a bouncy castle? Not to mention a bit old?'

Arlo laughed. They were on the landing now, and Natalie couldn't see his face any more. 'No way. You'd kill it, Dad. Not be as good as me, though. I can do actual flips. I'll show you.'

She heard Kit laugh. 'You're on.' She exhaled.

It needed to work. Today needed to be okay. It had to be. She had to face them all eventually, and she couldn't do it without Kit. It would be crowded, and jolly. They wouldn't stay long. And then it would be done, and it would start to get better.

30

Georgie had to smile as she walked around the side of
Annie's house and saw the party already well under way.
The event was, clearly, quintessential Annie, and the
weather had come out to support her. She'd been worried, the last time they'd met, about rain and an autumnal
chill – braziers and patio heaters were dotted about to
testify to that – but the sun was shining, and it was still
quite warm for October. By the time it got dark, Annie
had said, they'd untie the sides of the yurt, get everyone
into it and be 'super-cosy'. Supper was to be chilli with
all the trimmings, There was a bar serving mulled wine
and cider, and a dance-floor, behind which a DJ was trying to look cool while playing ABBA. Phoebe's wedding
a couple of months earlier had been polished and ele-
gant. This was an altogether different feel. A very Annie
feel. Annie's marquee was a yurt, her decorations were
homemade. It was, as Annie always was, all about family.
There was a bouncy castle, a candy-floss machine, toffee
apples and giant Jenga set up on the lawn.

Photographs of Annie had been printed out to A4
size, and hung wonkily around the tent in old frames.
Baby Annie in her mother's arms, schoolgirl Annie,
straw hat and bunches, Annie and her brother Giles at
the beach in Dorset. Annie in leg-warmers and a

headband, very Olivia Newton-John 'Let's Get Physical'. Then an absurdly youthful Annie and Rupert on
their wedding day, and Annie as a proud mum, with each
of the boys as newborn infants in turn. The most recent
had been taken that summer, at Phoebe's wedding.
Annie, Rupert and the three boys – their mother tiny in
comparison. The effect made you feel as warm as the
woman herself did.

Annie was talking to people near the entrance to the
yurt, bright and sparkling in a teal embroidered coat over
silk trousers. She saw Phil and Georgie approach, and
opened her arms to greet them.

'It looks amazing!'

'Do you think so? I'm really pleased. Knackered too,
mind you. The DJ arrived about ten minutes before
everything kicked off, and me and Rupert had to find
him a cable, then nail it in along these mats so no one fell
over it and died.'

She was talking fast, with the breathless nervousness
of the hostess. Georgie knew she'd never hold a party
like this – even if they had the space: she hadn't the confidence to pull it off. They hadn't this many friends, either,
she suspected. With another quick scan of the room, she
could see a number of distinct groups – she'd met a few
of the other guests over the years, from the hospital set,
Annie's old nursing friends, newer parent friends, from
when their boys had gone to boarding school at thirteen,
Giles and someone she presumed was a new girlfriend,
some of Rupert's family. It reminded her that she and
Phil had quite a little life by comparison – they came

from small families, and although they both had a friend or two from school and university, and a few from work, they were nothing like the collectors of people that Rupert and Annie patently were.

She'd come to accept that she and Phil weren't as appealing. Not easy entertainers, not good storytellers. Not as warm, not as welcoming. She might have minded once upon a time, but she didn't any more. For her, her fifties had brought menopause and crow's feet, but they had also gifted her a serenity and acceptance about who she was that had eluded her in her thirties and forties. She loved being there, being in the orbit of women like Flick and Annie. It was enough that they wanted her to be there. She didn't mind, now, that she wasn't just like them. Phil had taken her to Windermere for her fiftieth, a few years back now, and they'd had a lovely weekend. She hadn't needed, or wanted, a big celebration. Quiet suited her.

Now, she squeezed Annie delightedly. 'It looks fab. You've smashed it!'

'So glad you're here, darlings. I think the others are too – at least, I've seen Flick and Andrew, and Vanessa and Ross. I know Dom and Sarah are on their way. Go, drink cider. My gorgeous boys are here too, somewhere. I've seen Louis and Theo, actually, but not Will yet. He might be a bit late. Bless them – they must have better things to do on a Saturday night, but they've indulged their old mum. Have a bounce on the castle.'

'With my pelvic floor?' Georgie raised an eyebrow.

Phil winced, as Annie chortled.

'Did I hear my name?'

Will had appeared from nowhere, and crept behind his mother. Now he leant around and kissed her cheek. She hugged him delightedly. 'Darling! You're here!' She did a double-take when she saw Mia beside him, then warmly embraced her too. 'Mia! Sweetheart!' She looked quizzically at Will.

'I brought Mia.' He gestured at her, OTT, like a magician might introduce his assistant, but said nothing else.

'Yes. You did.' Annie beamed, not quite understanding, but not in the least perturbed.

He winked at her, then turned to shake Phil's hand and kiss Georgie's cheek. 'Hello, Coopers. Good to see you. How's Liam?'

Georgie shrugged almost imperceptibly at Annie, who stroked Mia's arm. 'I love this top.'

Dom couldn't find anywhere to park. The Hawtreys' driveway had evidently filled with guests' cars some time ago, the grass opposite too. Cars lined both sides of the road. 'Dammit.'

Sarah put one hand on his forearm. He was gripping the steering wheel tightly, both arms out straight. 'Relax. It's okay. Just go up here a bit. We'll find a gap eventually.'

'Their poor neighbours.'

'If I know Annie and Rupert, most of the neighbours will already be there.' She gestured to the garden. 'Besides, who gets uptight about a fiftieth birthday party? It's not like they do this every weekend.'

Dom, apparently, got uptight about a fiftieth birthday party. He'd been in a foul mood all day, resisting her attempts to be kind. He'd wanted to wear a particular shirt tonight, and he'd been disproportionately irritated to find it in the ironing pile she'd been planning to tackle the next day. When she'd stopped getting ready herself to iron it for him, he'd managed only a grudging thank-you, as though he wasn't quite over the fact that it wasn't hanging in the wardrobe when he'd gone there to look for it. It wasn't like him. Correction. These last couple of months, it was like him. She'd finally flown off the handle – he'd been a real pig about the shirt. She'd asked what was bothering him. Was something going on at work? Did he feel unwell? But he'd brushed off her questions with brief responses, mumbling an apology about the iron. They'd finished getting ready more or less in silence, and he'd hardly spoken to her on the way there. He hadn't noticed the new dress she'd bought with Mia. He'd barely looked at her when she'd come downstairs, ready to leave.

And now having to park two hundred yards up the road and walk back to the party seemed like the end of the world. As if it was him in high heels. She was looking forward to getting inside, finding her friends, and ditching him. Let someone else cheer him the hell up.

By the time Natalie and Kit arrived, of course, the queue for chilli had formed, snaking around the tables to the lawn outside. She hadn't been sure, until he appeared dressed, that he'd go through with it. Arlo had chatted excitedly all the way there. They'd left him, now, with a couple of young girls, one of whom she vaguely remembered as being a niece of Rupert's. There was a kids' tent, with their own food, and face painting and, of course, the bouncy castle, lit now that it was getting dark with some spotlights in the grass. He'd gone off happily. Natalie felt strangely relieved that the kids at the party were separate. She'd been here only five minutes, but she was already agitated. They shouldn't have come. Kit was right – it was madness, trying to force normality. It was too soon. She kept scanning the crowd for Dom. Vanessa waved Natalie over. She hadn't seen her since the walk.

'Hi.' She kissed her. 'You okay?' She looked her in the eye.

'Getting there.'

Vanessa smiled, not unkindly. 'Kit with you?'

She nodded. 'And Arlo, whooping it up in the kids' tent.'

Vanessa squeezed her arm. 'Okay. Good.' She must have seen the anxiety on Natalie's face. 'You've got this. It's okay. We've got that table over there.' She pointed to the corner. She smiled again, back in normal mode. 'Smells delicious, doesn't it?'

Natalie couldn't imagine she'd be able to eat, however good the chilli smelt. Kit had left her side the second they'd come in through the tent. She looked about the marquee anxiously. He'd found Andrew. They were in conversation with people she didn't immediately recognize. Kit's back was to her, so she couldn't catch his eye. She still hadn't seen Dom.

Suddenly, though, Sarah was by her side. 'Great dress. New?'

Natalie nodded.

'You look fantastic.' Sarah kissed her. Jo Malone. Her stomach lurched.

'Are you okay?'

'Fine. Yes. Late.' She rolled her eyes self-deprecatingly.

'You're good – you've only missed the mingle-schmingling. Not dinner!'

Natalie stood between Sarah and Vanessa in the queue, and tried to pay attention to what they were saying, conscious that Vanessa was overcompensating. Something about Mia being there with Will. How Sarah hadn't known she was coming. Natalie wasn't good. And she was beginning to wonder why on earth she had thought they needed to be there, how quickly they could get away without it being weird.

Somehow she got through dinner. Kit was largely ignoring her, but it wasn't obvious, in a rambunctious gang. He was drinking. Too much, she thought, with a small stab of fear. Dom had appeared, with a plate of chilli, but he was across the table from her on her left. So far, she had refused to meet his eye.

When the plates were cleared, Rupert took to the dance-floor, a hush descended, and the DJ handed him a mike. Natalie looked at her watch, but it was too dark to read, and wondered how much longer they'd have to stay after Rupert's speech. After some laughter and heckling, as he managed feedback and figured out how far from his mouth he needed to hold the microphone,

Rupert raised a hand for silence. 'We're here tonight to wish my beautiful wife Annie a very, very happy birthday with a nought on the end.'

From her table at the front, Annie, hands cupped around her mouth, shouted, 'Fifty. Five-oh. Fifty and fine with it.'

The crowd whooped and cheered.

'Fifty, and fabulous!'

'Okay, okay!' Rupert quietened them again. 'I've got some soppy stuff to get out before the dancing, so sssh.' He raised a finger to his lips. He beckoned to Annie, and she sidled slowly up to him coquettishly, taking his hand and standing by his side, beaming. 'It's no secret to most of you here that I was gone from the moment I saw this woman. Love at first sight. It's a thing. What you might not know, and I had almost forgotten in the mists of time, is that the first moment I laid my eyes on her just happened to be at her eighteenth birthday party. A friend of mine was a friend of hers, and I can't remember now how I snagged an invite.'

Annie leant over to the mike. 'Because my friend said you were a dish. And a medical student. Double point score.'

Everyone laughed.

Rupert shrugged. 'Guilty. Both charges. What can I say? Anyway, there she was. In a strapless pink dress. Very Bananarama, I thought she was. There's a picture somewhere around here on the side of the tent – look for it later. And I was done, from the first time I danced with her. To UB40's "Red Red Wine". The twelve-inch, mind you. Corny, yes. True? Absolutely. So, I realized, this is not only Annie's fiftieth birthday party, but it is also the thirty-second anniversary of the day I fell in love with her. I think that's right. So, I'm the luckiest man in the world. I love you, my Annie. More and more with each passing year, in fact. These young things think they have the monopoly on romance and passion. But they absolutely bloody don't. Happy birthday, darling girl.'

The yurt erupted into loud cheers, while the two of them kissed.

'That's it for me. But our boys have a little something for their mum.'

Will, Louis and Theo joined their parents from different parts of the room. Will took the mike from his dad, while his brothers shooed Rupert and Annie off the dance-floor into their front row seats. Theo nodded at the DJ.

'So, we wanted to do something for our mum. She's a brilliant mum. We love her to bits. And most of you know, if you can manage simple arithmetic, that Mum was born in 1970. You might not all know, though, that Mum is a big Elvis Presley fan. One song in particular. Which happens to have been the biggest hit in the year she was born. And if you were at their wedding, and I think some of you here definitely were – I'm looking at you, godparents – you'll know it was also their very first dance as a married couple. Not sure if it was the twelve-inch, though, Dad.' He inclined his head in his father's direction and gave him a knowing look, which made everyone laugh. 'And so, with our sincere apologies to the King and, frankly, all of you who are about to sit through this, we'd like to wish her a happy birthday with our own version of that very song.'

The DJ pressed a button, and the opening notes of 'The Wonder Of You' filled the tent.

Annie clamped her hand over her mouth, and Rupert, laughing, put his arm around her shoulders as the boys delivered their version, some of the words rewritten especially for her. Their audience was rapt. With the final chorus, they brought the whole crowd to its feet to belt it out. Then everyone erupted into rapturous applause and cheers.

The DJ put on a floor-filler and, from around the tent, people took to their feet. Annie and Rupert made their way to where Natalie and the others were sitting.

Will, his cheeks still flushed from his triumph, came over with Mia. Their table gave him a little extra clap, and he bowed theatrically.

'That was the best thing I've ever seen, Will!' Vanessa gushed.

'Brilliant,' Andrew agreed.

'So. We're glad to have you all together.' Will looked around the table. There were a couple of empty chairs but he'd started now, so he carried on. 'Most of you, at least. We have just a little announcement to make.' He took Mia's hand. Everyone looked at them both expectantly. 'Mia and I are officially boyfriend and girlfriend. A bit more than just that, actually . . . I . . . Well, it's a bit serious, I'd say.' He raised her hand to his lips and kissed it – a little old-fashioned gesture.

Annie clapped her hands together. 'Darlings! How wonderful!' She leant into Rupert, who was sitting beside her. 'I'm so very happy for you both.'

'How long has this been going on, then?'

'Well, technically, only a couple of months.'

'Since the wedding?' Vanessa sounded triumphant, and looked knowingly from Annie to Sarah.

'Well, I suppose it started there. We've been seeing quite a bit of each other in London.'

'Ever since,' Mia interjected.

'You never said a word, you dark horses.'

'Well, my mum knew. Just her. I made her promise she wouldn't tell anyone.' Dom looked sharply at his wife, who ignored him. 'It seemed like we should get used to it first. We were a bit worried, actually, that you might not approve.'

'Why on earth would we not approve?' Flick wondered.

Annie shot a look at Sarah. 'You knew!'

Sarah shrugged. 'I made a promise.'

'And, more to the point, why would you give a hoot if we did?' Andrew put in.

'You know – the whole growing-up-together thing. Even I thought it was a bit weird at first.'

'She did take a bit of persuading to give me a go, that's true,' Will added ruefully.

'Turns out,' Mia giggled, 'not weird at all . . . like falling for a really, really good friend.'

Will put his arm around her, and kissed her.

Flick gave a small cheer. 'That's fan-bloody-tastic.

267

You beautiful people. Happy for you. Very, very happy for you. The world needs more lovers.'

Natalie stood up, and took her handbag off the back of the chair. Kit looked at her. 'Need the loo,' she explained, hurrying off.

'What do you think, Dom?' Will asked. 'Do I have your blessing?'

It took Dom a moment to answer. Vanessa was watching him closely. He was staring at Natalie's back as she disappeared. Vanessa nudged him, and he snapped back to look at his daughter. Then he stood up, and formally offered his hand to Will, who shook it. 'Not that you need it, young man, but yes, yes, of course . . .'

'So, this is serious?'

'Oh, leave the poor kids alone! They don't need the Spanish inquisition. They're just dating.'

'If you *do* need a wedding planner, though, Andrew's available.'

Everyone laughed.

Will raised a hand. 'Enough of that, you mad buggers. Don't make me wish we hadn't told you.'

Outside, Mia threw her arms around Will's neck, and kissed him deeply. 'Will you sing like that for me one day? You were unbelievable.'

'I absolutely will. On your fiftieth birthday, Mia, if not before . . . Hell, before. On all the high days and holidays and birthdays and every day . . .'

Suddenly serious, they gazed at each other, their faces close together. 'Promise?'

'I promise.'

She hugged him again.

'And the Olds took it well.'

'They love it. Didn't doubt it for a second. Maybe we've started something. Who'll be next, do you reckon? They'll be wanting to marry us all off. Dylan and Zoë?'

'Hey? Who said anything about marriage?'

They raised their eyebrows at each other. 'Not me.'

'Not me.'

Dom was loitering when Natalie came out of the toilets and made her way back to the tent. He'd been watching her. She'd stuck so close to the girls, refusing to meet his glances throughout dinner and the Hawtreys' performances, but he'd known there would be a moment when she was alone so he'd waited, and now here she was. He'd barely registered Will and Mia's announcement. Done that stupid formal handshake thing that must have looked weird. He could only think about her. He didn't have a plan. No rehearsed speech. He lost reason when he saw her. When she saw him, she speeded up, but he stepped towards her and made her see that he wasn't going to let her go back in without speaking to him. She wouldn't want to make a scene. He cocked his head, and she followed him around the side of the yurt. There was a heater, with a huge tube that was pumping warm air inside. He walked to the far side of it, where they were at least partly obscured by the equipment, and she followed him.

It was properly dark. All the lights were on the other side. That was good.

For a second he couldn't say a word. He had so many in his head. They stood, facing each other, their arms by their sides.

'Dom . . .'

As soon as she spoke he raised his hands and held each of her arms.

She tried to shrug him off, but he tightened his grip. Her voice was a quiet hiss. 'Dom. No. What are you doing?'

'We have to talk, Natalie. You *have* to talk to me.'

'Not here.'

'Where, then? When? You won't answer my calls. You haven't replied to my messages. You haven't even opened them.'

'I'm sorry. I don't know what you want me to say.'

'Something. Anything. For Christ's sake, Nat, you can't just erase the past few months. You can't pretend nothing happened. And we can't go on as before. Just carry on.'

'We have to. Please, Dom.'

He took his hands off her arms.

Something made Natalie turn around. Kit was standing stock still, watching them. She had no idea how long he'd been there, what he'd seen, or how he had known to look for her there. She sprang backwards, away from Dom, almost stumbling as her heel caught on the grass. Suddenly, the others appeared behind Kit. It felt like everyone was watching Kit watching them. There was no way for what they were doing to be innocent. It was, by definition, clandestine. Her racing brain immediately filtered and dismissed any and all excuses for being behind the heating unit with Dom. It was obvious.

Natalie walked towards her husband, Dom following.

She was acutely aware of the music, suddenly, loud in the tent. It felt like the Black Eyed Peas were the surreal soundtrack of this piece of theatre. When she got close enough to see Kit's face, she knew at once that he had connected it, figured it out. She went directly to him, thinking that if she could get him away to where it was quiet, and they could talk, she could explain. Make it right. Not right, of course. It could never be that. But before she got to him, he stepped forward.

Afterwards, it was like it had happened in slow motion. Thinking about it later, Georgie realized she'd never before seen one man hit another in real life. The sound made her feel sick. The whole thing did, actually. It had happened so fast it was confusing. One minute, all had seemed well. The next Kit, drawn up to his full height, suddenly agile, had sprung at Dom.

'You bastard.'

It had to have been a joke. But Kit's face was deadly serious, rage etched on his features. She thought for one horrible moment that he was going shove Dom backwards, but then it got much worse. Kit drew his right arm back from his shoulder, his elbow high, and hit Dom. Just hit him. The blow caught him on the side of his face.

Dom sprawled backwards onto the grass. Kit turned and walked slowly away. Dom seemed to lie on the ground for too long. She was afraid Kit had knocked him out, but he was awake.

'What the hell?' Ross pulled Dom to his feet. 'What

271

was that for?' he called after Kit, but he'd already disappeared from view.

Vanessa put her hand on her husband's arm. 'Sssh.'

'What's going on? Are you okay, Dom? Natalie?' This
was Rupert, holding Annie's hand. Someone must have
told the DJ to turn the music off. It was eerily quiet
compared to what it had been just a few seconds ago.
What did they all think had happened? That someone
had had a heart attack? Or choked?

It felt as though the entire party had spilt out onto the
grass. Even some of the kids had been distracted from
their high jinks.

Natalie panicked. 'Where's Arlo? Who's got Arlo?'
She knew she sounded wild.

Will took a step towards her, his hands raised, as if
she was an animal to be corralled. 'It's okay, Nat. Mia
took him. They're inside.'

Arlo knew Mia well. She'd babysat him in university
holidays, when he was tiny, and they'd always been fond
of each other.

Will led Natalie now, as if she didn't know how to get
to the house from the garden. The others all seemed to
pivot at once, like a shoal of fish, to watch them. The
music started up again as they approached the house.
Natalie imagined Annie frantically 'striking up the band'
to distract everyone. She wondered how much had been
obvious to how many of them. She hadn't been able to
meet anyone's eye. Not even Vanessa's. Will kept his hands
up, almost as though he was afraid of her, but didn't speak.

Arlo and Mia were in Annie's sitting room, facing

each other, cross-legged on the rug by the fireplace. Arlo's face had been painted like a tiger's, in orange, white and black stripes. There was orange paint on his jumper, and he had half a cupcake in his hand, still in its paper case. He was laughing at something Mia had said, so Natalie forced herself to calm down, rearranged her features into something less stricken. She tucked her hair behind her ears, smoothed her dress, and took a deep breath. He looked up as she came in. There was no distress on his face, and she was relieved and grateful. Mia must have thought fast.

'Darling!' she said brightly. 'Ready to go home?'

Arlo frowned. 'You said you'd come and watch me on the castle.'

'I know, darling, but it's late . . .'

'Where's Dad?'

She had no answer for him.

Will, every inch Annie's son, rescued her. 'I think your dad has probably already gone home. I think most people are going soon, Arlo. Including the castle man. I'm going to drive you, okay? You and your mum.'

Natalie remembered as he said it that Kit had their car keys. Please God let him not do anything stupid. Please God let him be there, at home.

Arlo considered arguing, but decided against. He threw his arms around Mia for a hug, giggling when he deposited a smear of face paint on her cheek, and stood up compliantly. Mia didn't look at her until Arlo had turned towards the door and couldn't see her face. Then the change was frightening. Her chest suddenly heaved with anguish, and she looked at Natalie with fury and astonishment.

To know that Mia had worked out what was going on and had still rescued Arlo from the unsavoury scene was a fresh punch in Natalie's gut. Anything anyone did that was good made her feel worse.

'I'll be back in a few minutes. Sit tight and wait for me, okay?' Will addressed Mia now, his arm on her shoulders. She nodded at him, with a small tight smile, and turned away.

Will and Arlo talked cars the whole short journey home. Will asked him what his favourite model was, and that was it. Natalie was grateful. It reminded her of when Will and his brothers, and Liam, Callum and Marley had all played Top Trumps incessantly. Top speed. Cool factor. Engine size. She could see them so clearly. When he pulled in at their house, Kit's car wasn't there. She didn't know whether she was relieved or terrified.

'Thank you, Will.'

His face was concerned, not judging her. He, too, had noticed that the driveway was empty. 'Will you be okay now?'

She could barely smile, and she couldn't speak. She knew she'd cry if she did, and she badly wanted to get Arlo into bed. She nodded, and put her arm around her son's shoulders, turning him towards the front door.

Flick and Georgie looked for Sarah the second they grasped why Dom had been flattened on the grass. But Sarah was already gone.

31

Sarah was sitting in the driving seat, with the keys already in the ignition, but she hadn't turned the engine on. She was waiting. She wasn't sure what for. For her hand to stop shaking. For tears to come. For answers. For Dom.

She held the car keys in their family. It was how they did it. How they'd done it for years, since the kids were small, and Sarah had broadly given up drinking. Toddlers and hangovers didn't mix. Dom always drove to parties. She always drove them home. She always kept the car keys in her bag.

Dom opened the passenger door, and leant in. 'Is this okay?'

When she didn't answer, he hesitated, looking up and down the road, then climbed in. In the artificial overhead light, she could see a single livid mark along his cheekbone where Kit had hit him. He sat ramrod straight, hands on knees, facing forward. The rest of his face was unnaturally pale. His knees twitched up and down. Then the light went out and they were in the relative darkness.

She almost laughed. It was ludicrous. Farcical. She was so used to feeling sorry for him when he was in pain, to taking care of him, that she almost did now. Her hand almost wanted to reach across the gearbox and still his knee. She almost wanted to put the back of her hand gently on his cheek to soothe him.

Her pain wasn't a mark across her cheekbone. She imagined it hurt more than that. She wondered if he wanted to ease it. Her mind ricocheted flashes of memory around like ball-bearings. Dom bringing her ice chips in a paper cup as she laboured with Mia. Her finding him behind a green curtain in A and E when he'd fallen off his road bike and smashed his kneecap. Both of them holding a white and wailing Dylan the time he'd tumbled out of a tree and broken his collarbone. Dom's impotent, protective rage the first time someone broke Mia's teenage heart.

This pain, though, did not unite them, and they could not help each other. It separated them. He'd caused it.

She'd twigged so instantaneously that she wondered if she'd known. Everybody else had worn a mask of shocked confusion and incredulity. Could they have seen what they thought they'd just seen? And what did it mean?

But she had understood immediately. Dom had been sleeping with Natalie.

'I can take a taxi.'

She turned the key in the ignition and didn't answer him.

She saw Ross, Rupert and Andrew out in the road as she passed the Hawtreys' driveway. They were looking for them. They stared at the car, but neither she nor Dom waved or smiled.

When Mia and Dylan were younger, the car had always been a good space to talk to them. More importantly to listen. With the mechanics of driving, and the facing forward preventing eye contact, it had felt safe. Now, Sarah struggled to know where to start. The silence was oppressive.

Dom spoke first. 'I'm sorry.'

'About which part?' She heard herself speaking in a monotone. If she let emotion into her voice, she'd scream and she might never stop.

'What?'

'I'm asking which part you're sorry about.' To her, her voice sounded cold and calm. She was surprised to hear it. It was the opposite of how the questions sounded inside her head. In there, she was screeching. 'About the scene? About getting hit? About the fact that you've obviously been sleeping with Natalie? Which part?'

He turned his head at Natalie's name. Perhaps she was further along in her understanding of events than he had imagined. 'About all of it.' His voice was quiet.

'Oh, I think it's probably easier this way.'

'What do you mean?' He sounded nervous.

Sarah shrugged. 'Well, we don't need to worry about a drip-feed of poison now, do we? I mean, everyone else knows. They all know I know, and so on. Even the kids probably know. It's all out there, plain as day.'

'Sarah,' he pleaded.

'Don't.' She put one hand up, her tone icy, and he stopped.

She drove the rest of the way without speaking again.

At home, with the engine off, neither of them made to get out of the car.

'How long?' She remembered the tiny red bikini.

He paused. 'Not long.'

His vagueness made her impatient. She used her teacher voice. 'How long exactly?'

'Can't we talk inside?'

'Answer me, Dom. Please.'

He sighed. 'Since June.'

'Where?'

'Oh, God.'

'Just tell me. Here? In this house?'

Dom shook his head. 'Never. I wouldn't . . .'

Sarah remembered. 'Ah. She has a flat. I'd forgotten. How incredibly convenient. A London shag pad.' She turned to look at him. 'So . . . there?'

He nodded, but couldn't return her gaze.

'Just there? Not at her and Kit's? No hotels?'

'Does this help you, Sarah?'

She laughed, but the sound was brittle. 'I've no idea.'

'I'll tell you whatever you want to know. I'm just not sure now is the time.'

She ignored him. 'Is it just sex? Or do you love her?'

He didn't answer.

'Did you say you'd tell me anything? Did you just mean details? Not feelings?'

'Please come inside.'

She opened the door and stepped out of the car, slamming it behind her. She unlocked the front door but didn't turn on any lights. She kicked off her shoes. Behind her, Dom shut but didn't lock the door. He moved gingerly.

She sat down in the wing-backed armchair in the

278

sitting room. Dom came in and perched on the edge of the sofa.

'Stop following me.'

'Don't we need to talk about this?'

'Didn't you just tell me it wasn't the time? Change your mind on the long walk from the car? Now you want to talk. Just so long as I don't ask you any difficult questions.'

'Listen, Sarah. You're angry. Of course you are. You have every right to be.'

She picked up a small glass paperweight from the side table next to her and threw it, hard. She aimed for the other end of the sofa, but still Dom swerved. The orb landed against the cushion with a dull thud, then rolled onto the floor. 'Don't you fucking patronize me. Don't you tell me what I have every right to be. Don't you dare.'

'Okay. Okay.' He was breathing fast. 'Do you want me to go? I can go.'

'No. Turns out I can't talk to you tonight. I can't even look at you. But, obviously, there are things to say.'

'I'll sleep in the spare room.'

'Yes, you will.'

'And we'll talk in the morning.'

She nodded.

'Thank you.' It was an odd thing to say. He stood up. At the threshold he turned back. Sarah had drawn her legs up into the chair. She didn't look at him again.

She wouldn't have been able to say how long she'd sat there, but eventually she hauled herself out and went to the stairs. She never went to bed without her phone – the kids might need her. But when she took it out of her bag now, the screen was full of messages she didn't want to read and wouldn't be replying to, so she left it on the bottom stair, switched to silent mode. She thought about Mia. Poor Mia. But she was so tired and heavy. Mia had Will. She couldn't. She just couldn't.

The door to the guest room was closed. In their room, a light came on automatically when someone went into their bathroom. She looked at her reflection in the mirror. She still hadn't cried. Strange. She still looked much as she had when she'd checked her reflection in the same mirror a few hours earlier. Even the winged eyeliner was intact. She'd thought she looked pretty good, actually – it was one of those evenings when she'd had time, and when her hair had done what she wanted it to. He'd been in before her and taken his toothbrush. His dressing-gown was gone from the back of the door, and when she looked at the bed, she saw he'd taken his pillow too. He was fussy about pillows. His neck ached unless the pillow was very firm, and he couldn't sleep with long pyjama trousers on, because he hated how they bunched around his knees. These were the things you knew after thirty years. You knew what a person liked on their toast, which journalists made them shout at the TV, how they voted in an election. You knew what scared them most, what their favourite season was, and what might make their face light up as they unwrapped gifts on their birthday.

Except you didn't. A person was themselves, after all. Love, and habit, and longevity weren't clairvoyance. That person's thoughts and feelings were still entirely their own. To confess or manipulate or keep to themselves or change completely. And you would never know unless they confided in you. Unless they wanted you to know. Or unless one of your best friends' husbands whacked them at a party and with that one blow shone a bright light on a great betrayal and shattered everything you thought you knew about your life.

And a friend? Ah, well, there you were on even thinner ice. That one may smile and smile and be a villain. She couldn't think about Natalie tonight. Dom was a mushroom cloud in her brain, and the dust would have to settle before she could think about Natalie's betrayal. But she knew that when she did it would hurt her almost as much. She was like a car in the middle lane, already blindsided by one crash, bracing for the impact of the next oncoming car.

Good that Dom had had the presence of mind to brush his damn teeth. A lightning flash of rage cut through the cloud. Bastard. Bastard. She wasn't anywhere near that together. She felt catatonic. She stood by her side of the bed in the darkness and stripped off her clothes. Make-up, jewellery stayed on. Naked, in winged eyeliner, she pulled back the duvet, not so much climbing as falling into the bed.

32

Dom was up and dressed in last night's clothes when she came down to the kitchen the next morning. Sarah had slept fitfully, but not until the small hours. She felt ghastly, as if she was in shock. Anger, sadness, humiliation, and lack of understanding were a potent cocktail, and sleep seemed impossible. She wondered if she'd ever sleep again. She'd cried, silent, wretched sobs of frustration, and her eyes were swollen and sore. She'd taken a long shower, running the water as hot as she could stand, and letting it cascade on the top of her head, the back of her neck. She'd pulled on a tracksuit, but her hair was still wet, just brushed back from her face. She knew how dreadful she looked but she didn't care. Let him see how he'd made her feel, if he even cared.

He smiled when she came into the kitchen, gesturing towards the counter. 'There's tea in the pot.' The milk was on the counter, and he'd put out a mug for her. She poured without speaking, stirring in a teaspoon of sugar, although she didn't usually take it, then came over to where he was sitting and pulled out a chair opposite. She put her phone down. There were messages from Annie and the others, several from Mia. She wondered, absently, who had messaged him. Was he giving Natalie a blow-by-blow on how it was going here? Checking on how it was going there?

The mark on Dom's cheek was still there, with a bluish tinge this morning. Kit had hit him hard. Good for Kit. It was bruised enough that he'd be asked at work on Monday. What would he tell his colleagues? A DIY incident? Exuberant dancing?

'Can we talk?'

She nodded. 'We better had.'

He was evidently relieved at the tone of her voice. 'If it's okay, for now I don't want to talk about Natalie.' She hated him saying her name. 'I'll answer any questions you have about that. I owe you that, I realize.' Sarah snorted derisively. 'But it's not about that. I want to try to make you understand.'

She looked at him, challenging.

'Is that okay?'

Last night, she'd had so many questions. Right now, she didn't want to ask a damn thing. Dom took a deep breath and broke the look, staring down at his hands on the table. When he spoke, he sounded rehearsed.

'The awful truth, I'm afraid, is that, irrespective of what has happened, I'm not in love with you any more, Sarah.' He waited for the blow to land, but Sarah didn't react. 'I feel huge love for you, for our children. I feel gratitude, and fondness, and sadness. But I think I've realized that I haven't been in love with you for a long time.' He put air quotes around 'in love' and her eyes narrowed in something a lot like hatred. It was a short speech, after all.

'You utter bastard.'

'I want to be honest.'

'Now.'

'What?'

'You want to be honest now. Is it a relief to say those things, Dom? Have they been on the tip of your tongue for the longest time?'

'It's not that.'

'For God's sake, Dom. Listen to yourself. You're a cliché. Next thing you're going to say is that you have a right to pursue happiness. That it's you, not me.'

'I didn't say that.'

How dare he sound defensive? How dare he? She felt anger rise and she was glad. It was better than this awful empty void. 'No, but you were thinking it. Listen to yourself, you stupid, stupid man. You sound like an entitled, idealistic teenager.'

He raised his hands in surrender. 'You can throw all the insults you want at me. I deserve that, and more. But you know things haven't been like they should be for a long time now.'

'And what did you do about it? How did you try to fix it?'

'How did you?' The reasonable, conciliatory tone he was clearly trying so hard to maintain had wavered.

'We had a life, Dom. A whole life. And now you've decided, have you, that you need more, that you deserve more than that life, and now, just like that, you're in love with Natalie?'

'You make it sound like the two things are connected.'

Sarah laughed at his absurdity. 'Don't be bloody ridiculous, Dom. Of course they are.'

He shook his head in disagreement. 'I've gone about it so badly. And I'm so incredibly sorry for that. Believe me when I tell you I'm ashamed of that. This is my mess, not yours. But you're wrong about this. Me falling out of love with you wasn't because I was in love with her. I *could* fall in love because I was free to. If that makes sense.' She winced. 'I'm not trying to hurt you, Sarah. I'm trying to explain.'

'Very convenient for you. You never thought of leaving to be by yourself? Have some air between your "love" and your "in love"?'

'Sarah.'

She knew she sounded deeply sarcastic. 'Course not. Men don't leave to be alone, do they? Better to settle until you find something better.'

'You make me sound so calculating.'

'You've lied and lied. You must have done. I don't even know the half of it yet, do I? You've snuck around and made a fool of me. For months now. And you couldn't even go any further afield than our friends. My God, Dom. My God. My friend. She was my friend.'

'I know. I'm sorry.'

For a moment she thought he was going to cry. 'Oh, stop saying that. Please. I don't want to hear you're sorry. It's pathetic. More than that, it's utterly and completely meaningless to me.'

'Nothing happened until this summer. We never let it before.'

She laughed ironically. 'Oh. Oh, thanks for that. I'm so grateful that you held yourselves back. Lucky me. What a great guy I married. Let me guess, you waited until Dylan had gone to university. Until the nest was empty? That's how it goes, isn't it? So you only have to leave me.'

'I wasn't waiting.'

'No, but less guilt attached, for you, I guess. You think it's just me you're letting down, huh?'

He shook his head.

'You're wrong, though. So wrong. Our children are young adults. They're on the cusp of their lives. Deciding what they want, who they want to be with. Learning to love, and to trust. This isn't the best time to do this to them. Better you'd left years ago, if that's what you were working your way up to. Yes, actually, when was it that you had your big revelation about not being,' she made exaggerated air quotes, '"in love" with me? This year, last year, five years ago, ten?' She stared at him, eyebrows raised.

He looked broken. 'This year, last . . .'

'Well . . .' she paused '. . . I had a good run, then. Mustn't grumble.'

Dom pushed his chair back and went to stand at the window, facing the garden. His shoulders dropped. 'I don't think we're really getting anywhere. I don't recognize you like this, Sarah.'

'And I don't know you at all, Dom.'

'I hate this.' His voice cracked.

'Am I making you feel bad? I'm sorry. And when you've been so honest.'

'I think I'll go.'

'You should. I really need you to be somewhere else right now.'

'I'll pack a bag.'

'Pack a big one,' she shouted at his back.

She wanted to ask him where he would go, but she didn't let herself. She stayed in the kitchen, nursing a cold mug of tea, ignoring her messages, staring out at the autumn leaves collecting on the lawn, until he left.

33

Mia was grateful to find the flat empty when she let herself in. She stood in the door of her bedroom and wondered if she should pack everything. It would be weird to stay here, now.

It was a nice flat, for a rental. The landlord had whitewashed everything. It was a third-floor walk-up, as an American would say, so quite a climb, but that meant it came with roof lights that flooded the space with brightness, and a small terrace, which was pretty rare. And she'd had fun here, when she'd been around. She'd always loved Stella. At least, since they'd been adults. The age gap that had seemed so vast when you were young closed up remarkably quickly when you were living independent lives, with jobs and flats. But they'd always got on. Stella was cool. So was her friend Joanna. She hadn't met Sal, whose room she was staying in. Joanna worked crazy hours in some kind of eco start-up, so she was a bit militant about recycling and one of those slightly smug vegans who are on a mission to convince you that aquafaba can do anything an egg white can, but she was nice with it. And out a lot. Mostly at clothes swaps and meetings about climate change. She and Stella had had some laughs, here, smuggling in Nando's and ordering dresses on ASOS when Joanna wasn't there, watching *RuPaul's Drag Race* and chatting into the night more than once. Stella didn't ask too many questions about where she was on the nights she didn't come home, and Mia liked her for it.

But it was ruined now. She just couldn't stay. Stella couldn't, obviously, be held responsible for what her mother had done, but it would be weird. It had only ever been a stopgap. She was going to stay with Will, short term at least. It was too soon, probably, to move in together. They'd only been a couple for a matter of months. But he'd offered, straight away, and it would give her time to get her head together. It was more than that. He offered a kind of comfort and support she knew she needed right now, more than even a great flatmate could. He held her at night, when she cried.

The capacious blue IKEA bags she had used when she moved in were shoved into the back of the wardrobe. With a sigh, she pulled them out, and began taking work clothes off hangers and folding them. She'd taken a lot of stuff home when she'd given up her last flat so there wasn't too much. Will had said to give him a ring when she was ready, and he'd come and collect her and the bags.

She heard footsteps running up the final flight of stairs to the flat, and a key in the lock, before Stella burst in, pink-cheeked and smiley. Mia had sort of hoped it would be Joanna.

'Hiya,' Stella sounded breathless, 'you're home! It's just me,' and pleased to know she was there. Her face fell when she put her head round the door and saw Mia surrounded by clothes and bags. 'What's going on?'

She didn't know. Oh, God. Somehow, she'd imagined Stella would know, would be expecting her to be packing her stuff. It seemed cowardly of Natalie not to tell her. And sad that Kit hadn't.

'You doing a flit?'

'No. No. Course not. I was waiting for you,' she lied.

'Is everything okay?' Stella was clearly worried – concern etched on her face.

'Oh, Stella. No, it's not.' She cried so easily since it had happened. She felt wobbly, all the time.

'What's wrong, Mia? Tell me, please.' Stella sank onto the edge of the bed.

'You don't know, do you?'

'Know what? You're scaring me.'

'It's not really my place to tell you . . .' Mia was torn. She didn't want to be cruel, but she didn't want to say, either.

Stella's voice rose. 'Fuck sake, Mia. Just tell me what's up.'

Mia sat down next to her, close enough for their thighs to touch. 'I'm really sorry this is coming from me, Stella. Really. But . . .' she exhaled sharply, and felt herself shudder slightly '. . . can't quite believe I'm saying this, but your mum has been having an affair with my dad.'

'What?'

'I'm so sorry. It's true.'

'It can't be.' Stella laughed nervously. 'That's just ridiculous. They're friends. They're all just friends.'

Mia spoke gently. 'I know it's a shock. Trust me. I was exactly like you. It's bloody awful. But it's true.'

Stella was clearly bewildered. 'How do you know?'

'God. Long story. I can tell you, if you want, but it doesn't really matter. Trust me when I tell you that everyone knows. All the adults, anyway. It came out at Annie's birthday party. In a very public way. To be honest, I thought you'd know by now.'

Stella had her hand across her mouth. 'No.'

'Yes. Your dad hit my dad. In front of everyone.'

'Fuck.'

'Like I say. *So* not me you should be hearing this from. But I think I need to go.'

'God. God.' She was clearly stricken. 'Is your mum . . .?'

'Okay? No.' Mia shook her head. 'Not remotely okay. She's in absolute bits. I'm sure your dad is too. And probably Nat and my dad. It's a shitty mess. Dad's not at home right now . . .'

'My dad?'

'I don't know, Stella. I'm sorry. I don't know what's going on with them.'

Stella was still trying to process the information. 'Was there a scene or something? Before the fight, I mean?'

Mia sighed. She understood Stella's need for details – she'd have been the same if she hadn't seen it with her own eyes. She just wished the details didn't have to come from her. 'I don't know, really. Your dad threw a punch at my dad. An actual punch. He must have seen or heard something that made him see red. That's more or less what I know.' Her recollection was vivid. She could visualize all of their faces – the horror and surprise, the dawning realization, the fury in the half-light down the side of the marquee. She could hear the sound of Kit's fist on her dad's face, and picture him reeling backwards.

'Fuck.' Stella rubbed her forehead. 'Fuck. That's so bad. I've never once seen my dad angry enough to do that. He never even slapped any of us. Not once. It's just not him.'

'Fuck indeed.'

Stella picked her phone out of her pocket, and scrolled through the screen. 'No missed calls. No messages.'

'Listen, this is very new. I guess they're all trying to decide what to do.'

'But *you* knew.' Stella looked completely confused now. 'So how? Who told you?'

Mia sighed. 'No one told me. I was there. Because I went with Will.'

Realization dawned slowly on Stella's face. 'Hold up. Is he the guy . . .?'

Mia gave an awkward smile. 'Full of revelations, today, huh?'

'Christ. You are. Okay. So I feel like I want to make a fuss about you and Will. You know, girly stuff. I want to be happy and excited for you, and slightly dazed that it's our Will, but . . . I can't. I'm sorry. I'm in shock . . .'

'Hey. Of course. I get that. I was exactly the same. I pretty much cried all night, after it happened.'

'Is that where you're going now? To Will's? Or are you going to your mum's?' She pointed at the bags.

'Not Mum's. I don't know what's going on with any of our parents right now. Or what's going to happen, for that matter. I just think it makes sense for me not to be here. I'm going to Will's for a bit.'

Stella nodded her understanding, but her face was sad. 'I liked you being here.'

'Me too.'

They leant into each other for a moment.

When Stella spoke, her voice was quiet and small. 'What the hell are they playing at? They're the adults.'

'I really don't know, Stella.'

'Stupid bloody idiots.'

'Yep. I wonder if they've even thought of how far the ripples of this are going to travel.'

'They can't have done. It's the most selfish thing I've ever heard. Bad enough to do it. To do it like this?' She sounded disgusted. 'They shouldn't have done it.'

'Are you going to call your mum? Or your dad?'

Stella hesitated. 'I suppose. Yes. But I don't have a bloody clue what to say to either of them.'

'I know what you mean. I haven't spoken to my dad. I'm too angry.'

Stella whimpered, and started to cry. She had never sounded less angry. 'Oh. My poor dad.'

Mia put an arm around her and, for a while, they just sat together on the edge of the bed amid Mia's sweaters and dresses.

34

Straight after it had happened, Vanessa, Flick and Georgie had huddled together, pale with shock, whispering to each other. Annie joined them once she'd done a circuit of the party, trying half-heartedly to save it. 'I knew.' Vanessa had confessed immediately, told them about the hunch and the walk and Natalie's confession. 'I believed her. I didn't think I should say anything. She begged me . . .' Her eyes moved about the group, seeking understanding.

'I think I'd have done the same thing.' This was Georgie.

Annie said emphatically, 'You had no choice, Ness.'

'She bloody did. I'd have told.' Flick wasn't angry. But she was determined. 'I wish I'd been told. That's why.' But her eyes were not unkind when she turned to Vanessa. 'It's a scruples question.' She touched her friend's arm. 'You were trying to protect people. I know.'

'What do we do now?'

'Buggered if I know. Will's taken Nat home. I suppose that means Kit took their car. Not even sure he was safe to drive. Damn it. Rupert just told me he saw Sarah and Dom go together.'

'We have to leave them all to it. It's nothing to do with us.'

'Isn't it everything to do with us? We are their friends. They are ours.'

'Natalie?'

Annie was silent.

'None of us would do what she's done. I absolutely believe that.'

'Are we convicting her, then? Before we've even spoken to her.'

'Vanessa spoke to her.'

'And she swore it was over. There was no justification from her. Not at all. I think she was disgusted by herself. I honestly do.'

'And you believed her? That it was over?'

'I did. I don't know what happened tonight.'

'Well, I'm not reaching out to Natalie. Not now, anyway. That just feels too disloyal to Sarah, I'm afraid. Nat's made her bed.'

'And Dom? What about him?'

'Yeah. This isn't all on Nat. Takes two to tango.'

'And they were both bloody dancing.'

'Oh, God. What a ghastly mess.' Annie was tearful.

'Your lovely party, Annie . . .'

Annie waved away the concern. 'Oh, I don't care about that. I care about my lovely friends.'

They were all there the next evening when Sarah knocked on Annie's door. She'd answered Annie's text first, apologizing for ruining the party. Annie had called her at once, only half expecting her to answer. She'd been shocked at how different Sarah sounded: her voice was almost unrecognizable. She'd offered to go round, but Sarah had refused. Annie begged her to come to her, to eat something. She promised Rupert and the boys were gone. Sarah already knew Mia was with Will and had asked her not to come home. At first Sarah had told Annie she couldn't face anyone, especially Mia. Already, the mother in her had ruled that Mia mustn't see her like this, not because of something her father had done. Annie, kind and patient, had finally negotiated just a cup of tea.

She'd called Flick to talk about how to move forward. They couldn't leave it like this. It was Flick's idea to pick up Georgie and Vanessa – her suggestion that they should all be there when she came. She told Annie she had a muscle memory of needing as much physical support as she could get when she had been struggling with her first husband's affair all those years ago. Of how much it had helped to have people who loved her around her. If Annie wasn't entirely sure that Flick's way would be Sarah's way, she wasn't unsure enough to challenge Flick, who was, after all, the only one of them who had had a husband cheat on her.

It was meant to feel like a show of support, loyalty and solidarity, the four of them. They didn't consider that it felt to Sarah like an ambush. When she walked in she looked as ghastly as they had imagined she might. Flick would have said, 'Very Mrs Rochester,' if there had been room for even a scintilla of lightness. There wasn't.

Annie instantly regretted the decision. She could see how it looked to Sarah. She'd been still and calm at the door. But she'd become instantly agitated. Defensive. And angry.

'You knew? You all knew?' She wasn't herself. Her hair was wild, her eyes too. She was a dervish, Flick realized. It was frightening.

She reached out, as though Sarah were a wild animal who'd broken free of chains. Made her tone soft, coaxing. 'No. No, Sarah. We didn't. Wait just a minute, will you, please? Calm down.'

Sarah snarled, 'Don't you dare tell me to calm down.'

Flick didn't put her hands down. She heart was racing but she forced herself to take calm, measured breaths, hoping Sarah would too. 'We were just figuring out how to handle it.'

Vanessa nodded vigorously. 'We just found out.'

Sarah rounded on the new speaker. 'When? When did you find out?'

'You need to breathe, Sarah. Please. Breathe.' Annie's voice was tremulous.

'I am bloody breathing, Annie. When?' Her wide eyes scanned the room. For a second, none of them wanted to be the first to speak.

Then Vanessa said, into the heavy silence, 'I suspected. For a while.'

Sarah scoffed dramatically.

Vanessa spoke fast now. 'Just suspected. I didn't know for sure. What was I supposed to do? Come to you throwing around wild accusations about what was basically just a feeling? Really? I didn't know anything for sure. Not until the wedding.'

Rage was replaced with surprise on Sarah's twisted features. 'What? What's the wedding got to do with it?'

'I saw something. At Phoebe's wedding.'

Sarah stared up at the ceiling. She was very still now. 'Are you kidding me? What were they doing? Snogging behind the marquee, for Christ's sake? Shagging against the Portaloos?'

'It wasn't like that.'

But Sarah had digested what she wanted to from the confession, and now she whirled around to square up against Annie and Georgie. 'And you two?' she almost sneered.

Annie stared at the floor, tears in her eyes, wringing her hands. Georgie was hugging herself, her fingers digging into the soft flesh at the top of her arms. This was hideous. 'Vanessa told us, but not until Annie's. Not until after you left. She told Flick first and the two of them told us. We've been just – we were trying to work out what to do.'

Sarah held up a hand. 'Stop. Stop talking. It's inexcusable.' It was such a Sarah word.

'Sarah . . .' Annie implored.

'No. No. You knew, didn't you? You must have done.' She looked at Vanessa. 'And you weren't working out what to do. You were just protecting her.'

Flick sounded almost angry: 'Hey. That's not fair. That's not it at all. You're wrong about Vanessa.'

Annie was crying now. Georgie's eyes were full of tears. She went to Sarah, and put a hand on her arm. Sarah shook it off angrily. 'Don't touch me.'

'This is awful.'

'Have you spoken to her?' Sarah spat.

Vanessa stepped forward. 'Just that once. I'm sorry, Sarah. I was furious with her. I didn't want it all to blow up.'

'Warned her, did you?'

Flick had had enough now. 'Right. You're being a bitch, Sarah. Christ knows you're allowed to be, and you can say what you like to Vanessa, to any of us. And we can take it and we can forgive it, however horrible it is. We're your friends. You can be a bitch, and we'll still be your friends. But then you need to calm down and talk to us. Let us talk to you. Okay?'

Sarah laughed, but the sound was hollow and shrill. 'You must be joking. I'm not going to stay here with you lot. What do you think? We'll have some wine, chat about it. You can fill me in on the details. What the hell? I've got to get out of here. I'm going. Right now.'

'That wasn't what we wanted to happen.'

'What did you want? Is this an intervention?'

'This is your friends, wanting to help. That's all. Stop twisting it. There's no conspiracy here.'

'I'm still leaving. I can't do this now.'

'Okay. Take some time. At least let one of us drive you. You're in no fit state.' Vanessa's voice was firm.

'I'm fine. That's ridiculous.' Sarah was pulling on her jacket.

'You're not fine. And you're not driving yourself home. If you're going – and I don't want you to, none of us does – then I'm taking you. You needn't say a word the whole way. But I'm taking you. Your car stays here.'

Some of the fight went out of Sarah, and she visibly slumped, as if she'd been punctured. As if rage had flowed around her skeleton and now nothing was left to hold her up.

Vanessa had picked up her handbag, and was fishing in it for her car keys. Her hands was shaking.

'Is Dom there now?' Annie's voice was gentler.

'No. I told him to go. And he bloody well went. He's with her, for all I know.'

'I'm sure he's not. Where would he go, do you think?'

'I don't care.'

Georgie persisted. 'But you know? Know where he is?'

Sarah pinched the bridge of her nose. Then she sighed. 'He'll have gone to his brother's, I suppose.'

'Shall one of us ring? Check he's okay? Do you want that?'

'I don't care if he's okay.'

'I know. I know.' Annie spoke softly, moving quietly towards Sarah. 'But you do, really.'

'I have to stay angry. Don't you see? If I stop being angry, I – I don't know . . .' Sarah stepped back, then stopped, and suddenly let Annie hold her. The first cry was strangled, painful. For a long time, she sobbed, and the sound was anguished and ugly. Annie stroked her hair down onto her back, long, slow strokes, smoothing, and eventually the cries subsided. 'Can we sit? Please, Sarah, let's sit.' Annie tried to lead her to the sofa.

There was no anger in Sarah's face or voice now. She looked around the room at them. 'I'm sorry. I really am. But I can't do this now. I am . . . I can't speak. I can't face anyone. Can't say another word. Not even to you all. I just want to go. I'm sorry.'

'Of course. Come on.'

To Vanessa, Sarah seemed almost catatonic as she climbed into the car. She started to pull the seatbelt across her chest, but her movements were listless, feeble. Vanessa grabbed it and clicked it in. She put her hand on Sarah's as it lay in her lap, squeezed it once, then switched on the radio. It was tuned to some talk radio station, two politicians rowing about something, so she spun the dial, and then there was music, inappropriate gaiety filling the space and the silence. She turned it down a little, started the car, then concentrated on driving. She looked at Sarah every few seconds, out of the corner of her eye, but Sarah was staring out of the window, and she couldn't see her face.

They pulled into Sarah's driveway a little less than ten minutes later. Sarah hadn't spoken a word. Vanessa put the car into park, and turned off the engine.

There were no lights on and Dom's car was gone. Vanessa was relieved. She didn't want to see him, and she knew, instinctively, that Sarah probably shouldn't. Not while she was in this state. The house was as neat as it always was, as it always had been, from the pristine standard roses flanking the front door in their terracotta pots to the immaculate painted door, the gleaming brass knocker. It didn't look as though something seismic had shifted within its walls. It should have looked shelled and dismantled, not peaceful and tidy.

'I can stay, if you want.'

'No.' The sound was very small.

'We needn't speak. I'd just be here . . .'

'I don't need you to do that.' Sarah's voice was a quiet monotone, as though speaking hurt.

'Are you sure? I'm not comfortable leaving you alone, when you're this upset.'

Sarah smiled at her. A tight, dead smile. 'Yes. You can leave me. It's safe. I'm not going to do anything stupid. I'll close the curtains and go to sleep.'

Vanessa didn't want to push, but her face must have spoken her resistance.

'I promise.'

She nodded decisively. 'Okay. You know you can call me, right? Any time. Three a.m. Whatever. I know that goes for Annie, Flick and Georgie too. Right?'

'Right. Thank you. For that and for the lift.'

Vanessa tutted. 'I know how I'm feeling is the last thing you want to think about, but I just need to say that when I confronted Nat I thought I was having a go at her about, you know, flirting. Being inappropriate. That's all. I was completely shocked.'

'I wish you'd told me.'

'I wish I had too. I felt like I was doing the right thing. I wasn't, I suppose. I was scared, I'll admit. That's pretty shitty news to impart to someone. She said it was over. She swore.'

'And you were willing to be complicit in shoving it under the carpet?'

'That sounds awful.'

'Supposing it hadn't blown up. Supposing it had just

ended and we all just carried on. You were always going to know that about them. How would that have worked, Vanessa?'

Vanessa shrugged. 'You're right.'

'It doesn't matter now. It's not your fault.'

'Still. I'm sorry.' Then, 'We love you. You know that, too.'

But Sarah was opening the door now, and climbing out. She gave the same smile, briefly, and shut the door without another word. Vanessa watched her as she walked, ever so slowly, to the door, turned her key in the lock and let herself in. She waited for a light to go on, but the house remained in darkness as the door closed behind her.

Vanessa didn't know whether the girls were expecting her to return, and she didn't know whether she should, or whether she could even face going back. And she didn't know whether she should drive away if the lights weren't on.

She dialled Ross. He answered on the first ring, as though he'd been sitting with his phone in his hand. 'You okay?' He sounded tense and worried.

'It was bloody awful, love. I've just dropped her at home. I offered to stay but she wanted to be alone.'

'That's fair enough.'

'She hasn't put any lights on, Ross. She's been inside for, like, five minutes. And she's still in the bloody dark.'

'Let her be, love.'

'I feel horrible.'

'She's a grown woman. Come home. She'll be fine.'

'How do you know?'

He repeated, 'She'll be okay. Just come home to me.'

Vanessa sighed and switched on the engine, pushing the gear stick into reverse. She didn't stop looking for a light until she had backed out into the road, and pulled away, but there wasn't one.

It wasn't completely dark in the house. The moon was big, and the curtains weren't drawn at the back. No one had been home, so of course they weren't. The moon was centred in the dining-room window, big and white and close, and it shone a ghostly light into the hallway where she stood.

Sarah couldn't see clearly, but she could make out the frames of the photographs on the hall table. She knew the pictures by heart. The photographs of their lives. Their wedding, Mia and Dylan's christenings, graduations, sports trophy days. There had to be fifteen frames there. Dom always said there were too many. He preferred a minimalist aesthetic. She'd ignored his objections: his view held sway in most of the house. This bit was hers, she said. The gallery there sparked joy, she said. And Marie Kondo was all for that. It was true, too. Especially when first Mia and then Dylan had moved away. She'd often stop at the bottom of the stairs, en route from bedroom to kitchen, to look at all their precious faces. She didn't even mind dusting them. Sometimes she played a game – dusted them in order of their happening, not according to where they were on the table: 1991, engagement; 1993, wedding; 1995, baby Mia . . . Even the console table was sentimental to her. They'd bought it before they were married – they'd been on a weekend away, and she'd persuaded him into one of those antiques warehouse places, and she'd loved it at once for its curves and patina. They'd had to put the back seats down in the car, and borrow some rope from the dealer to tie it to the open boot, and Dom had said it was more trouble than it was worth. It had sat in the hallway of all three of the homes they had lived in since then – the flat they'd moved into after their honeymoon, the house they'd first brought Mia back to and this one, where they'd been for the past fourteen years.

Now, she let her jacket fall from her shoulders onto the floor, and left it there, dropping her bag beside it. She picked up her favourite photograph – a black-and-white portrait of the four of them, taken when Mia was about eight. They were sitting one in front of another, Dom at the back, Dylan striking a six-year-old pose in the front. She had her arms around Mia's waist, her head on her daughter's shoulder. They were all laughing at something. Probably Dylan's pose.

She held the photograph to her chest, and climbed the stairs. She didn't want to go to their bedroom. Dylan's was the first she came to. It was still full of his stuff. She kicked off her shoes, and lay down on the covers. It smelt of her son. Sports kit and Lynx and laundry. She put the photograph on his bedside table, curled up on her side, and waited. For sleep, or for more tears, or for neither. She had never been so exhausted, yet so far from sleep, in her life.

Vanessa felt completely drained as she pulled in at her own home. As she started writing a text to the group

WhatsApp she shared with the girls, she realized it included Sarah . . . and Natalie. She took a deep breath, input Flick, Annie and Georgie's numbers and rewrote the brief message: *Dropped S at home. D not there. Will call her in the morning. I've gone home as feel like shit. Speak soon.*

As she pressed send, she flicked the switch on the side of the phone to silent. She couldn't cope with their responses, or with anything else tonight. The front door opened, and Ross came out. He opened her car door, and, once she'd climbed out, held her in a long, silent embrace.

She mumbled, 'I love you,' into the side of his neck. She didn't say it often enough. There was something bubbling in her, something she hadn't analysed completely but it felt a little like panic. He knew, right? He knew how she felt? He still felt that way too? *They* were all right, weren't they, the two of them?

'I know. I love you too.'

'I really, really do.'

He laughed, and pulled back to look at her face. 'I *know.*'

She smiled apologetically. 'Can we talk about it tomorrow?'

'We can talk about it whenever you want to.' Ross nodded emphatically. 'Come on. I've poured you a humongous glass of wine, and I've run you a very deep and very bubbly bath. You go on up, I'll fetch the wine.'

Vanessa dropped her bag on the floor, and let her coat slip off her shoulders, slinging it across the chair in the hallway. 'Oh, my God. Perfect.'

Upstairs, she stripped off gratefully, and climbed into the bath. Ross knocked once, and came in. He sat on the edge, and stroked her cheek.

'You're an angel.' She took the glass, but she didn't really feel like drinking now. She was tearful. 'Ross. It's so fucking awful.'

'Sssh.'

'Her face . . .'

'Stop.'

'I got it wrong. So wrong.'

'You were trying to get it right. I know that. Sarah knows that, deep down. If she's shooting the messenger, or the not-messenger, in your case, that'll be temporary. She knows you.'

Vanessa hugged her knees.

'You're not the one in the wrong here, love. You're not.' He picked up a sponge from the side of the bath, held it beneath the water, then squeezed it out across her shoulders and her back.

'I feel so shaken up by it.'

He carried on what he was doing, without speaking. 'Of course you do. We all do, I guess. It's so bloody close to home, and it's made such an unholy mess.'

'And nothing is ever going to be the same again, is it?'

Ross sighed. 'No. Not entirely.'

He bent down and kissed the nape of her neck. 'But you and me, honey? We're solid. Okay?'

She loved a lot of things about her husband but his knowing, without her saying, what she needed to hear was very near the top of the list right now.

35

Mia and Ruth were laughing when Will let himself into the flat. They were both curled into opposite ends of the sofa, their hands curled around big blue-and-white-striped mugs. At the sight of him, they went off in fresh peals.

It was good to see Mia laugh. Will sat down on the arm of the sofa, still in his coat. 'What's so funny?'

'Oh, I'm just hearing about you at uni.'

He looked mock-sternly at his flatmate. 'Don't listen to Ruth's stories.'

Ruth put her hand up. 'I'm only telling the PG ones. Don't panic.'

Mia play-acted shock and horror. 'You mean there are X-rated stories?'

'Course not. I was a choirboy.'

Ruth snorted. 'Don't make me laugh while I'm drinking tea.'

He kissed the top of Mia's head. 'Sorry I'm late.'

She took his hand, brought it to her mouth and kissed it. 'Bad day?'

He shook his head. 'No. Busy.'

Ruth looked at her watch. 'Actually, it's late! I gotta get going.' She stood up.

'Going out?'

'I am indeed. Much as I'd like to stay here and play

gooseberry to you young lovers, cramp your style, you know, I do have a life.' She pulled on ankle boots.

'Oh, God. Are we that bad?'

Ruth smiled broadly. 'Not at all. I think I'd actually rather live with Mia than you, Will, to be honest, so if three's a crowd, you know who's looking for alternative accommodation.' She grinned. 'Just saying.'

Will grinned back. 'My name on the lease. Just saying . . .'

Mia wasn't entirely used to their banter yet. She looked at Ruth. 'You would say, though, if I was overstaying my welcome?'

Ruth patted her shoulder. 'Course I would. You'd be out on your ear, sweetheart. I mean, Will has a different girl here every month. Every week sometimes. I always ask the ones I don't like to leave.'

Will pulled the scarf from around his neck, balled it up and threw it at her playfully. 'Get out!'

'Going! See you later.' She slung on her cross-body bag, put on her coat, and left, throwing a wave over her shoulder as she pushed in her earbuds.

As the door closed behind her, Will slid onto the sofa beside Mia, and pulled her into a deep kiss. He loved the way she smelt and the way she felt in his arms. It was still a wildly exciting novelty, yet entirely as though it was always meant to be. He loved that contradiction.

'I missed you.'

And the truth was, he loved coming home and finding her here every night. He was a little surprised at how quickly he'd grown used to it.

And he knew Ruth didn't mind because he'd asked her straight, and if she said she didn't, you knew she really didn't. The two of them had gone for their usual Sunday-morning run – 'the weekly stagger', Ruth called it – the first weekend Mia had been there. She'd declined their invitation to join them – she was more of a yoga and Pilates girl, she'd said. They tried to do it every week – Ruth had done a Couch to 5K the year before, and become evangelical about the health benefits. They were up to 10K now, the natural competitiveness of their friendship pushing them both to be better. They did the same loop, and often stopped at the coffee shop a hundred yards from the flat for a takeaway. They'd drunk this one leaning on a low wall, and he'd asked her if she was okay with it.

'She's great, Will. I mean, objectively speaking, too good-looking.'

'What do you mean?'

'No woman wants to get up in the morning and wander in to find another woman who looks freaking gorgeous first thing. She makes me feel like a troll.'

'I'll have a word with her about that.'

'Piss off.'

'Seriously, though, Ruthie?'

'Seriously, though, Willie, she's brilliant. She's funny, and she's not messy, and she's a thousand times better cook than you. What's not to love?'

'Right?'

'And you're great too.'

'What d'you mean?' He'd cocked his head at the compliment. Ruth didn't give them out easily.

'The actual you. You know? Normal. Not all weird and showy and shit.'

He knocked her shoulder with his own. 'Gee, thanks. You say the nicest things.'

'She going to be a permanent fixture?' He'd told her Mia was staying because things were weird at her place. He hadn't elaborated, and Ruth hadn't asked. She was good like that.

'Would semi-permanent be okay? For now?'

Ruth had laughed. 'I actually meant in your life, not in the flat, dingbat. But fine with me. I've got my own irons in the fire, just so you know. I got prospects. Not planning on growing old with you in that flat, Will Hawtrey.'

'Good to know. Happy to offer an impartial, objective opinion on any potential long-term prospects.'

She raised an eyebrow. 'I assure you, you'll be among the very last to know.'

He'd brought Mia here the night of the party, after he'd dropped off Natalie and Arlo. She'd messaged her mum, and Sarah had replied, but only something along the lines of Mia not needing to worry that she was going to do anything daft, because she wasn't, and her wanting to be alone. Mia had sat at the table between him and his mum, and Annie had held her hand, and told her that Sarah not wanting to see her right now was precisely because she was her mother, and that she wanted to protect her from the full force of her own upset. That was what being a mother meant. And that Annie had Sarah – they all had her. They were all here for their friend. That she thought she'd be better left, just for the night. The boys had reported that Dom and Sarah had departed together. Give them a chance, Annie had counselled, to talk it through.

She'd suggested they both stay there, quick and kind to add that they could have Will's old room, but there were still too many people milling around, and it felt weird to be there together for the first time under such circumstances. Will had just wanted to rescue her. Ruth was back home for a week's holiday, so there was no one else to think about. That first night, back at his flat, he'd tucked Mia into his bed and made her tea, then climbed in beside her, and held her while she cried. She'd come back here after she'd seen Sarah and Stella and every night since. Annie had said to him, before they left that night, that he should let Mia talk about it as much as she wanted, but only when she wanted to, and he had followed that piece of advice. Tried to listen. Tried to make her smile.

It had fast-tracked them, he knew, not just the proximity and the domesticity. Mia was grieving, in a way, and he understood. They had in common that they came from strong, united family units. At least they'd thought they had that in common. He knew how devastated he would be if it were his parents. However common it was, however okay he knew it could be eventually. He understood her sense of loss, and her anger towards Dom. Will wanted to look after her. And he didn't care if it was too soon. It felt right.

And now, he wanted her never to leave.

36

Natalie hadn't been sure how Sylvia would be with her. She'd been barely coherent when she called, after the party, her confession spilling from her like lava. She'd put Arlo to bed, moving like an automaton, speaking to him without really knowing what she was saying, deflecting questions about his father. Kit had already been and gone – his open drawers in their room told her so. He must have moved fast. She couldn't have been more than twenty minutes behind him. Maybe he'd already had a bag packed. Like people kept a grab-bag in case of a fire. Maybe he'd been thinking about leaving her all along. Planning. Maybe he even had somewhere to go. She couldn't think about that.

Once she'd kissed Arlo and softly closed his bedroom door, she'd curled into the corner of her bedroom to call Sylvia and the words had tumbled out in a whispered, tearful rush. Her mother had been so angry with her, she knew, so disappointed in what she'd done. She felt Sylvia's feelings reflecting her own back at her, and she was utterly wretched. 'Come to me.' That was all Sylvia had said.

She'd lied to a mum from Arlo's class – said her mother was sick. The friend had agreed to have Arlo for the day, and she'd held herself together on no sleep at all until the front door of the friend's house was closed and she'd climbed back into the car. Kit hadn't read any of the WhatsApp messages she'd sent. She had no idea where he was. She'd judged some of her friends for having their husbands on FindMyFriend – been glad she and Kit weren't like that when she needed to keep her awful secrets. Now she'd give anything to be able to see where he was. She'd cried all the way to Sylvia's house.

And now Natalie didn't know what to expect. But when her mother opened the door, her face was soft, and she opened her arms to embrace her. Natalie burst into fresh tears.

'Don't be kind to me.'

'You shouldn't have come, if you wanted cruelty. I'm your mother.' Sylvia stroked her hair.

'I'm sorry. I'm so pathetic. I'm a mess.' Natalie sniffed hard, and ran her fingers under her eyes, where she knew her mascara would have run.

'Darling, I'm your mum.'

'And I've let you down – let everyone down – and disappointed you. And messed everything up.'

'Sssh. Calm down. Let's get you inside.'

Natalie sat at the kitchen table, and watched her mother make tea, then slice a lemon drizzle cake onto small plates. Natalie couldn't remember a time when she hadn't had cake in the house. She put a napkin and a cake fork at each of their places. The ritual of tea time was comforting and familiar, and for a few minutes they didn't speak. Classic FM was playing from the radio on the windowsill – something gentle and calming, she didn't know what it was. Natalie knew Sylvia was letting her get herself together, and she was grateful.

When she finally sat down next to her daughter, and picked up her fork, she patted Natalie's hand. 'All right. So tell me again, all of what has happened. It was more than a little garbled the last time.'

For long minutes, she just listened, carefully attentive, to what had happened at the party, and afterwards, nodding from time to time, and calmly eating her cake. She didn't interrupt, and she didn't ask any questions. When Natalie had finished, she waited a moment, then stood up. 'Poor you. Poor Kit.' Natalie rested her head on her mother's belly, and Sylvia smoothed her hair again. 'It sounds awful.'

'I don't know if he's coming home. I think he's left us.'

'You have to give him time.'

'I don't know what to tell Arlo. I can make the others understand, maybe. But I also think they might hate me. Stella ...' She had wanted to say how angry she knew Stella would be, how protective of her father, but the rest of the sentence disappeared in a sob.

'She will not.' Sylvia was stern. 'I will speak to her. She'll be sad. And, yes, she'll be angry, and she's entitled to be, but only to a degree. None of those things are hate, Natalie.'

'And Temple. My God. Temple.' Natalie held her head in her hand. 'Could the timing be any worse?'

'Temple is an adult. It's not one size fits all. She's not so simple a creature as to see this as binary. She'll listen to you, like you have listened to her. She'll try to understand what you choose to tell her. I'm not going to tell you they're fine. I'm not going to tell you that what you've done hasn't affected them. You know it has. But they'll all be okay. They are adults, Nat. You are no longer the centre of their universe. They can, and they will, form opinions and make decisions, and you cannot control that. You have to let go of it.'

'But Arlo? He's too young to understand.'

'So don't tell him. He's young enough to believe what you say and not figure it out. You say you don't know if Kit's coming back. But you will. You can't stay in this limbo indefinitely. You can deal with Arlo then. For now, right, Dad's working away. Buy yourself some time. He's been away before.'

'Do you think he'll come back?'

She smiled. 'I have no idea. I know that you have to let him lick his wounds.'

Then: 'I want to show you something.' Sylvia walked through to the other room. 'Something I made.'

She came back with a blue plate, which she held carefully, almost reverently. About twenty centimetres across, Natalie could see that it was glazed in blue ombre, darker towards the edge. But as she got closer, she could see that it had cracked in three or four places, the cracks running like lightning strikes across the china, as though it had been dropped and put back together. The fault lines were gold-coloured. Natalie looked at Sylvia, confused.

'This is a piece of *kintsugi*. It's Japanese. It means "gold repair", or "golden joinery".'

'Okay.' Natalie looked from the plate to her mother's face. 'It's beautiful. You made this?'

Sylvia nodded. 'It's more beautiful than you know. Not mine, although I think it's pretty good for a first attempt, the art of *kintsugi*. There's a whole philosophy behind it – quite fascinating. You see, the Japanese believe that damage is part of an object's history. That you shouldn't hide it, but celebrate it. Celebrate flaws. That's why they fill the cracks with gold. Sometimes silver or platinum. They make it with lacquer dust. Some of it is quite exquisite. They make a feature of the cracks, see, a virtue. Because it makes the history of the plate richer. Do you understand?'

Natalie took the plate and held it up, moving it back and forth in the light to make the gold shimmer. Then she put it down carefully on the table. 'I don't think I cracked my marriage, though, Mum. I think I smashed it. I think there'd be more gold than porcelain.'

'You don't know.'

'And it's Kit who must decide.'

'You have to make him understand, not how sorry you are – I'm sure he knows that. You have to beat yourself up about that, of course, but not to a pulp. You're not the first. I feel like Dom was a perfect storm. I'm not absolving you, but I understand why it happened. And I know that you stopped it. And I know how sorry you are. This self-loathing might be helping you now, but it won't get you anywhere, my girl. What you have to make Kit understand is how much you want him to stay in your life. Not because it's too messy otherwise, or because you're scared, but because he makes your life beautiful. Because of what you and he have built together over so many years. That you don't want him to throw it all away because of what you did. That you *can* get past it.'

'Do you think we can?'

'I do. I read another thing about gold the other day. It was a woman, setting down the advice for life she wanted to pass on to her daughter, before she died. The daughter was young. Her mother said she wanted her not to mistake tinsel for gold. One is real and precious and valuable. And one is not. Kit is gold. You and Kit are gold.'

'Quite the philosopher, huh, Mum?'

'Darling. There is no earthly point getting older if you don't get wiser. I have time, and I have some understanding.'

'Did you and Dad ever . . .?'

Sylvia tutted. 'No. No. Not this. Not so far as I know, at least. But don't imagine for any moment that a marriage worth having, a marriage that lasts, doesn't face different tests. I always find those smug people who claim their marriages thrive because they work at them make me cross. It's luck. Luck that you choose the right person in the first place. Luck that you stay in love. Luck that you continue to want the same things, and see the world in the same way – not as each other, you understand. Life is spicier if you sometimes disagree. No, I mean see the world the same as you did. Grow together, not apart. It's luck. But sometimes, my Natalie, you have to make your luck. And some affairs are survivable, my darling. Some behaviour is forgivable.'

Natalie smiled weakly at her mother. 'You should charge by the hour.'

Sylvia harrumphed. 'You couldn't afford me.' They laughed. 'Besides, don't therapists never tell you what to do? I wouldn't last five minutes. I'm telling you what to do.'

37

No one used the big Apple computer on the desk in Dom's study any more. It was almost as old as the century. Everyone had a laptop or an iPad. Sarah had been talking about getting rid of it for ages. It was the photographs that had stalled her. Everything else was obsolete, but for the last almost two decades, all their photographs had been downloaded onto this machine. All everyone else's too. It was the chronicler of their family history. They had pictures on there going back to the first year they'd had it.

Funny that everyone said modern photographic technology was better. She didn't agree. When photographs had been taken on film, and processed at Boots, she'd stuck them into albums that were still lined up neatly on the shelf, labelled, 'Sixth form', 'America', 'Teacher training college', 'Hen and stag dos', 'Wedding (day)', 'Wedding (evening)', 'Mia'. And there they stopped. From then on it had all been memory stick, upload. And now around twenty-seven thousand pictures were stuck in the computer, and no one, it seemed, had the will or the time to do anything with them. No one had ever edited them. When you had twelve, twenty-four or thirty-six exposures, you tended not to have ten different but almost identical shots. Mia's prom dress photo call alone accounted for maybe a hundred. It was always on the to-do lists Sarah wrote in the notebook she kept by her bed. Sort photos. Always at the end, after the more practical, easier jobs. Never tackled.

She was sitting here now. It had been dusk when she started, but now it was properly dark and there were no lights on anywhere downstairs, just the blue light of the screen in the room.

She couldn't stop. Her hand held the mouse, her finger click, click, clicking through the pictures. It was almost a trance. She couldn't stop looking for photographs with Dom and Natalie in. When one appeared, she leant forward and studied it intently. She was looking for clues, like a policeman would. Hoping that the camera had captured something she, in real life, in real time, had missed. This thing they'd had between them. Could they prove it?

Here we are in the pub in 2004. See how we're looking at each other. Look at us on this beach. Hadn't you noticed we're very, very close together as we lean on the groyne and laugh at a long-forgotten joke? Is that Dom, second row, that side, watching Natalie in the mother's race at sports day? Look how brown her legs are, how toned. She's winning, of course. She makes the other mothers look frumpy and plain. She makes me look frumpy and plain. Why wouldn't he be staring at her? Why wouldn't he want her? Why is Natalie wiping ice cream from Dylan's face? She isn't his mother, is she? It isn't her job. Is she playing a part? Is it some sick kind of foreplay? Something animalistic . . .

There were lots of pictures of the six women together, but very few with just her and Natalie on their own. Here was one, though. Taken one Christmas time, maybe ten years ago, in Natalie's kitchen. Everyone had brought an element of the meal, and she and Natalie were serving onto plates laid out on the island. The others, except whoever had snapped the candid shot, would have been next door, laughing and joking around the table while they waited for their food. They had aprons over their dresses, and paper crowns from the crackers on their heads, and they'd looked up from their task to beam for the camera, Natalie's arm thrown around Sarah's shoulders, a spatula held aloft in the other hand. Sarah didn't study the picture. She didn't want to look at the two of them. It hurt.

She didn't even know why she was doing it. What would that prove? How would it help?

Look at us. Dom and Sarah. Mum and Dad. All those happy photographs. I'm always on his left. I fit just under his arm so I can stand upright in a picture. I always put my left hand up and on his chest. We look good together, don't we? We look happy. Don't we?

38

Stella launched her attack the moment Natalie pressed the green button on the phone. Her voice was furious, indignant. 'What the fuck are you playing at, Mum?'

She'd dreaded this, even as she had known that for every hour she stayed silent, this became more likely. 'You know.'

'I know. Yes.' Natalie kicked herself. She'd wanted to tell her. She should have told her. She knew her daughter. She knew she'd have worked herself up. Of the two of them, Stella was more like Kit. Natalie could get angry every half an hour and it never had any real impact. Kit got angry maybe twice a year, and it was fearsome. The force of Stella's rage was powerful, even down a handset.

'Stella. Please. I'm so sorry. I wanted to tell you myself.'

'Plenty of time for you to have done that, Mum.'

'I wanted to see you. To tell you to your face.'

'Sounds like a convenient excuse. Where were you?'

'You're angry. I get that you're angry.'

'Don't do that. I hate it when you say stuff like that. Like you swallowed the parenting manual.'

'Okay.' Natalie had to let the blows rain down. 'I'm sorry. Did Mia tell you?'

'Yeah.'

'For that, I'm truly sorry. You are right. It was cowardly. I should have known she'd get to you first.'

'You make her sound like she was gossiping. That's not fair. She didn't want to tell me. She was moving out. I found her. She had to explain why, didn't she?'

'You're right. Completely.'

'You should have called me, Mum. Imagine how that felt for me.'

'I'm sorry.' It was really all she had to give. Even she didn't want to hear herself say it.

'Does Marley know?'

'Not yet.'

Stella sneered. 'You waiting for one of Will's brothers to do it?'

'That's unfair.'

'I feel like being unfair.'

'And I'm not allowed to tell you that you're entitled to.'

Silence.

'Bit bloody late for that, though, isn't it? A bit sodding inadequate. Sorry. You're sorry.'

'Of course it is. Wholly inadequate.'

'That all you got?'

'That depends on you. What do you want?'

'What do you mean?'

'You don't want me to say I'm sorry. You're not buying that. Fair enough. You don't want me to tell you you're entitled to any of the feelings I know you're having now. So do you just want to shout at me some more and then slam the phone down on me? Or do you want me to explain? Do you want to try to understand or to stay furious?'

That question seemed to floor Stella. When she spoke again, her voice was smaller, and less angry. 'I wanted it not to be true.'

'You and me both, darling.'

'But you made it true. So why? Why did you do it?'

Natalie exhaled. 'It's a complicated answer, my sweetheart. I don't have a soundbite.'

'And I'm not capable of understanding?'

'I don't know. Perhaps you can. Perhaps you will.'

'I don't know how you could do it to Dad. He must be devastated.'

'Yes.'

'Where is he?'

'He's not answering my calls. Maggie's, I guess. Maybe at a friend's.'

'I called him first. He didn't answer. I left him a voicemail.'

'He's hurt and he's humiliated. Give him time.'

'Don't think you're in any position to be handing out advice on how to handle Dad, do you? It's your fault.'

'Yes.'

Another long pause.

'You and Dom. Are you?'

'There is no me and Dom. It was over before your dad found out. I swear, Stella. It still is. If I lose your dad, it will still be over.'

'I can't believe it, Mum. I honestly can't. I never thought you'd do a thing like that.'

'I don't know what to say to you, Stella. I'm as ashamed and as sorry and as fucking furious with myself as I have ever been in my entire life. But I can't change what I've done.'

'No, you can't.'

'I can only try to make up for it. Make it right.'

Stella snorted.

'Can I come and see you?'

'No. I don't want to see you. Not yet.'

'Okay. I understand.'

'And I don't want to talk to you.'

'I have no right to argue with that.'

'Okay, then.'

'Will you talk to your gran, though? Please. She knows what's happened. She loves us all. She has wise words to say, Stella. Please? And keep trying your dad? Temple? I want you all to talk, to each other, even if no one wants to talk to me. You need to. Promise me?'

Stella's answer was more a grunt than a word, and then she hung up.

39

The marquee had been taken down, leaving just a large brown patch of grass in the garden. No one had heard from Sarah since the day the four of them had seen her, although they had all tried. She wasn't responding to texts or emails, and she wouldn't answer the phone. They hadn't talked to Natalie either. Or to Kit or Dom. It was like the whole group had been holding their breath for five days, absorbing the shock of what had happened.

It was Flick who broke the unbearable silence. With Georgie and Vanessa at work, she agreed a plan with Annie. No one knew whether Sarah had been going to work. On the Friday morning, Flick texted her: *I'm coming to pick you up from yours at 4 p.m. on Friday afternoon. I'm taking you to Annie's house so we can talk. It will just be the three of us: you, me and Annie. It's not an ambush this time. It's just friends who need to see you. No arguments, please. We all love you, Sarah. xx*

The text showed as delivered, but Sarah didn't respond.

At the appointed time, Flick pulled into Sarah's driveway, right up to the front door, and honked the horn. For a couple of minutes she thought Sarah would ignore her. Her car was there, but not Dom's, unless it was in the garage. She was deliberating how far she could legitimately push, but then the door opened and Sarah came out. She looked ghastly, but she was there.

Sarah opened the passenger door, and climbed in, then sat impassive in the seat, staring forward.

'Hello, you.'

'Hi.'

'I'm glad you're here.'

Sarah turned her head to meet Flick's gaze. 'Me too.'

Annie must have been waiting by the front door. It opened as soon as the car pulled in, and she came out into the garden. 'Hello, my darling friend.'

Sarah let Annie hold her in a firm embrace. Her shoulders dropped. Flick thought she might be crying.

'I'm so sorry about your beautiful party, Annie.' Sarah's voice was muffled.

Annie pulled back, and clasped her by both arms. 'Don't you dare apologize. Come on in.'

Sarah sank into the deep sofa. She was clean and tidy, and she'd even put some make-up on, but the dark circles under puffy eyes and the pale skin gave her away. Flick felt desperate for her. 'How are you doing?'

'Not great.'

'Are you sleeping?'

'When I get tired enough.'

'Have you been going in to work?'

She nodded. 'Sort of on autopilot but, honestly, it's a good distraction. Tires me out. I don't think I'd sleep at all if I wasn't going through the motions every day. It's half-term next week. That'll be a relief.'

'Do you have a plan?'

'No.' She shook her head. 'We'd talked about doing something, but we never booked. We were going to sort it last minute, depending on the weather.' She snorted, and stopped speaking.

'Sarah . . .'

'Perhaps he never meant to go anywhere. Why would he want to?'

'Where is Dom?'

'I was right – he's at his brother's. Have you seen Natalie?'

'No. *No.*' Flick's tone was incredulous.

Sarah looked relieved.

'Do you know the full story?'

Sarah nodded. 'I think so.'

'Do you want to talk about it?'

'I don't know. I haven't tried. I suppose I need to tell you . . .'

'Only if you want to.'

'It started in the summer, I gather. So it's been going on for a few months.'

'And is it still going on?'

'I don't know. I threw him out. I'm buggered if I'm going to ask Natalie.'

'No.'

'And you had no idea?'

'We hadn't had sex in ages. Before all this happened. Me and Dom.'

She just blurted it out. For a moment they were all shocked that she'd said it, including Sarah. A deep flush crept across her chest and up her neck to her face.

Annie spoke quickly into the silence. 'So what, love? That's probably true for most of us. We're not kids any more, are we?'

Flick, though, leant forward, and put a hand on Sarah's knee. 'What do you mean by ages?'

'That's none of our business, Flick,' Annie admonished her gently.

'Oy! Sarah started this conversation, Annie.' Flick sounded sharper than she meant to. 'I assume that means she wants to talk to us about it.'

'Don't fight, you two. Please.' Sarah stared at her hands in her lap, sounding close to tears.

Flick threw a warning glance at Annie over her head. 'We're not fighting.'

'Sorry, Sarah. We're listening.'

'So what do you mean? Ages?'

Sarah took a deep breath. 'I mean maybe five, six times in the last . . .' She hesitated. 'Five or six years.'

'Fuck.' Flick's response was involuntary.

'Flick!' Annie was horrified.

'Sorry. I thought you were going to say year.'

'I know. I know.' Sarah laughed tearfully. 'I've been so ridiculous about it. Such a bloody ostrich . . .'

Annie stood up. 'I'm going to make us some tea. We probably need cake. I'll be back in a bit, okay?'

She left the room, and they watched her go.

Sarah turned to Flick. 'I'm sorry. I don't mean to make everyone uncomfortable. I guess she needs a minute. Funny, isn't it? We've been friends for so long. But we've never been that kind of friends. The kind that tell each other everything. The really, really personal stuff. Do you think anyone does? I mean talk about that stuff all the time.'

Flick thought of Zoë and Phoebe. 'My girls say their generation do. Big on details. They seem to do full debriefs. All that.' She shuddered involuntarily. 'I'm not really sure how many women our age do.'

'Maybe I should have done. Talked about it.'

Flick touched Sarah's knee. 'I think you should have talked to Dom about it, love. Did you?'

She shrugged. 'Not really. Sometimes. But never really properly, I suppose.'

'And do you know why not?'

Sarah shook her head.

'Sarah . . .' Flick prompted. 'Hey, honey, you've started now, so you might as well tell us.'

'Okay. You're right, I know. It's just hard. So . . . humiliating.'

'Don't let it be. We're your closest friends.'

Sarah smiled gratefully. 'That probably makes it more embarrassing, to be honest.'

'What choice do you have, hey? Bottling it up hasn't got you far.'

They laughed a little.

'There must be something wrong with me. And there was obviously something wrong with "us". I feel like an idiot.'

'You're not an idiot. Who the hell knows what goes

on behind closed doors? We might think we do, but we don't. Only two people really know what goes on in any marriage.'

'It was gradual, I suppose. It wasn't just like we turned off a tap. First of all, it's life, isn't it? We were fine, when the kids were little. When they were teenagers, it got harder – making time, getting in the mood, all that. So it slowed down. I sort of assumed that was normal. I stopped initiating it completely. I acknowledge that. It got so I sort of gave in. That sounds awful.'

She looked at Flick, who smiled encouragingly. 'I know what you're saying.'

'I mean, I loved him. Still loved him. At least, I thought so. We had a life, you know?' Flick nodded. 'A good, happy life. I told myself it wasn't that important. And the sex, when it happened, it wasn't bad or anything like that.' She cringed. 'I just . . . I absolutely could have gone without and not minded. Weeks turned to months. I think I sort of forgot about it. Certainly forgot how to. I mean, forgot how it came about. That probably sounds ridiculous. It got so I almost couldn't imagine us doing it. Like it was an impossible distance from where we were to where we'd need to be, if that makes sense . . . Do you understand?'

Flick took a deep breath. 'Darling. I wish I did.'

'It's not like that with you and Andrew?'

'No. No, it's not. I want to be as honest with you as you are being with me. I would have to say that it's still important to us, to both of us.' Sarah looked stricken. 'Don't get me wrong! We're not jumping off the wardrobe thrice weekly.'

'But it's like it used to be?'

'A bit less often, probably. Definitely. When we were first together, it was pretty much every day. That's just not sustainable. Definitely less athletic.' She laughed. 'We're probably no longer working our way through the *Kama Sutra*. But, no, not less important than it ever has been. It's important. It's part of who we are as a couple.' She shook her head. 'I'm sorry. Not trying to rub your nose in it, I promise.'

'I know. That's what I would have guessed. Probably. Did you guess about us?'

'Never. Of course not. Were you . . . trying to guess about all of us?'

Sarah smiled ruefully. 'I suppose I was, yes. There's an element of curiosity. When things are that way with you, you wonder.'

'So you knew it wasn't right, really?' Flick's voice was gentle.

'Deep down I suppose I must have done.'

'Oh, Sarah. Bless you.'

'I don't know if it helps that you lot didn't think anything was wrong or not. I'm not even going to ask Annie. She and Rupert are so lovey-dovey.'

Flick sighed. 'Ask her or don't ask her. You don't know. I don't know. That's all I'm saying. Or Vanessa. Or Georgie.'

'Or even Natalie.' Flick wouldn't have spoken her name. Sarah said it bitterly.

'Okay. I'm going to say something. And you have to promise to listen to me, Sarah. Whether you and Dom were happy together, whether you and Dom were at it like bunnies . . . whatever . . . it doesn't excuse what Dom has done. It does not somehow grant him permission.'

'But does it *explain* it? Partly, at least.'

'You aren't going to blame yourself for what he's done, not even partly. I won't let you.'

'Me neither.' Annie, fierce with loyalty, was suddenly in the doorway with a wooden tea tray. She came in and set about pouring cups, passing cake on small plates, talking as she did so.

'What about Dom? Even if the change between you originated with you – and I'm saying *if* – he's surely culpable in not forcing you to face it sooner.'

'Exactly what I was going to say. There's counselling. There's couples therapy. There's help out there.'

Sarah looked contrite. 'He probably tried. Not recently. Back along.'

'Probably?'

'Okay. Definitely. He definitely tried. I didn't want to do any of that. I mean, come on! How excruciating would that be? Sitting in some smug counsellor's office talking about this completely private, personal stuff . . .' She stopped when she realized what she'd said. 'Sorry, Annie. No offence.'

Annie smiled easily. 'Hey. It's okay. But I hope I'm not smug.'

'You wouldn't know where to begin being smug. Nor would Rupert. It was a stupid thing to say.'

'Sssh. I know what you mean. Lots of people feel that way about getting help.'

'But they do it anyway. Far braver people than me, clearly.' She started to cry. 'Shit. Shit. What a bloody mess . . .'

Annie's eyes were filled with tears too.

'What am I going to do?'

'What do you want to do?'

'I don't know. I'm so bloody angry. All the time. I feel this – this rage. All of the time. I'm furious with Dom. I'm furious with Natalie. I'm furious with myself. I cannot seem to stop being angry. And I don't want to because, as wretched as the anger feels, I'm far more afraid of what will come behind it, after it. I feel like the anger is what's keeping me alive.'

'I so get that. I remember feeling that way with Craig. It's a million years ago, but I know exactly what you're saying there. I was pregnant, full of righteous fury. I was so scared that when I gave the anger up, I'd just melt away entirely and be this pathetic, useless puddle.'

Sarah stared down at her hands in her lap. She splayed the fingers, looking at the band of gold on her wedding finger. 'You're going to tell me I have to, though, right?'

'No one is going to tell you how you have to be. This isn't happening to any of us. It's happening to you. It isn't our right.'

'Annie's right,' said Flick. 'I will tell you one thing. It's a tunnel. Like some video game. You know, like the boys used to play – a room with levels. A tunnel with road-blocks. Whatever. You have to go through the levels. Anger isn't the most painful bit, or at least it wasn't for me. You hold on to the anger as long as you want to, as long as you need to. Don't do anything about the next stages. They'll still be there. I became that pathetic, useless puddle. I think it was always going to happen, however long I'd stayed mad. You know labour – first stage, transition. Remember transition? How much it stings?'

Annie winced. 'That's when women say they've changed their mind. Say they'll come back and do it tomorrow. Or that they know they can't . . .'

'But they can. They do. And it gets worse, and then it gets better.'

'And then they put your baby into your arms. Happy ending. That's not what this is. No happy ending here . . .'

'It's a tunnel you can't turn around in. That's my point.'

Annie wasn't sure how much Flick was helping. The thing about being in a tunnel was that it was often really, really dark. 'How are your babies doing?' It was a weak link, but it was a tangent.

Sarah exhaled slowly. 'Mia's okay, I think. Upset. Of course. She's pretty pissed off with her dad. Will's been extraordinary, it sounds like. And Dylan doesn't know yet. I don't want to tell him on the phone.'

'Okay.' Annie and Flick nodded.

'I'm so glad, Annie, about our kids. I meant to say before.'

Annie took her hand. 'Me too. They seemed so easy together.'

'He's been unbelievable with Mia, she says. So kind.' Sarah smiled. 'I think he loves her.'

'And her him. Lucky buggers. All seems so easy, doesn't it, when you're young?'

'Don't do that,' Flick said. 'Don't let it make you cynical.'

'Too late for that, I think.'

'Too soon to say.' Flick winked. 'What are you going to do about Dylan, though? You know secrets are like feathers, right? You don't want him to find out.'

'I told Dom he'd have to tell him. His mess. His confession.'

'Is that what you want?'

'No. Of course not. I don't want him to mess it up. He'll be back soon. I'll tell him. Face to face. God.'

'They're adults, Sarah.' Flick's tone was gentle.

'They're barely adults. And they'll always be our babies, I suppose.'

40

Natalie almost couldn't face Temple, who had so much reason to judge her, viewing her behaviour through the prism of Max's infidelity. Almost. It was unlikely that Temple would find out. Who would tell her? But she couldn't risk it. Not a third time. She knew from Sylvia that Marley knew, although she was sketchier on the detail of how he'd found out. Sylvia had spoken to them both. She'd relayed bits of their conversation to Natalie. Kit was staying at Maggie's, as she had thought. Stella and Marley had both seen him. He hadn't assassinated her character. Not at all. He'd refused to talk about the detail of any of it. But Marley, she knew, was united with Stella in wanting to punish her by not giving her a hearing. Sylvia's counsel was to leave them, for now. She said it with the same calm confidence that she'd always pronounced on things. 'They'll come back to you, darling. They are yours. Both of yours. And they always will be.'

Natalie understood Stella's fury, although their phone call had left her bruised and fragile. It was hurting her to give Stella the space and time she'd insisted on, but she had no choice. All she could do was be ready for whatever came next. She forced herself to engage with the full realm of possibility, despite Sylvia's certainty, because how could she be so sure of everything, when Natalie was no longer sure of anything? But estrangement seemed impossible to her. These were her babies – they were all her babies. It was unimaginable that they wouldn't forgive her. It was unbearable. She wanted to bang her head, over and over, against a hard wall. This was all so obvious. This was always going to happen. She remembered talking to Dom about it. Giving them both reasons not to do it. So why had she? Why had she been so weak, selfish, and so very stupid? It was the most dangerous thing she had ever done, the highest stakes she'd ever played. How could she have been so wantonly oblivious to what she stood to lose? How could it ever, ever have been worth it? The affair played out in her mind in slow motion, like a dummy lurching forward in a seatbelt test.

Although she'd arranged to meet Temple at her flat, where she could rail and rage as much as she wanted, in the end, Temple wasn't angry like Stella had been. Natalie had blurted it out, almost before she'd taken off her coat and scarf, a stream-of-consciousness confession. She didn't cry until she talked about the night in the shepherd's hut, the horrible moment of realization.

Temple listened, then poured them both a drink. Drank deeply and wordlessly. Natalie felt as if she couldn't breathe. Then Temple walked around the table to where her mother was, and put her arms around her. Natalie heard herself sob.

'I've done to Kit what Max did to you. How can you be kind to me?'

'Come on, Mum. It's obvious you're being harder on

yourself than I could ever be. Look at you, for Christ's sake. What would be the point?'

Temple pulled her mother over to the sofa, and they sat down, cross-legged, facing each other. Gradually, Natalie's breathing returned to normal.

'Did you love him? Dom? Do you?'

'For a while I thought so. But no. Not really. It was infatuation. I see that now. All very intoxicating. All very pathetic and cliché and middle-aged. I felt *seen*. I felt understood. I felt young and excited. I felt like a prize. I thought I felt more me.'

'Does he love you?'

'He said so.'

'Said?'

'We haven't spoken. He wants to. I can't.'

'Doesn't seem much point, if you don't love him.' She paused. 'And do you love Kit?'

Natalie took a deep breath. 'Very much.'

'Not just love. In love?'

'God. Are middle-aged married couples ever really *in* love?'

'I bloody well hope so, Mum.'

'I'm not sure they ever ask themselves that question, honestly. I truly don't know what would happen if they did.'

'What does he say?'

Natalie sighed. 'He's deeply hurt. He was angrier than I've ever seen him, the night it all came out. He left. He won't talk to me. I only know where he's staying because the kids told your gran.'

'This is new, though, right?'

'He's known for a while. He guessed. I don't know how. He wouldn't let me tell him anything. No names. No details. He didn't know who it was.'

Temple cleared her throat. 'I don't get that at all. I wanted to know every last tiny detail about the woman Max slept with. I was obsessed. I could see myself stalking her. I made him tell me everything. The most intimate stuff.'

'Not Kit. He didn't go, at first. I sound like a total fool. But I hoped we could get past it –'

'How?'

'What do you mean?'

'How were you trying to get past it?'

'I wasn't making big declarations or grand gestures, if that's what you mean.'

'I'm not sure they belong in real life. They're more film and TV.'

'And they wouldn't work on Kit. I was trying to show him I knew how good our life was. Does that make sense, or sound pathetically inadequate?'

Temple didn't answer. 'And then?'

'And then Dom cornered me at the party. I don't know why or what for – I was trying to get away. I wasn't even giving him airtime, but Kit saw, and figured it out, and, oh, God, it was the most hideous moment.'

'So he was humiliated.'

'Yes.'

'I won't pretend to you that I don't think it's a million times worse that it was someone you both knew. Max's was a nameless, faceless stranger to me. If it was me, I'd be going over everything, torturing myself with when and how and how long.'

'That's why I wanted to tell him everything. The truth couldn't have been worse than what he might have been imagining.'

Temple stood up abruptly. 'Right. We're going to need more drink. Possibly crisps and nuts, if I can dredge any up. Be right back.' She kissed the top of Natalie's head. 'I'm glad you've come, Mum. I'm glad you can talk to me.'

Natalie took her hand, and kissed the back, laying it against her cheek. 'I shouldn't be. I'm your mum. I'm supposed to be here for you, not the other way around. I'm supposed to have my shit together.'

'Mum. How come you don't you know this by now? No one has their shit together.'

41

If Will had been planning to say it, there might have been a romantic dinner, flickering candlelight, a glass of wine, something like a speech rehearsed in the bathroom mirror. But he hadn't, so there was only one shared plate of Marmite toast and a ridiculous story of something that had happened at Mia's work that he'd never be able to remember afterwards but that had made them laugh uproariously, and her beautiful face with the sparkling eyes and a crumb on her lip. 'I love you.'

'What?' Her eyes widened, and she leant back against the sofa cushion.

Will held himself stock still. 'Sorry. That slipped out.'

'Say it again.'

'Really?'

She nodded slowly, leaning in again.

'Okay. Mia, I love you.'

She narrowed her eyes. 'How do you know you do?'

'Strange question. Not what I was hoping for.' Now he drew back, just a little, and his cheeks coloured slightly.

'I'm serious, Will. How do you know? Don't say you just do.'

'Okay.' He laughed nervously. 'Give me a minute here. This is big stuff. Have I blown it? Said it too soon?'

'I didn't say that.'

'But you don't necessarily believe me when I say it?'

She was looking at him with her big brown trusting eyes. He took her hands and held them tightly in his. 'Look, I don't want to rush you, Mia. I know you've had a crappy time. And I know that even if you hadn't had a crappy time where the bottom pretty much fell out of your world, we've only been seeing each other for a bit. I don't want to take advantage of you feeling vulnerable and overwhelm you with how I feel. I don't want to be the intense, crazy man who scares you away.'

She laid a hand on his shoulder. 'You won't scare me. Tell me more.'

'How much more, Mia?'

'As much as you've got.'

Will took a deep breath and exhaled in a whistle. 'So, I've been biting the three incendiary words back for weeks now. There have been so many moments when I've had to stop myself saying it out loud, but I've been saying it in my head for ages. And you say I can't say I just do, but, Mia, that's kind of the point. It's not transactional. It's not an analytical thing. It's a feeling. It's a groundswell of feeling. It's that sense of . . . peace. That doesn't sound exciting. Not flattering, maybe. But peace. Yes. That's it. I do, I'm afraid. I just know. It's *you*. You are her. You are for me. Best I can do.'

For a moment, she just stared at him. Started smiling, a smile that grew from shy and faint to a wide beam. She was still smiling broadly when she kissed him tenderly. 'I love you too.'

'Oh, in that case, I have more. So much more.'

She laughed now. 'Go on.'

'I want us to move in together on our own. Find a place that's just for us. With high ceilings and big windows and something green to look out on. I want to spend Sundays testing sofas in Loaf and cooking roast dinners with you. I want to learn to strip wallpaper and lay flooring and argue about paint colours with you, even if you're showing me ten colours that look exactly the bloody same.'

'You do?' She was delighted. She wriggled with joy, like a child.

'I do, but I know it's too soon.'

Mia made a mock-serious face. 'What else?'

'Okay. I want to sit on planes with you and hold hands when there's turbulence, and see all the places we want, all the sunsets, all the endless views, all the turquoise seas. I want to go to our friends' weddings and exchange knowing glances while they exchange vows. I want to talk about what names our children would have, and how many puppies would be too many.'

'Yeah. That's definitely crazy-intense-man territory.' She was teasing, though. 'More than two is too many, just FYI . . .'

'The point is, I think about our life together, Mia Bennett. I think about it all the time. Where we'll live. How we'll live. All the places we can go. I want to dance with you in our kitchen. I want us to have a song. I've got a list, by the way. I want to feed you ice chips and have you break the bones in my hand, squeezing while you have contractions.'

She laughed loudly now, and covered her face with her hands.

'Too far?'

'Yes! Way too far, you crazy, intense man.'

'Really?'

'No! I love all of it. Every single word.'

'Promise? You're not going to wake up in the morning and be totally freaked out?'

She thought for a moment. 'Nope. I like the picture you're painting, Will. I like it very much. Think you're stuck with me.'

Will let out the breath he'd been holding. 'Thank God.' She slid off the sofa into his lap, straddling him, and took his face in her hands to kiss him deeply.

Ruth padded out of her bedroom in her pyjamas and thick socks. She raised an eyebrow at them as she headed towards the kitchen.

Will took his hands from where they had been, and raised them in a gesture of surrender. 'Sorry. I thought you were out.'

'Clearly. Will you two, please, for the love of God, get a room? What am I saying? You have a damn room. Use it.'

They laughed, stifling the sound in each other's necks. 'About that flat . . .'

42

Natalie knew it would be the last time she saw him alone. Ever. She was determined of that, but she also knew it had to be face to face. She had to make him understand that it was over. To do that she also needed to make him understand that it hadn't been, for her, what it had for him. He needed her to do that for him. Too much was left unsaid and unexplained when she'd broken it off at the hotel. Undefined. It wasn't fair. She owed him clarity. She could see that now.

The night at Annie's party had been a catalyst for them both. But in such different ways. She'd ended it, yes, at the hotel that evening. But like an idiot she'd wanted him, all over again, at the wedding. She'd made a decision, but she'd betrayed herself with how seeing him had made her feel. This was different. This ended it, absolutely and irrevocably, for her. It had become, for her, about her family, and about Kit. About making up for all the hurt and about winning Kit back if she could – about repairing her family and her life the way Sylvia had the plate.

For Dom, she knew, it had been a different kind of junction. She'd learnt that from his messages. Texts and voicemails she had wanted to read. It felt like she was still cheating, reading them, but not on Kit, now – Dom never once mentioned him by name. On Sarah. The messages told of how he'd made up his mind he didn't love her. How he'd told her so. How he'd tried to let the children down gently. Of how he wanted a future with Natalie. Loved her. It amazed her that he would write those things with no encouragement at all from her. Lay himself so bare.

She had to make him stop. She could block him, she knew. She also knew that wouldn't stop him. She was afraid that if she did that, he'd start showing up. She had to tell him.

He'd wanted to meet her at the flat. There'd been a tense and terse exchange of messages. When she'd flatly refused to do that, he'd tried for a restaurant, or a pub, one evening. Outside. It needed to be outside. It needed to be cold and uncomfortable and public.

Park benches were where spies met to exchange information, furtively looking left and right before they sat, each at a far end, to speak quietly and efficiently before they sloped off again.

It wasn't that she didn't trust herself. The spell was broken. Shattered. It had begun ending, she knew now, the second it had started.

'Can I speak first? I need to say something to you, and I want to get it out,' he implored.

'Dom, I think l might know what you're going to say, and I just don't want to hear it.'

'Please, Natalie. Let me.'

She raised her hands. 'Okay.'

Dom took a deep breath. 'I wish I had met you first. Before you met Kit and before I met Sarah. Years ago. I wish I'd married you. If I'd met you first, I'd have wanted you instead. If I could choose you now, without hurting anyone, without making an enormous fucking mess, I would. I feel like I didn't know I was settling with Sarah because I hadn't met you. And I would go away with you now, if you agreed. I would leave everything. Start again with you.'

She shook her head. 'You're talking nonsense.'

'Why don't you believe me?'

'You don't even believe you. Not really.'

'What do you mean?'

'I think you're trying to make this something it never was, Dom. You and me – we're not so different. I think we both hate what we did. Hate the disloyalty, the unkindness. The people it makes us. Because we don't hurt people. And we have. And I think that you're trying to make this some big, grand love affair, because then it will have been worth what we did to the people we've hurt. The people we love. There might be nobility to it. But there isn't. That's not what it was.'

He just shook his head.

'So, yes, I'm not denying we had something. My mother would call it a glad eye. We fancied each other. Yes, we let ourselves indulge in stupid adolescent fantasies, and yes, we have to own the tawdry fact that when we were both a bit vulnerable for whatever reason we just gave in to them, Dom. To fantasies. And we had a dirty little affair.'

'No!' He looked wild, and he was almost shouting now. 'That wasn't what it was. It wasn't.'

Natalie forced herself to keep her voice low and calm. 'Yes. Yes, Dom. Yes, it was. I can't keep trying to convince you about this. I'm going back to my life now. My real life. I'm going to try my best to salvage what I can from the wreckage that you and I have made of it. I'm going to try to get Kit to trust me again, to look at me how he used to before **I** did this to us. And I'm begging you, if you have any real feeling for me, to leave me alone. Don't call me. Don't message me. Don't come to the places where you know I am. Just stay away from me. But be very clear. It's not because I don't trust myself around you. It's not because I'm afraid you can turn me. That *will never happen again*. Because I don't want you. I don't love you, Dom. I don't. I love Kit. And my life with Kit. I want Kit.'

Natalie stood up and walked away. She couldn't look at him. She'd had no choice. She'd had to close the door so firmly that there wasn't the slightest chink of light.

Winter

43

Sarah had forgotten that the supermarket would be crowded. It was Friday afternoon. There were queues at all the tills, even the self-service ones, and the aisles were full of mothers, babies in the front of their trolleys, accompanied by meandering and unaware children in their school uniforms, whining for treats, or trying to be helpful. She almost turned tail and went straight home. Except she knew the fridge was pretty much bare. She'd barely cooked in weeks. Cereal and milk for supper. It was the dinner of students or, at a push, exhausted new parents. She'd had it three times in the last week. Still, she wasn't eating it for breakfast. For years, she'd nagged and cajoled Mia into eating 'the most important meal of the day'. Mia would be wide-eyed if she could see her now. Not so much as a banana. She'd stood on the scales for the first time since Annie's this morning, while the shower ran hot. Down ten pounds. It hadn't raised so much as a smile, and the naked woman she forced herself to confront in the long mirror on the back of the door didn't look good. She was gaunt.

So, she'd made a promise to herself. Spoken it out loud to her own reflection. She'd go after school today. No excuses. She would shop, and when she got home, she'd cook. And she'd eat.

Her basket was full of things she liked. There was no one else at home whose tastes must be catered for. No one who hated anchovies or peas. She was stalled, now, in front of the big display of cut flowers and house-plants. She'd always loved cut flowers in the house. All her life. Even as a student on a tiny budget, she'd spent some on whatever blooms she could afford. Having a small jug of something bright and fragrant made even scuzzy student digs better. Her whole mood better. Daffodils dotted everywhere in March. Coral peonies, as many as she could justify in their short season, in April and May. Whatever she cut from the garden through the summer, and then the hothouse flowers in winter. At Christmas she'd fill her arms with amaryllis, red roses and eucalyptus stems. She'd done a course once, years ago, and she knew how to strip the stems, how to plan an arrangement, how to make a criss-cross top on a wide vase with tape to hold delicate stems in places. In another life, perhaps, she might even have been a florist.

She hadn't bought flowers in weeks. They hadn't matched her mood. There was no one to see them but her. And she was sleepwalking through life, so even she might hardly notice them. Today, she forced herself to choose. Reaching out, she picked up a bunch of orange roses. They were the small ones with no smell. They wouldn't open, fragrant and expansive, like the ones she grew at home. They were mean roses, really. But they were a start.

She turned towards the tills.

And that was when she saw Natalie. Christ. She hadn't

anticipated it and now it seemed obvious that she'd be there. Of course she was. Sarah had the oddest sensation. She felt as though she was standing stark naked in the middle of the crowded shop. She didn't know how long Natalie had been watching her, but she was walking towards her now. She seemed to be alone – at least Sarah couldn't see Arlo, or anyone else. She looked stylish and fresh, like she always did, a stack of bracelets on each arm, and pretty drops in her ears. Good hair, held back with the glasses Sarah knew she needed, now, to read labels.

She was close enough to speak. She put up her hand, and the bracelets made a familiar noise. Natalie looked as frightened and as horrified as Sarah felt.

'Sarah. Sarah . . . I . . .'

She knew she couldn't listen. Not here. Not now. She put the basket down, turned to drop the roses back into the bucket she'd taken them from, and walked away.

Natalie followed her to the door. 'Please, Sarah.'

She turned back once more, raising one hand as if she was trying to shield herself. She heard her voice, strident and fierce. 'No. No.' Then she walked away as fast as she could, almost breaking into a run.

She was shaking when she climbed into her car. She switched on the ignition and pulled out too fast. Behind her, someone honked angrily, and a woman with a push-chair shook her head at her. Sarah ignored them both and tried desperately not to cry as she changed gear, and forced herself to breathe slowly in and out as she drove out of the car park and home.

*

44

'Are you here because Flick asked you to be?'

Andrew smiled and put the two pints of beer he'd bought on the table. 'Only partly. Is it that obvious?'

Dom raised an eyebrow and lit a cigarette, then put his lighter back into his jeans pocket and took a deep drag. 'Not sure we've had a beer, the two of us, in the shadow of Waterloo station before. Not in the – what is it? – twenty odd years we've known each other.'

Andrew ignored his sardonic tone, and the truth of what he'd said. 'How are you doing, Dom? It's not just Flick who'd like to know.'

He gave a tight, false laugh. 'Oh. I'm peachy.'

Andrew took a drink. 'We don't have to talk about it. I can talk rugby, or Brexit, easily enough while I down this pint sharpish, if that's what you want.'

'Let's, though. Talk about it. I'd like to know what you think.'

'About what, precisely?'

'About the colossal shitstorm of my life. The steaming pile of crap I've landed myself in. Life imploded. My daughter's not talking to me, and I'm sure my son won't be either, once he finds out. I'm looking for a flat to rent, for Christ's sake, living out of a sodding duffel bag in a mate's spare room.'

'Whoa.' Andrew raised a hand. 'If I'd known this was a pity party, I'd have worn my party shirt.' It was an in-joke, although neither of them was laughing. He'd appeared once in a lurid rainbow-striped shirt. Paul Smith. Untucked. They'd all made fun of him – it was the least Andrew garment any of them had ever seen him in. Andrew was a symphony in navy blue and storm grey. Flick wore the colour in that family. Flick had rounded on them indignantly. 'I bought it, if you don't mind. It's for parties.' Henceforth it had been the party shirt, and he wore it ironically at least three times a year.

'Ouch. I asked for that.'

'What did you think would happen? Honestly? I mean, come on. You and Natalie would ride off into the sunset on a white charger and everyone would say, "Fair enough, she's hot," and be happy ever after for you?'

Dom squinted at him. 'Something like that.'

'You're dreaming. You're an old fool. You're a bloody cliché. It makes us all nervous, to be honest, mate. You're bringing us all into disrepute. Were you that unhappy, Dom, that you had to go after your friend's wife? Humiliate Sarah like that. Really?'

'He's not particularly my friend. He's someone I've spent time with.'

'When it suits you to say so. Is Phil not? Rupert? Am I not your friend?'

'Our wives are friends. Haven't we all spent the last twenty years going where they tell us to go, thinking what they think? Sleepwalking.'

Andrew was suddenly angry. 'For Christ's sake,

Dom. Listen to your bullshit. If that's been your life, that's on you. Don't feel the need to tar all of us with the same brush. Not me. I'm very much awake. I'm grateful every day for Flick and for the life we've made together. I lost one wife, mate. I actually watched her die. Did you know that? Not sure we ever covered that in the twenty-odd years we've apparently been pretending to be friends. I watched Phoebe's mum bleed to death while I stood against the wall and held a baby barely ten minutes old. Tends to cure the cynic in you, that kind of experience.'

For a moment there was silence. Dom looked shamefaced. 'I'm sorry. I find I'm saying that a lot these days.'

'What about Sarah? She didn't deserve that.'

'She didn't. You're right.' Dom sighed. 'But she didn't deserve to spend the next thirty years with a man who didn't love her, either.'

'You're not trying to make that sound noble, are you?' Andrew scoffed.

'No. Not noble. But am I wrong?'

Andrew sighed. 'Are you so sure you don't love her?'

Dom stubbed the cigarette out slowly in the ashtray. 'Crystal clear. I had a hideous moment of absolute clarity, Andrew. Completely distinct from the vague dissatisfaction with life that has plagued the last few years. That was easy enough to ignore. This was sharp and vivid. I wasn't looking for it. I promise you that.'

Andrew shook his head. 'Okay, then.'

'It isn't okay. I know that. I broke it all. Just me. It isn't the kids' fault or Sarah's. Sarah is . . . Sarah was a good wife. I do know that. It's me. I changed. I wanted more. Bloody Oliver Twist.' The hubris had deserted him. 'I wanted Natalie.'

'And now?'

'She doesn't want me. She wants Kit.'

'You're a bloody idiot.'

Dom almost laughed. 'Yeah. So. I'm guessing my name is mud with you lot.'

Andrew whistled through his teeth. 'You're top of the shit list. No surprise there, I'm sure.'

'And Natalie?'

'None of them are having much to do with her. No one really knows what's going on with her and Kit. They've all rallied around Sarah, of course.'

'Of course they have. That's the right thing. She's the injured party.'

'But you're all hurt.'

'And I don't know how to fix any of it. Mia and Dylan . . .' For the first time, his voice broke. 'My kids.'

Andrew didn't have an answer. For a while, they sat and drank their beer.

'I thought I'd feel relieved.'

'And you don't?'

'I don't feel anything much right now, if I'm honest with you. I feel numb.' He lit another cigarette.

Andrew had finished his pint. He looked at his watch. He tried to do it surreptitiously, but he knew Dom had seen. There were three trains an hour. Trains that took him to Flick, and his warm, loving home. It was cold. If they'd been inside, fair enough. Dom's damn smoking.

Andrew could hear Sarah's disapproving voice, the short tut sound she'd make.

'You need to make a move? It's okay.'

'I'm all right, if you want another drink.'

Dom laughed. Andrew was a lousy liar. 'You go. I'm shitty company.'

Andrew stood up awkwardly. 'Look, Dom. I don't know how any of this is going to play out. You might want to walk away from all of us. Maybe that's best. I'm just saying I think you're wrong about us. We *are* your friends. I think the others would agree with me. Keep in touch, huh?'

They both knew he probably wouldn't. That it was just a thing you said. Andrew held out his hand, and Dom took it, and they shook in an awkwardly formal, strangely final way. Then Andrew headed for the station and his life.

Dom looked down at his phone. Flicking through, he saw that Mia hadn't opened his most recent messages. It was too early to go back to where he was staying. His old university friend Steve had married much later than him – his kids were still school age. He didn't like to go back until they were in bed. He might be imagining the judgemental glances Steve's wife Stacy gave him, or the edge of tension in the voices they were using with each other, but he didn't think he was. He needed to sort something else soon.

He walked across Hungerford Bridge and, from there, along the Strand to Trafalgar Square and up towards Piccadilly. His desire to keep smoking was at odds with his desire to warm up. Cold won. He ducked into a place he vaguely knew, and took a seat at the long bar. He ordered a Negroni.

He'd thought it would be different. He'd really believed Natalie might come with him. He'd imagined a new life for them, in some detail. The places they'd go. The home they'd make. The nonsense of it embarrassed him now. He hadn't even factored in Arlo, he realized. Selfish bastard. Had he imagined Kit would keep him? That Natalie would give him up? He knew he was ridiculous.

Even if Sarah would have him, would he go back? It would be a lie, wouldn't it? He'd felt suffocated by the view of the rest of his life. Now he couldn't picture any of it. And it wasn't invigorating, and it wasn't exciting. It was humiliating. And it was frightening.

At the other end of the bar, two young women were drinking cocktails. They were brash, self-conscious types, spending more time looking around than talking, trying to catch the eye of one of the blokes at the tables behind them. He would never have been interested in them. Too obvious, too much make-up, too pleased with themselves. He could tell, though, that now they looked right past him.

For just a moment, he wondered what Sarah and Natalie would think of him, pathetic and invisible in a Mayfair bar on a weekday evening. He closed his eyes against the thought, and drained the Negroni in one.

45

Natalie was watching the ten o'clock news, trying to summon the energy to climb upstairs and fall into bed when her phone started vibrating next to her on the sofa. She never ignored it, but she wished she could. Please let it not be Dom. She literally had no other weapons in her arsenal for him. Please let it not be one of the kids with a problem. She hadn't the strength for it. She had never been so tired in her whole life. She woke up tired, and went downhill all day. She pulled her glasses down from the top of her head to read whatever her phone screen said, determined to ignore anything except a mayday call.

'Sarah' flashed on the screen. Your best friends were like Beyoncé in your phone: no need for last names. She threw the handset like it was a hand grenade. It kept ringing. Frantically, she pushed the button that declined a call, and it fell silent.

She stood up and paced. Her heart had raced instantly, and she knew if she looked in the mirror she'd have coloured up in red blotches across her chest. She didn't know whether Dom had gone home to Sarah. She had no idea what he might have told her.

The phone started ringing again. She picked it up, put it down again, seriously considered throwing it out of the window. She shook herself. For God's sake, Natalie.

Get a grip. 'Woman up.' That's what Temple would say. 'Woman up, Mum.'

It had always been inevitable that she'd have to face Sarah. She was never going to be ready.

She took a deep breath, and pushed the button that accepted the call. 'Hi, Sarah.'

For a glorious moment there was silence, and she thought Sarah had rung off. Then she heard her voice, faint and muffled. 'Natalie?'

'Yes. I'm here.'

'Natalie. What have you done to me?'

Sarah's voice was slightly slurred, but not necessarily like she was drunk. She was so seldom drunk. It was more like she was dazed.

'I'm sorry, Sarah. Like I said. I'm so very sorry.'

Sarah seemed to consider the apology. 'I was thinking about everything. And I wanted to ask you something.'

'What?' She knew she had to answer whatever question Sarah had.

Sarah exhaled loudly. 'Last spring bank holiday, when we were all at Annie's, you wore that red bikini. I'm sure you remember. I bloody do. That amazing red bikini. I was just wondering whether you wore that bikini for Dom. For my husband.'

Natalie had been pacing at speed up and down the carpet, but now she sank onto the nearest chair, like a deflated balloon. 'Oh, Sarah, no.'

Sarah's tone was surprised. 'You weren't plotting? Planning how you could seduce him?' She said the word theatrically, like Blanche DuBois.

'It really wasn't like that.'

'How was it, then? He hasn't told me, you see . . . details. You know how girls like details. Maybe you'll tell me. How was it?'

'Sarah. You know this isn't a good idea.' Perhaps she had been drinking after all. Natalie wished she hadn't answered. Now she felt she had to let Sarah say whatever she wanted to say to her.

'But sleeping with my husband was a good idea?'

'No.' Natalie shook her head, although Sarah couldn't see her. 'It wasn't. Of course it wasn't. You have no idea how much I wish that had never happened.'

'Come on, Nat. Apparently, you guys had a thing for each other for years. Years and years. Dom told me that much at least.'

Natalie struggled to explain. 'We had . . . there was – I don't know how to describe it. An attraction. A connection. Yes. There was. We never did anything about it.'

'That was good of you. What changed your mind? Bored at home?'

'Sarah. You don't sound like you.'

'I'm not me, Nat. Not any more. You're not you, either. We're none of us who we were, are we?' Her voice was very quiet.

Natalie wondered if she'd finished. 'Sarah?'

When she spoke again, her tone was almost normal. Almost chatty. 'You know, the other day I was in some shop in town. I can't remember which one. They were playing that Dolly Parton song. You know the one. "Jolene". I was particularly struck by one lyric. "Please don't take him just because you can." You know the one? Did you take him just because you could?'

'I haven't taken him.' She wanted to shout, *I made a mistake. I don't want him.* It wouldn't help, though.

'Oh, but you have, Natalie. Doesn't matter what you do with him now. He's not ours any more. He's not mine. So you have taken him.'

'I don't want him. Please listen to me.'

'What a waste.' Sarah laughed.

'I know I can't fix it between you and me. I've done irreparable damage.'

Sarah snorted. 'Yes. I think you have.' Her voice was almost wistful.

'I'm sorry.' It felt stupid to keep saying it. 'I don't blame you for hating me.'

'Ah, Nat. That's the thing. It would be easier if I did.'

Then the line went dead.

Natalie went into the kitchen and filled a glass from the tap. Her hand was shaking. She drank the water. She sat at the table, staring at her phone, wondering if Sarah would call back. Minutes passed. It was too late to ring her mother, and she was too knackered to speak, anyway. The tiredness she'd felt earlier had been rewired into something that was still exhaustion but she was utterly incapable of sleep. She laid her head in the crook of her arm on the table.

Eventually, when her neck started to ache, she forced herself to go upstairs. She pulled off her clothes, letting them fall onto the armchair next to her bed, and tugged on her pyjamas. In the bathroom, she brushed her teeth half-heartedly without looking in the mirror. She really hated herself tonight, and she didn't want to see her face. In his room, lit by the owl nightlight plugged into the wall, Arlo was sound asleep, curled towards the door, one foot out from under the duvet. His thumb had fallen out of his mouth, and the ear of his toy elephant was obscuring half his cheek. She smiled at her beautiful boy, envious of his deep, innocent sleep. Sighing, she pulled a bean bag from the corner over to the small rug by his bed, gently so she didn't wake him, and carefully pulled off the red fleece folded at the foot of the bed. He stirred slightly and she froze, but then he was still and peaceful again. She lay down on the floor next to him and closed her eyes.

46

Sarah had cooked Thai green chicken curry for dinner tonight: her speciality. It had been a family favourite for ages. They'd been to Thailand and Cambodia the year before Mia left for university. It was probably the best holiday they'd ever had together – certainly the grandest: Dom's father had died, leaving his son a portion of the proceeds from the sale of his house, and for once they'd decided not to be sensible with all of the windfall. It seemed like the right time, with Mia in the upper sixth. She'd be leaving in less than a year. At that stage, they hadn't understood that the leaving involved a fair amount of returning. It had felt like a last chance. They'd spent a few days in the incredible buzz and energy of Bangkok, then flown to Siem Reap to visit the temples at Angkor Wat, top of Dom's list of places to see before he died. Dylan, around fifteen then, and quite a Kevin the teenager, had been deep in a Tomb Raider phase, and he'd been beside himself with excitement at the spooky jungle temple – the one where nature had overtaken entirely. It was like they'd got him back, for a glorious little while, from monosyllabic adolescence.

They'd ended the trip with a few days at a swanky resort inside the Bay of Thailand – the hotel had run cooking courses and she and Mia had learnt how to make *nasi goreng, pad thai* and *tom yum goong* while Dom and Dylan had spent so long swimming and snorkelling that she joked they'd grow webbed feet. She'd learnt to make the chicken curry from scratch there too. Making it now seemed almost to transport her back to the happiness of the trip – those lazy, indulgent days of water drunk from fresh coconuts, and dominoes played by the pool. It was also delicious. She could do it plain, almost with her eyes closed, or fancy. Tonight, she was doing the fancy version, with the coconut sticky rice, smashed miso cucumber and radish salad, and prawn crackers on the side. A high-days-and-holidays version, requested whenever exam results, or job interviews, or league-finals matches called for a celebration. She usually loved cooking it, the process of making the spice paste, mixing the marinade, slicing vegetables into almost translucent slivers.

Now it felt almost masochistic to be preparing it for this evening. She almost wanted to laugh. Funny how close tears and laughter were. Did this really count as a family occasion? There was certainly nothing celebratory about it. She was dressed up too – under her apron, she was wearing a silk dress. Matching underwear, for God's sake. When had she last done that? The table was laid – the rectangular one in the dining room, not the round one in the kitchen – with napkins, and wine glasses, as if she was planning a dinner party. What the hell had she done it all for?

Because it was a big night. A momentous occasion. It was important.

And now the 'guests' were all there. Dylan had been

due home anyway. Term had almost ended, and he'd handed in the big assignment he'd been working on for the last couple of weeks, so he had been planning to leave a few days early. He'd called that week, and said he might go with some mates to another friend's house – somewhere in Yorkshire – for a few days. She'd asked him to come home first, just for the weekend, on a promise of clean laundry, keeping her voice light. He must have heard something in her tone, though, because he agreed without arguing. He'd drive up on the Monday, he mused. No worries.

That was very Dylan. He'd looked at his parents – both uptight in their own way – and taken the line of least resistance, almost hippie-like in his geniality. Very different from his sister, who had her mother's tendency to plan and organize. He always got himself home, and in that respect he was also quite distinct from her. Mia had never taken herself to and from university – except for the odd weekend mid-term. Each journey had required an obscenely full car-load – clothes, toiletries, fairy lights and bean bags. With Dylan, Sarah and Dom had gone once at the start of his first year, more because they felt the need to settle him than anything else, and once when he took up a tenancy in the summer before his second year. Even then, the car hadn't been full. His room was almost monastic, his wardrobe a rotating combination of three or four pairs of jeans, hoodies and some sports stuff. And not a milk frother or twenty-four-aperture photo frame in sight. He had bought a huge khaki sack thing from an army-surplus store and gone back and forth on the train with it. That independence was very much part of his schtick. It amazed her. He'd been a clingy toddler, and quite a sensitive little boy. It had taken some getting used to, his lone-wolf persona. She missed him.

It was the right thing to do, to talk to them together. And that was 75 per cent of why she was doing it. The other quarter wanted to see Dom suffer. To see him diminished in the eyes of his children. She wasn't proud of it, but she did. She wanted to see him squirm in front of them. She'd never thought of herself as a vindictive person, but he deserved it. Mia and Dylan would be hurt either way: she couldn't protect them from this, because it was happening.

She knew Mia had wanted to speak to Dylan. She'd begged her not to. He'd be home in less than a month, she said. Mia thought it was risky – everyone had seen what happened at the party, but she let herself be persuaded. If Dylan had heard anything since then, he hadn't said so. Their communication had been exactly the way it normally was since Annie's party: Sarah texted him once or twice a week, and he responded relatively monosyllabically, compensating for the lack of information with XXX at the end of a short message. Once a week he called – usually at the weekend, when he was walking back from football practice. She kept the chat light and inconsequential. He never asked for Dom, so there was no need to lie about his whereabouts. Dom knew she wanted him to get through term without being disrupted, and weirdly, she trusted him not to go against her wishes on that. She had no idea how much or how little the two of them spoke. She thought mostly it was sport talk, or the exchange of puerile humour. Dylan loved his dad, she knew, but he still came to her for serious stuff.

Mia wanted to bring Will. She didn't ask. She announced that he'd be coming. At first Sarah had hated the idea. Her pride was already so bruised. But she didn't want to say no to Mia. If Mia wanted him there, Sarah needed to get over her own feelings about it. Then she reasoned that he'd be a civilizing presence. The memory of Kit's punch was still fresh. It horrified her to have been involved in something so . . . rough. She imagined Mia told Will everything anyway. And she was so grateful to him for the way he'd cared for her daughter since it had all happened. She knew Mia had refused to talk to her father in the aftermath of Annie's party. Perhaps she had by now, but Sarah hadn't asked. It wasn't fair.

Dylan arrived in the late afternoon, depositing a pile of washing from the khaki bag on the utility-room floor, and heading straight upstairs for an unfeasibly long shower. She always forgot how long a twenty-year-old boy could spend in the bathroom. She forgot how tall he was too. A good five or six inches above her, these days. In her mind, he was still her little boy, but he could easily lift her, and she had to tiptoe to kiss his cheek.

Mia and Will came at six, when she'd invited them. Will had driven them both. They'd probably dropped in at Annie and Rupert's beforehand. Mia had brought her flowers and Will handed her a bottle of wine. It was still strange to see them together – to think of them as an item. They looked good, though. Will was so much like Rupert. He was a little stiffer and more formal than normal Will, as if he was on probation with her, although she had known him most of his life, and she found that nervousness endearing. It meant he cared. She remembered him as a little boy: he'd been earnest and kind, the least boisterous of Annie's trio, perpetually with a cricket bat in his hand. She'd dug out a sweet photograph of him and Mia, crabbing at the beach, in matching striped terry-towelling ponchos. Will had evidently taken her bucket from her while she jumped across a stretch of water, and the picture caught her, knees bent, in mid-air, Will smiling at her, squinting against the sun. She'd sent it to Mia. Now she poured the three of them a drink, and the kids sat at the kitchen table while she fiddled with things at the counter. Everything was ready.

'So it's true . . .' Dylan appeared in the doorway, his voice low and sinister. 'You and my sister.'

Will looked vaguely scared until Dylan laughed, and slapped his shoulder. 'Your face, man.'

Mia giggled. 'Who told you, Dyl? Mum?'

Sarah raised her hands. 'Not me!'

'I think it was maybe Louis. Liam? Can't remember.'

'And . . .' Mia tilted her head.

Dylan helped himself to a prawn cracker from the big bowl. 'Bit incestuous, but go for it.'

'Not you too!' Will protested. 'I already spent some considerable time and effort convincing your sister that we are *not* actually siblings. Do I have to give you the same spiel?'

Dylan took a beer out of the fridge. 'I'm totally joking. You kids go for it.'

'It's all totally legal and legit. Our parents are mates. We spent time together growing up. That's literally it. You could get something going with one of the other girls. Jasmine? Zoë? Mia could put in a good word for you.'

Dylan grimaced. 'You're all right. I'll leave it to you childhood sweethearts.'

'Shut up.' But Mia looked pleased.

'Where's Dad?' Dylan asked, as if he was just now realizing Dom wasn't there.

Mia shot Sarah a look.

Before she had to decide how to answer, Dom's car turned into the driveway. The light from the headlamps briefly illuminated the hall, where she hadn't closed the curtains.

'That's him now. There's the car.'

Dylan wandered into the hall. Kids could be so gloriously incurious, Sarah thought. She heard Dom greet his son. The backslap of their manly hug. She took a deep breath, and gripped the counter, watching her knuckles turn white with the pressure.

Mia had come over to where she was standing. She stroked her arm gently. 'You okay, Mum?'

She nodded briskly. 'I'll be fine, love.'

'Are you sure it's okay that I'm here, Sarah?' Will sounded anxious. She squeezed his arm across the counter. 'It's fine, Will. I find it's surprisingly okay.'

374

'*I*'m glad you're here.' Mia took his hand. 'Stop saying "fine", Mum. Nothing about it's fine. I've got you.'

Sarah smiled at her gratefully, then took off her apron, and laid it on the counter. She took a long drink from her glass.

Dom looked good. She hated him, for a moment, for not looking tired or tearful, or just slightly unkempt and uncared-for. He'd had his hair cut. She didn't recognize the sweater he was wearing. How odd. He hadn't shopped for clothes without her in decades. He hated shopping.

He kissed her hello, and she let him, because Dylan was there, although he wasn't really watching now. The kiss hit her cheek, dry and quick, but his hand went to her hip in a familiar gesture, the way it had done a thousand times. She shrugged it off. She couldn't bear his hand on her. 'Just in time,' she said, in a *Stepford Wives* voice, high-pitched and highly strung. 'Dinner's ready.'

She'd rehearsed how the conversation would go, over and over, in her head, on the long nights when she couldn't sleep. Couldn't stay asleep. She fell asleep easily, as though she'd run a marathon, only to wake in the small hours. She knew how she wanted it to go, this awful conversation. She'd make him say it. Now, though, she was surprised to realize that she wasn't quite as bitter in real life as she felt in her head. Or maybe she was just being a mother, programmed to protect her children, however old they were.

She'd thought maybe they'd finish the meal, but it was, she found, completely unbearable to be sitting with them all, in this room, in this house, eating this meal that normally transported them to a happy time and place, everything seemingly normal, habitual, when in reality nothing was normal and never would be again.

She put down her fork and coughed. She hadn't a clue where to start.

On her left, Mia also downed tools. She put out her hand, and Sarah took it.

Dylan smirked. 'Are we doing a "Kumbaya" or something? Have we started saying grace since I was last home?'

'Shut up, Dyl,' Mia reproved him.

Sarah, suddenly, badly did not want Dom to say the words. 'We need to talk to you.'

Dylan looked instantly frightened. 'What is it? Is someone ill?'

Sarah couldn't bear the expression on his face. Words spilt out. 'No, darling. No one's ill. I'm sorry. We don't mean to scare you. Your dad and I, we've split up.' It really was that simple, Sarah thought. She hadn't said it aloud many times. The words sounded silly. As if she was a fifth-former after a fight at a dance. Damn him – he had made her so foolish. She didn't trust herself to look at Dom. Beside her, Mia's eyes had filled with tears. She saw Will reach under the table to touch her, and it was almost painful to see that kindness, that caring between them.

Dylan struggled to digest the information. He looked from one end of the table to the other, his mouth open. 'No! What? You're getting a divorce?'

Sarah was taken aback. 'We haven't – we haven't

exactly talked about that. No hard and fast decisions have been made yet.'

'So you could get back together?' He sounded anguished. Angry.

'I didn't mean that. I don't think so, sweetheart. I'm sorry. That's not going to happen.' She couldn't look at Dom.

For a long moment, no one spoke. 'But I don't understand it. You were good. Things were good.'

She tried to take his hand, but he pulled it away. 'Well, they aren't any more. You don't always know what's going on, love.'

'I know that! I'm not an idiot.' He sounded incredulous, his voice rising high.

Dylan was agitated. Sarah hadn't expected him, somehow, to take it like this. What had she expected?

From the other end of the table, Dom cleared his throat and spoke now, his voice tremulous. 'It's me, Dylan. My fault. I'm sorry.'

Mia glowered at him. Sarah felt an unexpected flicker of gratitude.

Will flushed, the rash travelling from where his shirt buttons started up his neck. He abruptly pushed his chair back from the table, not meeting anyone's gaze. 'I'm going to step out.' He touched Mia's shoulder. 'I'll be right next door.' She smiled up at him, and nodded. He shut the door behind him.

'What the fuck, Dad?'

'Don't swear, Dylan.' It was a reflex, the correction. But it sounded ridiculous to all of them.

'Seriously?' Dylan's voice dripped with sarcasm.

'I've been unfaithful to your mother.' So old-fashioned. 'I had an affair. She asked me to leave. Quite understandably. And so I left.'

Dylan stood up suddenly. His chair tipped back and fell against the wall. He picked it up, but it had left a long, shallow indentation in the paintwork. For some reason, the name of the paint colour came into Sarah's mind: 'Setting Plaster'. She remembered laughing with an incredulous Dom about how absurd it was to pay a decorator a fortune to paint a wall of fresh plaster the colour of . . . plaster. She couldn't stop staring at the mark.

'You cheated on her, Dad?'

Dom nodded. He looked ashamed. It didn't give Sarah the frisson of pleasure she might have imagined, after all. She just felt very, very sad.

'Oh for Christ's sake, Dad. You idiot. You sleaze.' His breath caught in his throat. 'How could you?' His voice broke.

Please don't cry, Sarah thought. I cannot bear it if you cry. My boy.

He rounded on his sister now. 'And you Mia? You don't look shocked. I guess you knew all about this?'

'Only recently, Dyl. I promise. Mum didn't want to upset you while you were finishing the term. That's why she didn't tell you. It's not a phone-call kind of thing. She wanted you to come home before you found out.'

Dylan rounded on his father again. 'Did you get caught?' It seemed an odd question, almost as if Dylan was trying to solve a difficult puzzle.

'I didn't confess.' An odd answer. There'd be time, Sarah supposed. Perhaps Mia would tell him what had happened. She hoped she wouldn't have to – hoped he didn't fixate on details. It wouldn't help. And she would know.

There was a long pause.

'So are you leaving Mum to be with this other person, then?' He spat out the words angrily.

Dom hesitated. Then, 'No. I'm not.' The sadness in his voice was like a blow to Sarah's ribs. It seemed clear to her now that leaving her to be with Natalie was what he had wanted.

Natalie had told her the truth. She'd turned him down.

Just as quickly, she let it go. She almost felt it flow out of her. Who cared? She heard herself laugh and she sounded like a crazy person. It wasn't in the slightest bit funny. She felt 105 years old, so exhausted that she doubted her ability to put one foot in front of another, to pick up the plates of uneaten dinner and scrape them into the bin.

Dylan slumped into his chair, staring at his plate, unable to look at either of his parents.

'Who was it with?'

Another long pause. Then Mia answered so neither of them had to. He'd find out. 'With Natalie.'

His incredulity made his lip curl, and his voice an ugly falsetto. 'Marley's mum?'

Dom nodded.

'One of Mum's best friends?'

'Dylan, I –'

379

Dylan raised a hand to stop his father. Smashed it down angrily, so the plates and glasses on the table shook. 'Wow. Wow. You complete bastard. I don't want to hear it. I don't want to hear anything else right now, Dad. I don't even want to be in this room with you.'

He stood up again, and went to the door Will had closed. As he opened it, he rounded on Dom, as though he wanted to hit him, his hand curled into a fist. Sarah put her hand to her mouth. Please no. But the rage was warring on his face with something softer and more vulnerable, and the fist loosened. 'How *could* you?' and then he was gone. They heard his heavy footfall on the stairs, and his bedroom door slam. Then the dull thud of angry music.

Mia picked up her wine glass, and laughed bitterly. 'That went well.'

'Mia . . .' Dom implored.

'You know what, Dad? I'm sure there are a lot of things you want to say. Truthfully, though, I just don't want to hear any of it tonight, any more than Dylan does. I've had more time to think about it than he has. He's shocked. He's angry, and he has every bloody right to be. You've fucked us all over, Dad. Not just Mum. This whole family. Our lives. All our lives. Me. I was *living* with Stella, for God's sake. I mean, how exactly do you think that is for me? For us? Most of all, though, whatever it feels to us as a family, you did it to Mum. What in the hell were you thinking? You're a loser.'

Dom winced, and opened his mouth to speak, but said nothing.

'But you're my dad, and I know that. We *will* talk. We will try to find a way through this. Just not now. Don't dare ask for it now. I'm not ready to be reasonable with you. I don't want to try to understand. And I cannot imagine forgiving you. Right now, you just need to know that I'm Team Mum, all the way.' Her eyes were bright and fierce, and her tone brooked no argument. 'You've made your bed, Dad. You're going to have to lie in it now.'

And, Sarah realized, there was not the remotest mite of pleasure in it at all. Dom looked defeated. She had been wrong, earlier, she realized, when she thought he looked good. He looked smaller, now. Older. He looked ashamed. Close to tears. And completely alone. And there was no pleasure in it. There was only hurt and damage.

Dom put down his napkin by his place setting. 'I'll go.' He stood up slowly. Neither of them tried to stop him.

Sarah and Mia sat at the table and listened to the sound of the front door opening and closing again, heard the noise of Dom's car starting, and then leaving. And then it was quiet, apart from Dylan's faint soundtrack. It felt odd, like a bad, miserable play – Dylan up in his room, Will anxiously waiting in the sitting room, Dom gone. Sarah looked at the table. Five platefuls of uneaten food. Sighing, she picked up Dylan's, and started to scrape the chicken and sauce onto her own plate. 'Such a waste.'

'Stop, Mum. Let me do that, please.'

'No. I'll do it.'

Mia was insistent. 'Will can help me.'

'It's such a mess.'

They both knew she wasn't talking about the remnants of the meal. Mia slid the fork out of her mother's fingers, laying it on the tablecloth. 'Sssh, sssh . . .' She stood up and moved to Sarah's side, her arms closed around her mother's shoulders and she rocked her gently. Roles reversed. How many times had Sarah rocked and shushed and consoled Mia, as an infant, as a child, as a teenager? Comfort sought, comfort given.

While Mia and Will stacked the dishwasher, Sarah went upstairs and knocked gently on Dylan's door. 'It's me. Mum. Can I come in?'

'Okay.'

The contents of the khaki bag were strewn everywhere. Dylan's wet towel lay on the floor. It was comfortingly normal. Two hours earlier the room had been immaculate.

Dylan lay on top of his covers, facing away from her. He was too long for the bed. He didn't turn over, just shuffled a little nearer to the wall, to make room for her, in an unspoken invitation.

'I'm sorry, honey. I didn't know how to tell you. Maybe I got it wrong. Perhaps I should have driven up and told you when it was just us.'

'Why are you apologizing? This is all on Dad.'

'It isn't, you know.'

'What do you mean?'

She ruffled his hair. 'You're very young, love. You still see life in absolutes. Black and white. Right and wrong. It isn't quite like that.'

'I can't believe you're defending him.'

'I'm not. I'm furious with him. I'm heartbroken. I'm just saying that marriages are complicated. I'm not sure it can be a hundred per cent one person's fault when they go wrong. I don't think it works like that.'

'I don't know about any of that. But cheating is cheating, Mum.'

'You're right there. I'm not defending him for that. I hate it. But he's your dad.'

Dylan rolled over to face her. 'I don't want to see him.'

She nodded, understanding. 'You will, though. And that's okay. He won't stop being your dad. Ever.'

Dylan sat up, and let her hug him. She thought he might be crying in her arms, but she didn't want to draw attention to it. They'd all cried.

'What's going to happen? Are we going to move? Will you be all right, you know, for money and stuff?' Thoughts were tumbling out of him.

'Sssh.' She stroked his back. 'My darling boy. It'll be all right. I don't have all the answers yet. But I don't want you worrying about those things.'

Eventually, he sniffed hard, and whispered, 'I'm so sorry, Mum.'

She kissed the top of his head. 'Me too, love. Me too.'

47

'I've never been here in winter before, Annie. It's a whole different kind of lovely.' Georgie was looking out of the kitchen window, across the front lawn.

It had been dark, and very, very cold when they'd arrived at Annie's Dorset house last night. The four had agreed to come in just one car, and since Vanessa had been held up at work, it had been after seven when Flick picked up the last of them, and after ten when they'd pulled in. Annie's 'lovely lady in the village' had come in to turn on the heating, but there was still a chill around the edges that made the thick duvets and Welsh blankets on the beds very welcome. They'd all been tired, so they'd lingered in the kitchen just long enough for a hot drink before they got into bed.

The early night made for an early start, although Georgie had been up first. Now Annie and Vanessa had padded down to the kitchen in thick socks in search of tea. Flick's room was on the ground floor and they could hear the shower running. There'd been a heavy frost overnight, and the grass was white, but the sky was cobalt blue, and the sun was shining. It made everything from the lawn to the cobwebs in the window frames sparkle magically.

'I sometimes think I like it best at this time of year.'

Annie joined Georgie by the window. 'It's so laid-back and cosy.'

It was Annie's house, but it had been Flick's idea, hashed out over the phone a week or two ago. They all felt oddly bruised, she knew, by what had been going on. They'd been moving carefully in each other's orbits, dazed by the revelations and high emotion of events. Flick thought they needed to reset, and Annie had readily agreed. They'd invited Sarah, of course, or Annie had, but she'd said thank you but no, she couldn't face it. Not yet. That she was planning to go for a long walk with Mia. And, in truth, each of them was a little relieved that she wasn't there and they didn't need to walk on eggshells. No one said so – it felt disloyal – but the atmosphere in the car last night had been lighter and less tense, even though most of them were tired after a full week's work.

Now, after a good sleep, waking up somewhere different, they were all relaxed. They pottered around making drinks and toast and enjoying the nothingness. Even so, it was almost impossible not to think about Sarah and Natalie and what had gone on.

'Do you think it was going on when we were here?'

'I don't know,' Annie said. 'I'd forgotten, until my party, but then, weirdly, I just remembered that they went to town together, didn't they? On Saturday morning. To buy bread. I didn't think anything of it. Don't know if it means a thing.'

'It feels like ages ago, that weekend. More than six months, at least.'

'Everything before the party seems ages ago, right? A different lifetime.'

'I still can't believe Kit hit Dom. In front of everyone.'

'It was not an edifying spectacle.'

'At least Dom didn't hit him back. They'd have been like Hugh Grant and Colin Firth in *Bridget Jones*.' Flick sniggered.

'Don't,' Georgie reproached her.

'Oh, come on. Sarah's not here, or Natalie. We don't have to be so po-faced, do we?'

'He deserved it. I know violence is never excusable but, my God, if I'd been Sarah, I'd have wanted to belt him myself.'

Annie put a finger to her lips. 'Sssh. They're all friends of ours. Things are never going to be the same as they were before for any of us. I don't find it all that funny.'

'And I'd rather not talk about it at all. Just for a while. Can't we just take a break from it?'

'Good idea.'

'Seconded. Now get your arses in the shower so we can go out.'

After that, they were a little giddy with not having to talk about it. Annie suggested Sherborne, for a change. They spent the morning browsing the antiques shops and independent boutiques. Flick talked Georgie into a red jumpsuit, suspecting that she wouldn't wear it unless Flick showed up at her house and talked her into it all over again, and Vanessa found a piece of pottery she thought just might be Bernard Leach for a total bargain in a musty rabbit-warren dealers' market. Annie had phoned ahead and booked lunch in a trendy pub with good write-ups and a roaring fire, and over the meal, they chatted easily about what they'd been reading, and watching, about Harry and Meghan and *Line of Duty*. Then they looked at photographs of Phoebe and James's honeymoon, and the new flat they were hoping to move into. Even Georgie blathering on about Liam felt good.

They filtered easily through the details of each other's lives, as they always had, studiously avoiding the subject of Natalie and Sarah. Talked about Vanessa's new extension, which none of the others had known was happening, and how her neighbours had objected. How her youngest, Callum, was planning a volunteering trip to Costa Rica next summer. It had been ages, they realized, since they'd caught up on what the kids were doing. Annie spoke about how happy Will and Mia seemed together, and Georgie said that she wished Liam would find someone. He hadn't had a girlfriend since his second year at university, she reminded them, and she thought he was losing his nerve. Flick nudged her and said it was like riding a bike, and she shouldn't worry.

Afterwards, full of food and bonhomie, they walked as far as the deli at the end of the high street to buy cheese and nibbles for the evening, croissants and pains au chocolat for the morning.

The sky had clouded over. By the time they got home, it was colder and dark, and a grey mizzle in the air frizzed their hair, chilling their bones. Annie put *The Notebook* on the DVD player in the sitting room, and they all curled up to watch Noah and Aly. Annie was audibly sobbing by the time the end credits rolled. Vanessa smiled and put her arm around her on the ancient Knole sofa. 'You're so soppy. How many times have you seen it?'

Annie laughed ruefully. 'Oh, about a dozen. Once a summer, for sure. Can't usually get anyone to watch it with me, though. Rupert is more of a *Die Hard* man.'

'Oh, God. Twelve times? Really?' Flick groaned, and switched off the set. 'I think that's probably the first time I've seen it all the way through. She makes advanced Alzheimer's look pretty glamorous, that Ellen Barkin, huh?'

Annie frowned. 'Best film ever. Such a gorgeous story. Love beareth all things, believeth all things, hopeth all things, endureth all things.' Annie blew her nose hard. 'Gets me every time.'

Later, when they'd all changed into their pyjama bottoms and sweatshirts, they sat around the table in the kitchen picking at the food Annie had laid out and drinking a couple of bottles of what Rupert always referred to as his 'not unpleasant' red from the cellar.

'Phil slept with someone else.' Georgie spoke to no one in particular and with no preamble. She'd been quiet since the film ended, unusually so, even for her. It burst from her now, louder than her voice normally was, as though she'd just found the courage to say it, and had to speak before she lost her nerve. Her hands were folded in her lap, and she couldn't look any of them in the eye at first.

They all froze. No one spoke for a long moment, and the silence in the room was strange. Then Flick blew out her cheeks and exhaled. 'Christ.'

Annie looked like she might cry.

Georgie, realizing they'd misunderstood, held up her hand. 'Not just now. Sorry. Dramatic. I didn't mean to be. Not recently. This was years ago.'

'What are you talking about?'

'I'm saying Phil had an affair.'

'I can't believe it. Phil?' Annie's tone was incredulous, confused.

'When?' Flick asked.

Georgie raised her eyebrows. 'After Liam was born, and before the breast cancer.'

'Shit.'

'You never said anything! We were friends, then. Weren't we?'

Georgie nodded emphatically. 'We were. I didn't find out for a long time. A long time after it ended. And no. I never said.'

'Why?'

Georgie shrugged. 'Pride. Loyalty. Humiliation.'

'Oh, love . . .'

'We hadn't been friends for that long, truthfully. I'd tell you now.' She smiled at them. 'We weren't that close. At least, I was afraid we might not be. You know, close enough for the washing of dirty linen. Besides, everyone else seemed so happy together. I supposed I was just too embarrassed.'

'I hate that.' Annie looked genuinely crestfallen.

Georgie smiled warmly at her friend. 'It's fine. I'm saying now. And I'm saying because we got past it, didn't we? It can be got past. That's my point. If we can, then maybe they can. All of them.'

Flick sucked in her breath sharply, then decided against speaking.

Annie looked from Flick to Georgie. 'Will you . . . can you . . . do you want to tell us about it? Sorry. I'm being nosy.' She took a deep breath. 'I mean, if it isn't too painful. You don't have to.'

'I started this conversation. It's fine. I want to. It *is* still painful. I suppose it always will be. You forgive but you don't forget. You don't forget any tiny detail of it, what happened, how it felt.'

'I know I couldn't.'

'Forgive?'

'Forgive.'

'You could, though. If you really wanted to. That's the point. That's the part you're in charge of. You control it. It was all a bit of a cliché. That embarrassed me too – it was all so soap opera. So low rent. It was a younger girl – someone from Phil's work – and it started at a sales conference, some swanky country-house hotel. God. Still makes me cringe. So fucking óbvious.' Georgie never swore. A flush moved up her neck.

'Did you know her?'

'Not really. We'd met. At the Christmas do. She hadn't been especially memorable, to be honest. Her name was Ashleigh. Ashleigh with an IGH. She actually said that, when we were introduced, as if I was ever going to need to write it down. She was about ten years younger than him – an office junior. She wasn't particularly gorgeous, or even sexy, I didn't think.' She snorted. 'What did I know? Or crazy bright, or vivacious or funny.' Her voice trailed off, and she stared into the middle distance. 'I think it was that she just wasn't me.'

'Oh, Georgie.'

She waved a hand in front of her face. 'Oh, I'm all right. The thing is, I had a lot of time to think about it. It wasn't all his fault.'

Flick's fierceness was undiminished. 'I'm sorry, but I just don't buy that crap for a second. Of course it was his fault. It was Dom's fault, and it was Natalie's fault.'

Georgie was emphatic: 'You're wrong, Flick. You're being too simplistic.'

'Well, I couldn't get past it. I know I couldn't.' Annie's face was haunted by the very idea of Rupert cheating. It seemed so unlikely to all of them. Then again, hadn't Phil seemed an impossible adulterer until five minutes ago? Hadn't they all, until they'd found out about Dom? The foundations were shaking.

'I'd cut Andrew's bloody balls off. He'd be out of the house so quick he'd leave skid marks. I couldn't go through it again. Couldn't. Wouldn't.'

'Oh, God, I'd almost forgotten it had happened to you.'

'Well, it did. And I'll tell you something – it wasn't my fault my husband chose to put his penis into another woman when I was pregnant with our child. It really, absolutely, totally wasn't my fault at all.'

'Flick,' Annie pleaded.

Flick stretched her arms, and her tone softened. 'Sorry, Georgie. I'm not talking about you.'

'We're all different. The marriages – they're all different too. And so are the affairs. That's sort of my point. I think you have to decide whether it's the kind you can get through, or not.'

'So how did you? Get through?'

'Like I said, in our case, and I'm only talking about us, I realized it wasn't all his fault and I confronted that. We'd had a shitty few years. We'd got married in 1989, and we'd started trying for a baby in 1992. Didn't panic, not at first – I wasn't even thirty. But a year went by so, you know, you begin to wonder. You turn thirty. Your friends start having babies. You go to the doctor to get checked out. And then they tell you you're not being silly or impatient. That there actually is a problem. Even then, you don't immediately freak out. I didn't, at least. I had this childlike faith in the doctors. They had to know how to fix it. One round of IVF, and I'd have my baby. I really, really believed that. But it didn't happen. And then we were locked into this cycle – this extraordinary loop. You've no idea how consuming it becomes when you want a child and you can't have one. It – it dehumanizes you, somehow. And in other ways it superhumanizes you. I know that's not a word. Part of it is all the science and the medical stuff. It's incredibly invasive and exhausting and impersonal. Everything about you, about that most private part of you, becomes public property – your sex-life, everything. Forget romance. Forget spontaneity. Forget sex being about sex. Let alone about love. And, God, the hormones. I wasn't even really me any more. You feel like you're a piece of meat. A science experiment. They're amazing, the doctors and nurses, and even the damn receptionists – they're mostly all nice and compassionate and sympathetic – but that is how it feels, even as they're being kind to you. And then there's the other side. You're obsessive. You really, really try not to be. But you're just faking. Because everything is about babies. The babies in your life – and they're every-fucking-where – the babies in your head. And you're not you and he's not him. Not how you were before.

'And then the miracle happens. There's a baby. And the weeks and months pass and there's still a baby. It should end there. You got what you wanted. You got your dream.' She laughed. 'But I knew I was only going to get this one baby. And it had taken so long, and cost us so much to get him. I couldn't relax. I couldn't put him down. I couldn't leave him alone to sleep. I was ter-rified to walk away from him. Phil bought one of those mats that you put under the mattress in the cot, the Moses basket, whatever – the kind with the alarm that goes off if the baby stops breathing.'

'We had one of those.' Vanessa nodded.

'Didn't make any difference. I used to hold a hand mirror up to his face to see if I could see breath on it. Every night, at least once. With a torch. Eventually, Phil insisted he go into the nursery, out of our room. I cried all night. Didn't sleep.'

Annie smiled sympathetically. 'I think we all had a bit of that, the worry. They're so small, so vulnerable.'

'With me, though, it just never wore off. If anything, it just got worse as Liam got older. There was so much in the world that could hurt him. I anticipated disaster all the time. He'd fall, he'd run out in front of a car, he'd choke on a sodding cherry tomato. There were a million ways I could lose him and I couldn't stop thinking about all of them. When bad things happened to kids and it was on the news, it was almost . . . it was almost like it was inevitable, you know, that something like that would happen to Liam.'

'You needed help. That's catastrophizing. It sounds like depression.' Annie shook her head.

'I know that now. I think it was. God, I kick myself for not talking to someone. I felt this huge guilt – I'd got what I'd wanted so badly, and I couldn't enjoy it because I couldn't shake off the dread. Phil tried – he really tried – to get me to go to the GP, or find a counsellor. I thought it was disloyal of him, unsupportive. I kept saying, because I kept trying to believe, that it would go eventually – the awful fear. And I suppose I made him feel he wasn't doing enough to understand me, or to help me.'

'And did it? Go?'

Georgie looked at them frankly. 'You tell me?'

They laughed fondly.

'Yep. Exactly. Not completely, not to this day. I'm the original helicopter parent.'

'You are shocking.' This was Flick. 'With the texts and stuff.'

'I know!' Georgie sat up, ramrod straight. 'I'm Georgie. I can't cut my apron strings.'

'You're not saying, are you, though, that that was why Phil cheated on you?'

'I am. I was hell.'

'Don't you dare say it was your fault. You drove him into the arms of another woman with your psycho behaviour?'

'I'm not saying that. I'm just saying I understand. How someone like Ashleigh with IGH, who thought he was great, and wasn't this neurotic, overanxious mess, making him feel a bit of a failure as a man . . . Ashleigh must have seemed – light.'

Flick snorted.

'Look, we didn't go out for dinner or anything for the first two years. Phil tried. My mum tried. I physically could not leave Liam. Two years.'

'I get what you're saying.' Annie glared at Flick. 'I do.'

'What happened?'

'It lasted just a few months, I think, their affair. I don't know a lot about the where and the when – I never wanted to. Mostly at her place, I suppose. I don't know what they did together. All I know is that he ended it the day after I was diagnosed.'

'Oh, my God.'

'When did you find out?'

'Much later. After I'd finished treatment. Do you remember we went away for that holiday? You had Liam for us, Annie.'

Annie thought for a moment. 'That's right. To celebrate the end of radiation. You went to the Lake District, right?'

'Windermere.' Georgie smiled. 'He told me then. On a walk.'

'Why, do you think? When he'd got away with it. We're talking more than a year, right? You didn't need to know.'

'I think he thought we needed a clean slate. And I think he felt guilty. Too guilty. And the guilt was between us. I think it was eating him. It just sort of blurted out, halfway up this fell. Tears, the works.'

'He shouldn't have told you. That was almost as selfish as having the affair in the first place.'

'You're being really harsh, Flick.'

Flick was unrepentant. 'I know. But she didn't need to be burdened with that. He'd ended it. It was over, she says. She'd been to hell and back. Don't you remember?'

They all remembered. Georgie had been as uncomplaining as anyone could reasonably be about her gruelling treatment, and it had worked, thank God, but it had left her frail and pallid, like someone much older. It had been another year before she was even vaguely as she had been before.

So Annie saw her friend's point. Had confessing been about Phil or about Georgie?

'I'm glad he told me. Imagine if he'd stayed silent. It would have made everything that came afterwards a lie, wouldn't it? For us to have any chance of getting through it, I think I had to know.'

'You're a better woman than me.' Flick still sounded unconvinced, but Georgie's confidence had grown while she was speaking, and she smiled at her friend.

'I'm a more pragmatic woman, perhaps. Trust me – if

I'm making it sound easy, I'm not explaining myself properly. It was not easy.'

'I'll bet.'

'It took a long, long time.'

'Do you think either of them can get through this? Honestly?' Vanessa frowned.

Flick was unrelenting. 'I couldn't.'

'We don't know. I don't want to speculate. It feels wrong.'

'And can we? The six of us?'

'No way. Whether they put their marriages back together or not. Surely the damage done to this group is beyond repair. What we had is ruined, isn't it?'

For that question, none of them had an answer.

48

Natalie was finding it hard to concentrate on what the doctor was telling her. She hadn't let herself concentrate on what he might have to say, not since the phone call earlier telling her Sylvia had been brought in by ambulance. She'd driven there on autopilot, all the windows lowered, with Talk Radio playing too loudly in the car, letting the shouty presenters and irate callers fill her brain. And now she was here, in front of him, and she was still struggling to take it in. Random thoughts intruded. Had she locked the front door? Had she put the handbrake on properly when she'd parked? How young this sweet doctor looked. Her hands were shaking, and her bracelets jangled. She tried to hold her arms still against her sides.

Beyond the curtain, staff bustled to and fro. Telephones rang, and trolleys squeaked on linoleum floors. Somewhere nearby a small child was crying, angry, indignant sobs. Within the cubicle, though, it was oddly quiet. The dominant sound was her own blood rushing through her ears. She could feel that she was breathing fast, too. It made her feel light-headed.

On the gurney beside her, her mother was strangely peaceful. Natalie had been afraid that she'd be somehow grotesque, that her face would have been distorted almost beyond recognition by the stroke, one half dragged down by invisible threads. But apart from a slight droop at the corner of her mother's eye and her mouth, she looked the same. The expression was almost wry. She was very, very pale. That was the biggest difference.

Natalie had her father's olive complexion – but her mother had always been English-rose pale. All through her childhood, on holidays, she and her father had tanned deep and dark and carefree in the strongest sunshine while her mother retreated under an umbrella or a wide-brimmed hat. She used to joke that the sunshine came around corners to burn her if she wasn't vigilant. But she'd been so glamorous. She'd always worn make-up on that pale, translucent skin – bright blush, lipstick, a flick of eyeliner, and always, always mascara.

Her dressing-table had been Natalie's favourite place to play, with its powder puffs and potions. She sometimes thought it was part of why she'd fallen in love with acting. It was ritual. The cool touch of Pond's Cold Cream and the scent of Estée Lauder's Youth Dew. Her mother's tinkling laugh as she'd played along, applying red lipstick to her tiny mouth, blotting it with tissue, holding up the mirror with the handle to show her, her father mock-disapproving from the doorway. She'd always been desperately proud of her mother when she came to school – delightedly conscious of her nipped-in waist, shiny smooth hair and her carefully made-up face. She made the other mothers seem dowdy. She'd never stopped wearing it, either. Older women often did. If they didn't, it sometimes looked heavy and pantomime dame-ish on their lined skins. Not Mum.

She'd softened everything. Less, maybe. A different colour palette, certainly. But never nothing. She honestly could not recall the last time she'd seen her mother without 'her face' on.

Now all of that was gone, and her mother's pallor was the strangest thing about her. Her lips were almost the same colour as her cheeks, and thin now, without the touch of liner. Her hair had been grey for a long time but now, against the blue NHS pillowcase, it looked almost white, and her skin was almost white too, and thin, like parchment. Her eyelashes, without their customary slick of black, were invisible, and her eyebrows sparse. She looked ten, maybe fifteen years older than the last time Natalie had seen her, and that was shocking enough, without the tube that was taped to her open mouth, and the wires that hooked her up to the machines either side of the bed. She'd be so cross, Natalie realized, so embarrassed that the stroke had caught her in the early morning, before she'd had a chance to make herself up. She'd hate anyone seeing her like this.

The doctor was still talking. His face was kind. He was doing his best to translate his medical language for her as he spoke. They'd need to do tests, he was saying, to determine what had caused the stroke, whether it was ischaemic or haemorrhagic. Intracerebral. Subarachnoid. It was an overwhelming deluge of information. She tried to say the words again, in her head. He obviously realized how incomprehensible what he was saying was to her, but she supposed he was obliged to explain. He used his hands a lot. She felt like she was listening from inside bubble wrap. Or as if a bomb had exploded close to her ear, and she was temporarily deaf. The sound was muffled and she couldn't clear it. And she was trying really hard.

He stopped talking. 'Do you have any questions?'

She had a thousand. And, really, only one. 'Is she going to get better?'

He looked at his shoes while he considered his answer, so she did too. He was wearing black Crocs. She hated Crocs, but she knew them to be comfortable, and you were allowed to wear ugly shoes if you were on your feet for twelve hours. He could wear anything he wanted if he gave her the right answer to her question.

'I'm sorry. It's too early to tell.' He paused. 'The next twenty-four hours are critical. But I need to be clear. This has been a massive stroke. Even if your mother survives, she is, in my opinion, extremely unlikely to make a full and meaningful recovery.'

'So she's gone?'

'As the person you knew, yes, I'm very much afraid that she has.'

A sob caught in Natalie's throat. 'Oh.'

'I'm very sorry I can't give you more positive or more definitive news.'

'Is she in pain?' She didn't look like she was.

He shook his head vigorously, on safer ground now. 'No. Not at all. She is most likely completely unaware of what is going on, and will have been from quite early on.' So she didn't know they were all seeing her bare-faced, without even mascara.

'Can I stay with her, please?'

'Of course you can. We're going to move her up to the ward. That will take a few minutes. A bit longer, maybe. Things can seem to move frustratingly slowly in here, I'm aware. But we are doing what we can. The nurses will tell you where you can wait, and then you're welcome to go up and sit with her. Someone up there will talk to you more in due course.'

'Thank you.'

He smiled kindly. 'I really am very sorry.'

Left alone in the cubicle, Natalie didn't quite know where to put herself. She lifted her mother's hand from where it lay inert on the bedspread, to hold it, but it felt strange and limp so she laid it down carefully, and stroked the back briefly. She thought she might be sick. There was a grey cardboard kidney dish on the table. She took deep breaths and the nausea passed. She sat down in the chair next to the bed, but only for a moment, then stood up again, and went to the curtain. A nurse in blue scrubs stopped. 'You okay, love?'

'Sorry. Yes. Just waiting. Sorry.'

But she wasn't. She wasn't okay. This wasn't okay.

The doctor was right about things taking a while. Nurses came in every ten minutes or so, briskly efficient in their checks, but it was forty minutes before a porter came to wheel away her mother's gurney.

'Give 'em a bit of time to settle her in up there before you come up,' he advised, patting her the arm, fatherly. 'Go and get yourself a cuppa, sweetheart. You look all in.'

She followed the signs back to the coffee shop by the hospital's main entrance, and joined a short queue to order a cup of tea. She'd come in through the Accident and Emergency doors and didn't automatically know the way. The young man handed her a paper cup with a wooden stick as a spoon. She stirred for a long time before she removed the stringed teabag and added milk from a small jug on the counter, but the tea was still horribly grey and weak. Mum would have called it 'water bewildered'. Natalie had never known why she said that. The thought almost made her smile. Why had she never asked her to explain?

She had a sudden, vivid memory of Kit talking about his dad's death. Natalie had never known his father – he'd died when Kit was a young man, long before he had met her. His birthday had been Boxing Day, and it seemed that the same thought occurred to Kit every 26 December when he invariably raised a glass of something to his father. 'I never asked him about the war,' Kit would tell her, and whoever else was gathered at the table, tutting at his own foolishness. 'Six years, he did. *Six years*. And I know almost nothing about it. I know he was in Africa, then Italy, in France at the end. I know he had medals. We used to play with them when we were kids. Can you believe that? But I don't know anything about how he felt, about what actually happened to him. I never asked him to tell me about it. Why the hell didn't I?'

Natalie sat at a table in a corner of the café now, nursing the water bewildered, and wondered what she should have asked that she never had. That she probably never would. What might she regret not knowing about the woman who'd given birth to her in the days and weeks that lay ahead?

They'd been close, hadn't they? People liked to say they were. 'We're very close.' They said that about their parents, about their children, even, when they wanted to seem good and balanced and healthy. If they wanted to seem mysterious, they might say their relationship had been complicated. But weren't most mother-daughter relationships both of those things? And didn't you remember mostly the high highs and the low lows anyway? Not the thousands of ordinary days. If she closed her eyes, let her mind wander, wasn't her mother leaning over her as she held Temple, hours old and still sticky with birth, in her arms, her eyes shining with emotion, stroking each of their faces in turn, exclaiming at how clever she was, how beautiful her baby girl was. But let it wander a little further back, and wasn't that the same mother, sitting, tight-lipped with anger, at the kitchen table, furious, disappointed and frustrated that she'd fallen pregnant so young, demonstrated such a cavalier attitude to how she would look after a child when she was still a child herself. It was all there. She just daren't unpack it now.

She should make some calls. That was what you did. She needed to be practical. She pulled her phone out of her bag. Kit. Should she call Kit? Would he even answer? That thought hit hammer-hard. It was many years now since Kit had *not* been the first person she'd call about most things that mattered. Now, she didn't even know if she would want him to pick up. The phone had a low battery: 20 per cent, it reproached her. YOU ARE UNPREPARED FOR THIS. It was the first time she'd felt close to tears since she'd arrived. For God's sake.

Who else was there, after all, to tell? Not her father, not her partner, not a sibling. If there was anything to be done, or even to be decided, it was just her who must do it. Her finger hovered over Temple's name in her contact list. But she hesitated. Better to wait, perhaps, until she knew more. The same with Stella and Marley. They'd be going about their lives. Life was odd and off kilter enough, with what was going on with their dad. She wouldn't tell them just yet. She could protect them from this for a while longer.

Arlo. She felt a tremendous urge to hold her youngest child in her arms and smell his sweet head. Arlo. She looked at her watch. Shit. He'd need to be picked up from school in a couple of hours. Shit.

She had never felt more alone than she did in that exact moment. It would have been a reflex – call one of the girls. Hadn't each of them done it, for one reason or another, a hundred times? Vanessa or Georgie or Flick or Annie or Sarah . . .

She'd called Annie first when she went into labour with Arlo, eight years earlier. Kit had been – sod's law – a long train ride away, with work. Arlo was early – not very, but enough that plans weren't in place: she hadn't packed a bag, and Kit had said yes to a meeting he perhaps wouldn't have done once she was past thirty-six or thirty-seven weeks. This was thirty-five.

Annie had swung into action, leaving William in

charge of Louis and Theo in her own house, arranging for Stella and Marley to go home to other people to do their homework and have their tea, even as she was driving over to pick Natalie up. Natalie had sat on her yoga ball, breathing, while Annie scurried around the bedroom and the adjacent nursery, packing the things Natalie might need in hospital. With each contraction, she'd stopped, crouched down in front of the ball, and breathed it with her, never once breaking eye contact, gently reminding her that she'd done this before, that she'd do it now, that she was not on her own.

So it was Annie she called. The phone rang two, three, four times before she answered.

'Nat?' Annie sounded worried from the get-go.

'Annie. I'm sorry to bother you.'

'Are you okay?' Her voice must have given her away. She tried not to cry. 'No. I'm not. Not really.'

'What's happened?'

'It's my mum.'

'Your mum?'

Natalie nodded, although Annie couldn't see her. 'I'm at the hospital. She's had a massive stroke.'

'Oh, Nat. I'm sorry. Is she . . .?'

'I'm not with her right now. I mean, I was.' She knew she wasn't making sense. 'She's still alive.'

Annie exhaled.

'I wouldn't have bothered you, but . . .'

'You're *not* bothering me. What do you need?'

'It's Arlo. He's at school, but I'm not going to be able to get there, I don't think. To pick him up . . .'

The help came instantaneously. 'I can get him.'

Natalie felt flooded with relief. 'Oh, Annie. Thank you . . .'

'Who's with you? Is Kit there? Temple?'

'No. No, not Kit. I haven't called Temple. Or the others. I don't want to until I know what's happening. No one. I'm by myself. I'm in the coffee shop. They're just moving her up from A and E to the ward upstairs.'

'What have they said?'

'It's too soon to tell. They've got to do some tests. It doesn't look good, though. The doctor I spoke to thought it was . . . catastrophic, but he didn't want to say so.'

'How wretched. Poor woman.'

'She's unconscious, whatever, out of it, anyway. He said she's not in any pain.'

'And you? Are you okay?'

Natalie took a deep breath. 'I'm all right. It's a huge help, not worrying about Arlo . . . I'm very , very grateful, Annie.'

'I've got him, Natalie. Call me later. He can stay with me as long as you need. I've got him.'

Natalie felt the tremor in her voice. 'I'll call you later, okay?'

'Okay.'

Annie went to the kitchen and looked at the clock. She had someone due for a session in a quarter of an hour. That would be an hour-long appointment, ten minutes for faffing and small-talk either side. It would still leave her plenty of time to get to school and pick Arlo up. She opened the fridge. She'd been planning a quick salmon pasta for dinner when Rupert got home around seven-ish. Probably not Arlo's thing. There was a Pizza Express margarita in the freezer. That would do. She filled the kettle, and made a pot of tea. She felt jittery. Her brain was whirring. She took a sip from her mug but the tea was too hot and it burnt her lip. Her own dad had died after a massive stroke. It was years ago now, but she remembered, acutely, those first agonizing hours in the hospital after it had happened – her and Giles either side of a bed in which their father seemed so small. She felt a rush of empathy for Natalie. They were very hard days.

Back in her office, she punched Flick's name into her phone, willing her friend to be home, free and alone. Georgie and Vanessa would be at work. She obviously couldn't call Sarah. That thought was a tiny, sharp stab of awfulness. So Flick was her best hope.

'Annie!'

'Thank God I got you.'

Flick's tone changed to match hers. 'What's up?'

'It's Natalie.'

A brief pause. 'What about her?'

Annie couldn't read her friend from the three words. She'd been the most adamant. The most damning. She was probably the reason the rest of them hadn't reached out to Natalie before, almost as much as Sarah was. 'She called me just now from the hospital. Her mum's had a stroke. It sounds very bad. She needed Arlo collected from school – she's obviously going to be stuck there for a while.'

'And she asked you to do it?'

'Yeah. And I said I would, of course.'

Flick was quiet for a second.

'The thing is, Flick . . . she's by herself.'

'Is she?'

'I asked her if she'd called Kit or Temple or Stella. Marley, even. She sidestepped the Kit question, said she hadn't wanted to tell the kids until she knew what she was telling them . . . Makes sense, I suppose. But she's all alone there.'

Flick sighed, relenting. 'How did she sound?'

'Really shaky. Shocked. Of course. Who wouldn't be? Been there. Done that. But I had Giles. And Rupert.'

Now Flick exhaled very slowly. She'd been there too. You were never too old or too grown-up to be utterly derailed by the death of a parent. It was elemental. 'I'm sorry.' And she meant it.

'Right. Ghastly. The thing is, Flick, I can't bear to think of her at the hospital going through this alone. She's bound to be, you know, extra fragile, with everything that's going on.'

Flick knew what was coming.

Annie continued: 'I wouldn't want any of you, any of us, to be going through it alone.'

'And you want me to go?'

'Well, if that was what you wanted.' Annie was thinking on her feet. 'Or you could pick Arlo up, so I can go to the hospital. Take him home, give him some tea. I'm supposed to see a client, but I can rearrange that, maybe, or just go straight afterwards.'

There was a very long pause while Flick considered. 'Okay. That would probably be better.'

'Oh, Flick, thank you.'

'It's okay.'

'And one more thing. Do you think one of us should maybe call Kit? Let him know what's happening?'

Flick drew in her breath. And when she spoke, the sternness of before had returned to her voice. 'No, I do not, Annie. I have no intention of doing that, anyway. It's not our business. Take my advice. Stay out of that part of it. Helping in a crisis is one thing. Anything else is just interfering, and it's not up to you or any of us.'

'You're right.' Under the tirade, Annie surrendered, although she wasn't sure she agreed.

'I think I am, love.' Flick's voice had softened again now. 'I know you, Pollyanna. I know you want to fix everything and everyone. But you can't, you know.'

'I know. But I can do this for Natalie. With your help. And I do know that's a big deal for you right now. Thank you.'

Flick put the phone down on the kitchen island, and regarded Sarah. She couldn't even pretend at subterfuge, and she didn't want to. This was all bloody complicated enough.

Sarah, who had called earlier that morning and asked whether Flick had time for a walk. Flick hadn't, particularly: she had two deadlines to honour before Friday, and was meant to be seeing an old friend from work for a gossipy lunch she'd been quite looking forward to, but it was the first time in ages that Sarah had asked to meet up, rather than just submitted to repeated requests, and she sensed from that she might be ready to talk, so she'd rearranged her day to make it possible. The friend had been put off for a couple of weeks and the deadlines could wait.

Except it had started raining hard just as Sarah pulled into the driveway, the bright morning unexpectedly giving way to a grey, forbidding sky, and a horizontal deluge that would deter the hardiest walker, which neither of them was. They'd always been the more coffee-and-cake type, until middle age and peri-menopause had hit and everyone else had abandoned cafés to yomp through the hills, for some unknown reason. They'd immediately abandoned the walk, and Flick had planned to knock up Welsh rarebit for a late lunch.

'Do you remember the kids going on and on about pathetic fallacy when they were doing their eleven-plus?' Sarah had half-heartedly joked. 'The grey sky is a pathetic fallacy.'

'Yes! I remember that.' Flick shuddered. 'Yuck. Similes. Metaphors. And describing things with all five senses. I'd completely forgotten.'

Sarah smiled. 'Do you remember when Dyl wrote that story about pizza?' She adopted a deep, belligerent tone. '"It smells like a pizza, it looks like a pizza, it sounds like a pizza" – tenuous – "and . . ."'

'"When I eat it, it's going to taste like a pizza." Yes.' They laughed. 'That's around the time all Zoë's stories ended with someone falling into a bloody river and becoming a water baby.'

'Bless her. Dylan was a little bugger. Such utter disdain for box-ticking in one so young! That's what his teacher said at parents' evening.'

'Little scientist would have been fairer, surely. He was never very interested in English, always the other stuff.'

'That's true.'

'And look at him now.' A brief flash of maternal pride passed across Sarah's face.

She looked rubbish, Flick thought, up close. Big dark blue circles under tired eyes. She'd lost weight, too, and her cardigan hung off her shoulders. And she didn't have it to lose. She'd pretty much always been on a diet, Sarah, at least as long as she'd known her. This one was the most effective Flick could remember. Heartbreak diet. And, after all that, being nine stone sopping wet didn't suit her. Flick had never dieted, heartbreak or otherwise. When Craig had buggered off she'd used being pregnant as an excuse to eat her feelings. She'd given birth to six pounds ten ounces of beautiful baby Zoë, and the rest of her was all cake.

And that was just about as far as they'd got, before Annie called. Gentle, fond, easy small-talk. Safe territory. Sarah had agreed to eat melted cheese on toast with her, and that felt like a small victory to Flick.

So Annie's timing was really bloody crappy.

'What's happened?' Sarah narrowed her eyes. 'I know that was about Natalie.'

Flick repeated the salient points of her conversation with Annie.

'Did she know I was here?'

'She had no idea.'

Sarah nodded.

'But, knowing Annie, she'd have phoned me anyway. You know what she's like.' Flick sighed.

'Kind to a fault. Loyal to a fault.'

'Don't do that,' Flick warned her, with a wagging finger. 'Don't put me in the middle of that.'

Sarah put both hands on her cheeks, and gently slapped herself. 'Sorry. Sorry. Mean and unkind. This year, I will mainly be wearing bitter.'

Flick chuckled. 'Doesn't suit you as well as cornflower blue.'

They smiled at each other.

'I haven't seen her, Sarah. As far as I know, the others haven't either. But this is different. You see that, I know you do. You're still you.'

Sarah stared into her coffee mug. 'Am I? Not sure about that. I know it's different. Of course. I know. You guys are stuck in the middle, and I'm sorry.'

'You don't need to be sorry about that. Or anything else.'

'But I am.'

The wind had changed direction, and suddenly the rain was pounding sideways on the kitchen window, incredibly noisy.

Sarah tried to smile at her, but the corners of her mouth stayed turned down. 'Poor Natalie. You have to go. You should go. It's the right thing.'

Flick slid off the bar stool and went over to where

Sarah was sitting. She put one arm around her friend's shoulders, and Sarah leant her head on hers.

The car park at the hospital was as rammed as ever, and the pay machines as complicated. Why did they have to make it so expensive and so difficult? People were already anxious. Annie felt stressed by the time she walked through the hospital's automatic doors. She just wanted to get to Natalie now. She'd messaged that she was coming but the message still showed as unread. She didn't know this hospital. She had no idea where she was going. There was a short queue at the main reception desk, then a long walk through the labyrinth of corridors to the right lift, to the right floor. Then another set of signs to follow and another receptionist to explain to.

Eventually she reached the right place. She wasn't allowed onto the ward, of course, just ushered into a small waiting room while someone went to tell Natalie she was there. A couple on the small television bolted to the wall were 'escaping to the country', and Annie tried to concentrate on the rolling hills and staggering sea views of Pembrokeshire. It wouldn't help Natalie if she was uptight.

The door opened, and Natalie walked in, as dishevelled as Annie had ever seen her, and paler. She seemed almost to crumple as she saw her old friend, and for a horrible second Annie thought she might actually fall to the floor.

'Annie. You came.'

'I came.'

'Oh, thank you. Thank you.'

Annie sprang towards her, and Natalie sank into her arms, crying now. 'Sssh. Sssh. You're all right. You're okay.'

She guided Natalie to a chair, and took a packet of tissues out of her handbag, pressing one into Natalie's hand. 'Let me make us a cup of tea.' There was a small machine and a tray of cups and teabags on a table by the door. Annie busied herself with the buttons and eventually produced two paper cups, which she took back to where Natalie was. She hadn't said a word, but she'd stopped crying now. She blew her nose hard, and balled the tissue in her hand.

'Here, drink this.'

Natalie took the cup. 'You're so kind to come.' Then, with some alarm, as if the thought had just occurred to her, 'What about Arlo?'

Annie patted her hand. 'Don't worry. Flick's collecting him from school. She'll keep him.'

'Really?' She sounded amazed, and pitifully grateful.

'Hey. I know we're all going through something weird. I know it's crap. But this is different. This is bigger stuff than that. None of us wouldn't help, Natalie. I'm sure. We're all better than that.'

Natalie looked like she might cry again.

'How's she doing, your mum?'

'No one's said much since I spoke to you. They're very nice, and kind, but I don't think they know, to tell you the truth. She's out of it. All tubed and stuff. I don't think there'll be an answer, as such, tonight at least. I'm not sure why I'm staying. I don't think she's got the vaguest clue I'm here.'

'Ah. No one knows what she can hear, what she can understand. Besides, you're here because you need to be, Nat.'

Flick texted that she'd drive Arlo over when Natalie said she was home from the hospital. Natalie didn't want to leave Sylvia, but the doctor said she should go home and rest. Someone would call if anything changed. And there was Arlo, anchoring her. She messaged from the car, sitting in her own driveway. Flick pulled up ten minutes later. The biblical rain of earlier had subsided, but now there was a persistent cold drizzle. Flick wound the window down, but she didn't get out of the car.

Arlo climbed out of the back seat, dragging his school satchel and a drawstring sports bag behind him. Natalie held out her arms to him, and he submitted to a brief embrace before he wriggled away.

'How are you doing, Nat?'

Arlo waved to Flick and slid past his mother at the doorway into the house.

She folded her arms, pulling a baggy cardigan tightly around herself.

'Arlo's okay,' Flick told her. 'We didn't talk much about why it was me picking him up. I wasn't sure what you'd want him to know, so he thinks you were just held up somewhere. I haven't said a thing about your mum.'

'Thank you. I'm so grateful. To you and Annie.'

'That's okay. How's Sylvia doing?'

'It's too soon to tell. Not good, I think. It was a pretty massive stroke.'

'I'm so sorry.'

'Thank you, Flick.'

Flick smiled, and it was a kind smile. 'It's really okay. Let me know how she is tomorrow. If you need more help . . .'

For a moment the two women just looked at each other. Then Natalie took a step back inside, mouthed a final thank-you, and disappeared behind the door. Flick sighed deeply, and rewound her window.

49

Later, home again, drinking a glass of red while Andrew sliced courgettes, Flick told him what had happened. 'I feel crappy about it. I really should have got out. I should have stayed with her even. Maybe . . .'

Andrew put down the chef's knife and took a sip from his own glass. 'You don't know if she'd have wanted that.'

'But it was cold, wasn't it? I didn't even get out of the sodding car.'

He leant against the work surface, close to where she was sitting. 'Hey. You did practical things. You know as well as anyone else that that's the important stuff, at a time like this. It's the best thing you can do. You took care of Arlo so she didn't have to worry about him. You picked him up, and fed him tea, and did his homework with him, and you took him home. That says a lot more than whether you got out of the car. To me and to Natalie. Stop beating yourself up, will you?'

'It's stupid. I'm so sorry for her. I know how this feels, and it's ghastly. But I'm still so angry with her.'

'One doesn't cancel out the other.'

'Doesn't it? Really? I'm not sure . . .'

'Stop. Enough.' He stood behind her, his arms around her waist, and she leant back against the solid warmth of him.

'I'm kind of surprised Kit wasn't there.'

'Do you know for sure he wasn't?'

'No car.'

'He might not even know.'

'Really?'

Flick shrugged. 'I don't know whether they're talking or not.'

'That's mad.'

'That's adultery. That's separation. That's the damn mess you make when you do what she and Dom did. The mess we've all been dragged into.'

Andrew shuddered. 'I know you're right. But still . . .' He made a sharp gesture – something being severed. She knew exactly what he meant.

'Annie wanted to message him.'

'And?'

'And I said it wasn't up to us. That we shouldn't interfere.'

Andrew nodded slowly.

Flick was quiet for a moment. 'And that was wrong of me, I realize. I'm going to message him.' She pulled her handbag off the back of her chair, and delved into it for her phone.

Andrew frowned, but didn't speak. She answered the question he hadn't posed. 'He needs to know. This concerns him. Right?'

'You're right. I guess. You know, though, that the messengers get shot, right? Sometimes?'

'I'll take my chances.' She took a big gulp of wine, and then she began texting: *I'm not sure you'll know, Kit, but*

Nat's mum had a big stroke today. Not sure whether she'll get better. She's in her local hospital. We thought you should know. Flick.

She held out the phone. Andrew wiped his hands on a tea towel, and took it to read the message.

'Who is "we"?' he teased.

She shoved him gently. 'You and me. We. All of us, for God's sake. They're our friends, right? They *were* our friends. Before this whole shit show.'

'You're right.' He touched send, and handed her the phone. The he leant his forehead against Flick's. 'Never leave me.'

'No immediate plans.'

'Good.' She tipped her mouth up to kiss his, then pushed the phone and the uncomfortable feeling to one side.

incessant questions about why she was downstairs, and whether he could have Nutella on his toast for breakfast. She felt as though he'd dragged her up to consciousness from a deep coma. Arlo didn't seem to notice that his mother was a zombie.

She got up to the ward just after ten. No change, the nurse said. She'd had a quiet night. Then they left her alone with Sylvia, pulling the striped curtain around the bed. Natalie sat down, and took her mother's hand, which was limp and cool. She laid her head on the mattress, and put Sylvia's hand on her own hair. Nothing. All of her life, her mother's hand had patted her head, smoothed her hair, cupped her cheek. But the last time had really been the last time. And you never knew. You never knew last times were just that. Natalie had never felt lonelier in her entire life. It was an engulfing sad feeling, and a vast ache.

She was with Sylvia when she died, but it wasn't dramatic or traumatic. It was more peaceful than she had expected. Everyone moved quietly and gently around them. She was glad she had come back and, actually, that it was just the two of them. Perhaps it wasn't selfish after all. She was her mum's only child, and her mum was her only mum. It was okay that it was the two of them.

The nurses were kind. Someone brought her a plastic cup of tea, and she was allowed to sit with her mother's body for a time. She had no idea how long until she came out, checked her phone and saw that it was lunchtime, although she hadn't been hungry since yesterday. She'd read somewhere that it was important to sit and be with the body for a while – to let your mind adjust, a bit like you let your eyes get used to darkness or light. She held her mother's hand, and watched her perfectly still face and chest. When she trusted her legs to carry her, she stood up, smoothed a strand of her mother's hair away from her forehead, and kissed her once on the cheek.

There was remarkably little to be done, in a practical way, today. She'd never had to do any of this – when her father had died, she supposed her mother must have taken care of everything. She didn't remember. A nurse explained, kind and painstaking, the next steps. Her mother would be taken downstairs to the mortuary. Once arrangements had been made, the funeral director would collect her and take her to the chapel of rest. A telephone call to a soft-spoken undertaker. A few pieces of paper to sign.

A different nurse, slight and younger, with a surprisingly strong Welsh accent, handed her a plastic bag with her mother's watch and her thin gold wedding band, along with the clothes she'd been wearing when she came in. Someone had folded them neatly for her. A woollen jumper, a tweed skirt, an old-fashioned petticoat, her underwear. Natalie hadn't seen her mother's underwear for years, so it was strange to see it now, although whoever had carefully folded the whole outfit had discreetly tucked the bra and knickers inside the slip. She didn't want to think about her mother's body, naked under the hospital gown. The jumper, when she lifted it to her face, smelt of her. She hadn't even had her handbag with her, when she was brought in. She'd have hated that. Everything was in a carrier-bag – they must keep some for just this purpose. It was an odd thought.

She thanked the nurses, and took the lift down to the ground floor, then went out of the hospital into the fresh, cold air.

She didn't cry until she got into the car. As the door closed, a flood of emotion swamped her and she sobbed quietly, gripping the steering wheel. A woman holding a young boy by the hand walked between Natalie's car and the one next to it, and the child stared in at her for a few seconds, until his mother pulled him away, her face apologetic and sympathetic.

She wasn't just crying for her mother. A tidal wave of misery had rushed in over her head. It was a bit frightening. Life seemed bleak. She suddenly wished the kids were there. She wanted to hold them. She wanted Kit. She wanted him to hold her.

It was a long time before she felt safe to drive, so it was after two when she got home. She felt exhausted, heavy and slow with fatigue. She had an hour before she needed to collect Arlo. She would have to tell him about his grandmother. She'd done her best to prepare him last night, but he hadn't seemed to grasp what she was saying, and she had seen no point in pressing him to absorb the possibility – the likelihood. She hadn't had the energy. Now there was an absolute to report. And she would have to deal with his reaction. Then she would have to call Temple, Stella and Marley and deal with theirs too. It felt overwhelming. She just wanted to lie down, but she was afraid that if she did, she'd fall into a sleep so deep she wouldn't hear an alarm. She wondered if a shower might be better.

Before she put the key into the lock, the front door opened and Kit stood in the doorway, watching her walk towards him. Her Kit. Opening his arms, then enclosing her within them, holding her so tightly.

'She died.'

He made a small, sympathetic noise close to her ear. She felt as if he was holding her up.

Inside, he poured a stiff whisky from the decanter in the sitting room, and handed it to her. 'Here. Drink this.'

She sank into a chair, and rubbed her face as he poured a second glass. She smelt like the hospital, but now she wasn't sure she had the energy for a shower. 'I'd better not. Arlo . . .'

'I've sorted Arlo. He's at Jake's and he's going to sleep over there. Jake's mum – Adele, is it? She knows what's going on. She'll take him in tomorrow. I've spoken to him – he's fine.'

'Poor Arlo.'

'He's fine. More than fine. You know him.'

'Our flexible, adaptable little bonus baby. Passed from pillar to post since birth.'

'That's the one.' He raised his glass briefly, then took a gulp. Natalie drank too, feeling the burning liquid warm her throat, relieved she didn't have to compose herself for Arlo after all. People were kind.

'I need to tell him about Mum. I need to tell the others, too.'

'Do they even know about the stroke?'

She shook her head. 'I didn't want to scare them until I knew what was happening. Perhaps I should have done. Given them the chance to say goodbye. I didn't know it would be today.' Tears threatened again.

'Hey. You were coming from a good place. I don't know that any of them would have chosen to see her that way, rather than how she was the last time they were together. You can call Temple, Stella, Marley if you want to. If you can face it. Or I can call them, if you like. But don't worry about Arlo for now. Let him be. We'll tell him together, tomorrow. He doesn't need to know today.'

He was right. 'Will you be here tomorrow?' she asked tentatively. She couldn't believe he was here today.

He nodded. 'I'll stay.'

'Thank you.'

His voice was gentle. 'It doesn't mean anything, Natalie. My staying. I don't want you to misunderstand.'

She smiled weakly. 'It means you're a good man.'

Kit paused. 'I'm the man I've always been, Nat.' He looked unutterably sad.

'I know you are.'

He'd always been there, she realized. For the hardest moments. With his quiet, kind strength. She'd taken it for granted. She'd missed his presence at the hospital. She knew he would have been practical – he'd have helped her to remember the right questions to ask. He'd have just been there. She'd felt bereft, driving home. Seeing him, she felt just a little less bereft. A little less alone.

She realized something else, something perhaps more unexpected. She'd wanted him to be there. In these two ghastly days, she'd never once wanted Dom. She hadn't even thought about him.

51

Natalie had never organized a funeral before. The funeral director was all compassion and helpfulness, but there were so many decisions to make. Sylvia had known that, of course. There was a letter, thank God. Sylvia had told her, a while ago. She remembered waving away the conversation, not willing to talk about such an eventuality, but Sylvia had persisted.

She'd gone to her mother's house alone, letting herself in with the spare key she'd kept at home. Sylvia's navy leather handbag, so conspicuous by its absence at the hospital, was on the stool by the stairs. In the kitchen her breakfast dishes were stacked on the drying rack. A cup and saucer, a plate, a knife. Not a single crumb from her toast on the counter. Natalie smiled fondly. Sylvia had a dishwasher, but she hadn't approved of using it every day. In the sitting room, there was a book on the side table, with a tasselled bookmark keeping her place. She picked it up. Something about Princess Margaret. Very Mum. There was a small desk behind the sofa, and Natalie briefly looked in the drawers. Papers were neatly filed in plastic folders, each labelled in her mother's elaborate round hand. UTILITIES, STATEMENTS, CONTACTS. She was in no state, really, to think about any of those things. It was too soon to deal with it. She'd get to it. She'd have to – there was no one else.

Up the narrow staircase, in her mother's room, the bedcovers had been vaguely straightened, presumably by the kind neighbour who'd found her up there when she'd let herself in, worried that the milk was still outside. Sylvia had always made the bed smooth and neat, after breakfast, when it had had a chance to air, so it couldn't have been her. It wasn't tidy enough. The timing of her stroke was so clear – she'd risen early, eaten her breakfast and dressed. But she hadn't had time to make the bed, or to put on her make-up. It felt so strange, and so awful, picturing her. Was she frightened? Natalie smoothed the quilt, and tidied the pillows. Her mother's dressing-gown lay on the stool at the foot of the bed. Natalie gathered it up and brought it to her face, but it smelt only of clean laundry. She sat down and opened the drawer of the bedside table.

The envelope with her name on it was there, as she had thought it might be. She leant against the uphol-stered headboard, and took out the letter.

My darling Natalie,

I hope you know how much I love you, and how much I love Temple, Stella, Marley and Arlo. You, along with your father, have been the great loves of my life, and the source of most of my joy and my pride. (A little, I confess, has been reserved for my fabulous art.)

Natalie could hear her voice, ripe with self-deprecating laughter, and a theatrical gesture at her latest pastel canvas or coil pot: 'My fabulous art.'

Please do not be too sad to be reading this. I was old. And it's been a rather lovely life. I am only sad to be leaving you, my love. I remember how overwhelming it was to make decisions after Dad died, so I've written some thoughts to help. I shan't haunt you if you do it differently. It's just in case you wanted to know.

I think I know how much you'll miss me, because I would miss you exactly the same. Such is life, sweetheart.

All my love, Mum

On a separate sheet was the most Sylvia list Natalie could have imagined. Reading it was like listening to her shouting it from the next room.

Navy suit, white blouse: not the one with the lace on the front, the plain one.

No jewellery, except my wedding band. I don't think you'd get that off if you tried. Such a waste to put me in anything else. Sell the rest, if you and the girls don't want it. Wear it, if you do.

'Jerusalem' and 'Abide with Me' in the church. And absolutely not the crematorium. But only if you can get the whole choir out. Nothing worse than an insipid 'Jerusalem'. And I appreciate 'Jerusalem' has been 'cancelled', so uninvite anyone who is going to be 'triggered' by it. Except Marley. He has to come. Consider earplugs for Marley.

Crematorium after church. Just you lot since I think someone has to show up.

I would like a willow coffin, never mind the squeaking, and I would like proper pallbearers to carry me, no exceptions.

Christina Rossetti poem, please. There's a book on the shelf. You choose: I love them all, the romantic ones especially.

For God's sake (and yours), get caterers for the wake, if you really want to have one. There's money to do that.

And a letter of wishes about certain things. Spoiler: it says you must each choose something you like and sell the rest of the furniture and things to buy shoes. No point leaving you my shoes. Stella makes it very clear what she thinks of my shoes. She'll understand, when she's old and her feet hurt. I've always hated wakes, but of course I'm not invited, so up to you. I'd much prefer you to head home with fish and chips and drink champagne. You have lovely taste, Natalie, so whatever you do, I promise I'll like it. I hope I told you enough that you have lovely taste. Sometimes I wonder if I was too much stick not enough carrot as a mother. I hope you knew how great I thought you were, darling.

Scatter me wherever you like. I've always thought it would be rather good fun to be released as dust from your trouser leg like they did with the tunnel dirt in The Great Escape, preferably while you were walking around somewhere glorious like Lisbon or the gardens at Blenheim. But that's probably impractical.

Trust Sylvia to make her laugh from beyond. Ridiculous, glorious Mum. Natalie folded the paper and returned it to the envelope, then tucked the envelope into the back pocket of her trousers. She opened the first in a row of fitted cupboards in search of the navy blue suit and the plain white blouse, and her quiet chuckle turned immediately to tears.

Sylvia had been preoccupied by her when she died, Natalie knew. If not exactly angry, then disappointed, frustrated and worried. She tried to push away the persistent fear that the emotional conversations of the last few weeks had contributed to her mother's vulnerability to the stroke that had killed her. The doctor had said not, had cited her age, and the high blood pressure she had never admitted to, but how could Natalie ever entirely believe that she hadn't played a part in it?

She'd been thinking about her mother's letter since she'd left the hospital. Had she hoped for an addendum – some post-Dom postscript? Some last wisdom? There was no such comfort. Sylvia had died knowing only that Natalie had most likely broken up her own family. It was a horrible, hollow feeling in her chest.

'I'm sorry, Mum,' she whispered to the empty bedroom.

52

Walking into the small church, Natalie was taken aback by how full it already was. Small groups in brightly coloured clothes filled almost all but the two front pews. She was glad – there was almost no family beyond her own. She'd dreaded an empty, echoey space – although as per the instructions Sylvia had left, disguised as suggestions, she had secured the whole choir. But she needn't have worried. Not for the first time in the weeks since Sylvia had died, it struck her how full Sylvia's life had been. It made her feel she'd let herself get stuck in no man's land. She could never regret any of her four children. But between having Temple at eighteen, and Arlo at forty, she'd been parenting above all else for more than twenty years. Arlo wouldn't leave home for at least another ten. She'd be almost sixty. Would she have the energy then to build the kind of life Sylvia evidently had done?

It was a bitterly cold day – there'd been a heavy frost that morning, almost like snowfall – but the sky was bright and clear. The organist was playing sombre music in the background, which made her want to weep.

Temple had arrived early, wrapped in an oversized black coat, and a floppy felt hat. She was sitting at the front, staring forwards. When Natalie had gone to her, she'd leant wordlessly into her mother, and blown her nose on a tissue. Natalie kissed the top of her head. There wasn't very much to be said. It was all just to be got through. Maybe some people could make a funeral a celebration of a life well lived, but she wasn't ready for that. She felt utterly bereft. She missed her mother more than she would have been able to explain. She knew Temple understood.

In the porch, Marley looked charmingly unlike himself in the navy suit she'd bought him for a stint of work experience in the sixth form, and didn't think he'd worn since. He'd brushed his hair and shaved closely, and she loved him for it. He hadn't said a word about 'Jerusalem'. He and Stella were greeting mourners, handing out the order of service Stella had helped the funeral director with. On the front, there was a colour picture of Sylvia, happily surrounded by the six of them a couple of years ago on a holiday weekend. On the back, they'd chosen her black-and-white wedding photograph: a quintessential sixties glamourpuss, with a full veil attached to a pillbox hat, arm in arm with Natalie's dad, puffed with pride and slicked with Brylcreem.

The door opened, and Kit came in, hand in hand with Arlo. She'd wondered about him being there, but he had said he wanted to come. It was the sort of thing she would have talked to the girls about. Annie, certainly, would know the best thing to do. She would have leant on all of them, in different ways, and it would have helped. A familiar wave of self-pity lapped at her. Kit believed Arlo would be okay if he came. She thought it was more about not being left out of something the rest of them were involved in, but she'd agreed. He was smartly dressed too – not in a suit, but in khaki cords and his navy duffel coat. Like Marley, his neat hair threatened to undo her. Kit smiled at her. She kissed Arlo, then watched them walk slowly down to the front. The congregation was anxious to be warm, and sympathetic, turning to smile and nod. Arlo waved back.

When they got to the front, she saw Temple beckon and stand up, and she watched her hug first Arlo and then Kit. A huge lump formed in her throat. How the hell was she going to get through this without losing it?

She looked at her watch. The service was due to start in a couple of minutes. Gesturing at Marley and Stella to put the last orders of service by the prayer and hymn books and take their places, she nodded to the vicar. She knew Sylvia's coffin had arrived. She hadn't expected to feel so panicky. She fought to control her breathing, and her tears, and walked up to where the rest of her family were, trying hard not to meet anyone's eye.

Stella stepped out into the aisle, and Natalie took her place, between her and Marley. Kit smiled at her encouragingly. Her children took one hand each, and didn't let go.

She heard the doors open, and didn't dare turn around to watch the coffin's progression. But it wasn't the slow, measured gait of pallbearers she heard. It was the clip of heels on ancient tile, moving quickly. She turned to see Annie, her face apologetic, trotting in as dignified a manner as she could muster to take the only empty pew that remained, a third of the way back from the front. Behind her, Vanessa, Georgie, Flick. And, last, Sarah. They'd all come.

She was turning back to face the front, just as the music changed, and the pallbearers appeared at the door with Sylvia's wicker coffin on their shoulders. And now she cried.

Temple had asked if she might give the eulogy, and Stella and Marley were not about to argue. Stella said she knew she couldn't get through it without sobbing, and Marley hated any kind of public speaking. Temple spoke beautifully, her voice breaking with emotion, but not so much that she became incomprehensible, about the grandmother she had so adored. There were observations that elicited fond smiles and nods from the congregation, sweet stories from her childhood, and from Stella and Marley's – the three of them had talked and compared notes. Arlo had contributed an anecdote about Sylvia wading into a boating lake, in tights, to retrieve something he'd thrown in, and people laughed. Temple reserved the end of her address for Natalie, and looked straight at her while she spoke. 'My mum and my gran had a beautiful relationship. It was amazing to watch the two of them together, both of them always immaculate, always talking. She always spoke her truth, my gran. My goodness, she did.' She paused, to general acknowledgement from the pews. 'But she spoke it with such love, and such understanding, such humour and such tenderness that it never hurt. And it was most often real wisdom. Really, really worth listening to. And heeding.' She smiled ruefully. 'I know how very much my mum will miss her, that wisdom and that love. More than any of us.'

Everyone wanted to shake Natalie's hand at the end, and to talk with her. She was surrounded by well-meaning friends of her mother. They all seemed to want to tell a snippet of a story about Sylvia. They'd taken her advice about the wake, so there was none, and as only family would be at the ghastly crematorium, Natalie had no choice but to listen to everyone and thank them in the church. Kit took Arlo home, as they had agreed he would, so it was just her and the three older children, chatting to and smiling at strangers. Of the girls, only Annie came briefly to the throng. Natalie watched her warmly hug the kids, and pat Kit's arm. She excused herself and went over to her. 'We're off, lovely. We can see you're swamped. I just wanted to give you a cuddle, from all of us. I've told Temple she did a wonderful job. Sylvia would have loved what she said.'

Natalie gripped her arm. 'I can't believe you came.'

'Of course. We wanted to.'

'Sarah came.'

Annie took her hand. 'And no one made her. She wanted to be here.'

'I . . .' Tears welled again.

'Sssh.' Annie pulled her into a hug, and held her for a moment. 'We're all still us, Nat. We're all still us.' She stepped back, turned, and left, briefly touching Stella's arm.

Yes, but I'm not sure I'm still me, she thought.

*

Flick, Sarah, Georgie and Vanessa were waiting for Annie by the car. It was freezing, and they stamped their feet. Vanessa opened the boot so they could put their coats in, and then they all climbed in. Sarah sat in the middle of the back seat, flanked by Annie and Georgie. Vanessa fiddled with the heater until warm air started to blast into the space. Annie took Sarah's hand. 'Well done, you. That cannot have been easy.'

Sarah was staring straight ahead. 'Nope.'

'Is she okay, do you think?' Flick asked.

'She's a bit overwhelmed – a lot of people in there clamouring for her. I remember feeling that too, at my own parents' funerals. Both of them. You're sitting there, desperately trying to keep a hold of yourself, and everyone else seems to try everything to make you lose it. Those particular hymns. Sob. Eulogy. Sob. Their sodding favourite song. Sob. Sob. When one parent is still alive, you at least have them to worry about – to focus on. But when the last of your parents dies, it's worse. I remember sitting at my mum's and thinking, I'm an orphan. Daft, really.'

'Not daft. It's an odd, horrid feeling. I had it too. My brother chose "Let It Be" and I totally lost it. You'll remember my mum thought she'd discovered the Beatles, right? I don't know why we try not to cry, either. Why hide how we feel? And if we really want to hide how we feel, why have a funeral in the first place? Just to prove how stiff we can make our upper lips? You don't have to have one, do you?'

Georgie shuddered. 'I hate a funeral. But, more than

437

that, I hate the idea of nothing. There's something to be said for collective grief, don't you think – shared experience?'

'What happens if you don't have one, anyway?'

'An aunt of mine didn't. Still cost her kids a small fortune to get her body collected from the hospital and cremated without a service.'

'Can't the hospital just, you know, pop 'em in the incinerator? With the legs and bits and all the other stuff they have to get rid of?'

Georgie grimaced. 'Nice.'

'I actually always want to laugh at funerals.'

'Same thing, really. They can be pretty closely related.'

'Some cultures do death much better than we do, if you ask me.'

'Who is it that digs up the dead every year to have a little shindig with them and change their outfit?'

Flick laughed out loud. 'I have no idea. Not sure that constitutes doing it much better.'

'Just for the record, you are so not in charge of planning my funeral!'

'Ah, go on . . .'

They fell silent.

'They were close, Natalie and her mum, weren't they?'

'She was a piece of work, was Sylvia.'

'Did she know what was going on, do you think?' Sarah asked.

Annie chose her words carefully. 'You can imagine what she had to say about it. I know Natalie told her. I think right after the party. She was beating herself up about it when I saw her at the hospital. I think she genuinely believed it was part of what brought the stroke on – Sylvia being disappointed, and worried. And cross.'

'I'm sorry. That's horrible.'

Georgie patted her arm. 'Not your fault. And not true, most likely, anyway.'

'And what about Kit? Did you know he was going to be there?'

Annie shrugged. This was the first time Sarah had asked. 'I thought he would. I'm not sure how much to read into it. I know he came back when Sylvia had the stroke. Natalie must have asked him to. But I don't know if it's permanent. She and I haven't had that kind of conversation.'

'I texted him. When it happened.' Flick looked at them from the front seat.

Sarah smiled. 'That was the right thing to do.'

Flick smiled back.

'I don't hate her, you know.'

'I might, in your shoes.' Flick winked.

'I don't, though. I don't want to give it that energy. It's taking all I've got to get through the days. I just don't think I have the bandwidth to loathe Natalie for what happened.'

'You couldn't do it, could you, though? I've thought about this. I mean, it's unimaginable. Sleep with Ross, or Andrew, or Rupert? I know I couldn't. And I don't think any of you could, either.'

'Okay. But I don't think she set out to hurt me.'

'Of course she didn't. No one thinks that. No one is

baying for her blood, least of all me. But she had to know what the collateral damage would be. She can't be let entirely off the hook, can she?'

'We don't live in isolation. Our actions have consequences. That's what we teach our kids, isn't it?'

'I don't want to wade in on her. Especially not today. And I think hurt people hurt people.'

'Oh, come on. That's a very simplistic view.'

'And true. Besides, isn't it Kit Natalie hurt? Natalie didn't cheat on me. Dom did.'

'She did, though, and I don't want to wade in on her either. But she cheated on your friendship. She cheated on all our friendships.'

'And so what? Are we going to punish her for ever?'

'It's not about punishment. Not for me, anyway. It's more about trust.'

'Is it?'

'What do you think? Ah, well – we've been friends for twenty years. She's only slept with one of our husbands.'

'You sound like you think she'd go through them.'

'I don't mean that.'

'Look. We're talking in circles. I can't tell all of you what to do about Natalie. I can only tell you what I feel. I can't be close to her again. I know that. I'm not naïve. For me, it can't go back to being how it was – of course not. But if I stay furious with her, that only eats me. I don't even want to be angry with Dom for ever. I don't want to be angry.' She looked at them. 'Can you understand that?'

'I think you might be a better man than me, Gunga Din.'

Sarah laughed. Flick reached over her shoulder and Sarah took her hand. They stayed that way for a moment. It broke the tension in the car.

Georgie smirked at them. 'Who even was Gunga Din?'

'Isn't he some guy in a Rudyard Kipling poem?' Vanessa shot the answer back from the driver's seat, as they had all known she would.

'Him that wrote "If"? As in "You'll be a Man, my son"!'

'Him indeed.'

'Hold up, though,' Sarah said, to the inevitable accompanying groans. 'Hasn't Kipling been cancelled?'

53

After Sylvia, after the year and everything that had gone on, Natalie had no real enthusiasm for Christmas. She felt as if she was auditioning for a role. Playing a role. It was the same muscle memory from all those years ago. The same nerves, the same care over how you delivered your lines, the same breathless, terrified anticipation of your reviews.

They still hadn't talked about the future, if they even had one. Kit had simply come home that night, the night of the day her mother had died, and he was still there. But she had no idea why. And she was too frightened to ask. Or beg, which was what she really wanted to do. He had been kind, and practical, and gentle. But self-contained. As days became weeks, she started to hope, but hoping scared her. She had no right to be forgiven.

She told herself he was here for his children. For the time of year. That, come January, he'd go again, and this time he'd stay away for ever. She forced herself to believe that it was a combination of pity for her, love for the kids, and just the time of year that kept him there for now.

He was sleeping in the guest room. It would normally be where her mother slept at Christmas. Stella and Marley still had their own rooms, and Temple usually stayed in the small annexe on top of the garage on the driveway.

They hadn't kissed, and barely touched since that first extraordinary hug he'd given her in the doorway the day Sylvia died. He was like a house guest. He never came into the bedroom they had shared for years.

Christmas was mostly all about Arlo, of course. The last almost-believer in the family. He knew, really. He'd sussed the Tooth Fairy long ago, and someone in the class had been in the middle of telling them where babies come from before the teacher had interrupted. All the myths were getting busted. But he was in the hinterland where the fear that acknowledging the truth might cost you presents gripped you, and he really, really liked presents, so he encouraged the theatre of the season, like the worst ham actor ever, and Natalie was very grateful to him for it.

She was watching him like a hawk. She remembered Sylvia, so sure he was immune, so confident they could minimize the damage they'd done to him by sheer force of love. She wished she believe it as emphatically as her mother had.

Because of Arlo, the Elf on the Shelf had to be moved every day. Sometimes twice, once Marley got home from university. He liked to arrange the Elf in compromising positions and the trick was to find him and release him from the Barbies or change the suggestive angle of the Beanie Baby before Arlo found him. Because of Arlo, there were reindeer prints to make in flour sifted onto the floor around the wood-burner. There were mince pies, a glass of milk and a carrot on a plate, and someone had to bite the carrot and leave crumbs of pastry.

Stella and Marley were very much Kit's. They'd been hers too, briefly, when Sylvia had died. But now she felt a million miles away from them. She'd tried to talk to them. Marley couldn't look her in the eye, let alone enter into a conversation about what had happened, and his coldness was almost worse than Stella's wrath. Stella was angry about all of it – from the fact that she'd found out from Mia, to Sylvia's death meaning she couldn't shout and rail against her mother. She was attentive to Kit in a way none of them were used to, and she avoided being alone with Natalie. She'd already said she was going back to her flat after Boxing Day.

Natalie missed her mother. She tried to remember every word of the conversation they'd had in the kitchen that day. She'd brought the plate with the gold back with her, and propped it on the oak mantel above the fireplace, like a talisman. She felt sad all of the time. There were a few seconds when she woke up each morning and didn't remember. Then it all flooded back. The whole awful mess, the loss. She'd lost everything, or that was how it felt, and it was all her own fault.

By the time Temple arrived on Christmas Eve, she was ready for more rejection. She'd half expected her not to come. This mess wasn't her problem. This family Natalie had decimated was only half her family anyway. She'd missed a lot of the good bits. Even if she'd understood what Natalie had told her, managed not to judge her too harshly, why would she volunteer to come into the chaos? Risk the toxicity? She thought she'd choose to spend the day with her dad instead, although she didn't know whether he was even in England, but she daren't interpret her coming as support. Natalie picked her up at the station. She couldn't find a place to park, so she hovered anxiously on a double yellow, the passenger window down, craning to spot her among the throng pouring off the London train. She saw her first. Temple scanned the layby.

'Darling. I'm here.'

'Mum.' They hugged uncomfortably. Someone behind honked in a very unfestive manner, and Temple turned and stuck two fingers up at him. Natalie laughed.

'Here, park here.' Temple gestured to a space. 'The inspectors have all gone home. We'll be all right for a minute. How are you doing?' Her face was full of concern, and love.

'I've been better, as the saying goes.'

'Kit? He's still at home?'

She nodded. 'He hasn't said what will happen after Christmas. I think maybe he's just staying for Arlo. I suspect he's waiting to leave me.'

'Has he said that?'

'No.'

'Is he acting like that?'

'He's been lovely to me, since Mum. Careful, and sweet, and lovely. But that's because he *is* lovely. Doesn't mean anything, does it?'

'Oh, Mum.' Temple put her arms around Natalie, who dissolved into tears. For a moment, Temple let her cry. The engine was off and the windows steamed up. Then she gently pushed her mother back into her own seat. She fished in her coat pocket, and produced a tissue, which she handed to her.

'Here's what we're going to do, okay? We're going to go one day at a time. One hour. Gran rang me, you know . . .'

'I thought she might.'

'Did she tell you she knew you and Kit were going to be okay?'

'No.' Natalie half laughed.

'She told me. She said she knew you loved each other, and that Kit would stay, and that you two would be all right.'

'She did?'

Temple nodded. 'And I agreed with her. I still agree. Some classic Sylvia guff about gold and tinsel – didn't really get all that – but I agree with her. You guys love each other. You fucked up. Okay. You're still the person he loves. It's going to be okay.'

'I wish I had your faith.'

'I'll lend it to you. Besides, I'm here now. And we're going to drive home, and we're going to have a good Christmas – all of us. And it will be okay. That's just that.'

54

At the Bennetts' house, no one really had a clue how to play Christmas. Dom had expected to come for the day. He'd raised it a week or two before. He'd made a face like a clubbed seal's when she'd said that, no, he couldn't come. She wouldn't stop the children seeing him, not that she could – they weren't children, anyway – so they could see him Christmas Day if that was what they wanted to do, or any day either side. As much as they liked. But the notion of going through the motions of a happy family Christmas for the sake of the children was obscene to her. Or, indeed, for the sake of Dom. He couldn't expect to cherry-pick the part of life with her that suited him. It was almost laughable. No. Just no.

The indignant anger had dissipated quickly, though, and she'd started to dread the day. If it weren't for Mia and Dylan, she'd have ignored it, or volunteered at the homeless shelter or somewhere where they'd keep her too busy to think. They usually saw friends and family, clustered, in ten days or so around 'the big day'. Godparents, old university mates, aunts and cousins. Sarah realized she drove most of those plans. It was her, sending emails and making calls through the autumn to fill their diaries. Without her, there were precious few plans.

She'd stalled over invitations received rather than

extended. It wasn't festive, was it, telling people she and Dom had split up? Maybe she should write a round robin for the Christmas cards, tuck the news in at the bottom, along with the singsong snippets about the kids' achievements and the garden progress. She hadn't found a way of saying it that felt comfortable. It was like being naked under a coat and suddenly opening it wide, showing everyone everything. Nobody could receive that news without asking questions or expressing sympathy or just being discomforted by it, and she found it almost unbearable. She would honestly rather everyone gossiped about her behind her back so she didn't have to tell them herself. That would be better. Christmas was just a microscope on the slide of your life, magnifying everything. She'd cancel it.

But she couldn't pull the curtains and leave the lights off. So instead, she overcompensated for Dom's impending absence and for the fact that she'd find it difficult to raise a smile on the day. She did all the things she did every damn Christmas, but more so. She knew she was doing it, but she couldn't help herself. In a normal year, she might curate the boxes of Christmas decorations that came down from the loft. This year, every single ornament and gold macaroni decoration came out. She bought two Christmas trees. They never had two Christmas trees. She'd always been rude to Flick, who always had an ostentatious nine-footer, chosen and cut by Andrew, in the hall of her house, kept a rose-gold-tinsel fake tree in the kitchen, and had yet another, a small real one, in her bedroom on which to hang all of Phoebe

and Zoë's homemade things (where she could feel sentimental but it didn't ruin the look downstairs). Now
Sarah, too, had one in the hall and one in the sitting
room, each fully loaded. She iced a big, boozy fruit cake,
although no one but Dom really ate it, and filled the
freezer with mince pies that didn't taste as nice as the
ones you could buy.

She bought too many presents for the kids. Mia's
favourite perfume, a huge haul of Zara clothes, things
for her flat. Dylan got new AirPods and the Stan Smiths
he wanted. What a cliché she turned out to be.

She bought herself a handbag. It was a spiteful pur-
chase. Dom had always disliked designer labels on
principle. He wouldn't buy a sweater if it had an ostentatious emblem on the chest. Vanessa and Flick both
had a few smart bags, and he'd been snide about them.
Natalie had a Prada. She presumed, hearing the bitterness in her own head, that he'd been willing to make an
exception for her. She went, on her own, to Bond Street
and browsed the boutiques, feeling the buttery leather
and the heavy hardware of the bags. She settled on a
Mulberry, and tried not to look anxious when the sales
assistant put through the staggering transaction. They'd
always had a bank account each, and one between them
that they paid into for the mortgage and bills. She used
the joint account.

Back at home, she wrapped the smart green box in
Christmas paper, tied it with wide gold ribbon, and put
it under the tree with the other gifts.

In the end, they made it work. She and the kids had

agreed an alternative menu. 'Please can we skip the turkey? Does anyone actually like turkey anyway?' They had silver-dollar pancakes and bacon for breakfast, late, and told stories of Christmases past, of the time when Dylan had fervently believed he'd spotted Santa at the end of his bed a week early, and told everyone in his class, and the year Mia had sulked all morning because he *hadn't* brought the pink patent DM boots she'd gone on about for months. They had bought them, of course, but they kept the gift back until just before bedtime – Sarah couldn't really remember, any more, why they'd wanted to tease her like that.

She knew Dylan and Mia spoke to Dom on their mobiles. She knew he was with his brother, not alone, and she refused to let herself feel sorry for him. Ghosts of Christmas Past kept floating in her brain. Dom, tying one end of a ball of string around a shiny new bike in the garden and the other around the end of Mia's bed. Dylan's face when Dom casually switched on the TV one Christmas, telling them it was time to watch the Queen's message, and instead the Nintendo Wii sprang into life. Dom was there, whether she let him physically join or not. You're so stupid, Dom. She thought it several times. You're so, so stupid. It required iron control to get through the day. She couldn't let herself think about Christmas Future. One day at a time. She almost whispered it to herself. A mantra and a promise.

After they opened their presents, they had steak with Béarnaise sauce and oven chips for lunch, but they still pulled crackers, wore the paper hats and told the bad jokes from the tiny scrolls that sprang out. Mia went to Annie and Rupert's in the afternoon, promising to bring Will back in the evening, and Sarah was glad that he would be there ('Four is enough for games'), and Dylan helped her wash up. 'See? It's a Christmas miracle, Mum!' he'd teased. He plugged his phone into the speaker in the kitchen, and made her listen to songs he thought she'd like, and they ended up, quite giggly, with her subjecting him to Phil Collins and Kate Bush.

On Boxing Day, Georgie had asked her to go for a walk. Liam and Phil were glued to the Test match on Sky, she said, and she'd love the company. Sarah was glad to be out of the house, in the crisp, cold fresh air. Dylan had suggested she get a puppy. He'd been suggesting that, to be fair, since he was about five years old, his pleas largely falling on deaf ears, but perhaps now, at last, she might think about it.

Coming around the side of her own car to where Sarah was, Georgie beamed, threw her arms around her and held tight. 'You okay?'

Sarah smiled. 'I'm okay.'

They moved away from the car park, and other walkers, arms linked, just making Christmassy small-talk for a few minutes. The path they'd taken was steep and wooded until they got to the top, and then they were on the ridge, with a panoramic view. They groaned at the incline, and didn't talk much while they scaled it.

Then, breath recovered, Georgie looked sideways at her. 'So, did they tell you about me and Phil? I'm guessing so.'

Sarah nodded cautiously. 'Is that okay?' Annie had told her over a bottle of wine one evening. Sarah knew she'd desperately wanted to help her find a way through, and that she'd told her hoping it might help. She'd known, too, that her friend wanted a happy ending for everyone, but she couldn't promise that to Annie.

Georgie nodded. 'Yes! I wanted you to know. That's why I told them, really. I mean, I didn't want to chuck it down your throat. I didn't want you to hear it from me, because then you'd have had to react and make it about me. We were away . . . the time seemed right. But, yes, I meant it for you, really.'

'That's kind of you.' There was no pity on Georgie's face or in her voice, and Sarah was grateful for that. It *was* easier to face her, knowing where she'd been.

'Not kind at all. Look, this stuff is different for everyone. I haven't a clue how you're feeling, or what you want to do. I don't even know all the facts, probably. I don't need to. I just wanted to say that it can be survivable. I really believe that.'

'Do you?'

Georgie stopped. 'I'm not saying it's easy. It was bloody hard. For twopence, I'd have walked away, at first. Even though it was historical by the time I found out. That sense of betrayal. It was Liam, really, who stopped me doing that. He was much younger than Mia and Dylan. Not that older kids are immune to the hurt. I don't mean that. But we'd tried so damn hard to be a family. So I stayed. And my marriage is stronger as a result of having survived. Better. More honest.'

452

'Truly?'

'Yes. Truly. We came close to losing what we had, and that scared us both, I think. At least, it made us take a long hard look at our marriage and evaluate, I suppose, whether it was still what we wanted. I sound like a manual. Sorry.'

'No. I see what you're saying.'

Georgie paused. 'Have you done that? You and Dom?'

Sarah thought for a moment. 'I suppose *I* have. I can't speak for him. I don't know what's going on with him. I'm not sure I even know him well any more. I actually think he's been slipping away from me, from us, for years. I've had to be scrupulously bloody honest with myself. Unpack it all, really look at it. What happened with Natalie wasn't the start of our problems. I see that. So clearly.'

'What about you, then? Where's your head at? Do you have the same clear view of that, at least?'

Sarah took a deep breath. 'Oh, yes. It's over.'

'And are you really sure?'

'I am.' She sounded surprised, but she'd only been sure since Georgie had asked a minute ago. Christmas had confused her. But just for a moment. The answer had been clear. 'Yes.'

'And – tell me to mind my own business if you want to – but is it over because you think you can't get past him sleeping with Natalie, or is it over for other reasons?'

'I'm not going to pretend I could just get past what happened with her. I mean, you'll know how much that hurts.'

'To be fair, I think what happened to you was much

453

worse. I'd have wanted to kill Phil, if he'd come closer to home.'

'But that's a slightly separate thing. That's a double betrayal – yes. Dom cheated on me and so did Natalie.'

'Right.'

'But I've got to split them up. Not literally. I think Natalie's seen to that. I mean just deal with those things one at a time.'

'Exactly. You've got to be forensic about your marriage.'

'Yes.' Sarah sounded exultant. 'That's it. You've got to be forensic. That's what I've been doing.'

'And?'

'And it seems so clear, now. Things were wrong. A long time before the two of them scratched the itch they'd had for years. It was a thousand little things, you know? It was just a little less warm, a little less together, a little less kind . . . Nothing major. Just chipping away. It makes you less, it makes him less, and it certainly makes what you are together less.'

Georgie nodded encouragingly.

'They add up. And, ah, the lies you tell yourself. I'm a master, turns out. You tell yourself it's the same for everybody else. You tell yourself it's middle age and that it's inevitable. You tell yourself it doesn't matter. But it does. And the pride. My God, the pride. It's the last taboo. I mean, you're all married, aren't you? All happy together. You feel like it must just be you.'

Georgie raised her eyebrows. 'I didn't know. You never said a word.'

'Pride.'

'Right. You don't want to be the one who fails. I know something about that.'

Sarah smiled. 'Of course you do. No. I really didn't.'

'Isn't that stupid? We're meant to be friends.'

'It's not stupid. And we are friends. You could have tried us.'

'And so could you, I suppose.' They smiled at each other.

'And then, even if you look yourself right in the eye and admit that you know it's changed, and for the better, you say, "At least we're friends. I'm living with my best friend, my teammate, and we have this inextricably linked life, and I don't want to dismantle it, and it'll be okay."'

'Except that it's not okay, is it?'

'No. The truth is, if you can't fix it, you should get out. And if you got out sooner rather than later, you'd salvage more of what you actually had.' She hesitated. 'I don't want to hate him, Georgie, and right now I feel like I'm on the edge of that.' It was the closest she'd come to crying. 'I can't bear that thought. I've liked him for so long.'

Georgie squeezed her shoulder. 'So don't. It's not compulsory, Sarah.'

55

By the thirtieth, Natalie's house had emptied again. Everyone had plans for New Year's Eve. Stella was flying to Copenhagen with a gang of friends, and Marley had planned a house party in Birmingham. Temple had work on the thirty-first, and then a dinner with her closest girlfriends from university, the ones she'd been to Île de Ré with. She'd offered to give it up but, of course, Natalie had begged her not to. Even Arlo was going to Maggie's, something of a tradition from years back to when he was an infant: Kit and Natalie had invariably had plans. She'd wondered if he'd rather stay at home. He'd talked about Sylvia a lot across the holiday. He wasn't weepy, and the questions had stopped, but it was clear he missed her, and she instinctively wanted to keep him close. But he'd begged to go to Maggie's so she'd agreed, reluctantly.

Natalie imagined that Kit would take him, then stay with him and his sister, and that she would be alone, and she tried not to mind, just as she tried to still the voice in her head telling her she deserved to be lonely. It had never been her favourite night of the year. Too much pressure, too much faux gaiety. She planned to take down the Christmas decorations – pack away the merriment – have a hot bath and be in bed hours before midnight in the hope of sleeping through the moment.

She was helping Arlo pack a rucksack when Kit appeared in the doorway of their son's room. 'Good to go, kid?'

'Yeah. Wait. I need my iPad . . .'

'No one *needs* an iPad, Arlo.'

Arlo smirked. 'Do you know where it is, Mum?'

She laughed. 'I do. It's on charge in the kitchen. I found it down the side of the sofa this morning, with no charge at all.'

Arlo ran out, Kit swerving to let him through.

She couldn't put it off any more. 'So, are you going to stay with Maggie too?'

'I wasn't planning to.'

She didn't know how to respond.

'I was going to come back here, Nat.'

She nodded.

'If you'll have me.'

Relief flooded through her. 'I'd like that.'

'Okay, then. I thought, if it was okay with you, that I'd pick us up some dinner on the way back. It's been a houseful. We haven't had much of a chance to talk. I think we should, don't you?'

'You're right.'

She couldn't read his face.

Arlo was back, breathless. He skidded across the floor, and shoved the iPad into his bag. 'Ready, Dad.' He hoisted it over his shoulder.

'Come on, then. Let's hit the road. Kiss your mum.'

Arlo threw his arms around Natalie boisterously. Sitting on her knees, she almost fell backwards. 'Love you, Mum. See ya!'

She held him a fraction longer than he would have liked. 'Be good for Auntie Mags. And have fun. You just be sure you remind her that you have to be in bed by eight.'

'Mum . . .' Arlo wasn't entirely sure whether she was joking or not.

'Okay, then. Nine.' But she ruffled his hair. 'Kidding. I do not want to know how late you're going to be. Happy New Year, my gorgeous baby boy. Happy New Year. I love you.'

'You too. I love you too.'

And he was gone. Kit turned in the doorway to follow him, then turned back. 'Curry or Thai?'

She smiled weakly. 'Whatever you want.'

He raised an eyebrow, and she laughed. 'Okay, curry. Please.'

'That's more like it.'

She was too jittery to keep still while he was gone. On impulse she decided not to take down the decorations. Let them stay one more night. She pushed through some more of the vast quantity of laundry a houseful for Christmas generated, and tried to make sense of the leftovers in the fridge. Passing the mirror in the hallway, she caught sight of herself. She looked older, less glossy. How long had it been since she'd had a long, hot bath? How long since she'd put on a full face of make-up, and carefully chosen what to wear?

It was no good, this self-loathing. It wouldn't help. Enough.

She carried the laundry basket back to the utility room, and went upstairs to run a bath.

She was still upstairs in her bedroom, in their bedroom, when Kit got back. She heard the front door shut, and then, a few minutes later, he called for her. 'Get it while it's hot.' He always said that. How many ordinary, wonderful nights had he come home with takeaway and stood at the bottom of the stairs and called for them? She stared at herself in the dressing-table mirror. Whatever he had to say, whatever he wanted to happen, she willed herself to argue for what she wanted. She had to make him understand. She had to beg him to stay.

Kit had laid the table. He'd turned off the overhead light, and switched on the side lights on the sideboard. A bottle of wine and two glasses stood next to the collection of plastic and cardboard containers of food.

In her place, on the plate, was an envelope, face down. For just a second she didn't recognize it, but she could see at once that the envelope was old. It was creased, and yellowed. Not stuck down. She picked it up, aware that Kit's eyes, across the table, were fixed intently on her, gleaming, and then she recognized the hotel address printed on the top left-hand corner, and she knew exactly what it was. Kit was smiling reassuringly at her now as she took out the contents.

It was a postcard of *Portrait of Madame X*, the most famous of John Singer Sargent's portraits. She knew the painting and vividly remembered the day she'd first seen it, hanging in the Metropolitan Museum in Manhattan, on their first holiday together in the late 1990s. Kit had arranged the whole thing as a surprise, conspiring with her mother, who had taken Temple for the few days they were away. She'd been to New York only once, years earlier, and he knew how much she'd adored the city, and longed to return. They'd had a sensational time. Kit was happy, he said, to go to as many galleries as she wanted, so long as he got a great dinner every night, and they'd already spent hours in the Frick, the Museum of Modern Art and the Guggenheim by the time they tackled the vast Fifth Avenue Metropolitan Museum of Art. Of all the pictures she'd seen across the week, this one was her favourite. She'd fallen in love with the woman's haughty, sensual expression in profile, and stood in front of it until Kit grew bored. 'Great dress. We should get you one like it. Let's go to Saks right now,' he'd begged, and she'd called him a Philistine and bought a postcard in the gift shop.

New York had been bitterly cold, notably so even for January. The security guard at the entrance had said he could smell snow in the frigid air. The sky had been grey when they went into the behemoth in the early afternoon, and by the time they came out several hours later, she'd been ecstatic to find almost half a foot of soft, powdery snow. The same security guard, triumphant now, had smiled benevolently at her obvious delight. 'What'd I tell ya?' They'd walked back to their hotel through Central Park, enchanted by each other, like new lovers are, and enchanted by how the snow made everything different and magical. She still vividly remembered how oddly quiet it had been, all sound muffled by the blizzard, and how beautiful, the snow fresh and untrampled. It had been like being in a film, and she'd hardly felt the cold with his arm around her shoulders. It was as if the city had laid on the snow especially for them.

Turning the postcard over slowly, she saw her own handwriting.

> I choose you.
> And I'll choose you.
> Over and over and over.
> Without pause,
> Without a doubt, in a heartbeat.
> I'll keep choosing you.

She couldn't remember where she'd first read it. Maybe she'd heard it somewhere. She had no idea who'd written it. But it said everything she had felt on that trip, so very eloquently, and so perfectly. She'd signed it at the bottom, just with an N, and three crosses.

Her eyes filled with tears. 'Oh.' She'd written it that night. The snowy night. Kit had fallen asleep. Their room had floor-to-ceiling windows, with a low, wide sill upholstered for you to sit on, and she'd opened the curtains so she could watch the snow. She'd sat for a long time watching it fall across the vista of water towers and advertising hoardings, and she'd written the card then, on her knee, her heart full of him, although she hadn't given it to him until much later, once they were home. 'You kept it.'

He nodded slowly. 'I kept it. And I kept everything else too. I have a whole box, you know.'

'I didn't . . .'

'I'll show you sometime. I'm a sentimental old fool.'

'No. Not at all. That's lovely. I remember that day so clearly.'

'So do I . . . So do I, Nat.' Kit reached across the table, to take her hand. 'I still want this, my love. What you wrote there. I want us to choose each other, Nat. Over and over and over. But we have other choices. We can choose to move past this. To stay together. To make things better. Best. How they were. Even better than that, maybe.' He smiled ruefully. 'We. Can. Choose. Together. I want us to choose to get past this. I believe we can get past this. If we try. If we both try.'

She heard herself sob. It was all she could manage, suddenly.

'We got lost, didn't we? But we're still us.'

'But I've done such damage to us.'

'We both have. We need to forgive each other.'

'I've got nothing to forgive you for.'

'We both know that's not true. It's more complicated than that. I've had time, believe me, to think about it. What you did – it was acute. What I did was chronic. I let it slide. I let you go. I'm not saying I deserved it. I'm not a saint. I'm saying I understand it.'

She was still crying.

'Look at me, Nat. Please look at me.' She raised her eyes and looked at his face. It was open, and imploring and so familiar. 'I forgive you. But now you have to forgive yourself.'

She smiled weakly.

'Say it. If you mean it, say it.'

'I love you.'

It was his turn to well up.

'I choose you.'

He stood up and came around to her side of the table. She got to her feet and the two of them held each other for a long, long time. 'I choose you. I choose you.' He repeated the words, into her hair, into her neck, his arms pulling her as close as he could.

'Thank you.' It was what she most wanted to say to him.

He laughed, took her face in his hands. 'Fresh start.'

She knew then, in that moment of clarity, and beginnings, that they couldn't stay in that house, in that town, in that life. Things needed shaking up. Things had to change. The one thing she knew for sure was that they both wanted the same thing. And that they needed to move away from all of this to keep themselves safe. And that was okay. It would be all right. They would be all right. They were both wide awake now. She put her hands on his face, pulling him down so their foreheads rested together. 'Fresh start.'

56

The Christmas lights were down already. Sarah had never made it as far as Twelfth Night in all their Christmases together. She started getting twitchy about needles and dust around the twenty-eighth, and the decorations usually stayed up only as long as New Year after a vocal campaign by the kids. He wondered if she'd hung everything this year. And who had helped her to take the boxes out of the loft and put them back again when everything was cleared away.

Dom wondered if he should ring the bell. They'd lived in this house for years, and he didn't think he ever had before. For a second his finger hovered over the button. Then he changed his mind, put his key into the lock, and opened the door. There was no sign of Christmas.

Just inside the hall, two big suitcases, his leather garment carrier and a large plastic crate were neatly lined up in front of the console table. He knew the contents would be clean and folded too: shoes in shoe bags, toothpaste smudges wiped from his washbag. Sarah was not a cut-the-sleeves-off-all-the-suits kind of woman scorned. She couldn't bear the mess or the waste of nail-polish remover on a car bonnet, or shredded shirts. He almost regretted that about her: punishment would have been almost a salve. A pile of unopened post with his name on it was neatly laid on top of the larger case.

Brutal, but eloquent. For that, he rather admired her.

Ignoring the bags for now, Dom went through to the kitchen in search of her. Sarah was sitting at the round table, nursing a mug. A cafetière stood half full in front of her, alongside a small painted jug. He knew the milk inside it would be hot. She would have ground the beans herself, this morning, probably, in the small grinder he'd bought her one Christmas or birthday. Instant coffee and cold milk made no sense to her, when you had time to do it properly. Sarah had a particular way of doing everything. Neat, thorough.

Was it any surprise that she was ending their marriage, at last, in the same way?

She turned to him, as he opened a cupboard and took out a mug. 'I'd like one, if that's okay.'

'Of course.' Her voice was calm.

He sat down opposite her, and poured coffee and milk, glad to be busy for a moment before he looked at her. Although it was early for a Sunday, she'd washed and styled her hair, and she was wearing normal make-up. She looked nice. She looked thin.

They'd sat here, in this niche, how many times? Hundreds. Thousands, maybe. Outside, plants that they'd nurtured marked their time here. The previous owners had not been gardeners – one large oak stood in the middle of the lawn, the only thing still as it had been when they'd moved in. Once, very early on, when the kids were both at birthday parties, they'd made love under its canopy on a sultry summer afternoon. It was memorable because it was rare, even then. All the rarer for being outside. The memory caused him a sharp fleeting pain behind the ribs.

Elsewhere there were acers, climbing roses, the hazel tree in the corner, all established now – they'd gone into the ground during Sarah and Dom's first year in the house, transplanted from small pots brought home from the garden centre in the back of the old estate car, long gone now. The garden was bleak on this wintry day, the oak like a diagram of lungs. Only the fiery red stems of the dogwoods along the back fence gave any colour to the grey day. It would take more months of winter before it sprang into life. And he would not see it. He'd never again come home and find Sarah in the garden in her old clothes and that silly floppy hat, pruning and watering, and the thought was more strange than sad at first, and then the newly familiar melancholia laid itself over him again. She'd covered all the wicker furniture, and taken the cushions off the old swing seat, but, looking out there now, he could see a teenage Mia sprawled across it, GCSE flashcards strewn around her, Walkman headphones firmly in, although if you walked past her you'd catch the violent thud of whatever she was listening to. On the lawn, perilously close to the flowers, a young Dylan with a silly hairstyle was endlessly rehearsing keepie-uppie. They were ghosts.

She followed his gaze as she sipped her coffee, hands nursing the mug. He wondered if she was seeing the same phantoms, remembering all that shared history. He hoped he hadn't made it all a lie for her. It wasn't. It hadn't been.

Dom sighed sadly, and forced himself back into the room. It was so quiet. Normally, *The Archers* would be on now, and they'd both be listening, then *Desert Island Discs*. He'd stop paying attention entirely while Sarah cooked Sunday lunch, and he read the papers that would be spread out on this same table.

Stop, he told himself. Stop torturing yourself, you prick. It's all gone.

Dom pulled his key fob from the pocket of his bomber jacket, and slowly took the house keys off the ring, putting his car key back, and laying the others in the middle of the table. Front door, back door, garage.

For a moment she just stared at them. Then she raised her eyes to him. 'What will you do?'

'For now, I'll rent somewhere. I'm not sure where yet. I haven't got that far.'

'I'd like us to sell this house. Not straight away. But next year.'

'Okay. That's probably easiest, if that's what you want.'

'It's far too big for me on my own. I'll buy somewhere smaller. With fewer bedrooms, and less garden.'

'The money should be all right.'

She waved away the remark. 'I know. I've never accused you –'

He interrupted, eager to make his point: 'No, but we've both known men who hide it and fight about it, and I need you to know I'm not going to be one of those.'

They'd certainly talked about it over the years. Someone

in his office, a girl from Sarah's yoga class, his cousin: their men had become completely unrecognizable in divorce, hoarding and hiding money.

'I hope you mean that.' She smiled at him, raised an eyebrow.

'I do.' He did. He desperately wanted to do the right thing now, having been so wrong, and to have her believe that he was going to.

At the end of it all, that was what made him saddest: that Sarah couldn't trust or admire him any more. He'd lost her love. He'd lost his place in their life. His home. His children's respect. But that was the worst: to be some-one she distrusted and viewed with disdain. It meant he had to confront not being the man he had always believed himself to be. He honestly didn't know, yet, how he was going to rearrange his own view of himself.

How many times had his father tried to explain him-self after he'd left Dom's mother? Dom had shut him down every time: he hadn't wanted to listen to him – hadn't been ready to, at least. He wished his dad was still alive. He wanted more than anything to listen to him, to have him listen back. He wanted someone to tell him he wasn't all bad.

'How are the kids?'

Sarah's brow furrowed. 'Aren't you talking to them?'

He exhaled sharply. 'They're not that keen on me right now.'

'You've got to give them time.' Her tone wasn't unkind. 'I know.'

'I'm not encouraging them to be angry with you.'

'You'd be entitled.'

She didn't disagree. 'But I'm not. They'll come around. They love you. They know you love them. You're a good father, Dom.'

It seemed a long time since he'd heard anything good about himself, even inside his own head. He was horrified to find himself suddenly tearful. 'Thank you.' He sniffed, rubbed his nose and blinked away the tears. For a second he wondered if she would reach for him, but she didn't. Of course she didn't. 'I'm sorry. I'm pathetic. A ridiculous wreck.'

'It's okay.'

It wasn't. Not at all. 'You're the last person I should be looking to for comfort. I'm absolutely the architect – boom, boom – of my own misery.'

'And yet, somehow, I'm still also the most obvious person. Ironic, isn't it?'

He nodded, not trusting his voice.

Sarah sighed. 'Listen, Dom. I'm not Mother Teresa. I'm not sure I've quite finished being angry with you yet. It's quite the process, this. It's like food poisoning. You think you're finished, then . . .' She aped retching. 'But I'm not feeling sorry for you. And I'm trying not to feel sorry for myself, either. I've done enough of all this crap.' She threw her arms up. 'I'm really bloody tired of crying and being furious and feeling like a shell. Of everyone being afraid of hurting me, of inciting me, of me falling to pieces in their kitchen. I'm tired of all of it. I don't want to be that person any more. I want to move forward. So I have to want you to move forward too. Otherwise you'll keep dragging me back. It's hard to explain. When my mum died, she'd been ill for so long that I'd done a lot of my mourning before she actually went.'

'I remember.'

'This is the same. You didn't just explode a healthy marriage. We both know that. You threw the death blow, but it was already on the mat. It's taken a lot for me to admit that. I think I was just so bloody terrified of our life collapsing around our ears, around our friends, our kids, ourselves, I'd just been lying about it.' She smacked her sternum hard with the heel of her hand. 'In here, to myself. Too proud, too stubborn, too embarrassed . . .' Her voice trailed off.

When she spoke again, her tone was harsher. 'I can't forgive you for it being Natalie. Funny, but that's almost the worst of it, for me. You've done so much damage. Not just to us, to this marriage, but to other parts of my life. Parts that matter so deeply to me. But that's the bit that's unforgivable. The rest – that was just you being more honest than me, and I can't hate you for that. And, believe me, I have tried. But we both need to walk away from it now. Enough. We can try to be friends eventually. I don't know if I can, and I won't promise, but I'll try. I'll try for Mia and Dylan, and I'll try for all the life we've shared, for all the years that were good. We're always going to have those two in common. I can't imagine a time when they aren't the most important thing in the world to both of us. We're leaving the marriage, not the family.'

'That's what I want too. More than I can say,' Dom said.

'Christ. I sounded like Gwyneth Paltrow.'

Dom laughed, despite himself. She laughed too. The moment of levity helped.

'So go now. Please. It's hard to look at you, and it's hardest here. I don't mean to be cruel, but it's true. Give it space, give it time. Be a dad to our kids. Be a human being over the divorce.' He nodded, pathetically keen to agree with everything she was saying. 'And we'll see, hey, about the friends part? Eventually.'

'I'm so grateful to you, Sarah. You're – you're incredible.'

She stood and held up a hand to stop him. 'I don't want to talk about it any more. I'm sick of the sound of my own voice. And I've given you the wrong impression if I've seemed ready for your platitudes. Because I'm absolutely not. I'm going upstairs now, and when I come down, I would like you not to be here. Okay?'

He wanted to touch her, but she took the cafetière and her mug and put them by the sink, then walked out without another word. He heard her footsteps on the stairs, and then a door closed on the landing.

He sat for a moment longer. Then he put both mugs in the dishwasher, poured the coffee and milk down the sink, rinsed the jug and the cafetière under the tap, and rested them carefully on the draining-board. He used the tea towel to dry the sink, and folded it carefully over the oven handle.

Back in the hallway, he moved the suitcases and the

suit-carrier out onto the doorstep. The crate was heavy, and he wondered what she'd put into it. As he lifted it into the boot of his car, he flipped the lid and looked inside. On top of the papers, toiletries and shoes was his favourite picture of the four of them, taken on a summer holiday in Portugal when the kids were much younger, all of them smiling, sun-kissed and accidentally coordinated in white and blue. Except that it wouldn't have been an accident – Sarah would have planned it that way. He hadn't noticed that it wasn't still on the console. He laid his hand on the glass briefly, on his family. Then he put the lid back on the crate, closed the boot, climbed into the driver's seat, and drove away, without once looking back.

57

It was Annie, of course, who organized the walk. She'd talked it over beforehand, separately, with each of them except Natalie and Sarah. She knew she was probably the hardest to say no to, and she intended to use that quality. No one had completely nixed the idea. But Flick, her eyebrows arched, had said she didn't rate her chances, and Georgie had been rendered twitchily nervous by even the suggestion of the six of them together, even in the public space Annie intended. Vanessa had been the most vocally supportive. 'I knew you'd do it at some point, Annie. I'm so behind you. It's a good idea. Better out than in.'

She hadn't consulted Sarah before she issued the invitation about whether she would come or not. That was deliberate and manipulative. Let Sarah ignore the message if she wanted to. She was a grown woman who needed to make up her own mind about whether she wanted to confront things. She hoped she wouldn't ignore it.

The group WhatsApp they used had lain dormant for months. The last message felt very poignant – something from Flick about what to wear to Annie's birthday party – a jokey, emoji-laden exchange of the kind that went back and back and back to the beginning of

WhatsApp, and which previously had taken place via text and before that in person at the school gates. Back for years.

Their lives would always be like this now – everything that went before the party, and whatever happened between them afterwards. This was a salvage operation. They had to want to save whatever they could.

They all agreed to come, in the end, but it was hard to tell how any of them felt about it via electronic messaging. Communications were always a bit blunt, however many smiley faces and kiss hugs you put at the end of one in mitigation. Rupert had often laughed, not unkindly, as Annie pored over simple messages trying to translate them. 'Crikey. Women don't half make their lives complicated with this stuff.'

One by one their agreements pinged through. Sarah's message was the penultimate – it seemed as though Natalie had waited for Sarah, like she needed her permission, which she figured she did.

Five 'yes' messages for a walk at 9 a.m. on Friday. As she replied, easy and breezy, with details, Annie wondered what on earth she'd done.

Annie chose a National Trust car park they all knew. It wasn't somewhere any of them walked often, though – she wanted to minimize the chance of an audience of acquaintances. It was a sharply cold morning, with a hoar frost first thing, but bright and dry. She got there a few minutes earlier than nine, deliberately, and queued with the dog-walkers at the small kiosk serving hot drinks. Then she carried all six polystyrene cups to a picnic table and waited, hoping the drinks would still be hot when the others arrived.

Georgie, Vanessa and Flick pulled in within a couple of minutes of each other, and joined her. Everyone seemed nervous. Flick was wearing distinctly unsuitable footwear.

'No walking boots, Flick?' Vanessa raised an eyebrow.

'We're not actually walking, are we? We're just here for the big showdown. I'm going into town later.'

Annie was indignant. 'We might.'

Flick chortled. 'Then I suppose these babies will get muddy.'

Georgie had pulled her sleeves down over her hands, and was nursing her hot drink with both, skipping from one foot to the other. The others weren't sure whether it was nerves or cold. 'Well, Annie, I guess we're about to find out whether this should be filed under good ideas.'

'Don't! I'm nervous. I'm actually wondering whether it was the worst idea I ever had.'

'And I'm actually wondering whether either of them will turn up.'

'They will.' That was Flick, sage-like. 'Sarah turned up at the funeral, didn't she? She'll come today.' The others pondered the wisdom.

'Were there croissants or anything, Annie?'

'Not sure. Didn't look . . .'

'I'll go and check. Anyone want one?'

There was a murmur of general agreement to refined sugar.

Just then, Natalie appeared. They'd been watching Flick head for the kiosk in her townie boots, so they didn't see her until she was right next to them. There were echoes of how glamorous and polished she usually looked, but the bloom was definitely gone for now. Vanessa wondered if she had toned herself down on purpose, or whether she had just been through the emotional wringer. She figured it was the latter. She was such a pretty woman, even without make-up or glossy hair, but she looked tired and, this morning, anxious.

She hovered nervously by the table. 'Hi.' The women smiled and responded. Georgie gave a small wave. It was awkward.

'Sit by me.' Annie patted the bench. Natalie smiled gratefully and sat down. Annie handed her a paper cup, and she sipped from it, not quite meeting anyone's eye. They were all waiting for Sarah.

Sarah's car pulled in a minute or so later, and they watched their friend reverse park in a space directly opposite where they were sitting. For a couple of minutes she just sat in the driver's seat, as though she were making up her mind whether she could face them all. Annie was afraid she would drive away. Then she seemed to decide, opened the door and climbed out. Annie exhaled with relief, and tried to read her state of mind from the set of her face. She couldn't. If Natalie looked dialled back, Sarah looked ramped up. She had dried and styled her hair, and she was wearing more make-up than she ever normally would have done on a walk. Her cheek sparkled with highlighter in the bright sunshine.

The dark circles, however, she had in common with Natalie. Annie desperately wanted to hug them both, then take them home and feed them chicken soup.

She greeted her too breezily. 'I got us hot chocolate!' and stood up to give her a quick hug and a cup.

Natalie stood up too, and walked around the table to where Sarah was. The other women looked down at their drinks and at each other.

'I'm glad you came, Sarah. I really am.' Natalie's voice was tremulous. 'I've so wanted to see you.'

'Safety in numbers?' Sarah didn't mean her voice to sound as sarcastic as it did.

'The numbers was my idea, not Nat's,' Annie interjected. 'I'm sure you two still have things to say to each other, and maybe you will, some time when you're alone, but let's face it, we're all involved in this – it affects all of us – so I think we should all talk. I really do . . .' Her voice trailed off, and Georgie came to her rescue.

'We've been friends for such a long time. Surely we can do this. Can't we?'

Flick, back with them now, handed round brown-paper bags. 'Here, everyone, eat.'

She gave Sarah and Natalie a quick peck on the cheek. Sarah took the bag with a faint smile. 'I'm not sure I'm as civilized as you seem to think I am.' She was talking to all of them, but she was still looking at Natalie.

Natalie met her gaze squarely. 'So, be uncivilized. I can take it. Be as uncivilized as you like, because I sure as hell deserve it. Do you want to scream at me, throw things at me or hit me?'

Sarah laughed. It almost reached her eyes. 'Okay – I'm more civilized than that.'

The tiny joke just about broke the surface of the tension. Everyone relaxed their hunched shoulders.

'I don't deserve it, but I'm very pleased you're here.' She faced the group. 'I wanted the chance to apologize to Sarah, face to face, and I very much wanted to do that in front of all of you, as well as, if she wants to, privately with Sarah at some point. Whatever she'll allow. I don't know if she'll want to do that.' She looked at Sarah, who raised her hands, and shook her head. 'But Annie's right. I know I dragged you all into this bloody mess, and I know it's had repercussions for every one of you, for all of us. I'm aware. Painfully aware. And I'm sorry for that too. More than I can say. It's a very small word for a very big fuck-up. I can't make you believe me – that's up to each of you. But I do mean it very, very profoundly.' Her cheeks were pink, and although she said each word slowly and distinctly, she was breathless. They could each see what it cost her. But no one wanted to speak until Sarah had. In the hierarchy of hurt caused, Sarah was way at the top.

Natalie had more to say. 'I didn't deserve you all rallying around when my mum died, either. Helping out like you did. Coming to the funeral. But you did.' There were tears in her voice now, although she fought to control them, her hand at her neck. 'And so I wanted – I needed – to say thank you, too. You were unbelievable to me, and I will never forget the kindness. Never.'

Annie reached out and touched her arm.

'You've been the best friends I have ever had, or ever

478

will have. I'm sure of that. The very best. If I've destroyed that, well, I can't think of a worse punishment for what I've done.'

'We're not dead. Enough of the past tense.' Flick was characteristically flippant, and the others were grateful for her swagger.

Annie looked at Sarah, willing her to speak, but it was Georgie who answered. 'No one is trying to punish you, Nat.'

'I know. You stuck by Sarah. It was the right thing to do.'

Sarah sat down on the picnic bench. When Natalie stayed on her feet, Sarah gestured that she should sit too. They all climbed in, so they were huddled close together.

Sarah took a deep breath, staring at the gnarled surface of the table, and spoke without looking up. 'Dom's moved out for good. We're getting a divorce.'

'Okay.' This was Flick.

'Are you sure that's what you want?'

Sarah smiled slowly. 'Very sure. Not that it's what I want, so much as what I know is right. The truth is, as much as it might suit me, might have suited me, to blame you, Natalie, to paint you as some sort of sodding scarlet woman, you didn't destroy my marriage. You speeded things up, for sure. I hate you, a bit, for that. You cheated on me too. That's how it feels.' She gave a small, joyless laugh. 'But you didn't destroy my marriage. You flushed it out. Can't say I love your methods.' Her voice was heavy with irony. 'But I do know that it wasn't you who destroyed it.'

It was a truth maybe only Natalie knew for sure.

'No. But have I destroyed our friendship.'

Sarah sighed. 'I don't know. I'm not sure yet. I want to say you haven't. But I can't. It's still too fresh, this wound. We're grown-ups, all of us. We know about trust and we know about betrayal. It can't be brushed under the carpet for the sake of a group dynamic. However much any of us might wish it could be.'

They sat quietly for a moment. It would never be the same, they knew. It never could.

Then it was Natalie's turn to sigh. 'We're going to put the house on the market. Move away.'

She still had the capacity to shock them, it seemed. But after just a moment of absorption, it made sense to all of them. Sarah nodded slowly. 'You and Kit?'

She nodded. 'We're going to try and fix us.'

Sarah chewed her lip. Under the table, Annie took her hand and squeezed it tightly.

'Where to?'

Natalie shrugged. 'We're not sure yet. It's a pretty new decision. Somewhere different. Suffolk, maybe.'

'That doesn't make me relieved, you know. A couple of months ago I wanted it more than life itself. For you to be gone. Not even exist. It doesn't matter now. So I hope it's not just because of me? Penance?'

'No.' Natalie shook her head vigorously. 'Because it's the right thing for us. I didn't imagine anyone would object. But I'm not that selfless, I'm afraid. Truthfully, it's for us. We need to make a new start, don't we, if we're going to survive this? I haven't, it seems, quite destroyed my own relationship after all, however much I might deserve to have done. Kit wants us to stay together, to make it work. It's what I want too. We can't do that here.'

'I get that.' Georgie smiled gently. 'For what it's worth, I think it will help.'

'Thanks, Georgie.'

'It'll be very strange, you not being around. We've been the six of us for so long. These last months have been weird and horrid.'

'I'm sorry.'

'Stop. No one wants you to keep saying that, for God's sake.'

'I'm okay with it, actually,' Sarah deadpanned. They all looked at her, and then she laughed, and because she laughed, they did too, even Natalie, and the tension broke just a little bit more.

'Surely we can all keep in touch.' Annie was thinking about Dorfest. They'd never all be there together again. About Stella and Marley and Arlo. And Kit, only half listening to any conversation from the deckchair furthest from the pool, his hat across his face to disguise the napping. If only there was a way . . . But not even Annie believed it, really. That wasn't how it worked.

Natalie looked very sad, suddenly. 'Let's say we will, knowing we won't, hey?'

'We'll miss you.'

'I'll miss you.' Sarah's voice was very small.

She put her hand, palm up, into the middle of the table, still looking at Natalie. Natalie smiled, more like her old smile now, and put her own, palm down, into

Sarah's. One by one – Flick, Georgie, Vanessa, and finally Annie – they laid a hand on the pile, like a tower, and left them there for a moment. Annie's eyes glistened with tears. 'Oh.'

Flick sighed theatrically, and pulled her hand out, standing up as she did so. 'Right. Enough of this sentimental crap. We've come over a bit too *Steel Magnolias* for my liking, and it's getting creepy now. We all get it. We love each other. Even despite. End of. It's getting cold, and I want to make the most of this sugar high. I'm in the wrong boots, goddamn it, but I'm walking. Who's coming?'

'Oh, do shut up.'

He leant down and kissed the top of her head. 'They mean that it's going to be yet another gorgeous sunset. Take my word for it.'

And now it seemed everyone else had had the same idea. Families had spread blankets and unfolded picnic chairs in all the good spots, all facing the same direction. Kids who still had the energy after a day in the fresh air and the surf ran in circles. The older couple she and Will had chatted to a couple of days earlier had staked their claim on a teak bench just to her left. Mia watched as the man uncorked a bottle of something fizzy, and the woman held two glasses, laughing as he tried to pour the frothy liquid steadily. They were celebrating their fiftieth wedding anniversary, they'd said, back in the place they'd taken their honeymoon all those years ago. They smiled at her now, and raised their glasses. She waved.

Their chosen place was the end of the dock. Will had gone to get drinks from the bar at the end of the beach, leaving her to guard their spot. Mia lay down briefly, her head against a rolled towel. The old wood held the heat of the day. Her skin felt crispy from the sun, and she smelt coconut from their sunscreen. She'd piled her tangled hair on top of her head, and pulled a linen shirt of Will's over her bikini top and denim cut-offs. She closed her eyes and listened to snippets of conversation among the sounds of nature, feeling utterly relaxed. When she sat up again, she scooted to the edge, from where her legs just reached the water. She lifted one up and down languidly, enjoying the golden colour they'd taken on across the week, and the gentle splashing of the water.

The holiday had taken on its own rhythm. This was their seventh night. Time had done that odd thing of passing incredibly slowly and at warp speed all at the same time. They'd come here each evening to watch the sunset with drinks and crisps, then head back to shower and dress, but probably end up in bed and miss dinner altogether. Then they'd be ravenous when their room-service breakfast arrived on a vast tray, and they'd eat in their bathrobes on their balcony, watching the determined early joggers criss-crossing the boardwalk before the heat of the day hit.

And repeat.

She never wanted to go home.

It had been exactly what she'd needed. A perfect week.

She'd done the Interrailing, the backpacking, and she was glad she had. Lucky girl. She'd danced at a Full Moon party, navigated the Paris Métro, bartered in Vietnam. She'd even sort of shorn a sheep on a farm deep in New South Wales. Drunk fishbowl cocktails on a raucous girls' trip to Malia on Crete. Been scared, been brave, made some epically bad decisions.

Will Hawtrey wasn't one of those.

He might not be the first boy she had ever loved, but she felt so sure he would be the last.

Total happiness. Complete contentment. She marvelled at how her life had changed in the last twelve months. That this was where she was, and that Will was who she was with. It was true what they said: when you knew, you knew. She'd emotionally exhaled. He was her home now. No doubts, no fears, and no hesitation. She could not imagine her life without him, and she did not want to. It astounded her, and at the same time, it was wonderfully commonplace.

Her world had shattered when her mum and dad had split up. That was the truth of it, dramatic though it sounded. People didn't expect you to be so affected when you were in your twenties, when you'd left home and were living your own grown-up life. It wasn't a broken home if you no longer lived in it, was it? Maybe she hadn't expected it to hit her so hard. She was invincible, after all, at twenty-five. Wasn't she? But the plates of her life shook, shifted, broke apart, and altered the landscape irrevocably, past, present, future. She'd had no say. There was a time when she didn't know where to put everything it made her feel – she was furious with her dad, she ached for her mum, she hurt for herself and Dylan, she feared for what would happen to her parents. The effort of trying to understand, mediate and, eventually, to realize and accept there was nothing she could do but hold their hands, love them both, had exhausted her.

Will had been the person who stilled the maelstrom. She was almost frightened of who she might have become if he hadn't been there, pulling her out of the melodrama of her parents' relationship into something lighter, and sweeter, and beautiful. She couldn't be cynical when he was there, open-faced, loving her. She could still believe in love. Forever, whatever love. Because of him. She was so grateful for him, and she thanked her lucky stars every night for him.

She heard footsteps padding on the dock behind her, and turned to watch him walk towards her. He was barefoot, moving slowly, holding two opened bottles of beer in each hand. The pockets of his chino shorts bulged with snacks.

She laughed, and beckoned him. 'Come on. I thought you were gonna miss it!'

'Nah. I was watching. Here you go.'

She took the beers from him, and he sat down beside her in one easy, athletic move.

He nudged her shoulder with his. 'Told you it was going to be a smasher.'

'You were right. It's just . . . wow . . . Best one of the week, I reckon. I've taken a couple of pictures but I don't think they're going to do it justice. Those colours.'

'They never do. Let's just watch. And remember.' They clinked bottles and drank. She laid her head on his shoulder and they watched the changing sky parade its stunning riot of pinks and corals, silent for a while now.

Mia felt happiness expand inside her.

'D'you call your mum? Is she okay?'

'Yes.'

He squeezed her knee, and didn't push her for more. He always seemed to know when she wanted to speak, when she didn't. He wasn't always falling over himself to offer solutions. It was one of her favourite things about him.

'Oh, I forgot. I got us snacks. Those pretzel things you like, some nuts . . . Gimme a hand.'

He pulled a couple of packets out of his right-hand pocket, and leant on his right hand, lifting his left pocket in her direction. 'Can you just grab those for me?'

She smiled at his goofiness, and reached into the pocket, feeling a cellophane packet, and then, behind, a small hard box. 'What's this?'

She pulled it out. The pretzels fell onto the dock, unnoticed. Before she'd quite realized what he was doing, what was happening, Will had sprung up and was kneeling in an unmistakable pose beside her. He took her free hand and, when she put her beer down, the other one too.

'My mum would never speak to me again if I wasn't down on one knee for this. Even if I get splinters.' He coughed. 'Mia Bennett. I want to thank you for the best year of my life. I love you. I *really, really* love you. And I know I'm going to love you for the rest of my life. I know it. So, will you, please, marry me?' He took the box out of her hand, and opened it.

She'd pulled her hands away, covered her mouth with them, ignoring the ring. 'Really?'

'Really!' They were both laughing and crying at the same time. She crouched beside him and threw her arms around his neck. 'Are you serious, Will? Really?'

'Yes! Deadly serious. Yes! Marry me!'

Around them, other people had become aware of what was playing out against the painterly sky. Several started to clap, and someone whooped.

Will turned, suddenly made aware of his audience by the noise, and raised a hand to stop them, his cheeks pinking. 'Hang on. Hang on. She hasn't actually said yes yet.'

Mia hid her face in his neck, just as flushed as he was. Then she drew back, and put one hand on either side of Will's face, whispering, 'Yes,' over and over again as she pulled him in to kiss him, and they hugged. The clapping grew in intensity, until they broke apart and gave a small, theatrical bow. Will held their clasped hands aloft.

A few feet away, the elderly couple with the Prosecco stood to toast them, both beaming.

'Here's to both you beautiful people!' the woman said.

'Thank you.' They spoke in unison, delighted.

The old man put his arm around his wife's shoulders, and she leant into him. 'And here's to you kids, and your very own happily ever after.'

Acknowledgements

I owe a debt of gratitude to all the dedicated people who work at Michael Joseph and Curtis Brown, who always work hard, but who have worked hard these last two years under the most difficult of circumstances, ever resourceful, ever cheerful. And thank you to booksellers everywhere. How wonderful it was to go back into bookshops, the portals to all other worlds.

After a funny few unsettled years, five years ago we moved to our new house in the country, and I have never been happier – we found a warm and welcoming community that opened its arms to us, and we felt we were home. So to dear old ones, and to a host of wonderful new ones, thank you for the fun and the friendship.